THE EMPEROR'S PET
THE DISINHERITED PRINCE SERIES - BOOK FIVE

THE
EMPEROR'S
PET

DISINHERITED PRINCE SERIES
BOOK FIVE

GUY ANTIBES

SALT LAKE CITY, UT

THE EMPEROR'S PET

Published by CasiePress LLC in Salt Lake City, UT, April, 2017.
www.casiepress.com

Cover & Book Design: Kenneth Cassell

ISBN-13: 978-1545598634
ISBN-10:   1545598630

AUTHOR'S NOTE

The fifth book in the Disinherited Prince novels, The Emperor's Pet features a series of reunions. Pol continues to wonder about the alien 'essence' that continues to nudge him from time to time. Along the way the stakes are raised for Pol as he struggles with his identity and with returning Shira to Shinkya. I've been waiting since A Sip of Magic to write this book and now it's done.

I'd like to thank Ken for contributions on this episode and my wife Bev, who helped along the way.

— Guy Antibes

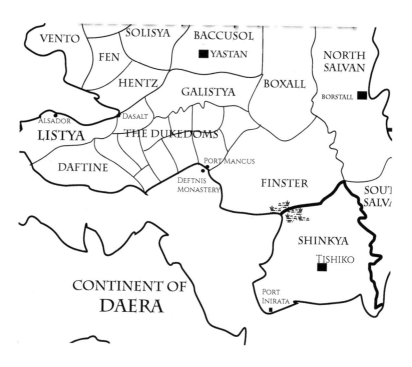

The Emperor's Pet

CHAPTER ONE

~

POL CISSERT HELD SHIRA'S HAND as they walked down the gangplank onto one of the many piers in the Alsadoran dockyards. The spring sun shone brightly, and all of Pol's party were thrilled to land on Imperial soil after their adventures on the Volian continent.

Pol looked back at Namion Threshell, their erstwhile Volian guide. He didn't consider the man part of his party. He had barely talked to the Seeker during their voyage from the Port of Ducharl, and that was fine with Pol. Namion didn't make himself very likable before, during, and after he had been ensorcelled by the Pontifer of the country of Botarra.

Fadden hadn't asked Namion to join them in Alsador, the capital of Listya, and Namion didn't volunteer to join them. Pol was certain that all the rest felt the same. He stepped onto the stone pavement and smiled as he walked on solid ground. He looked over at his friend Pakkingail Horstel, who looked like he wanted to kiss the ground. Paki had been sick for most of the way and his ordeal had finally ended.

"I can't say I know of a suitable inn in the city," Pol said. "The last time I stayed, the innkeeper of The Turning Wheel tried to steal all my belongings and hired thugs to beat me up."

"I suppose he didn't succeed?" Shira said.

"I suffered a few lumps, but I'm here."

Fadden Loria, an ex-Seeker nodded. "I know of a place."

"Loa and I are only staying for two nights," Kell said. He had had his own conversation with the captain of one of Kell's trading ships that had brought them from Volia. "Then we are going to visit my family. I'll meet you in Yastan."

"What's this?" Paki said. "You're leaving me with them?" He pointed his finger at Pol and Shira. "You never told me!"

"And make you more miserable?" Kell laughed. "Don't worry, you'll have Fadden to keep you company."

Paki made a face at Fadden and then put his hand on his head. "He'll have to do."

Fadden gave Paki a bit of a shove. "At least you won't have to learn a new language. There are other things I can teach you. Think of me... as a private tutor."

"I'll think of it," Paki said.

Fadden led them through the city once the rest of their belongings had been brought to them. "I stayed at a serviceable inn not far from the palace," he said. "It's not a long walk, but I don't trust my legs after four weeks at sea." He called the driver of the next wagon, lined up to transport goods. They put their packs and bags in the conveyance and followed. Shira and Loa were able to sit with the driver, and the other four piled into the back.

The wagon entered into crowded streets and moved at a crawl. Pol jumped off and walked just behind. "I have to admit, I'm a bit nervous, not knowing how well my brother is doing. I will have to visit him."

"I have a few contacts in the city if they haven't retired like I did. We'll have birds sent to Yastan with word of our arrival," Fadden said.

"I know the weapons master of the Royal Guard. His name is Wilf Yarrow. Val said he was the Emperor's man. He can send birds as well."

"Good," Fadden said. "Make sure you warn Ranno Wissingbel

about Namion. Who knows what kind of trouble he'll stir up, and I'll do the same."

"I smell something really good," Paki said, as they passed a street vendor.

Pol caught the aroma and called for the driver to stop, while they all bought skewers of meat and vegetables to munch on. The fresh food was welcomed by all, and that made Pol's mood all the brighter.

Alsador looked better than when he left it. The late Queen Bythia, King Landon's wife, had her South Salvan lackeys turn Alsador into a bureaucratic nightmare with lots of petty regulations and taxes when he had visited the city a year ago.

He had stopped Bythia from poisoning Landon and had to kill the former Chief Guard before the man, Regent Tamio, ran his brother through with a sword. It wasn't a pleasant visit. He hoped they wouldn't run into any trouble this time. It wasn't much longer before Fadden stopped the driver at a decent-looking inn. At least this one was different from the last inn Pol had used in Alsador.

Fadden and he walked in after Fadden settled with the cart's driver. Pol felt that most inns looked just the same in most of the countries he had been in on his recent tour of Volia. He never did have the opportunity to stay in an inn while they traveled through the Shards, but didn't really feel like he had missed anything. He had experienced enough of the Shards to last the rest of his life.

This inn had a dining room and a common room. Shira and Loa would like that. He noticed that the innkeeper was a woman similar in age to Fadden. He never had figured out what it was between Fadden and lady innkeepers, but the ex-Seeker had a penchant for them.

Each of them had their own room, and Pol smiled as he stowed his belongings underneath a tall bed. He laid back and put his hands behind his head to examine the floral-patterned wallpaper on the walls. He was ready to take a nap when he heard a knock at the door.

"Come in," Pol said.

Shira poked her head in. "Did I disturb you?"

"I was just going to take a nap, unencumbered by the rolling of a ship."

"The main market in Alsador isn't very far. Could you be my escort?" she said.

Pol couldn't help but smile. "As long as I'm not punished along the way. Could we have a truce for a day or two?" Shira liked to express her sentiments towards Pol with painful expressions of her emotions. He had suffered pinches and flicks of her finger, which had gotten tedious.

"It's a deal. Come on." She held out her hand and Pol put on his boots. He sealed the door with his magic, tweaking the door to the frame, and followed her down the stairs.

She had chosen to wear a long woolen skirt with a linen blouse covered with a vest. That was one of the Fassin purchases she had made. Shira took his hand. "The innkeeper said it was three blocks to our right and then two blocks left.

Pol smiled at her. He liked seeing Shira excited and smiling. The trip in Volia had been one peril after another. She had been abducted early in their tour, and after that they were running from the Pontifer's Hounds, a group of trackers and magicians in the employ of the Botarran monarch. He had hoped they would have enjoyed their Volian trip, but it wasn't to be. Now she looked loose and free. No Hounds in Alsador, Pol thought. He still walked armed in the city.

The innkeeper had given accurate directions, and they entered a large square filled with merchant tents. This visit would give Pol a good reading on how his brother had settled into ruling Listya.

He enjoyed walking around listening and understanding all of the conversations around him. Shira and he learned all of the languages of the countries they traveled, but one couldn't get a full vocabulary in such a short time. Now he enjoyed knowing all the words and picking up the nuances behind them.

Shira turned down a lane of tents and stopped in her tracks. Standing in front of a mapmaker's tent was a lithe man of shorter than average stature. Pol looked at the person through his magician's eyes and recognized a disguise. Shira had found a Sister, basically a Shinkyan spy, before they had been in the market for half an hour.

"Shall I go off on my own?" Pol asked, nodding towards the woman disguised as a man.

"No. There may be questions that I'd rather not answer."

Shira had taught Pol a little Shinkyan on the voyage back to the

Empire, but not enough to speak with any fluency. He followed her and watched the woman's eyes widen after she recognized Shira.

"You are Shira Graceful Willow?" the woman said. She looked at Pol and back at Shira.

"I am. I have just returned from Volia and would like a few words."

"As would I," the woman said in a low voice, but since Pol knew 'he' was a 'she' it was easy to pick up her feminine speech.

She led them into her tent and tied the flaps shut so they wouldn't be bothered. "I have a map of Volia. You can tell me of your travels. You had a safe trip?"

Shira looked at Pol. "I returned intact, but we had more than enough excitement along the way," Shira said, glancing at Pol.

They spent the next hour telling the Sister of their adventures. Shira didn't hold back anything except she had Pol talk about her abduction and rescue as well as saving Loa, the pirate chief's daughter. They finally came to the point where they entered into the Demron cave, and Shira took a deep breath.

"Tell her everything." She turned from Pol to the Sister. "What Pol has to tell you is very disturbing. I'd rather you hear the entering of a Great Ancestors' cave from his point of view." She grasped Pol's hand and nodded to him.

The story included everything except his standing at the portal, fighting with the alien intelligence that still seemed to swirl from time to time in Pol's head. He hadn't shared the extent of the invasion with anyone and certainly wouldn't with this Shinkyan Sister, the equivalent of the Emperor's Seekers.

"Cannibals," the woman sighed. "That will turn any number of Elders and Grand Masters on their heads. I have a hard time believing all this, but it must be true." She looked at Pol. "We suspected something of your heritage, but not this. There are those in Shinkya who would want to use you, Pol Cissert," the woman said. "We have a prophecy."

"No," Shira put out her hand to the Sister. "Don't tell him. I will in my own time."

"Prophecy?" Pol sighed. How many times had he studied religions where the gods will return? The Sleeping God in Fassin was supposed to wake and save Gekelmar. "I'm no savior," Pol said. He plucked his whitish hair. "This doesn't make me a Demron, and I have no taste for human flesh."

"You haven't tried any," Shira said. She moved to pinch Pol, but he grabbed her hand. "Supposedly the prophecy came over from Volia when we founded Shinkya. A Great Ancestor will return, and great changes will take place among us."

Pol nodded. "Of course, no one knows the time of the arrival of this ancestor, nor of the great changes. Am I correct?"

The Sister nodded but looked disapprovingly at Shira.

"I'm not the one," Pol said.

"But you could be," the Sister said.

He shook his head. "I don't want to be. I'm for a simple life."

"As a duke in South Salvan or as a former prince? Maybe you would prefer the life of a citizen personally known to your Emperor? You have no hope to lead a simple life," Shira said.

"And you don't either," Pol replied. He instantly regretted his words. He has studiously avoided any mention of Shira's royal connections.

"He knows that you are a princess?"

This time Shira poked Pol in the side and that made the Sister sit up.

"You're not supposed to know that," Shira said.

He sighed. "I'm a Seeker. I understand the pattern. I know all and see all," he said, trying to smile his way out of his blunder.

Shira snorted. "I am a princess. The seventh daughter of the Queen of Tishiko." She looked at the Sister. "My mother is still queen?"

The woman nodded.

"Seventh in line?" Pol said.

Shira looked at Pol with her head held high, but her eyes seemed a little watery. "You suspected all along."

Pol shook his head. "I knew you were noble, but not what rank. There have been hints and inconsistencies from the start. It doesn't affect anything on my side."

"But it does on mine." She looked sorrowfully at Pol. "Now you'll treat me—"

"Like Shira, the Seeker," Pol said. "Until you step into Shinkya, you are the same."

She grabbed his hand and squeezed. "You are a prince."

"Disinherited. But I may be a Duke in South Salvan, however." He tried to give her a reassuring smile.

The woman looked at both of them and sighed. "Now I see why you didn't return to Tishiko. This little love play is better than fighting the factions."

"And which faction are you?" Shira said.

"Fearless. As you know, we've been neutral about your mother's reign. All the Sisters have instructions to accompany you to Shinkya as soon as you return to Eastril," the Sister said. "That doesn't mean we have to go straight home, though, does it?" She smiled at them. "Tell me the rest of your story, and then let's get introduced."

Ako Injira stood up after they had finished. Pol looked upon her as a much older sister or young aunt to Shira. She was blunt in talking about the situation in Shinkya, which hadn't changed, but Pol could sense an empathy within her that seemed to be different from the hard-as-steel demeanor that characterized his other brushes with Shinkyan Sisters.

"Stay in Alsador for a few days so I can find a proper storage space for all this." Ako waved her hand at the books in her tent. She looked at Pol. "I suspect you'll be anxious about meeting your brother, King Landon, again?"

Pol thought for a moment. "What is Alsador like these days? Were you here a year ago?"

Ako nodded. "Alsador has been my home for nearly three years. Queen Bythia was a tyrant. It didn't take a Sister to figure out her motivations. The King has done a fair job, but he hasn't been as effective as he could be. I suspect he is getting conflicting advice. Recently there are signs of discontent rippling through the nobility. I haven't found out what it is yet. Perhaps we can work together to find out what it is."

"I have one request," Shira said.

"Yes?" Ako looked at Shira with interest.

"My friend, Loa, is leaving and I'd like you to appear as you really are."

Ako smiled. "I will show up at your inn in a day's time." She rummaged around her books and handed two to Pol. "Learn Shinkyan, if you'll be accompanying Princess Shira to Tishiko. One is a book on our language, and the other will teach you a basic collection of the characters we use to write." Ako looked at Shira and smiled. "I am sure your girlfriend or her new companion will help you through both books on the way to Yastan."

~ ~ ~

Chapter Two

~

POL LOOKED UP AT THE CASTLE. A year ago, he stood at this same entrance trying to gain entrance. Shira looked at him with a bit of concern as they approached the guards at the gate.

"I am King Landon's brother, Pol Cissert, the disinherited one. I landed in Alsador yesterday and would like to see my brother."

"Do you have any proof?"

Pol pulled the amulet that he wore around his neck and gave it to the guard. "Landon will remember this."

The guard looked more closely at Pol. "You worked in the castle around the time Regent Tamio was killed."

"And when Queen Bythia tried to poison my brother. Yes, I'm the one. I called myself Aron Morfess at the time."

The guard nodded. "Then the Captain of the Royal Guard will know you."

"Wilf Yarrow? Did he succeed Regent Tamio?"

The guard nodded. "He did. I'll take this to him. It might expedite an audience."

Pol didn't have to wait for more than a few minutes when Wilf Yarrow, now wearing a dress uniform, appeared at the gate.

"Pol Cissert? You were going by Aron something or other last year. King Landon told me that you were his brother. Come on in." He looked at Shira standing by his side. "You have a Shinkyan maiden at your side. I'm sure there is a story to that." Wilf scribbled something on the guard's notebook and led them inside.

The castle looked much the same to Pol as he walked behind Wilf.

"I'm your Shinkyan maiden, am I?" Shira said in Pol's ear.

"Yes, and I am your Imperial youth." He smiled at her and took her hand. "You get to meet another king and a brother who, hopefully still, is not out to kill me."

"Is that possible?" she said.

The smile faded from Pol's face. "I hope so. One should never underestimate Grostin's influence, even from across the continent."

Pol had walked the corridors of Alsador castle before, and it looked like nothing had changed. He wondered who stayed in their positions and who had left. Wilf took him past guards to the door to Landon's study.

He knocked. "King Landon, this is Captain Yarrow. I have someone important to see you."

"Come in." Pol recognized Landon's voice. The King didn't sound very energetic. His desk was filled with piles of paper, but he didn't look like he was working.

When Landon saw his brother he shot to his feet. "Pol! What are you doing in Alsador?" His eyes drifted to Shira and then he frowned. "Grostin told me about her."

"He didn't say anything good, did he?" Pol said.

"No, but then I wouldn't expect him to if she is your friend." His eyes turned back to Shira. "I am pleased to meet you. Have a seat. I'm sure Captain Yarrow has other things to do. Thank you, Captain."

Yarrow saluted his king and left the three of them alone.

"How has the last year been?" Pol asked.

Landon ran his hand through shorter hair than he wore a year ago. "I've made some progress in learning how to be a king, but recently, I've found I'm not as successful as I'd like to be." He went back around behind his desk and rummaged around in a drawer and pulled out a letter.

"You can read this and tell me what you think."

This time, Landon treated him like a peer. The change surprised Pol. The job of king seemed to be wearing on his brother. He actually seemed humble, but something else must have caused his lack of energy. Pol turned his attention to the letter.

Grostin ran on about the restrictions the Emperor had placed on his rule, especially in regards to the amount of troops in his standing army. Grostin's words expressed no appreciation for Hazett III saving the kingdom for him. Pol sat up straighter when Grostin began to discuss the amount of tribute that he expected Landon to pay North Salvan. His threat to undermine Landon's rule was rather blunt.

"This is preposterous," Pol said. "Tribute? Father never demanded such a thing, did he?"

Landon shook his head. "He initially wanted Listya as a vassal kingdom, but by the time the Emperor gave his permission, he had dropped that idea. Bythia wanted Listya for South Salvan, as you know. Now Grostin is asserting authority over me."

"You are the king of a sovereign land. You don't owe Grostin anything. I'm sure the Emperor will back you up. I'm going to Yastan and will make sure that Hazett III conveys that to Grostin." Pol didn't say what he really felt about Grostin's attempt to usurp Landon's power. It certainly fit with the pattern that he had created for his brother.

"He is an expert at stirring things up," Landon said, "just like Honna."

Pol didn't like the weakness in Landon's voice. Pol got up and walked around the desk, putting his hand on Landon's shoulder. That was enough to see a film of mind control back on Landon's brain. He eliminated it. Pol looked at Shira who raised her eyebrows.

Landon shut his eyes tightly and shook his head. "Somehow your presence reassures me. Funny, isn't it? I used to hate you and now we seem to be allies."

"Remember when I said you were under Bythia's spell? Little did I know that magicians can put suggestions into people's heads. It's something I learned at Tesna. I also learned how to create a shield. Let me put one on you. I think we won't be heading to Yastan quite yet. Someone put a spell on you, Landon, and we need to find out who."

He gripped the arms of his chair and raised his eyebrows. "What?"

"Grostin mentioned my act at removing mind control in his letter. You had a film of mind control right now. That's why you were probably feeling better by my presence."

"How? Why? Someone aligned with Grostin?" Landon looked very concerned and rubbed his head, looking shocked. "I don't know what to do."

"I think I can help," Pol said. "Shira is a magician of some ability, as well. Let my friends work with Wilf Yarrow to find what's happening in Listya."

Landon shook his head and took a deep breath. "Can you do that? I feel like a weight has been lifted from my shoulders. Grostin is really behind it?"

"Maybe not just Grostin," Shira said. "There may be others in Listya who would rather you abdicate your throne. In Tishiko, Shinkya's capital, there are many factions stirring up trouble. We can help you stabilize your situation. From what I can tell, the general populace of Alsador isn't after a change."

"I have a dinner meeting with my ruling council tonight. Come back with your friends at midday for lunch. I'd like to meet them and learn what Grostin failed to tell me. You weren't instrumental in Father's death?"

Pol shook his head. "No. I defended him until he fell to South Salvan treachery. We will talk of it tomorrow."

King Landon stood. "Whatever you did made me feel better. Let's meet again, but I have some preparation to do before my next meeting."

Pol rose with Shira. They left Landon shuffling through his papers. The king approached his work with a vigor that was lacking when they entered.

When they reached the courtyard in front of the gate, Wilf Yarrow stopped them.

"Do you have some time?" he said.

Shira squeezed Pol's hand and nodded.

"We do."

Wilf smiled. "Let me reacquaint you with a familiar office."

He led them to the Guard's administration building and into the chamber that Regent Tamio had occupied.

"I can't say that I have wonderful memories of this place," Pol said. He turned to Shira. "I used to have one of the desks outside to write reports and deliver messages for the previous Captain."

Shira smiled without showing her teeth. "You've told me."

Pol just nodded. "Anything special?"

Wilf pursed his lips. "The King hasn't been himself lately. I was wondering if you could help me find out why."

"I already have," Pol said. "You probably heard about King Astor's army?"

Wilf nodded.

"The Tesnan monks used mind control. Shira and I were placed in the monastery to learn all about it."

"I know you were involved, but I never heard the details other than you fought to defend Borstall and your father died."

"We just returned from a tour of Volia. It wasn't as pleasant a time as we thought it might be. That isn't important right now. Landon was under the control of Queen Bythia, who was a magician. I just removed a film of mind control from his mind."

Wilf's face showed alarm. "That means someone sought to control him!"

"Of course," Shira said. "It could be Grostin, his brother, or a more local faction."

"Both could be the case. There hasn't been a Court Magician here since King Landon rose to the throne." Wilf put his hand to his chin. "I can look at the log books to see who has been in the castle."

"Anything that might contribute to the pattern."

"Pattern? That is Seeker talk," Wilf said.

"We have a Seeker among our group," Pol said.

"Four, actually," Shira said.

Pol thought of Fadden along with Shira and himself. "Ah, Paki."

Shira gave him an enigmatic smile.

"Landon asked us to do some poking around. I'll have him make it official and include you," Pol said.

"I was going to ask the same," Wilf said. "It is beyond me that someone would resort to twisting the King's mind.

"Really?" Pol said. "You deal with enforcing the King's law. You know how twisted people can get."

Wilf laughed. "I didn't apply very much perspective to my thoughts. I put my own thoughts in the shoes of whoever assaulted the King. That isn't a very Seeker-like thing to do, is it, My Prince?"

"No talk of princes," Pol said. "Could you send word to Yastan that we are coming. That's my next stop. We plan to visit Yastan and Deftnis before Shira returns to Shinkya."

"After you've stabilized Listya?"

"I think you've overestimated my abilities," Pol said.

Wilf narrowed his eyes. "We'll see. Who is your ex-Seeker?"

"His name is Fadden Loria. We met him in Demina, the capital of South Parsimol."

"I've heard of him."

"You might have heard of Namion Threshell, too."

"He is a Seeker I have also met. Valiso Gasibli escorted him through Alsador and put him on a ship to Volia a few years ago. I didn't like him."

"He traveled with us on our journey through Volia."

"For some of the way," Shira said.

Pol nodded. "He came back with us but left to go his own way when we disembarked. If there is some way to tell those in Yastan, that he might not be very truthful with what he's done, I would appreciate it," Pol said. "Namion made our trip more difficult."

"I'll get right on it. I still keep Yastan informed on what's going on in Listya."

That brought a smile of relief to Pol. "I had hoped so."

Wilf rubbed his hands. "Have you learned any new tricks?"

Pol nodded. "Not all of them are admirable. Do you want to hear our story? I think it's time for you to listen to the lovely Shira."

That earned Pol a nudge from Shira's foot, out of Wilf's sight.

"So, we have a meeting with Captain Yarrow tomorrow," Fadden said as they all sat down at a farewell dinner for Kell and Loa.

The two of them would leave later that night on one of Kell's family ships to visit his parents in the country of Fen. They would head to Yastan on their own.

"My brother is understandably anxious to find out what is going on in his kingdom, as you found out at lunch today. Whoever put the mind control spell on him, merely muddled his mind and threw him into some kind of depression. I know what that's like. You all noticed he's better now, but I'm staying until I can find out what's going on."

"And I'll be joining you," a woman's voice spoke from behind Pol.

"Ako," Pol said. He rose and turned to see a woman a bit shorter and more muscular than Shira, but every bit as pretty for an older woman. "Everyone, this is Ako Injira. She is the Shinkyan equivalent of a Seeker." Pol introduced his friends. "We have decided to put off our journey to Yastan until my brother, King Landon, has the Listyan factions under control."

"Is that even possible?" Ako said, finding a chair to sit on her own.

"Our purpose isn't to solve his problems, just identify things. We will be working with Wilf Yarrow—"

Ako raised her hand. "I know Yarrow, but he doesn't quite know me." She smiled.

Pol looked over at Fadden, who kept his eyes glued to the woman. With Ako's looks, she would be hard pressed to work unnoticed in Alsador without a disguise. "We have a meeting tomorrow. You are welcome to come along." Pol could count on her local knowledge if she had been in Alsador for the last three years. He looked at her with magical eyes and made sure he could detect no traces of magic affecting her features.

"I have already closed my activities in Alsador and sent off the last of my dispatches. I think I can be of some help." She said it in a self-deprecating way. "King Landon was under the Tesnan kind of mind control, not one of those wards you encountered in Fistyra?"

Fadden pursed his lips. "She knows all?"

"Not all," Shira said, "but enough."

"I will see you all tomorrow. If you excuse me, I must secure a room and I don't want to upset your party." She rose from her seat and bowed to Kell and Loa with her hands clasped over her stomach. "I wish you well on your journey. I have been accepted as a companion for Shira and hope to know you better in Yastan." She turned and left the dining room.

"Are all the Sisters like that?" Fadden said.

Shira smiled. "No, definitely not. I can see why others might want her assigned to a foreign country and away from Tishiko. She is rather striking."

Pol didn't utter a word, but Paki grinned. "If I were a few years older," he said.

"She is more than a few years older than you," Shira said. "I'd say closer to Fadden's age."

The ex-Seeker turned red. "I suppose our mission in Alsador will be a little more colorful." Fadden tried to suppress a smile as he looked in the Ako's direction while she stood booking her room.

Pol didn't know when Fadden's wife had died or the circumstances, but he was definitely over any grieving period. If Ako was anything like Shira, Fadden might have some romantic ideas, but he wondered if his friend would have any luck in developing a relationship with a Shinkyan. It was time to get back to their farewells. Pol raised his glass in a toast to the departing couple.

~ ~ ~

Chapter Three

~

"I'M GOING TO MISS KELL," Pol said to Shira as they strolled to the castle.

"I'll miss Loa. I'm afraid Ako won't be the companion she thinks she'll be," Shira said. "Sisters aren't quite normal. That's why they become Sisters."

Pol left that statement fall to the pavement. He had no idea how Sisters were chosen to be Sisters. Was it voluntary or were women with magical capabilities forced to develop Seeker skills? They walked up to the guardhouse. A hulking guard walked up to Pol. A year ago, the man looked down at Pol, but now the pair of them looked eye to eye.

"Well, if it isn't Ossie. How are you today?" Pol said.

Ossie grinned. "Do you want to earn the right to enter the castle grounds?" The beefy guard had pummeled Pol a year ago at the very gate.

Pol smiled. "I came to see my brother."

"Brother?" Ossie said, furrowing his brow.

"He's King Landon's brother, Ossie."

The guard's head swiveled to his cohort standing behind him. "He is?" Ossie looked confused.

Shira laughed. "He is. I wouldn't tangle with him. He's learned a few tricks in the past year."

Ossie looked dumbfounded. "You're not the Seeker brother, are you?"

Pol turned invisible and stepped around Ossie and tapped him on the back. "I am."

Ossie tried to turn around, but his legs tangled and he stumbled to the ground.

"Does this count as earning the right?" Pol said to the other guard.

"You don't have to earn anything, My Prince," the man said. "Ossie never does know what's going on."

"Disinherited," Pol said as he took Shira's hand.

They arrived at the administration building and were shown to a conference room with tired furniture and the lingering smell of sweat and unwashed bodies.

Shira waved her hand in front of her face as if to ward off the odor as Wilf walked in.

"Oh," the Chief Guard's face reddened. "I guess I'm used to the smell."

"As long as you don't contribute to it," Shira said, smiling. "The others will be here shortly."

Wilf pursed his lips. "I suppose neither of you know of a tweak that will make a room more presentable?"

Pol snapped his fingers. "That's something useful they can develop at Deftnis." They all laughed. "At least your office isn't this aromatic. Fadden will bring along our fourth Seeker."

After a bit more small talk, Fadden walked in followed by Paki and Ako.

"Another Shinkyan?"

"And our fourth Seeker," Shira said.

"I thought Pol said Paki was the other."

"I'm not a Seeker," Paki said.

"I am a rather accomplished Seeker, but in Shinkya we are called Sisters." She bowed to Wilf. "I am called Ako Injira."

"The bookseller?"

She smiled and lowered her head.

"I like this disguise much better," Wilf said. He grinned, and then cleared his throat while offering them seats.

The chairs creaked when they sat, and Pol wondered what the sounds would be like when a whole squad of guards, including Ossie, would sit at the table. Wilf opened a few windows that brought in some fresher air.

"So there are two of us familiar with Alsador," Wilf said. "How should we divide up the tasks?"

"Let's determine what we want as our outcome. Our final pattern," Pol said. "Then we work on determining the present pattern and bridging the two should reveal the state of Alsador and perhaps of Listya."

"What are the major factions?" Fadden asked.

"Greenhill leads one," Ako said. "He wants a weak monarch. King Landon has certainly filled that role. Lord Wibon acts as the South Salvan ambassador. He is a relative of the new South Salvan queen. He skillfully kept his head during the South Salvan purge, although he lost his position at the palace. There is a rumor among the servants in his house that he might be working as an agent for some other kingdom."

Wilf tapped his forefinger on the table and smiled. "Good work. You said you are leaving Alsador?" Pol could tell that the Captain respected the spy, but not the spy craft. Wilf continued, "General Donton wants a strong ruler, but my men haven't seen any rumors of a coup bouncing around within his forces."

"There are other factions?" Pol asked.

"Minor ones, but there are alliances among them. I'm not sure who the Chief Healer is aligned with, but she doesn't act happy around King Landon," Wilf said.

"I met all four of those people the last time I visited. Regent Tamio paraded me around as an heir to the throne so he could establish a desire to rule Listya."

"That didn't turn out to be an effective strategy for him," Wilf said. "You did the country a great service."

"What service was that?" Ako said. She looked at Pol with eyebrows high on her forehead. "You were the one who killed Tamio?" She laughed. "I never bought the story that King Landon fought and defeated him. Only another pattern-master could defeat him."

Pol pressed his lips together and remained silent.

"Don't spread that around," Wilf said. "It's a state secret."

Ako nodded, smiling at Pol. "I'll not tell a Listyan soul."

Her words meant the story would make it all the way to Shinkya. But that didn't matter to Pol. He would only be in Shinkya long enough to get Shira safely home.

"I don't see enough here to make a good pattern. A Tesnan monk has got to be involved somehow. Pol can detect mind control, so I propose he interview his old friends in behalf of the king," Fadden said. "How does that sound, Pol?"

"I agree. We can work in parallel, each of us taking one or two of them and determine the strength of the factions. Ako evidently has connections to Lord Wibon. I can take General Donton. I think I got along with him, best of all. Fadden, you can handle Greenhill," Pol said.

"I'll take Lord Greenhill," Wilf said. "As long as I can get some help from one of you to help me make sure he isn't under someone else's control."

"That leaves Fadden for the Chief Healer. Paki why don't you join him? If Shira agrees, she can assemble the information that you all develop and work on spotting a pattern," Pol said.

"With your help, since you are the best at that," Shira said.

"Why don't you help me with Lord Greenhill? A pretty face might distract him," Wilf said.

"I always enjoy being a distraction," Shira said through her teeth.

"He is a character," Pol said, "but he is very intelligent." He got up. "Wilf can make an introduction to the Chief Healer. I'm going to talk to my brother again. Come on, Paki."

Paki and Pol made their way into the castle via the kitchen. Pol's mouth watered at the smells of baking bread and simmering broths. He grabbed a snack from a cook who remembered him from the year before and introduced the staff to Paki, making sure the cooks knew that Paki's mother was a castle cook. Pol hoped she wasn't working for Grostin, now.

Pol had to wait while Landon was holding court. He tried to picture his mother walking the halls of the castle when she was a

GUY ANTIBES | Page 21

teenager, but he found it hard to imagine her as the Listyan princess. She would always be the Queen of North Salvan in his mind.

Greenhill passed him just before he reached the throne room and stopped Pol.

"You've grown, Prince Pol. Without the hair, I might not have recognized you."

"I'm not a prince, Lord Greenhill. I'm spending a short time in Listya before moving on to Yastan."

"I heard that you recently arrived from Volia. How did you find the people over there?"

"The same as the Empire, there are bad people mixed in with the good."

"Pretty women?" Greenhill said.

"Pretty ones mixed with those who aren't as pretty."

Lord Greenhill nodded to Pol. "Ah, it must be the same all over the world," Greenhill said breezily. "Enjoy your stay."

Pol bowed to the man and watched him walk down the corridor.

"Oily," Paki said quietly.

Pol chuckled. "I think he can be quite charming. Let's get to work."

"Seeking," Paki said. "I like it."

"Some of it," admitted Pol.

One of the guards walked over to the pair. "The king is about to end his session. You may enter the throne room now."

King Landon had to address a few more matters before guards cleared the throne room. Landon took off his state crown and put a thin gold circlet on his head.

"We can sit over there." Landon pointed with his chin to a table set with a wine carafe and two bowls of fruit by one of the tall windows that lined one side of the room.

The throne room looked impressive when Pol first saw it a year ago, but it didn't compare to rooms in the annex at the palace in Bastiz with their high windows and thinner columns.

"You've had something to eat?" Landon said as he poured wine for himself.

Pol noticed they were the only ones in the vast room. "We pilfered a snack in the kitchens.

"That's fitting, you are here with Paki, after all. Have you found the culprits yet?" Landon said in a quieter voice.

"There are three major factions. So far, we haven't found any that are after your throne, but we just started today. I drew Lord Wibon."

Landon's face grew a look of alarm. "Is South Salvan active against me? I've had reassurances from Queen Isa."

Pol shook his head. "You don't have to worry about her, but there might be others in South Salvan not happy with Bythia's death. I can see those individuals aligning with Grostin."

"I wish Bythia hadn't been so against me, but her death had to happen," Landon said. He sighed and concentrated on peeling a grape.

Pol checked his brother's mind shield and reinforced it, relieved that no one had successfully tampered with Landon's mind. He took a deep breath.

"As I indicated, there is a possibility that Wibon is keeping track of Listya for Grostin."

"Others could do that," Landon said.

"I'll find out. I'll be talking to him since there are rumors I have a dukedom in his country."

Landon laughed. "It's more than a rumor. Wibon told me Kelso Beastwell runs your ducal estate along with one of his own close by. I don't know any of the particulars, but Wibon would." He popped the peeled grape in his mouth. "Oh, I see. You even outrank him in South Salvan."

"Seekers start with a pattern and continually verify it. The more information, the better the pattern. If nothing else, our investigation may clear him, but you can't trust Wibon at this point."

"He would know Tesnan monks, wouldn't he?"

"Maybe. That is possible. A Tesnan monk needs to be a member of one of the factions that surround you. Many of them know how to apply mind control," Pol said.

Landon waved his hand. "We had factions in Borstall. Father tried to discuss them with me, but I wasn't too interested at the time. I should have listened, right?"

Pol nodded. It was odd giving Landon reassurance, but he preferred that to Grostin's antipathy.

"I made up a list before I left. I'm sorry, but the faction leaders were on the list, except for Lord Wibon."

Landon shook his head. "They all helped me get things going again. The only bit of advice I haven't followed is that I'm still not remarried. It's hard to meet eligible women when you are the king."

"You can always ask Hazett III to find you a wife. That's how Father met my mother."

Landon frowned. "You suggested that I marry a Listyan woman and I still think that is the best course. I thought I made some headway along those lines, but things went into a stall, lately. We both know why." He tapped his head.

The door opened, and a uniformed man walked in. Pol didn't recognize him.

"This is Carl, my chamberlain." Landon looked at Carl. "This is my brother, Pol, and his friend Pakkingail Horstel. They've been at Deftnis together."

Pol and Paki rose. The man looked very smooth, and that was to be expected, but Pol sensed a distinct chill.

"My King, the ambassador is here for your meeting." Carl turned to Pol. "I have heard a great deal about you, My Prince."

Pol reflexively waved away the title. "My brother tells me I am a Duke."

Carl's eyebrows shot up. "In Listya? You didn't inform me, My King."

Landon gulped down another cup of wine. "His domain is in South Salvan. I really must go, Poldon. I have matters to discuss with the Daftine ambassador. He is our closest neighbor, after all." The King shrugged and stood. "Keep me posted."

"We will," Pol said.

Landon patted Pol on the shoulder and left the two of them standing in the throne room.

"This might have been yours," Paki said looking around.

"And you might have been a gardener."

"Not me!" Paki said.

Pol laughed. "I will reiterate that I have no desire to be King of Listya. The sooner we find the magician who ensorcelled Landon, the sooner we can leave for Yastan. That's an adventure I look forward to. Neither of us has been there." Pol wondered if Amonna had made her way to the capital. He didn't like the idea of her living with Grostin. Who knew what kinds of things their brother was capable of.

"I set up an appointment for us with Lord Wibon," Ako said, as she walked into the lobby of the inn the day after Pol's meeting with his brother. "I would like to try to see mind control, but it would be easier if I know if Lord Wibon is controlled first."

"Is Shira included?"

Ako frowned. "Not this time. She's currently with Captain Yarrow. We should leave soon to make it to his townhouse in time."

Pol closed his Shinkyan language primer. "Maybe we can practice your language a bit on the way," he said. Everyone else seemed to have other things to do and the appointment brightened Pol's afternoon.

"First a word," Ako said, motioning Pol to sit. "I've observed Shira's behavior around you."

Pol gripped the arms of his chair as discreetly as he could. He was prepared for an uncomfortable conversation.

"I've noticed the way she expresses her affection towards you."

Pol furrowed his brow. "What do you mean?"

"I mean pinching and that finger-flicking she does. It is inappropriate behavior in Shinkya and in the Empire."

"I figured she was uncomfortable with our relationship and that's how she expressed her frustration," Pol said.

Ako looked at Pol and nodded her head with a vague smile on her face. "You are a Seeker. That is what she's been doing, but since you're not experienced with girls, you wouldn't know how out of bounds she is. I told her to stop it or she would lose you."

Pol was about to object loudly, toned his voice down. "That's not true."

"Do you really like the punishment?"

Pol shook his head. "I've endured a lot for her and she for me."

"You shouldn't have to endure anything. I believe the behavior will end. If it starts to get where you have to endure it again, don't let it slide. It will lead to cruelty if unchecked. She observed a few of her sisters doing the same thing. They now casually torment as a matter of course and it has made life difficult for those in close proximity to her sisters. When I pointed it out to Shira she begged for my forgiveness, but it's not my forgiveness that she needs."

"You told her to apologize?"

"She is not mine to command, but I suggested it. If she does, please accept it, but I suggest that you don't encourage her present behavior."

Pol sat back and wondered what bad behavior he conducted without knowing. "If I make a mistake with her, let me know."

"If I catch you in one, but I won't be looking for it. I am her chaperone, not yours."

Ako rose, and Pol followed.

"Shall we go?" she said in Shinkyan.

The walk to Lord Wibon's townhouse was long enough to exhaust most of Pol's new Shinkyan words. Ako seemed to be patient with Pol and kept correcting his pronunciation. Shinkyan was unlike any other language on Phairoon.

"He doesn't know you?" Pol said.

Ako nodded. "I made the appointment in your name."

"What if I was busy now?" Pol said.

"You aren't." She shrugged and used the door-knocker. It was in the shape of a lion, not the South Salvan money, but the animal.

A tall, thin, middle-aged woman dressed in black opened the door. "Yes?" she said, drawing out the word.

"Pol Cissert to see Lord Wibon," Pol said.

"Poldon Fairfield is his other name," Ako said. She looked at Pol and grimaced. Perhaps that was Ako's way of an apology.

"Lord Wibon is expecting you. Please come in." The woman led them inside.

Pol let Ako precede him into the house. The housekeeper, if that was what she was, showed them into a sitting room.

"Lord Wibon will join you in a few minutes." She bowed stiffly and shut the door quietly behind her as she left.

Ako wandered around the room and picked up pieces of art and read the spines on books.

"You can tell a lot about a person by the decorations in his or her house," she said.

"Wibon has a number of phony pieces that aren't sold in Shinkya." She picked one up and tossed it to Pol.

"How do you know they are fake?"

"He owns them. They are here. Look closely and if the pieces are not perfect, they are duplicates. Burrs on carvings, paint that doesn't follow the inscribed lines. There are a number of telltales, but if you compared them with the real pieces, even you could tell the difference. Think of your patterns. These have irregularities that you'd never see in ours."

Pol examined the wooden image of a cat. Carved lines delineated different paint colors, and he could see exactly what Ako meant. "A noble Shinkyan would never own these?"

Ako nodded. "South Salvans have an attraction to Shinkya without understanding our culture," she said while still examining a shelf of books. "They mimic the Shinkyan style, but without knowing us, it all looks false to us."

"I've been to Covial."

Ako turned around. "Then you know what I mean. Shira must have pointed out their pointless imitation of Tishiko."

Pol smiled weakly. He didn't know what Ako was getting at, but there was a deeper meaning to her words. "She did. Do you consider humans an imitation of Shinkyans?"

The Sister went silent. She didn't move a muscle. Pol wondered what went on in her head.

"You received this insight in the Demron cave?" Ako said. "Shira and you didn't mention such a thing."

Pol detected anxiety in her question.

"Shira and I have discussed it. I haven't told you everything that happened in the cave."

Ako snorted in a very unladylike way. Perhaps it was a mannerism picked up mimicking a man for so long. "Neither has Shira."

The doorknob squeaked as someone turned it.

"We can save this discussion for another time," Pol said.

"Aron Morfess? Am I mistaken?" Lord Wibon put his head through the opening, looking confused.

Pol shook his head. "There is no Aron Morfess. That was a false name."

"So are you Poldon Fairfield or Pol Cissert? I'm confused by all of your names," Lord Wibon said as he entered the room. "Sit. Both of you sit."

Pol didn't believe that Lord Wibon was confused about his identity at all. Pol still held the yellow-painted cat. "From Shinkya?"

"From Covial," Lord Wibon said. "It is a poor rendition of a Shinkyan carving. An artist spent a season in Tishiko absorbing your culture." Wibon nodded to Ako and sat on a lemon-colored overstuffed chair. "He made quite a bit of money selling his book of Shinkyan designs. That was a hundred years ago. We still are making these. I think they are quite accurate, don't you think?"

"I wouldn't know," Pol said. "I've never been to Shinkya."

Wibon chuckled. "I hear that lack will be remedied before the year is out."

"It will. Ako and the young Shinkyan woman who accompanied me to Volia will be returning to their homeland after a visit to Yastan."

"You are Ako?" Wibon said.

"I am."

Pol wondered if she would have corrected Wibon's proud description of purloined Shinkyan designs, but she remained silent.

"I wanted to know if rumors that Queen Isa has made me a duke are correct. The last time I saw her, the Queen was on a ship heading for South Salvan."

Wibon bowed to Pol from his sitting position. "You haven't been formally invested, but the answer is yes. You now own General Onkar's estates. They were one of the largest in South Salvan, so she decided to award you a dukedom within South Salvan. The Queen thinks a great deal of you, My Duke."

Pol didn't bother to correct Wibon. "I think a great deal of her. We spent considerable time together last year."

"Your other Shinkyan friend did, too, I understand."

Pol nodded. "Our efforts met with mixed success."

"You are as modest as you were when you delivered messages to me while you masqueraded as Aron Morfess."

"I see you landed on your feet. I am surprised Queen Bythia's confidant survived Queen Isa's ire."

Wibon twittered. "Isa and I are cousins, don't you know. She would rather have me enjoying Alsador than plotting in Covial."

"Would you be plotting in your capital?" Ako said.

"Perhaps. We are always plotting about something or other, aren't we? It's the nature of royal families and the nobility. You should know, My Disinherited Prince."

Pol nodded. He shut his eyes and noted a film of mind control coating Wibon's brain. Pol nodded again to Ako. He walked over to the older man and gave him the cat. "I didn't mean to handle your heirloom," Pol said. He touched Wibon's hand as he handed it over and removed the mind control and placed a shield.

"What did you do? Did you just play with Order in front of me?" Wibon appeared very uncomfortable and twisted in his chair.

Pol returned to his seat. "The rest of the Empire calls it tweaking and I tweaked you, twice. Once to remove a mind control spell and another to shield you against another such indignity upon your person."

Pol glanced at Ako, who lifted her chin, winked. She had just received a little education.

"Mind control!" Wibon jumped up from his seat. "That's outrageous. I'm going to complain to King Landon."

"Do you know of any Tesnan monks who have taken up residence in Alsador?" Ako said. "Perhaps one of your former friends at the monastery…"

Wibon sputtered a bit and shook his head. "I, I…"

"If you remember any or if you are contacted by any in the next few days, please let Captain Yarrow know. We will want you checked again to make sure your faculties are unimpaired," Pol said.

"Faculties? What about my faculties?"

"The mind control spell didn't get there on its own. Whoever put it there had a reason. I'll be a bit more specific. If someone makes a suggestion that you do something that you wouldn't ordinarily do, remember their identity. King Landon wouldn't want to take extraordinary measures against you."

Wibon's eyes grew. "I'm an ambassador! You can't tell me what I can and can't do. I am my own man, not a Listyan subject."

"Possibly under the control of some other person. That makes you a potential danger to my brother."

Wibon wiped the sweat off his brow and sat back down. He took a deep breath, ostensibly to calm down. "I understand. I was going to ask if you would like refreshments, but forgive my rudeness. I think I now find the need to rest for a bit."

Pol and Ako said goodbye to Lord Wibon. The same housekeeper let them out. Pol stood in front of the townhouse and looked back at it.

"Honestly, Bythia could have put the mind control on Lord Wibon," Pol said. "You still have your contacts in the house?"

"She just let us out."

Pol whistled. "The woman is a great actor."

"She's never seen Ako Injira."

"Oh. In that case, you might have to return to your disguise. See if there was a time in the past few months when Wibon's behavior noticeably changed. That might help us fill in his pattern."

They began walking back to the inn.

"Did you see Wibon's mind control?"

Ako nodded. "I can't see inside his head like you can, but there seemed to be a haze around his forehead and temples."

Pol barked out a laugh. "People see tweaked images differently. I never asked Shira how she viewed mind control. I just assumed it was the same. Assumptions are not a Seeker's friend."

"You really are good at this. I feel like I'm working for an Elder," Ako said. "You have such a clear picture of things."

Pol chuckled. "No, I don't. I know any secret of how to make a picture clearer. To me it's a process, and we are still engaged filling in the pattern."

"Whatever you say," Ako said, smiling. "It's a shame you aren't Shinkyan."

~ ~ ~

Chapter Four

~

BACK AT THE INN, POL ASKED AKO to help him with diction, using the language book, when Paki flew through the door and stood at the common room table where Pol and Ako worked.

"I've been looking for you! Something happened to Fadden."

"Is he all right?" Pol asked.

Paki shook his head. "He's at the castle infirmary. He was talking to the Chief Healer when he twisted in his seat. The Chief Healer called it a bowel spasm. You need to see him."

Ako begged off to write a note to Wibon's housekeeper. Pol and Paki ran to the castle and found Fadden in a healer's ward. His face was red and sweaty."

He reached up and grabbed the sleeve of Pol's tunic. "Help me. I think I'm dying."

"Did you eat anything that might cause your cramps?"

Fadden shook his head. "The Chief Healer might have done something to me," he said.

Pol couldn't picture the woman harming anyone. "Let me see what I can do."

Working with soft tissue was not something Pol was particularly comfortable with, but Fadden writhed in pain. He grabbed a chair.

"Where is the pain?"

Fadden pointed to the lower right side of his belly. Pol put his hand on Fadden's stomach and closed his eyes. He didn't see any evidence of magic, but he did find a length of Fadden's intestine that appeared to be undulating. Pol examined a calmer part of Fadden's abdomen and sent a similar pattern of calm through the organ. He didn't know if that would work, but perhaps it might counter whatever spell the Chief Healer or someone else might have performed.

"That's better."

Pol used his magic to send more calming tweaks along the intestine.

Fadden's breathing evened out and it appeared the crisis had ended.

"I thought I was going to die," Fadden said.

"No hope of that," Pol replied. "You were made uncomfortable, but the malady wasn't dangerous."

"It felt dangerous," Fadden said, rubbing his stomach. "What did you do?"

Pol smiled. "I tweaked calmness. Think of me petting your intestine as I would a cat. The petting calms the feline. I just calmed your insides, and it seemed to have worked. Where did the Chief Healer go? Was she under mind control?"

"I didn't get that far. We introduced ourselves, and then my stomach took over. She helped me to this bed and then left. I sent Paki out to go find you."

It all seemed strange. "What about the other healers?"

"No one knew what to do other than to apply hot towels to my stomach. That didn't help."

A healer walked up with a basin filled with a steaming aromatic paste.

"He won't need that," Pol said. "What is it?"

"A mustard seed plaster. It has other herbs. We didn't want to perform an enema."

"It wouldn't have helped," Pol said. "I'd like to talk to the Chief Healer."

The healer looked defensive. "I saw her leave the infirmary." He looked at Fadden with a bit of surprise on his face. "Your friend looks much better."

"He's fine now." Pol turned to Fadden. "Can you come with us?"

Fadden nodded. He looked tired but had already begun to put his clothes back on.

"If you need him, he'll be at our inn. Wilf Yarrow knows which one."

Paki and Pol helped Fadden outside.

"You didn't tell Yarrow which inn we are staying," Fadden said.

Pol frowned. "Let's see if Wilf is around. I'd like him to ask the Chief Healer some questions before he tells her where we are staying, anyway."

Wilf was in the smelly conference room standing over a large sheet of paper. Shira must have glued a number of smaller sheets together.

"What's with Fadden?" he said.

Fadden sat down, but then had an alarmed look on his face. "If you will excuse me, my bowels are a bit too loose now." He ran from the room.

Pol watched him go. "Tweaking a pattern sometimes produces unintended consequences," he said. "What's with the paper?"

"It's a technique that Regent used, of all people. You write things down on a big piece of paper. It helps to keep things straight when you are trying to find a pattern. I work with the city guard on enough crimes and that keeps us all together on the right track. It's always good to have a competent scribe." Wilf smiled at Shira, who wasn't looking at him.

Shira lifted her head, an annoyed expression on her face. "Do you have something important to give me?"

The large sheet had the names of the interviewees spaced out.

"Under the Chief Healer, put a note that she tweaked Fadden's tummy," Pol said. "She took him to a bed and then left the building. Under Lord Wibon, put that our friends might have tweaked a film of mind control, but that might have persisted from when Bythia was here."

"A year?" Shira said. "Doesn't mind control fade away?"

"Do we really know? I've never really tested it. The only record we have of mind control dissipating was in the Tesnan texts. It's an open piece of the pattern. I can't see the Chief Healer playing a prank on Fadden, so she becomes a suspect and we will need to follow her movements."

"Are you sure she left the castle?" Wilf said.

"I only know the healer said she wasn't in the infirmary. I told the healer to get the name of our inn from you. I'm sure the Chief Healer will be wary of talking to Fadden, but she knows you and she might mention where she went after she left the infirmary."

Wilf nodded. "Good thinking. I'll do that. So we still have two suspects?"

"No, we don't. Lord Wibon had a film of mind control," Paki said.

"We can't rule him out as a suspect, because he might have asked for a touch of mind control to give him the courage to arrange something during an audience with King Landon. We can't close up that part of the pattern," Pol said.

"Oh. I didn't think that far ahead."

"It's not a matter of thinking ahead. We need to evaluate all the possibilities because we don't know what the actual pattern is."

Shira tapped her pencil on the paper. "Is there anyone not under mind control?"

"It's time to find out." Pol looked at Wilf. "Have you met with Greenhill, yet?"

The Chief Guard shook his head.

"Then let's get him out of the way, and perhaps pay a quick visit to General Donton. We will talk to them just long enough to see if they are controlled. We can call them courtesy visits on my part. Maybe along the way, we'll meet with the Chief Healer."

Fadden staggered in. "I think I'll make my way back to the inn." His face had turned white.

"I'll help you, Fadden," Paki said. "I don't want to get my guts twisted."

Greenhill was out, but Pol and Wilf Yarrow found General

Donton outside his office talking to an aide.

"General Donton," Wilf said.

The General's eyes turned to Pol. "King Landon's brother, Poldon? You've grown." His gaze returned to Wilf. "What is it? A chat? I have time for a short one. The Daftine delegation is still meeting with us, so I have to prepare something for your brother. Come in."

They followed the General into his chamber. An aide followed. "You may get the maps ready while I talk." He put his hand to his forehead in salute, dismissing the man.

"So what brings you back to Listya? Are you going to fight for your brother's throne?"

"I'm happy with King Landon being King Landon—"

"Once that witch Bythia was put aside," the General interrupted Pol. "You did us all a service, although it led to Regent's death."

"Listya is better after those events," Wilf said.

"Some think that," Donton said. He looked at Pol and brightened. "Is that a Shinkyan sword you wear?"

Pol smiled. "Would you like to handle it?"

The General's eyes lit up. "I would. I've never even touched one."

He stepped from this desk and took the sword from Pol, who touched the General's hand.

"The balance is wonderful, but I'm afraid it's a little light for me."

"It depends on your style. You could get used to one," Wilf said.

"You're a former weapons master, so you should know." He played with the blade for a moment. "Where did you get this?"

"In Tesna. I—"

"That's right. You were involved in the unpleasantness in the East. I hate the notion of controlling men's minds," Donton said.

"And yet, you are controlled, as we sit here."

Donton pointed the tip of the sword towards Pol. "What? How dare you!"

Pol stood, ignoring the General's aggression. "If you want it removed, let me touch your head once you're seated. Removing mind control can be disorienting."

Donton glared at Wilf Yarrow. "Do you believe him? I'll not be made a fool."

The Chief Guard nodded. "I do. Give him his sword and sit down. We will explain."

After another angry stare at Pol, the General sighed and returned Pol's Shinkyan sword and went to his desk.

"If you weren't here, Wilf, I would have run him through."

Pol sheathed his sword and put his hand on the General's head. He detected a thick film of mind control and removed it. The General had to close his eyes and put his head against the back of his chair.

"I know what you mean about getting dizzy," he said, his voice growling. "I've been manipulated, haven't I?" He sounded a bit mollified.

"We have suspected someone stirring the pot against King Landon," Wilf said.

Pol replaced the mind control with a shield and returned to his seat.

"Even with the King," Pol said. "I can't be sure if his mind control was from Bythia's time or recent. I didn't know about mind control last year. Lord Wibon was also under a spell. Can you remember anyone giving you instructions?"

Donton shook his head. "I deal with so many people trying to giving me advice, I have no idea who might have done such a thing." He still looked peeved.

Pol leaned forward. "But you were feeling angry with the King and had thoughts to replace him."

The General looked away. "I admit such things arise in many of my conversations, but they have even before your brother became King."

"But you didn't take them as seriously as before, right?"

"Of course not!" the General said.

"Have you organized anything specific?"

Donton shook his head. "I didn't go that far." He put his head in his hands. "What an idiot. I never thought I'd be the dupe to any man."

"Then don't," Wilf said. "Let us know if anyone gives you more specific instructions. We think there might be a Tesnan monk loose in

Alsador." Wilf stood. "You have your meeting. Make sure you represent the King's interests."

Donton nodded. "I will." He looked at Pol. "You are a good lad. I am sorry if I appeared weak."

"Someone made you that way," Pol said. "Remember that helping us helps the King. If you hear anything specific, let Wilf know."

~ ~ ~

Chapter Five

~

GREENHILL HAD RETURNED TO HIS OFFICE by the time Pol and Wilf made their way across the castle.

"I would like a moment of Lord Greenhill's time," Wilf Yarrow said to the Lord's secretary.

"A moment," the man rose, eyeing Pol and disappeared behind Greenhill's door. He served as Greenhill's aide a year ago.

Greenhill flew out of his office. "Yarrow, Poldon. Please come in. I am surprised you made the effort to snatch me from a moment of boredom."

They walked in. Papers were stacked on Greenhill's desk, and a pen lay on a half-filled sheet of paper in front of his chair. The man was anything but bored.

Lord Greenhill rubbed his hands and grinned. Pol noticed ink stains. "What brings you to my tiny cell?"

"I wanted to meet with you again under less hasty circumstances."

"Ah, the awkward hallway conversation. Yes, hasty. A good word to describe it."

"Forgive my surliness. Listya does not bring out the best in me," Pol said.

"Killing one of my dearest friends is evidence of that." Greenhill put out his hand and smiled. "But so few of us know the real details. I can forgive, too."

Pol took it and found no evidence of mind control. He didn't know what to think about that. Perhaps, like Grostin, he didn't need to be controlled to do the will of others.

"He was in the act of thrusting a sword in my brother."

Greenhill's eyes lit up. "I knew you did it!"

Wilf made a sound. "So skillfully done, as usual, Greenhill. It only took a goad to get Pol to admit he was behind saving his brother's life that night."

Lord Greenhill gave them a smug smile. "You need to sharpen up your conversational skills if you want to survive in Yastan, my lad."

Pol felt like a five-year-old. Lord Greenhill had bested him in the man's own way.

"Can we have a serious word?" Pol said.

"Of course. I'm always serious."

Pol wondered if that might really be true, behind his facade. They all sat down in chairs in front of an empty fireplace. Pol looked at Wilf to talk. He had inflicted enough damage to his self-esteem for one meeting.

"I'll get to it so you can return to your boredom," Wilf said, glancing pointedly at Greenhill's desk.

The lord tugged on his waistcoat. "I'm prepared for your onslaught, Chief Guard."

"Right, Lord Exchequer. King Landon is feeling uneasy. He thinks that the usual palace intrigue is coalescing into something more serious."

"That's apparent from his recent behavior, although King Landon has shown some life ever since Poldon has arrived."

Wilf nodded. "There is a reason for that. Do you know of anything that I can use to calm down the King?"

"Drugs? Gods know he needs a good woman. I can help him along those lines, but he doesn't trust me, does he?" Greenhill said.

"Does he deserve your trust?" Wilf said.

Greenhill poked his tongue in his cheek. "You know me better than that. He does."

"Then perhaps it's time you quit playing around with your circle of backbiters and do something positive."

Pol was taken aback by Wilf's harsh words. The two men knew each other much better than Pol had realized and their discussion was much more to the point than he expected for such a short encounter.

Greenhill looked at Pol and then back at Wilf. "I'm not about to abandon my style."

"I don't expect you to, Greenhill. Just play straight when you need to. King Landon needs your help and Pol is an apprentice Seeker and needs your help, too."

"Seeker?" Greenhill looked at Pol with appraising eyes. "You have too much heart and passion for a good Seeker, My Disinherited Prince. But you don't lack for courage. I could tell that last year. Regent was taken by you enough to consider a boy of your age a threat. That was quite a compliment, you know." He sighed. "I will keep my tiny wolf pups at bay, Wilf. They are all harmless enough."

"If they suddenly grow longer teeth let us know, Pol said. "Permit me to tweak a shield against mind control for you before we leave."

"Mind control. Wasn't that what the Tesnans threatened to use last year?"

"They did use it," Wilf said. "We have found a mind control spell on General Donton, and Pol knows how to craft a shield. I have one, so I can assure you it is painless.

Greenhill sighed and waved his hand. "Shield away."

Fadden recovered enough the next day to attend a meeting in Wilf's conference room. Shira stood next to the big sheet of paper that she had now pinned to a wall.

"No one has spoken to the Chief Healer again?" Fadden said as he sat down. Silence filled the room with Fadden's answer.

"So far, the only person that hasn't been touched with mind control is Lord Greenhill," Pol said. "That doesn't make him one of the manipulators."

"Where are we, then?" Wilf said, tilting his chair back, gazing at Shira's work.

"Something is going on for sure," Shira said. "What will happen once the monk finds that the mind control has been removed and replaced with shields?"

"What is your opinion of Lord Greenhill?" Fadden said to Wilf. "Pol thought you acted like close friends."

"We were," Wilf said. "I grew up on his father's estate. My father was the previous Lord Greenhill's steward. Greenhill and I played together. Although I was younger, he and I spent hours together when we grew up. When Greenhill's father died, he had to take over the estate. My father worked for him and at that point, the distance grew."

"Do you trust him?" Pol said.

"I used to, but when Regent Tomio came to Alsador, things changed even more. Greenhill isn't a bad person if that's what you mean. There have been no money issues since he took over the Exchequer's position five years ago and that included a very tense year when Queen Bythia essentially ran the country."

Pol sat back. Lord Greenhill played his own game, but as Pol struggled with being objective, despite his negative feelings for the man, Greenhill's pattern didn't indicate him to be at the center of any conspiracy.

"Let's assume that he is what he is, a leader of a grumbling faction and is not connected with the monk."

"For now," Shira said.

Pol noticed that Fadden nodded. "Ako, do you have any perspective?"

"I would agree with your assessment. Greenhill sometimes acts the fool, but he works hard for King Landon."

"So, General Donton?" Fadden said.

Shira looked at her own entries on the paper. "He is a necessary link to any conspiracy since he leads the armed forces—"

"Other than the Royal Guard," Wilf said.

Shira nodded. "A good faction in Tishiko has to have both political and military strength. We can assume that the faction intended General's mind control spell to provide them with military resources, should they need them."

"And that would indicate that the conspiracy could be working towards an overthrow of some kind," Wilf Yarrow said.

That made sense to Pol. "Let me throw in two possible outcomes. It doesn't look like the conspiracists want Landon to rule. The weak mind control merely muddled his wits and depressed him so he would look timid and ineffective. One possibility is that there is a local faction at fault. The other is that my other brother, Grostin desires to control Listya as my father originally intended, using Landon as a puppet."

Ako smiled knowingly. "I don't know of any pretenders to your brother's throne other than yourself. In my time here, I haven't noticed any real challenges to King Landon and before him, the North Salvan Regent, there was just a lot of grumbling."

Wilf narrowed his eyes in thought. "I would have to concur, but I don't get out much. There are no rumors that have reached me, but being in the Royal Guard, I've kept out of all that, unlike my predecessor."

"Something you should change," Fadden said. "You should hire a Deftnis Seeker or contact Ranno Wissingbel to see if a retired Seeker might want to work for you in Alsador. It's always better to anticipate threats than react to them."

"Would you be interested, Fadden?"

"Me?" Fadden looked surprised by Wilf's offer. "Perhaps it is something we could talk about after I've accompanied these fine folks to Yastan."

"Don't jump at the offer, Fadden. I think an Imperial point of view might be useful to my Fearless faction," Ako said.

Her smile looked more like a smirk, but Pol thought she might even be serious. He'd have to ask Shira. Pol knew that better relations with Shinkya involved more contact with the Empire.

"Something to think about when all of this is over?" Pol said.

Fadden cleared his throat and nodded. The man hadn't blushed when Wilf gave him an offer, but Ako's definitely had an effect. "We shouldn't give one alternative precedent over the other this early in our investigation, but it does give a direction to build possible patterns."

Pol examine Shira's work. Her handwriting had its own look that Pol hadn't really noticed before. He thought of Tishiko factions and from what she described, the situation in Alsador looked different.

"We have to find participants in the faction that employs mind control. Anyone serious about taking over the kingdom would need others. The nobility wouldn't accept just anyone." Pol said. "We need to talk to the Chief Healer—"

"Not me," Fadden said, clutching his stomach. Pol didn't know if Fadden was serious or not.

"A wider net. That means you will have to observe," Wilf said. "But we are all too well known."

"Not Paki," Shira said, "and the rest of us can disguise ourselves to some extent."

Wilf looked at Ako. "All four of you?"

"To an extent," Fadden said. "Pol, Shira and Ako are better at it than I."

Wilf put his hand to his chin. "Someone needs to observe Wibon's house. I can place you as servants to allow you to observe Greenhill and Donton. The last will need to find the Chief Healer. Anyone they contact could be a faction member."

"If my thoughts on the pattern are correct, there are at least two of them in league. I'm assuming the Chief Healer is one of them, but we need to verify that," Pol said.

Pol assigned himself to pursue the Chief Healer since he might be able to come up with a better defense against the bowel offense. Fadden, Paki, and Shira would be servants and trade off from time to time. Wilf would try to do some Seeking on his own, talking to nobles and their servants about attitudes. Ako still had the best contacts in Lord Wibon's household.

The Chief Healer hadn't returned after a few more days of observation of the infirmary. Pol walked into the lobby and asked after the Chief Healer.

"She hasn't been here for days," one of the healers told Pol.

"I need to contact her. Do you know where she lives?" he asked.

"We aren't supposed to give out information like that."

Pol pursed his lips and turned into himself. "Do I need a royal order? Do you know who I am?" He didn't want to go so heavy on the older man, but Pol didn't have time to fiddle around finding Landon.

The healer took a step back. "You are the King's brother. I remember you from a year ago." The healer seemed to be thinking. "If you will sign a note requesting her address, I'll give it to you."

Pol smiled as nicely as he could. "That would fine," he said. "Get me some paper and a pencil."

After composing the note, Pol took the paper with the Chief Healer's address from the other healer. "I'll make sure King Landon makes things right if you get into any trouble."

The healer nodded. "Thank you, My—"

"The name is Pol. No prince here." He gave the man a little bow and walked out into the bright morning. He lifted his face to the warm sunlight and hoped for good fortune.

He asked for directions from the guards at the gate. The healer's residence was only a few streets away. He realized that a good Seeker should have gotten the address sooner.

On the way to the house, Pol ducked into an alley to change his features into those of Nater Grainell. No one but Shira, Paki, and Fadden would recognize him in Alsador. He checked his attire to make sure he wore nothing in a Volian style that he brought back with him from his trip to that continent.

He paused across the street and took a deep breath. Pol wasn't particularly adept at walking up to strangers and talking. He could picture Valiso Gasibli assuming any disguise and approaching anyone. He fiddled with his hands before straightening his already-orderly clothes and crossed the light traffic to knock on the Chief Healer's door.

"Is the Chief Healer here?" Pol said to an older man dressed in clothes suitable for a servant. He hoped the man wasn't the Chief Healer's husband.

"She isn't taking visitors."

"But she is in. I tried to contact her at the Royal Infirmary."

"They let you in?" the man said, looking at Pol and seeing a teenager.

"I am a healer of some talent, a prodigy if you will."

My Lady doesn't hire people off the street, young man. You may go."

Pol fiddled with his hands again, but this time on purpose. "When will she return to the Infirmary?"

He looked past the servant and could see part of the Chief Healer's face at the landing of the stairs. He tried to keep his eyes from returning to her.

"My Lady doesn't use me for her confidences. You'd better be on your way," the servant said, shutting the door in Pol's face.

Pol stood there with his head down, in case anyone looked. He tweaked his hearing to hopefully hear what was said in the hallway on the other side of the door.

"Who was that, a messenger?" the Chief Healer said. Her voice was clear, so she must be on the stairway.

"A boy who claimed to be a healer. He made it past the castle guard, My Lady."

"That is suspicious," she said. "Did he have silvery-blond hair?"

"More of a dirty blonde turning brown, My Lady."

The Chief Healer must have paused in thought, for the conversation went silent.

"Is it all right for me to go out for a little bit?" the healer asked someone.

Pol had heard enough and moved to an alley across the street in view of the house. He changed his appearance again with darker hair and waited for the Chief Healer to leave her house.

In a few minutes, a woman, clutching a common hooded cloak around her, walked down the steps to the sidewalk and headed in the opposite direction from the castle. Pol proceeded to follow her from the other side of the street, a few steps behind, so she wouldn't inadvertently spot him.

Now he wished he had someone else with him. She wouldn't notice a couple trailing her as much as a 'teenager'. She turned down an alley. Pol couldn't follow without being noticed, so he had to run ahead to circle the block. He slowed up and took a deep breath before looking ahead. The Chief Healer walked in his direction but had crossed the street.

Pol paused to look inside a cobbler's window, watching her in the reflection. His mind continued to work finding ways to look unobtrusive. The street was too busy to resort to invisibility.

She passed by and walked into a general supply store. Pol slipped across the street and had to chance going into the business to see whom she might be meeting. By the time he entered, the Chief Healer had disappeared. He left the shop and ran around to the back, but no one walked the alley.

There was no possibility of her going through the shop, so she must have met someone inside. He walked back to the street but heard the squeaking of hinges. He hugged the side of a building and watched the Chief Healer enter the alley.

He grimaced and turned invisible. He had to touch the woman before she made it to the street on the other side of the alley. Pol ran as lightly as he could and touched the woman's hand, looking for mind control but not finding any.

"What's this?" the woman said, raising her hand to her face. "Who's there?" She turned in Pol's direction.

He had to withhold a sigh. This woman wasn't the Chief Healer. He'd been tricked. Pol stayed where he was for a moment and followed the woman from a distance. She walked back to the Chief Healer's house but went down a tiny alley and entered from the rear.

Pol walked back to the castle, making sure to return to his normal appearance.

"Any luck?"

Defeat weighed heavily on Pol. Success made Seeking more fun. He didn't want to say he failed, but he did. Luckily, Shira was the only one in the conference room.

After hearing his report and noting it on the large paper, she grabbed Pol by the arm. "Let's go out and walk around Alsador. You need a break. Show me the Chief Healer's house and the shop. I'm hungry, so maybe we can eat some street food. I haven't yet had the opportunity to really relax in Alsador."

Pol brightened up. Life was more than Seeking, wasn't it? They stepped out of the castle. He wouldn't change his appearance this time.

Pol guessed that even failures could be useful to Seekers. He looked at the pattern of deception and realized that he wasn't certain that the woman coming out of the Chief Healer's house was the right person. If it was the Chief Healer, then the general supply shop would be part of a conspiracy. If it wasn't the Chief Healer, then why the deception of the woman leaving by the shop's back door?

Either scenario made the behavior curious. Evasion of someone following was the common thread to both alternatives. Pol thought that if the Chief Healer had left her house and purchased something at the shop and emerged with her purchase, that there would be much less suspicion.

He wondered—

"Hey, come back to me," Shira said.

"What?"

"You were someplace, but it wasn't by my side," she said.

"Ah, yes." Pol smiled. "I was thinking."

"Deeply, it seems."

He nodded. "Let's pass the Chief Healer's house, first."

Shira bumped him gently with a thrust of her hip.

Pol glanced at her. She didn't look particularly apologetic.

"You know how to show a girl a good time," she said.

"How would I have learned that?"

Shira raised and lowered her arms in exasperation. "We've been together for a year and you've learned nothing?"

Pol cursed himself. He smiled at her and took her arm. "Let's go have a good time. I know of a square just past the house. Searl and I set up our healer's cart close by."

They walked along the street. Pol made sure to stop and let Shira peer inside shop windows along the way. They stepped into the street where the Chief Healer lived. He noticed someone pounding on the woman's door.

"That's the house," Pol said, pulling Shira along with him.

They arrived as a crowd grew on the sidewalk.

"I definitely heard a scream inside. No one answers. The door is locked." The man said as he frantically worked the door latch.

"Let me try," Pol said. He had to tweak the door open. Shira followed him inside. The scene wasn't pretty. The man who had opened the door lay dead on the floor. Further down the hallway, Pol found the Chief Healer's body. She wore a frilly nightgown that didn't quite match Pol's pattern of the woman, but then what did he know of the woman's style outside of the healer's robe that he had seen her wear?

He turned to the crowd standing at the door. "Someone call for Captain Yarrow of the Royal Guard. Quickly!"

He walked to the back of the house and found a plump woman in a dusty white apron on the floor. She barely breathed, but her face was pale and her lips were turning blue. Pol knelt at her side and found that someone had all but closed her windpipe.

After tweaking her windpipe clear, the woman's color quickly recovered. Her eyelids fluttered open and she raised her hands to fend Pol off. "Don't!"

Pol took her hand. "I'm not the one who did this. I just helped you breathe. This is Shira." He gave her hand to the Shinkyan and told her to let the woman recover.

The Chief Healer and the man both died of suffocation very recently. Perhaps the cook had screamed, scaring away the murderer. There wasn't anything he could do for the other two. Any trace of mind control would have dissipated with their deaths.

Pol looked around the main floor of the house. He found the cloak and bonnet that the Chief Healer or an imposter had worn lying on a chair in the kitchen.

Shira had Pol help the cook up to another chair.

"Some wine?" Pol said.

He looked around the kitchen and found a wine jug and poured it. The woman finished off two cups before she took a deep breath.

"Awful, it was," she said. "My Lady's friend came in the back door and had a heated discussion with Hubble." She shivered at the memory. "My Lady came down the stairs, and there was more argument."

"I stayed in here to prepare a lunch." The cook's eyes drifted to a cutting board filled with prepared vegetables. "The talk became more animated. My Lady didn't join in, but Hubble was livid. The arguing went on for some time." The cook raised her hand. "Don't ask me what was spoke. I purposefully don't have ears for my mistress's patter."

"Then you heard a scream?" Shira said.

"That scream came right out of my own mouth. I went to the drawing room asking about what drink to serve and both of them were laid out in the hallway. I turned around and looked right into that witch's eyes. Cold, cold, cold, they were. She never felt like a real friend to My Lady, even though both claimed her as such. That's when I screamed and could feel my throat tighten until I couldn't croak a breath."

"You wailing saved your life. A man passed by and pounded on the door," Shira said.

The cook looked around. "Do you think she is still here?"

Pol shook his head. "Look." He pointed to the back door. A sliver of light shone between the door and the frame. "She didn't even close it properly."

"Lad, are you doing all right in there?" the man who first pounded on the door said. He hadn't taken a step inside the house.

"Did someone fetch the Royal Guard?"

The man nodded.

"I am a personal friend of Captain Yarrow. Could you make sure no one comes through the door except for him, or call out to me."

"Do you know the Chief Healer?"

"We are acquaintances," Pol said.

He heard mutterings describing Pol as a person too young to be in the house by himself, but ignored them.

Pol walked back into the kitchen. He took the cook's hand. "Are you feeling better?" He took the opportunity to check for mind control but didn't find a thing.

"I am, thank you." The woman looked frightened, and why wouldn't she be?

The front door flew open. Wilf Yarrow and Fadden Loria entered along with two other guards. Pol went to talk to them, closing the door to the kitchen.

"An assassination?" Wilf asked, standing over the bodies with his fist on his hips.

"After a heated discussion, evidently."

"How do you know that?"

"We have a survivor?"

Wilf's eyebrows rose. "We do?"

Pol nodded. "The killer, a magician, tweaked their windpipes closed. The person eventually attacked the cook, who got off a scream, so the perpetrator left by the back door."

"Could the cook have done it?" Fadden said.

Pol didn't even think that far, but he quickly came up with the answer. "The woman who impersonated the Chief Healer might have been thinner."

Wilf shook his head. "You saw the killer?"

"Why don't you look at the bodies and talk to the cook, gently, and then we can go over the situation."

Wilf nodded. Both older men knelt by the Chief Healer's body. They turned it over without seeing any external injuries. They did the same to the male servant.

"Nothing here to contradict your observations," Wilf said before turning towards the kitchen.

"Let me introduce you," Pol said. "The cook has had a rough time."

He opened the door. Someone jumped up and ran out the door. Shira lay gasping on the floor holding onto her neck. Pol looked into Shira's throat and found it constricted as well. He tried to open it up and the windpipe began to convulse. Fadden had a similar convulsive spell on his intestine.

Pol put his hand on Shira's throat and tweaked to massage the affected area. Her body went limp, but Pol worked on and finally stopped the spell. By this time Shira had stopped breathing. Her heart still beat, so Pol put his mouth to Shira's lips and blew into her lungs. He kept at it until he noticed her muscles moving.

Suddenly, she put her arms around him and Pol's resuscitation method turned into a long kiss.

"Thank you," she said hoarsely. "We should have locked the back door. The cook had put her head on the table and closed her eyes. The next thing I knew there were hands touching my throat, and I had no breath. A woman took the cook away."

Pol looked at the closed door. He should have used his locator sense to see if the woman lurked nearby when he came upon the murders. He wasn't performing very well. He used it now and didn't detect anyone outside, but he went to the door and spotted the cook's body by the gate. The killer didn't bother with magic this time since a knife was quite visible and the cook's apron was no longer white.

~ ~ ~

Chapter Six

~

"WE'VE MANAGED TO STIR UP A HORNETS NEST,"
Wilf said, as he stood in front of King Landon. The rest of
the group were lined up behind him in the King's study. "Three dead
and Shira nearly made it four."

Landon scowled. "That's not the kind of news I wanted to hear."

"The Chief Healer must have been one of them," Fadden said.
"She was the person who mixed up my insides."

Pol shook his head. "I doubt the woman that you met was the
Chief Healer," Pol said.

"A disguise?"

Pol nodded. "The Chief Healer that I saw through the door was
wearing a night dress, and then she wore a heavy cloak on a warm day."
He should have noticed that at first.

"Come back to me when you've got this all sorted out," Landon
said. His brother spoke with more authority than Pol had ever heard.
He considered that a positive development.

"Let me check you," Pol said. He didn't expect any mind control
and was pleased that the shield was still in place. Pol reinforced it.
"We'll be back with a more cohesive story."

"Please do. Everyone may go except for Pol," King Landon said.

Landon waited for all of them to leave. "I did all right?"

Pol blinked his eyes. "Your anger was faked?"

Landon shook his head. "My anger wasn't, but my reaction was. I hoped I sounded genuine. I always thought tirades would be effective, but Father knew me better than I did myself and ignored my outbursts until our minds were controlled, I think."

"You're right about showing a little extra emotion…" Pol rolled the concept around in his head. "As long as it is applied sparingly. Make it part of your pattern and people will change their behavior to take your anger into account." Pol had ended up doing exactly that when he was under attack by his siblings, and ultimately his father, in Borstall. His thoughts also turned to Shira and her regime of incidental corporal punishment. Her behavior was something Pol had grown to overlook.

Landon smiled. Pol realized his brother was growing up. Now, the trick would be to protect him from whatever was happening inside his city. "What happens next?" the king said.

"The woman, if disguised, could just as easily be a man. There weren't many, if any, Tesnan monks who could assume a disguise when I was there."

"Why does it have to be a Tesnan monk?"

Pol pursed his lips. That was a very good question. "As far as I know, they are the only ones who know mind control." He thought for a moment. "That's not true. I sent Tesnan books on mind control with Val to Yastan. Any Imperial magician could have read them."

Pol would have to have a conversation with Fadden about twisting the insides of bodies to kill or disable. The Chief Healer's death certainly posed more questions than it answered.

Landon grinned. "I helped you, didn't I? The great Poldon Fairfield was assisted by his oldest brother."

Pol returned his brother's grin. "You did, and it was an excellent comment. Keep them coming. My job isn't to get direction from you, but get rid of this assault on your kingdom."

"I agree. I think you can go now. The others are probably waiting."

Pol took that for the dismissal it was. "Thank you, My King."

"No 'My King' business with you. Go!" Landon shooed him out of his study.

Pol found them all but Ako standing by the stairway leading down from the King's personal quarters. He joined them as they made their way to Wilf's conference room.

"He was really angry?" Wilf said.

"That he was," Pol said, truthfully. "Landon wanted a more personal assessment than he felt comfortable asking me in front of everyone."

Wilf smiled. He knew Landon better than anyone, probably better than Pol.

"He did ask me one pertinent question. Why does the magician who performed the murders have to be from Tesna?"

"Mind control," Shira said, but then she narrowed her eyes. "But that leaves out the Emperor's magicians who found a way to eliminate the spell. We have a saying in Shinkya. Be wary of what comes out of an unknown box." Shira snorted a laugh. "I've been burned by that one."

Pol looked at her, knowing she referred to their adventure in the Demron cave. "We are still looking for a magician. If the Chief Healer administered the mind control spells inside the castle, then the perpetrator could be anywhere."

"The supply shop that she went in was cleaned out by the time we got there," Wilf said.

"So that means we now have specific points in the pattern," Pol said. "The shop. Who owns it? Was it let out? What do the neighbors know? Did the Chief Healer leave any papers? Are there any other evidences of communication with the killer?"

Fadden smiled as they walked into the conference room. "Shira, are you going to get all that down?"

She nodded and began scribbling on the paper. "I didn't think we would come with anything." She stepped back to see all of what she had written.

Wilf sat down. "I'll have my best men talk to the relatives of the

Chief Healer's butler and the cook. Perhaps an inadvertent comment might lead to something."

"Did the Chief Healer have any relatives?" Pol asked.

"None in Alsador."

"Then maybe we should write letters. Any change in behavior becomes a pattern element." Shira said.

Fadden nodded. "Perhaps more interviews with Donton and Greenhill?"

"I'd like to have another conversation with Wibon," Pol said.

The investigation was expanding rather than contracting, even with one less suspect. Pol didn't know if they were gaining or losing ground with the demise of the Chief Healer.

These thoughts continued to run through his head as he stood on Lord Wibon's doorstep, waiting for someone to answer the door.

Lord Wibon greeted them himself and led them to the same sitting room Pol had been with Ako.

"A different Shinkyan maid?" He grinned at Shira. "I am Lord Wibon and you are?"

"Shira. I am a Sister apprentice."

"Sister?" Wibon looked confused and turned to Pol.

"Sister is the term Shinkya uses for their Seekers. The more powerful magicians in Shinkya are all women. Shinkyan Seekers are all magicians, therefore all Seekers are women and are called Sisters.

"I am young for a Sister," Shira smiled at Lord Wibon. It didn't look very sincere to Pol's eyes.

"The other Shinkyan from a few days ago?"

"A Sister," Shira said. "She is a good one."

"So you are a magician, as well?"

Shira nodded. "Perhaps Queen Isa mentioned me in her stories of the Tesnan war? I was disguised as a youth. That's where I met Pol."

Wibon looked at both of them. "And Shira and the other woman will be heading back to Shinkya?"

Pol nodded. "Has anyone contacted you?"

Wibon shook his head. He got up. "Excuse me for a moment."

In a few minutes, he returned with a small box. "I remember

the other Sister's comment on Shinkyan carvings. I have one that I'd like to present to you, Poldon." He opened the box and within it sat a frog carving in bright green. "This is a real Shinkyan carving. I have a collection of them in my private rooms upstairs." He put the box on the table in front of Pol and Shira and sat down. "Since you have lands in South Salvan, you should have a memento representative of our Shinkyan neighbors. Most South Salvans do, you know. Most aren't real, as I told you before."

Shira picked it up and looked at it closely. "Ako would know better than I, but this looks like something I could buy in Tishiko."

"I paid enough for it to be real," Wibon said. "It's a gift from me to you. I never did like King Astor and always worried for my cousin, Queen Isa. I don't expect anything in return."

Pol could tell the difference in workmanship. He looked at the carving through magical eyes and could see that the grains in the wood followed the shape of the carvings. It had been remade using a pattern. "I can see magical craftsmanship here, regardless of the frog's origin."

Pol didn't understand why Wibon would give him such a valuable piece, but then he remembered that he was a Duke in Wibon's home country and outranked him. He also wondered how close Wibon actually was to his cousin, Queen Isa. Diplomats curried favor and this gift might have been no more than that, especially since Ako had so easily identified the South Salvan copies as poor imitations.

Wibon smiled. "Now how can I help you in your investigation? I heard about the Chief Healer's death." He frowned and shook his head. "A tragic thing. She was purportedly the best healer in Alsador."

"Did you ever use her services?" Shira asked.

"Not really. We spoke a few times during state functions."

Pol put the frog back in the wooden box and laid it on the table. "She might have known the spell for mind control."

"She had access to everyone in King Landon's Court."

Pol nodded and looked at Shira. "She did. Since you last saw the Chief Healer, has anyone tried to change your mind on anything or made any suggestions that you felt odd?"

Wibon looked at both of them. "Yes, someone has."

Pol nearly knocked the table over when he shot to his feet. "Who?"

"A delivery man," Wibon said. "He walked into the house and told me to pay him a South Salvan Lion for a bouquet of flowers."

"Did you do it?"

Wibon nodded. "I remember you telling me about mind control, so I did as he asked out of fear what he might do if exposed, and then he left."

"That's it?" Shira said.

The South Salvan ambassador nodded.

Pol broke into a grin. "Good job. What did he look like?"

"Non-descript. He wasn't a big man, no taller than Shira."

"Did he speak with a soft voice?" Shira asked.

"Now that you mention it, his voice was strange."

Shira cleared her throat. "Like this? Did he ask you for money in a voice that sounded like this?"

Wibon's eyebrow rose. "Yes."

"A woman in disguise," Pol said.

Shira nodded. Now they would have to talk to Ako.

"We need to leave. Your information was invaluable," Pol said. "Thank you for your time."

Wibon bent over and gave Pol the box that held the Shinkyan carving. "Don't forget the frog, it is yours," he said, smiling. "I'm glad to have been some help."

Pol and Shira left and began walking back to the castle.

"Do you believe him?" Shira asked.

"I'd like to," Pol said, "but we will want to see if Ako has been watching or had anyone watch. What is it with the low voice?"

"Didn't you remember how I spoke when I was Shro?"

Pol snapped his fingers. "That's what a Sister learns? Could the culprit be a Shinkyan? That doesn't make sense."

"It doesn't, but that's how women are taught to impersonate men," Shira said, looking worried. "Definitely a woman, then."

"I don't know if that will make it easier to find her or harder. Let's go tell the others."

They found Fadden writing something down when they entered the conference room.

"Do you know where Ako is?" Pol asked.

Fadden shook his head. "I haven't seen her for a few days. Why?"

Shira looked at Pol with a defeated look. "Ako."

"Let's go to the inn and look at her room," Pol said. "Come with us, Fadden."

~ ~ ~

Chapter Seven

~

AFTER FILLING FADDEN IN ON WHAT TRANSPIRED, the three of them went up to Ako's room. Pol knocked but heard nothing. He tweaked the lock open, and they walked into the empty room.

Most of Ako's belongings were gone, but there were a few clothes strewn here and there. Pol looked under her bed and found a traveling bag full of weapons. Shira sat down on an unmade bed. "I can't believe it," she said. "Ako couldn't be turned."

Fadden shook his head. "Anyone can. If she left like this, I would say she is under compulsion rather than mind control from how you described it, Pol. A Seeker wouldn't have left a bag of tools."

"Nor would a Sister," Shira said.

"I'm afraid it turns our investigations upside down," Fadden said.

Pol was loath to admit defeat, but all they could do now was observe and wait until something happened. He put the Shinkyan frog in his room. He had only checked the mysterious woman for mind control and not compulsion. What a mistake! The facts of their problem assaulted Pol as he ran over them in his mind again and again until he just shut his eyes and tried to clear his mind of the frustration that he felt.

He threw himself onto the bed and didn't wake up until nightfall. When he went downstairs, Pol found Shira eating dinner with Fadden.

"You're awake," Fadden said. "Shira knocked on your door, but all she heard were snores."

Pol sat down and ordered dinner. They had all finished, but none of them wanted to talk about Ako or their investigation. Paki entered the dining room and rushed to their table.

"Come with me. I think I have found the magician!"

Paki led them through the streets of Alsador. "I found a comfortable drinking place."

"That has been a nightly duty for you. With games?" Fadden said.

Paki made a face. "I played a bit of dice, but I noticed a shaven-headed man playing with a marked lack of skill, so I sensed an opportunity and joined the game. He was a bit into his cups and let slip that he had bested a Shinkyan. I tried to ask him for details, but he came a bit to his senses. I won this from him." He showed them a worn South Salvan Lion.

"There are plenty of those in circulation in Alsador," Fadden said.

Paki shrugged his shoulders. "When a pattern is filling up, does it matter?"

The comment made Pol smile. Perhaps the pattern of the magician showed more that it should.

They reached the tavern. It wasn't exactly presentable, but the shutters and door had fresh paint and the sign looked new. The Stuck Pig, it read, showing a pig with a spear through its body.

"Nice," Shira said looking up at the facade. "A woman's place, for sure." Her voice dripped with sarcasm.

Paki grinned. "It depends on what kind of woman."

She hit him on the upper arm. Shira frowned and then she rubbed where she had hit him. That was new from her. Ako's advice to Shira might be working.

"He might be in there. Let me check your shields against compulsion." Pol reinforced everyone's shields including his own.

They all walked in and looked the place over. Just about everybody turned to the door. Pol recognized a familiar face.

He walked up to the shaven-headed man. "Did you think no one would recognize you without your hair and your beard, Manda?"

Shira put a freeze spell on the late King Astor's court magician. The tavern went silent. The customers began to slip out the front door.

"Does anyone know where this man lives?"

"Upstairs," one of the barmaids said. "He moved in a few days ago. There is a servant with him," she sneered.

"Ako!" Shira said. She moved towards the stairs.

"No," Pol said. "She might be in a dangerous state, and if she's under compulsion, removing the spell might kill her. Remember Val." Pol didn't consider that the murderer would be under compulsion, but that would explain the strange actions. Ako had shifted into a number of disguises, at least three, the Chief Healer, the woman coming out the back of the shop and the 'male' servant. He should have been able to expand the pattern to include disguises, but he hadn't.

Shira nodded. "We will have to keep Manda asleep. He's too dangerous."

"And we won't want to be interrogating him here," Fadden said. He turned to Paki. "Get Wilf and some guards to take this man away from here." He watched Paki run out the door and then looked at the unmoving magician. "I suppose you've had dealings with him?"

Pol grimaced. "He is powerful and helped King Astor try to take over the Empire. I don't know how he escaped from the Emperor's army, but I imagine he is resourceful." Pol put the man to sleep before he unfroze him. Manda slumped over the table.

"The pattern is filling in," Shira said. She didn't say another word.

"It's time to work on Ako." Pol said. He looked over at the bartender. "Which room?"

"Four," the man croaked. He untied his apron and hurried through the kitchen door.

The tavern had emptied out.

"Watch him," Pol said.

Shira and Pol walked quietly up the stairs. They stood at the door and looked at each other, holding hands. Shira nodded, and Pol tweaked a sleeping spell. He heard a body fall on the other side of the door and another downstairs. He looked over the railing and found his spell had downed one of the barmaids.

He tweaked open the locked door and found a slight man lying on the floor.

"Ako," Shira said.

Pol knelt at her side and put his hands on her head. The purple patch of compulsion was even larger than what Pol had removed from Val's mind. He took a deep breath and began to remove the compulsion a little bit at a time.

When he finished, the window glowed with the promise of dawn. Shira had fallen asleep on the bed.

He rose from Ako's side and gently shook Shira awake. "Go to the castle and make sure Manda stays asleep," Pol said.

Shira yawned and rubbed her eyes before she looked at Ako and then at Pol. "You must be out of strength."

Pol smiled. "Oddly enough, I'm tired, but I'm doing much better than I thought. Go. Manda shouldn't wake up until I'm there." He gazed down at Ako. "She comes first."

Shira nodded.

Pol worked on Ako for another hour until the sun peeked into the room. He sighed. As far as he could tell, Ako's compulsion was gone. He stood and stretched before he removed the sleeping spell.

Ako struggled for a bit before she opened her eyes. Her hands shot to her head. "It's gone?"

Pol nodded. "You were under a compulsion spell. Do you remember what happened?"

She nodded. "A man walked past the alley while I observed Lord Wibon's residence. Then..." she shook her head, "it was like I was an observer. I had no control over my body. He forced me to do some awful things."

Pol frowned. "Collapsing a windpipe is a Shinkyan assassination technique?"

"Shira!"

"I saved her."

"Impossible. Once the esophagus is closed it is ultimately..." She put a hand to her forehead. "No, I had to kill the cook twice. You saved Shira and the cook? You really did?"

Pol nodded. "I told you I knew how to heal. Why did you stay at the Chief Healer's?"

"You came while I nearly finished with the cook. I had to leave, but I couldn't because I hadn't killed her. What happened to me?"

Pol put his hand on her shoulder. Her eyes were rimmed with tears. "Manda put you under compulsion. It's a nasty spell."

"The Tesna compulsion. Like your Seeker friend."

Pol nodded. "He's the one. I did a better job removing your spell than I did his." He stood, still amazed that he hadn't fainted. "Did you ever deliver flowers to Lord Wibon?"

Ako shook her head. "No, but I did collect money from him. The magician boasted that he could make me do whatever he wanted, but he treated me like any other servant. He liked me in disguise. He didn't like Shinkyans, and I assure you, Shinkyans wouldn't like him."

Pol could only agree. "Can you stand?"

"Wait." Ako grimaced in pain as she turned back into her real self. She let out a sigh. "That's better. Can you help me up? I need something to eat."

He helped her down the stairs. There weren't many in the tavern so early in the morning, but a woman baked bread in the kitchen and gave what she could to Ako.

"I'll eat on the way," the Sister said.

Ako had to hold onto Pol's arm while they walked. They stopped at a street vendor selling hot apple cider and sweet buns in the early morning. Pol bought enough for the both of them. By the time they reached the castle gate, Ako could walk unaided.

She smiled. "Much better," but then the smile faded. "I'm not proud of what I did."

"Under a spell?" Pol said. "The fault rests with the wielder of the spell. A murderer isn't a sword, but the wielder of the weapon."

Ako nodded curtly. "Right. I'll have to remember that, but it doesn't make me feel good. It's not that I am without sin, but being used as a tool…" She shook her head.

"You don't have to be in on the interrogation," Pol said.

"I want to be," Ako said with a fierce expression.

Pol suspected that she might be seeking some vindication if she could participate. He didn't care if she was a bit rough on Manda. The South Salvan magician had been partly responsible for many deaths, including his father's.

Paki, Fadden, Wilf, and Shira sat looking at the still form of Manda, sleeping away on the conference room table when Pol and Ako entered. Chains bound the prisoner with a length leading from handcuffs to foot cuffs. Even if he ensorcelled everyone in the room, Manda wouldn't travel very far, unless he could unlock the cuffs, something that only Pol could do among the group.

Something needed to be done. Pol thought for a moment. "Can you put handcuffs on Ako? Manda probably won't know I removed her compulsion.

Wilf walked out and returned with manacles and placed them loosely on Ako's wrists.

"I'll place fresh shields on all of you, making sure he won't compel any of you or put you under mind control."

"Do you want to wake him up, Ako?"

The Shinkyan Sister pressed her lips together and closed her eyes. Manda began to stir and then popped his eyes open.

"Get these chains off me!" he said, looking wildly at the people surrounding him until his eyes locked on Pol. "Poldon Fairfield!" He stopped struggling. "What do you want?"

"Answers," Fadden said.

"Do you really want the answers I will give?" Manda said to Wilf.

"What do you mean?" Wilf said.

"I certainly didn't perform the murders," Manda said. The man seemed to be gaining confidence. He looked at Ako. "Put them all to sleep and then kill them."

"Why?" Ako said.

"Why? I ordered you!" Manda's confidence began to crumble. "What is this?" His eyes shot from person to person. The magician was thinking of a way out. "I didn't do anything. Why am I in chains? You should arrest the Shinkyan woman for the murder of the Chief Healer and her household staff."

"No, you didn't kill them personally," Pol said, "but you ordered a compelled magician to carry out murderous acts."

"You can't prove that," Manda said.

"Oh, I can. I removed her compulsion."

"Impossible. Only a few magicians could do that and they were killed at Borstall."

That admission made Manda's spell even more of a crime in Pol's eyes. "You have to cut the compulsion out, slice by slice and bit by bit, but I've done it before."

Manda nearly gagged with the news. "No. You're just a boy, powerful I'll admit, but it takes years to learn how to do that."

"A boy who can remove compulsion and see inside a body to heal," Fadden said.

"So Grostin spoke the truth," Manda said.

"When did you speak to my brother?" Pol said as casually as he could. Manda could have just given them what they wanted.

"Your brother? Oh, not your brother. I know another Grostin." Manda began to sweat.

"We will let the King decide, but I suspect you won't live out the day," Wilf said.

"No! No!" Manda cried out. "What do you want to know?"

Wilf put his face close to Manda's, but then he grimaced and held his head, swaying on his feet. Pol could feel the pressure of the spell. The magician was trying to tweak.

"He's shielded, Manda, against both mind control and compulsion."

Wilf blinked through his headache. "The boy is right. I want to know whom you are working for and why you are stirring up trouble for King Landon. Pol is the King's brother, and he has a right to know."

Manda looked at the people around him and sighed.

Pol never tried a truth spell before, but somehow he was inspired to tweak a spell at him. The form of the alteration of the pattern suddenly appeared in his mind.

"Whom do you work for?"

"I work for myself," Manda said.

"Why did you come to Alsador?" Wilf asked, looking at Pol as he asked Manda the question.

"To make things rough for King Landon so he would re-affirm his vassal king status to his brother."

"And if King Landon wouldn't agree, what were you going to do?"

Wilf said.

"Remove him from the throne one way or another."

Pol wanted to fill out the final pattern now that Manda was under a truth spell. "What is your relationship with Lord Wibon?"

"He provides me with contacts and his own observations."

"Money, too?" Shira asked.

"Yes."

Wilf nodded to Pol. "What is your relationship with Lord Greenhill?"

"He is a faction leader. I eventually plan to use him to oust King Landon."

"The same with General Donton?"

"Yes," Manda said.

Pol took another opportunity to speak. "Was the Chief Healer under compulsion?"

"No."

"Why did you command Ako to kill her?" Wilf asked.

"She broke my mind control and threatened to tell the King after I used her to place spells on King Landon's enemies. I replaced the mind control, but I couldn't trust the woman after that, so I commanded the Shinkyan to move in."

Pol looked at Wilf and the others. "So the Chief Healer must have thrown off the mind control again, and Ako was there to put an end to the household when she did," The Chief Healer might have had a strain of resistance in her, but it wasn't sufficient to keep her from spreading the spells around the castle. Pol said. "Is that enough?"

"It is for me with so many witnesses."

Fadden gazed at Pol. "I didn't know you could tweak a truth spell so effectively. I've never experienced an interrogation where the recipient didn't struggle with the truth."

The truth spell came on its own, or did it? Was the spell inspired by the Demron essence that still lingered in his mind?

Pol put Manda back to sleep. He sighed. Pol had come to the same conclusion that Manda had just confirmed, as soon as Ako's participation in the killings came to light.

"He will never wake up. I'll go to the King," Wilf said.

Pol got back up. "I'll go with you if the rest will keep an eye on Manda."

~ ~ ~

Chapter Eight

~

THE PAIR OF THEM FOUND KING LANDON in his throne room, listening to petitions.

"I have an urgent matter, My King," Wilf said.

"You have found something out?"

Pol nodded to his brother. "If we could speak privately for a moment."

Landon cleared out the space and stood, pacing back and forth until the last person left them alone. "What is it?"

"We found Manda, King Astor's court magician in Alsador. Under a truth spell, he admitted he had ensorcelled the Chief Healer. He used a compulsion spell on Ako Injira, who was forced to kill the Chief Healer and her household."

"How do you know she was under a spell?" Landon said.

Wilf looked at Pol. "She would never have harmed Shira otherwise, Landon," Pol said. "I personally removed Ako's compulsion. The more talent a magician has, the thicker the spell."

"I've never heard of thin and thick spells before," the King said.

"Magicians see spells differently. To me, compulsion is like a purple slab with tentacles going down into the brain."

Landon shivered and put up his hand. "That's enough of a

description. You removed it from the woman, so that's all I need to know."

"My King, there is more. Lord Greenhill and General Donton are not part of a group conspiracy. Manda had the Chief Healer put a mind control spell on Donton. Luckily, we arrived before he was ready to do real damage to Landon."

Landon put his hand to his chin and thought. "So Donton and Greenhill are still enemies?"

"I wouldn't call them enemies at this point, Landon," Pol said. "Now that the major threat is over, we can work with them to find areas of agreement."

"Diplomacy," Landon said.

"Right. Father mentioned a number of times that he needed to be diplomatic inside his own borders."

Landon's eyebrows rose. "I remember that from conversations in our family dining room."

Family dinners were always an opportunity for his siblings to abuse Pol, but he didn't bring that aspect up. Perhaps Landon had picked up some of his father's advice.

"Very well. What do we do now?"

Wilf took a deep breath. "Dispense Royal Justice. Lord Wibon has been working with Manda."

Landon sighed. "And who is behind Lord Wibon?" He looked at Pol with sad eyes. Landon already knew.

"Grostin," Pol said. "He had a two-pronged strategy. Get the factions to unite against you to force you to re-affirm your fealty to North Salvan—"

"That would never happen."

Pol put his hand on Landon's upper arm. "Remember, you were under mind control, too. If we hadn't arrived, how would you prevent it? You were pretty down when we met."

Landon nodded. "I was, wasn't I? I hate, hate, hate it to be Grostin. What was the other prong?"

"Manda was prepared to have you killed. If Ako hadn't shown up, he would have compelled some courtier to do it. Maybe even the Chief Healer would have been enlisted, but you would have known something was wrong with the woman if she was compelled. People lose their identity."

"The Shinkyan would have been the perfect tool," Landon said. He turned towards the windows with hunched shoulders. "The alliance with North Salvan is forever dead." He shook his head and sighed. "I'll notify the Emperor, Queen Isa and Grostin. With no hope of a union, we might not be able to speak civilly to each other again, but my loyalty is to Listya."

Pol agreed with that observation. Once Grostin became King of North Salvan, he lost his restraint. "If it wasn't for Paki's observing Manda in a tavern, we would have taken longer to find out," Pol said.

"Saved by the gardener's son. Once I would have been appalled by the prospect, but no more. I praise him for his effort." Landon looked at Wilf. "I'll sign an order to have Manda and Lord Wibon hanged. I hope Queen Isa will support me in that, after the fact." The King turned to Wilf. "It is my will, Captain Yarrow." Landon's fist balled up when he looked away and said, "Grostin."

Pol stood at the front door to Lord Wibon's empty house. No one knew how the South Salvan ambassador found out, but his personal possessions were gone. He walked up the steps and entered the drawing room. The Shinkyan copies were missing. Undoubtedly the real Shinkyan carvings were taken, too.

Wibon would not be welcomed in South Salvan if Pol had anything to do with it. Nothing of significant value other than the furniture and decorations remained in the house.

"My Captain," a guard said, rushing into the house. "Lord Wibon and his servants boarded a ship to Volia. It wasn't due to leave for another week, but he has gone."

"Volia," Pol said. "He won't like Duchary or Bossom very much."

"His actions gave us the answers that we needed," Wilf said. "Let's get Manda's execution over as quickly as we can."

They walked back to the castle. A gallows had already been set up in the guards' practice yard. Manda's execution would be a private affair.

The magician's chains were gone, replaced by ropes. Pol wouldn't have done such a thing. He took a sliver of metal out of his pocket and began to play with it while they put the rope over Manda's neck. The magician looked over the small gathering.

Pol felt the pressure of mind control as he observed Manda's bonds shredding. First, the noose frayed. As Manda began to work on his bonds, three of the guards assumed vacant looks. Pol recognized compulsion.

"Kill the king's brother!"

Those were the last words Manda uttered as Pol moved the splinter into Manda's heart. The three guards' froze in place while Manda struggled to breathe. His bonds loosened enough for him to clutch his chest as he toppled over.

The other guards looked on in astonishment. Wilf stepped over to Manda.

"He's dead. What do we do about them?" He looked at his guards.

Pol walked over to each one and removed the purple film on their brains. None of them had a lick of power and it only took a moment each to remove the spells.

They collapsed to the ground, swords clattering to the dirt when Shira or Ako unfroze them.

Fadden clapped Pol on the back. "I would have never thought the ropes wouldn't hold him."

"I had to put myself into his pattern. I failed the three guards, though. I should have thought to shield them as well," Pol said.

He'd made a mistake again that might have cost lives. But of more concern was the boost on the truth spell. That had come without conscious effort. What other surprises would come as a result of the mental fight he had with the Demron essence, as he thought of it?

Pol didn't hear any voices or insane laughter in his head, but something rolled around in his mind that he couldn't control and that unsettled him. He would have to put such thoughts behind him until another unexpected outburst of ability. That must be the reason his magical stamina had already shown startling improvement.

At least Manda deserved to die since he tried to escape while ordering the guards to kill them all. Pol thought back, once again, to the time Val killed the stable master in Borstall who had been instrumental in the death of Paki's father. He hoped he would never forget the feeling that shocked him.

The group assembled once again in Wilf's conference room to go over what they had learned. Pol sat forward in his chair, his hands clasped on the table, listening intently to the others. He looked at Fadden, who stood at the wall about to go over Shira's notes.

"I don't know how Shinkyans close their investigations, but where a group of Seekers have worked on an investigation, we go over the process to see what we did well and what pieces of the pattern we missed." Fadden looked at Ako, who responded by faintly nodding and smiling.

"This chart makes it easy, so let's begin," Fadden said.

Pol responded where he could, but Fadden and Shira seemed to take over. Fadden because he had done such a thing before and Shira contributed because she assembled the document and that duty brought its own special perspective.

Shira's notes helped Pol understand the pattern better than the one he had built in his mind. What he gained were details that he had missed when he was in the thick of the investigation.

All agreed they should have been more alert to Ako's disappearance, but the loose organization of the seeking involved didn't break any Seeker rules. She was experienced in her role, but still, thought Pol, Ako had suffered more than the others with the exception of Shira's near-death at Ako's hand.

The mistake of holding Manda with ropes, easy enough for a magician of his stature to break with tweaking was attributed to Fadden and Wilf underestimating the South Salvan's abilities. Pol kept quiet, as he would have never bound Manda with rope, preferring to keep him under all the way to the end. However, the incident was a good lesson to be learned by the others, and the review was held to identify such things.

All agreed that Paki's tavern-hopping had been the inadvertent act that brought luck into the investigation, although they might have found Manda's trail through investigating the sale of the shop. That was where Manda had lived for a few months in Alsador.

Fadden wrapped the session up with a final comment. "When Seeking, luck and coincidence does have a part. Keeping your eyes open to your surroundings often brings fortune. Identifying a drunken magician's idle boast is what made our investigation successful." Fadden had Paki stand while the others clapped.

Paki blushed. "I'm the least among you and was happy enough to do my part." He plopped down on his seat with a smile that wouldn't go away.

"I think you deserve another task seeking out the best ale that Alsador has to offer. Fadden and I will be observers, if you don't mind," Wilf said.

Paki looked at Pol, who nodded his encouragement. "I will gladly accept."

The three of them slipped out the door, leaving Ako, Shira, and Pol looking at each other.

Ako stood. "I think I'd like to do a bit of shopping. I'll need a few more things before we head to Yastan. Want to join me?" she said to Shira.

The pair of them left Pol sitting by himself in the conference room. He wondered if Landon had a bit of free time and sought out the King of Listya.

Pol found him in his study surrounded with stacks of papers.

"I guess I'm lucky you have a little free time."

Landon barked out a laugh. "I'm ready for a quick break. I have to finish reviewing these today. I'm amazed what I put off while I was under Wibon's control."

"We may never know who influenced you. That spell was mild, yet insidious. Perhaps it was a good lesson for you."

Landon shook his head. "I'm afraid I have had too many lessons in the past few years." The king sighed and joined Pol, sitting in comfortable chairs facing the fireplace. "I've never worked so hard in my life after Bythia died. She kept so much from me. I was complacent. I went along and enjoyed prancing around as Listya's King. Once she left, the reality was staring at me. Being a king, a good king, is hard. I never appreciated our father more than when I faced day after day dealing with stacks of paper." He pointed to his desk. "I don't know what Grostin is doing, but I feel the responsibility every day."

"You are close to being where you need to be," Pol said. "We just finished finding Manda for you. It was a group effort. Everyone on our team contributed. Without Paki, we would still be seeking the Tesna monk. Even you contributed since Manda wasn't really a monk. You need to use the same technique as you rule. Now that the unpleasantness of Manda and Lord Wibon's attempt to usurp your authority is over, you can go back to relying on others to lessen the load."

"I can't—"

"I always thought Father took too much on himself when he ruled North Salvan, but when confronted with King Astor's forces, he delegated the defense of Borstall to a team."

"But they failed," Landon said.

"Success was an impossibility. We all knew it. Our goal was to put off the inevitable as long as possible. We kept them out of the city for three or four days. Our effort limited King Astor's conquest of Borstall to three days before the Emperor arrived. I'm sure we saved more lives than were taken. There couldn't have been many reprisals. But Father died. He would have been the first killed and I would be the second." Pol smiled. "Maybe Grostin would be the second, who knows? I know we didn't fail and would have lasted longer except for a failure at the castle gate."

Pol thought of Seen, the South Salvan soldier. If he hadn't opened the gate, Pol would have been caught outside the castle, anyway. It was senseless to wonder what might have happened under different circumstances.

Landon nodded and sighed. "At least you gave him a decent sendoff."

"I did that." Pol reflected that burning his father's body was nearly as sad as watching his own mother's pyre.

After a deep breath, Landon looked at his hands. "What is next?"

"Patch up the factions so you can have a functioning government, then I have to leave for Yastan."

"You think you can do that so quickly?" Landon looked at his brother in disbelief.

"I'll present them all as dupes to Lord Wibon and his attempt at disrupting their country. If we can get General Donton and Lord Greenhill to support you, I think you can make the kind of progress you need. Both of them can still help you organize your kingdom to take some pressure off your efforts trying to rule on your own. You won't last long if you don't have allies. Count me as an ally. I probably have the clearest claim to your throne and I support you. Wholeheartedly, I support you," Pol said.

Landon gazed into the empty fireplace. "You know I don't deserve that."

"You are the rightful King of Listya. I don't have any desire to rule."

"Yet."

Pol shook his head. "Remember, I'm Duke Pol, whenever I set foot in South Salvan. That's enough for me."

Landon looked at Pol sideways. "I don't believe that, but I trust you, where I don't trust our other brother."

"See? We are allies."

They both laughed.

~ ~ ~

Chapter Nine

~

POL SHOOK HIS HEAD. He was amazed how Landon had grown up and he was more surprised that he actually liked Landon as a person. Pol never thought that day would come. He would do what he could to support his eldest brother.

Grostin didn't deserve any more than a fleeting thought, so Pol decided he would visit General Donton first. He wasn't in his office but was out of the city at the main army camp. Pol rode out of Alsador to find the General.

Pol located the camp a few miles outside the city walls. He decided to arrive fully armed and found General Donton observing his troops training in a large practice field. If any grass grew on the field, it was long since trampled into dust.

"General, I'd like to have a word with you."

Donton eyed Pol. "It looks like you've come to fight. I'll talk to you as long as you want if you defeat one of my men in a little sparring match."

From the expression on Donton's face, Pol didn't expect anything 'little'. "I'm willing."

Donton motioned for a nearby aide to come to him. He muttered something in the aide's ear and Pol watched the man run off.

"I heard your investigation ended."

Pol nodded.

"You killed the traitor yourself?"

Pol pressed his lips together and nodded. "Manda, the former Court Magician to King Astor in South Salvan stirred up a lot of discontent in Alsador. He suborned the Chief Healer and she was the one who tweaked your mind control spell. He broke free of the ropes that restrained him and ordered Captain Yarrow's guards to kill us. I had little choice."

"Like a mad bull in the city streets?"

Pol smiled at the simile. "You could say that."

Donton went silent as a group of men approached.

"Which of you want to go up against a teenager?"

Most of the men nodded and produced confident looks.

"Captain Yarrow said he gave him a good go."

One of the men stepped up. "Do you believe Yarrow, My General?"

Donton pushed out his lower lip before replying. "No reason not to. Any takers?"

Four of them raised their hands.

"You." He pointed to tallest man of the group. "First blood. Is that acceptable?" His eyes focused on Pol.

"It is," Pol said. He pulled out his Shinkyan blade and that brought a few murmurs.

"That sword is real," Donton said. "I've tested the balance. It is a worthy blade."

Pol opponent drew a serviceable sword. It was heavier and straighter than Pol's.

"I need to warm up," Pol said. He went through his exercises but didn't use any tweaks to improve his speed.

"Not bad," his opponent said. He didn't warm up at all, but Pol suspected the man had already trained for some time earlier in the day.

Donton nodded to both of them to start.

Pol backed up like he usually did. His opponent came at him causing Pol to parry a thrust right off. The man didn't waste any time being on the offensive. Pol realized that the man wasn't fighting him to spar, but demonstrating how he would fight on the battlefield.

That increased the danger to Pol as he fended off a flurry of blows. The man was fast, but not pattern-master fast. Pol began to use sips to anticipate the man's actions and to speed up his response. He began to slash down and slash up. Pol would have been eviscerated had he not used sips of his magic.

His opponent began to tire after his aggressive start. Pol had successfully defended himself and now it was time to go on the offense. His first thrust nearly caught his opponent off guard. Pol followed it up with a slash so fast that the man wasn't ready to bring his blade up, so Pol used the back of his blade to hit his opponent's hand hard enough dislodge the sword from the man's grip.

Pol stepped on the sword and pointed at the unarmed man's arm. He ran the edge just hard enough to slip through the sleeve of his light leather tunic to draw a tiny bit of blood.

"Are you satisfied?" he asked his opponent.

The man rubbed at his arm as a dribble of blood seeped to the edge of the cut. "If I didn't know any better, I'd guess you were a pattern-master."

"You know better now. I am a pattern-master and Deftnis-trained," Pol said.

"I guess you were playing with me."

Pol shrugged. "I didn't use my magic until you performed that two-way slash. There was no sense in either one of us getting hurt, was there?"

"No, sir," the man said. He looked at the tiny smear of blood on his palm.

"Dismissed, all of you." Donton looked at Pol. "I suppose you want to say something to me?"

"It will be more than me talking, General. I want a conversation that will take as long as it needs to."

The General took off his helmet and rubbed his head. "I suppose you earned it."

Pol grinned. "I did, indeed."

"Follow me to my quarters, we might as well talk sitting down."

An aide retrieved Donton's horse. It took them a bit of time to ride to the permanent camp buildings. Pol eyed the tall walls surrounding a camp with only a few two-story buildings.

"We practice on those walls," Donton said, following Pol's eyes. "There are plenty of cities with walls lower than these. My armies are always prepared."

"King Landon's armies," Pol said.

"And the King puts his armies in my trust," Donton said.

Pol didn't say another word until they entered Donton's quarters. He had set it up with furniture that might have come from a command tent.

"Roughing it?"

Donton laughed. "It reminds me how to live when I'm in the field."

The General impressed Pol. He liked the way the man thought. "You don't need my approval, but you have it, General," Pol said.

"Buttering me up, boy?"

Pol shrugged. "Take it as you may," Pol said as he sat in one of the collapsible camp chairs.

"What do you want to talk about?"

"My brother."

The General squinted. "What about your brother?"

"I'd like to know where you stand in regards to him. I know you have your own faction. You think he's a weak ruler, don't you?"

"The boy is blunt," Donton said, obviously referring to Pol. "But I like blunt. I saw how you used the back of your sword to end your match. You could have just as easily sliced his hand off."

"Why would I do that? He's useful to you and to King Landon, isn't he?"

"A mere tool?" Donton said.

"No, a useful person. He's an excellent swordsman."

"Who was beaten by a sixteen-year-old boy," Donton said.

"A pattern-master, Deftnis-trained, as I said. I've probably killed more men than he has," Pol said. "I'm not saying that to boast, but to give him credit for putting up a good fight."

Donton worked his lips together. "Well said. You fought in Volia?"

"For my life, a number of times. We were beset by the Pontifer of Botarra's Hounds, a group of magicians and scouts."

The General's eyebrows went up. "Even I have heard of them. And you lived to tell the tale."

"Too many tales, I'm afraid General. I'd like to prevent any tales like that in Listya. So, back to my question, you think Landon is weak?"

"I do. I'm sure he knows."

Pol nodded even though he didn't know if Landon knew to what extent or not. "I wouldn't call him weak as much as inexperienced and overworked. He is teachable," Pol said.

Donton looked away. "I suspect so."

"Then why don't you support him? Advise him. Take away some of his burden. Become a mentor. What do you have to lose? If he respects you, good things will happen for Listya. He has a brother, not me, who wants to take over your country. Grostin is no friend of Listya's. You would not enjoy working for him."

Donton pursed his lips waiting to hear more.

Pol knew he should wait to hear what Donton had to say, but he couldn't stop. "He is bad for North Salvan and would be worse if Landon relented and became a vassal-king."

"Hazett wouldn't permit it."

Pol shook his head. "I'm not so sure. Hazett treats his kings and dukes well. He gives them lots of rope and few hang themselves. I worry for Grostin."

"So what specifically do you want me to do?"

Pol leaned forward. "Protect Listya from Grostin. The best way to do that is to become a strength for Landon. I'm trying to get Landon to marry a Listyan. I gave him that counsel last year when I was here. He needs ties to Listya."

"I can't disagree," Donton said. "I wish it were you taking the throne. I'll not deny it."

Pol took a deep breath. "The throne of Listya is not for me. I have a dukedom in South Salvan I haven't even seen. I'd be a bad king because I haven't finished growing up yet."

"You seem pretty grown up to me."

Pol laughed. "Not really," he said. "I'll pledge my support for you as long as you support my brother as king. If I wanted the throne, I could have seized it last year. Certainly, you realize that."

"I do." Donton peered at Pol. "I'll do it for you."

"Not for me, for Listya."

The General nodded. "For Listya. That's a better reason for those in my circle."

"Of course it is." Pol rose from his seat. "I'll notify Landon. Be prepared to become more of a participant in the affairs of the kingdom." Pol had a thought. "By the way, were you in on the deliberations with Daftine? Or did you just stand by waiting to be called in?"

"I had my maps, but I didn't end up participating. Should I have?"

Pol smiled. "Start with reviewing whatever they decided. Stopping wars is more noble than prosecuting them," Pol said. "Do you agree?"

Donton looked down at the ground. "As long as I keep my men trained."

"A good defense is to keep your weapons sharp, right?"

Donton laughed. "That's right. I forgot, you read the right kind of books in Borstall."

"It seems that I did," Pol said, smiling back.

The same technique might fail with Greenhill, Pol thought, as he sought out the King's Exchequer. The man was home, so Pol had Wilf find a guard that knew where Lord Greenhill lived.

Pol knocked on the door and nodded his head to the guard, releasing him from his duty. An attractive woman answered the door.

"Oh, I thought you were one of my errant children," she said, blushing when she confronted a stranger on her doorstep. "Are you here to see my husband?"

Pol smiled. "I am if your husband is Lord Greenhill, madam." He bowed to her as he was taught.

"Ah, a boy with the manners of a courtier. Come in and sit while I find out where Bisom is."

Pol followed her to a sitting room. He spied the tip of a wooden practice sword peeking out from a settee. One of Greenhill's sons, he surmised.

He waited for a bit and heard the front door open and slam shut. A youth about Pol's age rushed into the sitting room.

"Excuse me," the youth said. "I left something here." He looked around, not noticing the sword.

"It's behind that settee," Pol said.

"Oh?" His mouth retained the 'O' for a bit until he spotted it. "Why are you here? Message for my father?"

Pol nodded. "That's close enough. Do you know how to use that?" Pol's eyes went to the sword. It looked like it was good quality.

The youth winced. "Just starting, actually. My father told me I was too young to learn weapons. He'd rather me be a magician, but there are problems."

Pol brightened. "I'm a magician," he said.

"You? How far along are you?"

"I'm not a disappointment," Pol said.

"I can move a penny halfway across a board. Want to see me?"

If the boy wasn't trained, that would be an excellent indicator of his talent.

Pol didn't know how long he would have to wait for Greenhill to show, so he let the boy grab a game board from a small bookcase in the room and pulled a penny out of his pocket.

"I just have to take a bunch of deep breaths to calm myself and concentrate." He did as he said and moved the penny close enough to prove what he said.

"Can you do that?"

Pol tried not to be smug. "I've studied at Deftnis for a bit," he said. "So my training is a little better."

"Deftnis? I'd like to go there. Father says the local magicians said I'd never be accepted."

Pol knew that the boy would pass the test for admittance, regardless of what Greenhill felt.

"Point to where I should move the penny."

The teenager frowned and then smiled. "I can do that." He put the penny on a corner of the board and pointed to the opposite side, the longest distance on the board. "That's a challenge," he said.

Pol nodded. He played at concentrating and tweaked. The penny rose straight up about six inches. Pol moved the penny to each corner of the board and ended on the one the boy pointed to and lowered the penny.

"I, I've never seen anyone do that." He said.

Pol tried to maintain a serious face. Plenty of Deftnis magicians could do what he did. With some training, the boy in front of him could, too. He leaned over and said. "They even let you train with real swords if you want."

The boy's eyes grew. "They do? My father couldn't stop me if I was at the monastery, could he?"

Pol shook his head.

"What if I wrote out a letter of introduction?" Pol said.

"They would take your word?"

Pol nodded. He had met enough acolytes to know the boy would fit in just fine. "I have a passing acquaintance with the Abbot."

"You do?" The boy's gaze turned to the doorway as Greenhill arrived. "Father, your visitor is Deftnis-trained. He says he would write a letter of introduction for me."

Greenhill looked surprised. "You would do that for me, Poldon?"

Pol nodded his head.

"You know him?" the boy said.

"He's the King's brother and was the one who killed Regent Tamio." Greenhill turned to Pol and bowed. "May I present my son, Robor."

Pol rose and bowed to Greenhill's son, who stood open-mouthed. "I am pleased to make your formal acquaintance."

Robor looked at his father with pleading eyes.

Greenhill shook his head. "Not now. I have business to discuss with Duke Pol."

"D-D-Duke?"

"Out," Greenhill said.

Robor bowed deeply and left, slipping out with his wooden sword behind his back.

"I must apologize for my son."

Pol sat back. "No apologies needed. If it wasn't for all my trials, I probably wouldn't be much different."

"Trials," Greenhill said. "I heard about a few of your exploits in Volia from Wilf. Trials would be an understatement. Now, what would you have of me?"

"I don't represent the King, but I come on his behalf."

Greenhill laughed. "You should replace him," he said.

"General Donton said the same thing and I'll give you the same answer I gave him. I don't want to rule Listya."

Greenhill looked at Pol with cynical eyes. "Your sights are higher? Are you to be Hazett's replacement?"

Pol shook his head. "Perish the thought. The Empire would crash down around my feet."

"I'm not so sure," Greenhill said.

"Even if I wanted to be King of Listya, I feel that I'm not prepared, not old enough," Pol said. "I have other things I want to do. I've never been to Yastan, and then I'm going to escort my Shinkyan friend to Tishiko."

"On your black Shinkyan? Where is he?"

Pol clamped his lips together. "I don't know. He disappeared when the Tesnan monks mobilized. That's a long story."

"I've heard part of it," Greenhill said. "More trials, I suppose?"

Pol nodded. "I'd like you to take more responsibility in helping Landon become a better king. He can be trained if he has the right mentors. I trust that you have done a decent job being the Exchequer, but Landon needs more of you."

"What's in it for me? A better title? I like doing what I'm doing. It's the right combination of responsibility, yet I have time for other pursuits."

Pol wouldn't ask him what those pursuits were, but looking around the house, Pol felt that Greenhill was more of a family man than his demeanor let on in the castle. That thought prompted Pol to come up with a possible lever.

"Shall we do a little trading?" Pol said.

"What kind?" Greenhill looked interested.

"I will write a letter of introduction to Abbot Pleagor of Deftnis for your son, Robor. He has been tested, I know, but his level of magic is acceptable to get him admitted. I think he would thrive there, from what little I picked up in our conversation."

Greenhill moved to the edge of his chair. "You'd do that? I tried to get the local magicians interested, but they declined."

"I am well known at Deftnis, although I've been gone from the monastery more than I've been there."

"Regent indicated that you were an unproven prodigy."

Pol nodded. "At this point, I would say I'm a proven prodigy. I know I can get him accepted."

"And what do you want in return?"

"Support King Landon. He needs mentors. I know he will take lots of advice, especially if it can get some of his paperwork reduced."

Greenhill put his hand to his chin. "I don't think that's enough."

So they were horse-trading. Pol bit the inside of his lip. He knew his negotiating skills were awful. He scoured his brain to think what else he could offer. He didn't think Greenhill would want a mistress, but that led him to another bright idea.

"Landon needs a Listyan wife. Do you know of any eligible woman of decent rank? Perhaps a relative?" The relative part was what Pol hoped would hook Greenhill. "Pretty would be a plus. I will give you the opportunity to function as a matchmaker. I understand I can't guarantee that Landon will choose whoever you offer, but it would solidify your position in Court and secure your position as Exchequer." Pol had to look at Greenhill to see how interested he might be.

Greenhill grinned. "A pretty girl. Good head on her shoulders, but not too forward?"

"Sounds right to me," Pol said.

He snapped his fingers. "I know just the wench. My wife's cousin is the youngest in her family, but as smart as a whip. Pretty, too. Blonde, just like the King. She couldn't come from a better background." Greenhill looked towards the door.

Pol couldn't help but smile. The man had said the last for his wife who must be listening in.

"Then I'll put your cousin into a position that Landon can notice and place your son in Deftnis. In return, I want you to make, along with General Donton, my brother the best king Listya has ever had."

Greenhill's eyes took on a faraway look. The man was thinking about Pol's offer. "I am tempted," he said. "I am tempted."

His wife barged into the room. "I am more than tempted. Consider the deal done."

Pol looked across the ballroom. Landon accompanied Allisor, Greenhill's niece, for five straight dances that Pol could count.

Shira stood by his side as pretty as ever. She smiled at the couple. "They both look like they are enjoying each other's company. I think we're looking at a royal wedding."

"I'm too young," he said with a smile.

Shira put her hand on Pol's wrist and plucked gently at his skin. "Not us, silly. Your brother is enthralled."

"And without mind control."

"Not magical mind control," Shira said giggling. "Feminine mind control."

Pol smiled and squeezed her hand. He had enjoyed the past few weeks in Alsador, but they would be leaving in the morning for Yastan. His letter had gone out to Abbot Pleagor recommending Robor Greenhill. He had told Greenhill to send Robor to Deftnis with another introduction letter signed by Fadden, Paki, and Pol at the end of summer, so the boy could start at Harvest Break. Greenhill's other condition looked like she approved of a match as much as Landon.

He sighed.

"What was that for?"

Landon's problems look to be solved, for now. "Our problems are just emerging. First an audience with the Emperor, and then your return to Shinkya."

"I know," Shira said. "I feel bad about that, but Ako would put me to sleep and ship me home if I exhibited any thoughts of remaining in the Empire."

Pol nodded. "Let's make the most of it them."

Shira led Pol out onto the balcony in the early summer evening and pulled him closer. "We can start with this." She kissed him on the lips and Pol was more than happy to kiss back.

~ ~ ~

Chapter Ten

~

T HEY DEBARKED FROM THEIR SHIP AT DASALT, the
capital of the little kingdom with the same name. Pol had been
here once before when Searl and he sought out the monk's daughter.
Could it have only been a year? His life had been filled with a lifetime
of adventures, yet here he was.

Paki looked happy to leave yet another ship. Fadden escorted
Ako and Shira down the gangplank. Pol didn't feel hurried. He would
have to savor his remaining few months with Shira. He had no idea
how long they would linger in Yastan. He was eager to introduce Ako
and Shira to Malden Gastoria and Farthia Wissingbel, but he dreaded
giving Akonai Haleaku the news of his mother's death.

The less he saw of the Emperor, the better. It wasn't that he didn't
like the man, but Hazett was unpredictable and that made being
around him uncomfortable. Fadden warned that the Emperor would
want a report of their travels in Volia and of what happened in Alsador.

After a deep breath, Pol gathered his personal items and trudged
down the gangplank. After milling around the dock, guarding their pile
of possessions, Fadden and Paki came into view riding atop a carriage,
of all things.

Pol was used to riding a horse, but perhaps that wouldn't be the case during their trip to the Imperial capital.

"We travel to Yastan in style," Fadden said.

Pol noticed a horse trailing behind the carriage.

Fadden followed his eyes. "We might need a horse for one reason or another," he said. "Perhaps we can do a little scouting."

They piled their belongings into the boot of the carriage and what didn't fit was stowed into a large flat covered box on top. When everything appeared to be stowed properly, Fadden ushered everyone to their places.

"Paki and I will get us through Dasalt, then any of us can drive the road to Yastan. Most of it is paved," Fadden said.

He seemed to be in good spirits. In fact, all of them were. Pol had felt a burden sliding off his back when they sailed out of Alsador's harbor. The responsibility of Landon's success lay behind and the excitement of his first visit to Yastan brought a smile to Pol's face as they took off from Dalsalt's harbor square and ascended the row of hills behind the capital.

"Did you recognize Dasalt?" Shira said. She sat next to Ako letting the sway of the carriage push the back and forth in the cab.

"I never came close to the docks before, so not really. Searl and I were in and out of the city and on our way to Alsador so fast that I didn't notice much." Pol looked out the window. "We approached and departed from the south side of the city, so I've never been here before." Pol noticed a river to the north. "That river divides Dasalt from Hentz. On the other side of Hentz is Fen, where Kell grew up."

"You said you've never been here before?" Ako asked.

Pol laughed. "Never, but I memorized a number of maps before I was twelve years old."

"So when is our next stop?"

"Memorizing a map and knowing the best places to stay are two entirely different activities. We will have to rely on Fadden, just as we did while we traveled through Volia. He said he'd been along this road a number of times."

"If we have to, we can sleep in here," Shira said.

Pol turned his head from the scenery. "Maybe the two of you can, but the rest of us are too tall. I don't know if Fadden has a tent, but as we move into the heart of the Empire, there will be plenty of villages to spend the night. This road is paved because there is so much traffic between Dasalt and Yastan."

"Do you have many paved roads in the Empire?" Ako said.

Pol knew what she really asked. "Yes, we do. The Emperor can quickly get to most countries in any weather."

"The Emperor and his forces."

"That's right. Is there something wrong with that?" Pol asked the Sister.

"No. Good roads aid your Emperor in keeping his Empire stable."

"That among other things," Pol said. "He rules with a light touch, but doesn't hesitate to pull recalcitrant states back into line."

"We all know about that," Shira said.

"North Salvan?" Ako nodded her head. "This is all quite different from Shinkya, isn't it, Shira?"

Shira cleared her throat. "It is. The bureaucracy runs Shinkya regardless who rules."

"And that's why factions can proliferate, I suppose," Pol said. "The government persists regardless of what intrigue stalks the royal family."

"What keeps the Empire from crumbling if the Emperor dies? Do the people elect a new Emperor?"

Pol shook his head. "One of the children of Hazett III will rule when the time comes. He has plenty of children, so there isn't a prospect of a political problem, at least for a generation or two. Sometimes an Emperor will adopt a child. Under Imperial rules, the adoption can only be for a minor, someone who hasn't reached the age to twenty, if he needs more heirs. It's happened enough times in the past."

"That leaves me out," Ako said. She smiled and effective ended the conversation by looking out the window.

Shira looked at Pol, but he couldn't figure out why. He smiled at her and joined Ako in observing the Dasalt countryside go by.

They crossed into Galistya. Pol drove with Shira sitting beside him atop the carriage. Fadden had ridden ahead to secure rooms for the night at a popular inn located at the heart of the Galistyan capital.

"Aren't you getting excited?" Shira asked.

"No. Well, I've always wanted to walk the streets of Yastan. You always build up in your mind what the city is like. I am sure I'll be disappointed. It will be like all the other capitals we've been to—"

Shira threaded her arm through his and put her head on his shoulder. "I like the 'we' and I dread losing it," she said. "The past week has gone by too quickly. Fadden said we turn north from where we stay tomorrow."

"Yastan is about due north. Two days, if the weather holds." Pol looked up at the cloudless summer sky. "I think it will."

Shira followed his gaze and sighed. "Yastan and then to Shinkya."

Pol grinned. "Not quite. We get to visit Deftnis on the way back. You'll see how much different it is than Tesna."

"I get to be introduced to all your monkish friends?"

"Paki is a monkish friend," Pol said.

"Somehow I think he is less monkish than the others. He has managed to find himself either a game or a girl in nearly every inn."

Pol laughed. "Deftnis monks have their vices. There is a port town across from the isle called Mancus where the monks can easily find girls and games."

"Did you frequent Mancus very much?"

He shook his head. "Acolytes have limited opportunities to go to Mancus. There is a small port on Deftnis Isle that does a good enough job at leading them astray. Paki took advantage when I was there. I can't say what he did when I wasn't. It's been almost a year since we both were at Deftnis together."

"And you aren't an acolyte any longer?"

Pol grimaced. "No, I'm not and that leads to problems. Abbot Pleagor was concerned that my youth got in the way at the monastery. Perhaps it's better that I've been gone. I was rated the second highest level at the monastery and they didn't know how to handle Gray sixteen-year-olds. They probably still don't."

"By the time you've delivered me to my fate and return you'll be seventeen, won't you?"

"Close to it, anyway." Pol sighed. "I'm not going to worry about it until the time comes."

"Maybe the Emperor will adopt you and Yastan will be your home."

Pol laughed. "And complicate my life even more? Not likely. I can always retreat to my ducal estate in South Salvan and wait a few years."

"We wouldn't be that far away from each other that way," Shira said, smiling and squeezing his arm. Gently, Pol noticed.

"As if that will matter once you return. Won't they lock you up or something?"

Shira's smile faded. "I don't know. It might be more like you were at Deftnis. They won't know what to do with a princess with too much experience. I already know more than I should."

Pol looked at the placid countryside with rolling hills covered with crops. It appeared peaceful like Fistyra did. Pol hoped the country was as serene as it looked travelling through the fields. He took Shira's hand and held it as he grabbed back onto the reins. She looked at him and smiled, then looked up towards the sun with closed eyes.

'Too much experience' she had said. Pol knew she referred to their experience in the Demron cave. Neither of them spoke of that experience any more than they had to, for different reasons, and that made Pol hurt inside a bit.

Perhaps he could put all that behind him as they made their way to Yastan.

Fadden intercepted them before they reached the Galistyan capital and took over the reins. Paki was eager to climb back up on the driver's seat.

"I can only be in that woman's presence for so long," he said to Fadden as Pol climbed down. Shira had already retreated into the cab. "She is too smart and everything she says makes me feel like she's making fun of me."

Fadden laughed. "Ako doesn't fall for your lame opening lines? If she wasn't a Shinkyan…" He let the comment fade and looked at Pol. "Make sure to tell the ladies to spruce up once we sight the capital. The inn is a very nice one, and they will want to look their best."

"What about us?" Paki said.

"We three are hopeless," Fadden said with a smile.

Pol let the two women know. They exited the cab and rummaged around in the boot looking for presentable clothes to wear. Soon, they were back on their way to the Galistyan capital with Pol riding behind.

The city was built on a plain alongside the river that flowed from the east side of Boxall, all the way to Dasalt. The five of them had traveled on the south side of the river and once they left the capital, they would cross a bridge and soon be in Baccusol, the country that gave the Empire its name.

It seemed that all of a sudden they passed village after village until the road changed and the carriage passed under a gate. The growth of the city had smothered the capital's walls. Pol evaluated the uniqueness of the Galistyan capital and found it prosaic other than its size.

No style proliferated. After the gate, all the buildings were made out of stone. The streets were reasonably clean. Even Alsador had more character than this place, Pol thought. Fadden turned down a broad avenue and pulled up at a four-story inn. The place reminded Pol of the Bossomian inn they stayed at in Missibes.

Pol dismounted as boys of much the same age as he grabbed the horses. He climbed up to the rooftop box, pulled out his possessions, and then jumped to the ground.

Fadden talked to a voice Pol instantly recognized. He dropped what he carried and ran around to the other side of the carriage.

"Malden!"

"You've grown." Malden Gastoria, the former Court Magician of Borstall, grabbed Pol by his shoulders. They stood eye to eye, for Malden wasn't the tallest person Pol had ever met. "How have you been?"

"I've had my ups and downs. I read your report. Your version was somewhat different than Namion Threshell's."

Pol grit his teeth. "I would imagine." He shook off his anger and looked at his old friend. "Is Mistress Farthia here?"

The magician grinned. "She is and dying to see you again. Come in, the inn's staff can see to your things."

Paki had climbed to the top and gave Pol the long metal rod from the Demron cave.

"What is that?" Malden said taking the rod from Pol.

Pol pressed his lips together. "A souvenir from Volia, Teriland, actually. It's something that I didn't put in the report."

Malden feigned a shiver. "Sounds ominous. I can't wait to get the details. Let's go in."

The anxiety that Pol felt when he learned that Namion had already told his tale, left when he saw his old tutor.

"Mistress Farthia," Pol said grinning.

She held out her hands and grasped both of Pol's. "Mistress no more. Malden and I are married."

Pol couldn't remember if he heard anything about that but shrugged. "I wasn't able to attend, but congratulations. It was bound to happen."

"Tell Malden that. I had to use extraordinary measures to get him to make the commitment. Can you introduce me to these two women?" Pol looked back. Ako and Shira stood just inside the inn's entrance. "I know who the younger one is, but not the older Shinkyan."

Pol motioned Ako and Shira over. "This is Shira. As you know, she fought the South Salvans at my side."

Farthia beamed at the two women. "I don't think I've ever seen two Shinkyan women in the same place." She put out her hand. "I am Farthia Wissingbel. My father—"

"Is the Emperor's Instrument. I am familiar with him. Actually, I've lived in the Empire for the past three years, in Alsador."

"A Sister?" Malden said.

Ako blushed. "Of course." She smiled but looked a little flustered.

"I am Malden Gastoria."

"Ah. The instrument of the Instrument, if I'm not mistaken," Ako said. "No wonder you know me as a Sister."

Malden examined Ako's face. "No disguise today, it seems."

"You are a magician?"

Pol stepped into the conversation. "He's rated a Black."

"Some in Shinkya would say that's a bad thing. I don't," Ako said.

"And you are with what faction?" Farthia smiled at Pol and Shira before turning her gaze to Ako.

"Fearless."

Farthia nodded. "Good. We can talk freely then."

"You know our factions?" Shira said.

Malden gave Shira a deep bow. "Yes, and we know who you are, Shira."

Pol couldn't believe the extent of Malden's information. "Did you know who she was when we traveled through South Salvan?"

Malden shook his head. "But we found out about the time you made it to Borstall. You travel with exalted company."

"Pol is exalted enough for me," Shira said.

Farthia's face turned serious. "For now, anyway."

"For now," Shira put her hand on Pol's arm. "For now."

Malden rubbed his hands. "We will be riding with you to Yastan. I thought it might be better to get your side of the story without other distractions. Farthia and I wanted to get out of Yastan, and I couldn't think of a better reason than getting reacquainted traveling along a friendly road."

Pol grinned. "I'm all for that."

Malden bowed to Ako and Shira. "We would like to treat you to dinner. This is the best inn in Galistya, in my opinion."

"Mine, too," Fadden said, just joining them from arranging for their rooms. "Ako and Shira will share rooms tonight. I'll be with Paki. Pol, you are on your own."

"Fine with me," Pol said.

Later at dinner, Shira wore a pretty dress that seemed to shout 'summer'. Ako had used cosmetics on Shira much to her advantage. He noticed that Fadden couldn't keep his eyes from admiring Ako's looks.

"We will keep ourselves to pleasantries if you don't mind," Malden said. "Although I will warn you that the Emperor will put you to work when we arrive once you have told your story."

"I thought I was through with the Emperor's tasks. I would rather look around Yastan, and then visit Deftnis on the way to Shinkya," Pol said. He tried not to sound truculent.

"Two weeks in Yastan. Summer may be a bit hot in Yastan, but you'll find enough to do with whatever Hazett has in mind for you and do some sightseeing as well. Besides, Farthia and I would like to spend some time with you. I'm interested in what your thinking was during your various challenges."

Pol nodded. He wouldn't mind putting off the inevitable parting from Shira. "If Ako doesn't mind hearing it all over again."

"Don't you need your girlfriend's permission?" Ako said.

"Yes!" Shira and Pol said simultaneously.

All around the table laughed as the pair blushed. Pol felt awkward around Malden and Farthia. They were married and Shira and he were together temporarily.

"I'm sorry," Malden said. "I'll make sure you two get opportunities to share Yastan."

Shira smiled. Pol thought Malden put that nicely.

Farthia kept up the conversation asking about the different cuisines they encountered in Volia. That was neutral ground and Pol was glad when Ako yawned, signaling an end to dinner.

"Pol, would you mind if I bought you something to drink?" Malden said.

Shira patted Pol on the back as Ako, Farthia, and Shira went to the lobby to sit and talk. Fadden eyed Ako walking away, but Paki stopped his gaze when he asked if Fadden knew of any gaming at the inn. The inn didn't have any, but another tavern down the street did. They left, leaving Malden and Pol alone.

"Follow me." Malden rose and went into the tavern part to find a more secluded corner.

"I'm sure you are wondering what to expect in Yastan?" the magician began.

Pol nodded, not knowing what to say.

"The Emperor is impressed by your actions in Volia. Both Fadden and Wilf Yarrow sent messages by bird with their impressions of your visit. We can talk about the details tomorrow with Shira. I definitely want to get her impressions. Tonight, I want to reassure you that Namion did nothing to sour the Emperor's opinion."

A barmaid took their order. Pol elected a fruit juice. He wanted to keep his mind sharp. Malden asked for a glass of wine.

"I'm not particularly interested in what the Emperor thinks of me," Pol said. He made a face. "That didn't come out how I intended. I haven't acted in order to curry the Emperor's favor. Do you understand?"

"I do and that is only to your benefit. The Emperor abhors toadies and he abhors liars. Namion's report was full of misrepresentations, if not outright lies. When we get to Yastan, I'll let you read his report. I also received a letter a week or two ago from the Prelate of Bastiz. You impressed him. His own description of the event of a council contradicted Namion's account. His name is Homan?"

Pol nodded.

"Prelate Homan apologized for trying to arrange your abduction. He had recommended you to the Council in Missibes and suggested that they spend time with you, but they mistook his message. I don't know if that is the truth, but he would like to initiate direct relations with Yastan, including allowing his magicians to train in the Imperial capital rather than in Missibes."

"I never read his message to the Commission, but Fadden and Namion seemed to think Homan wanted me to train others in the Bossomian Magicians Academy."

Malden waved his hand. "We can debate that with Fadden in Yastan. Suffice it to say, you have impressed many people and made enemies of others. Both of those are compliments considering your enemies."

"I don't know what to say," Pol said. He didn't like the attention that was for sure.

"There is one thing that you will be happy to know," Malden said, and then took a sip of his wine.

"What?"

"Demeron returned to Deftnis all on his own. He traveled through Shinkya on his way back to the monastery and brought along with him a major dilemma for Hazett."

"Is he safe?"

"The Abbot says he's a little scarred up from this travels, but he made quite a stir when he arrived."

"What dilemma?"

Malden grinned. "He brought over two hundred Shinkyan horses with him. Demeron says they were all wild or had escaped abusive masters."

Pol scoffed. "How can Demeron talk to anyone but me?"

"That's the interesting part. He says a Shinkyan Elder infused him with magic. Demeron thinks it has something to do with how you two bonded. He can speak to most magicians Gray or above."

"Really? Magic?"

"I don't know the details, but I'm sure you'll have stories to exchange when you get back to Deftnis."

"How is the Emperor going to deal with so many Shinkyan horses? Won't the Shinkyans want them back?"

"Demeron said they refuse to return. You talk to him and I think Shira is adept enough to talk to him as well. The Emperor will want both of you to address the situation when you take Shira back to Tishiko. You'll have the authority of the Emperor to do so."

Pol sighed. "I don't want his authority."

"Do I want to take over Ranno's position as Instrument? Yet, Ranno and Hazett are planning just that when Ranno retires. I think we both are going to have to take deep breaths and realize that we are destined to serve the Empire."

Pol swirled the fruit juice with his finger, wanting to change the subject and he had just the story to do that. "I had an experience in Volia."

Malden smiled. "You had many experiences."

"I mean something really, really different. Did Fadden tell you about the cave of Demron?"

The magician nodded. "Only that you found your alien relations."

Pol related the episode at the cave. "When I put my amulet to the podium with my hand over it, I fought with an alien intelligence."

"No one told me about that." Malden sat up straighter.

"We fought for dominance, over what I don't know, but I won when I convinced the intelligence that his race was truly dead. He gave up after that."

Malden's eyebrows went up. "Fascinating. How do you feel about that?"

"I'm still feeling. An essence of the alien remained inside me."

"What?"

Pol nodded. "I am more powerful than I was and my magic doesn't tire me nearly as easily. When I applied the truth spell to Manda—you know about Manda, don't you?"

Malden nodded.

"It was a different tweak to the pattern than I ever learned. I think the intelligence improved my ability to tweak."

Malden drained his wine glass. "I'd like to test you in Yastan, but do you detect any change in your personality? Has your relationship with Shira changed?"

"That didn't affect us," Pol said.

"But something did?"

"I'll tell you later. I think I've had enough sharing tonight."

~ ~ ~

Chapter Eleven

MALDEN SAT BACK IN THE CARRIAGE after Shira described the Magic Circle's ward defense of their fortress.

"We don't encourage wards in the Empire," he said. "Interesting."

"Not true," Pol replied. "The Tesnan Abbot warded his office. They use wards in Shinkya."

The magician returned to his upright posture as the carriage shook and rattled over the cobbled roadway. "Can you create wards for me?" Malden looked at Shira and then at Ako. "Either of you?"

Ako put up her hands. "Not me. I'm no expert at wards…" she smiled, "other things perhaps."

"Perhaps," Farthia said looking at the Shinkyan Sister with a doubtful expression, at least Pol perceived it that way. His former tutor sighed. "We won't ask you to expose any state secrets or force you to disclose anything you are unwilling to share."

"You sound as if you are part of the Instrument's staff."

Farthia smiled. "I am, actually, but I don't know anything about Seeking. I deal with information and providing political perspective. Don't I Pol?"

"She was my tutor for nearly five years before I left Borstall Castle," Pol said.

"He was a very good student," she said.

Shira giggled. "Very good. I've seen Pol in action."

"With wards, too," Malden said, turning to Pol. "But you didn't learn how to create them, did you?"

Pol shook his head. "I was too busy getting in and out. At the Council of Malcia, I had to remove wards while enemy magicians were placing them."

Malden pursed his lips in thought. "We need to get back on track. Let's continue with your time in The Shards."

By the time the carriage reached their first stop in Baccusol, Pol felt drained, and they stopped at the point when the group had just left Missibes in Bossom. He had told their story lots of times, but never in the excruciating detail that Malden and Farthia demanded. He looked over at the book of notes that Farthia scribbled. How she could have written anything down as they traveled over the roads astounded Pol.

Pol lugged his belongings into his room. The inn wasn't full so everyone got a private room except for Malden and Farthia. He sat on his bed, feeling wrung out. The worst part was to come and Pol felt a bit uncomfortable about describing the events in the cave. He would leave that description to Shira, but Malden and Farthia were so detail oriented, he knew they might want to extract every last detail from their story. At least he had already told Malden about the alien essence bouncing around in his head.

He walked down to the common room. This inn had no dining room, but it was comfortable enough. After a day's travel, everyone wolfed down a mediocre dinner.

"Want to go for a walk?" Shira said.

Pol put his hand over the lump of slivers in his pocket. He was armed well, even though he left his knives up in his room. They left the inn. The sun hadn't quite gone down, so it bathed the town in a warm golden glow.

"I never thought I would be considered to be an expert on Volia," she said after the pair walked down the wooden sidewalk, passing a few buildings before talking.

"Farthia was always thorough."

"So are you," Shira said, taking Pol's hand in both of hers. "What should we tell them about the cave?"

"Whatever they ask," Pol said. "I trust both of them as much or more than I trust anyone in the world. They both know how to act with discretion. Anyway, I've already told Malden about my experience with the alien intelligence, so we don't have to talk about that in Ako's presence. You haven't revealed my experience to her have you?"

Shira shook her head. "That's our own little state secret," she said. "Do you still get images?"

"No. But I told you about Manda and the truth spell. I never imagined I could suddenly come up with a different spell. The frustrating thing is I don't know how much it has affected me. Malden's going to do some testing when we get to Yastan."

"It's better that you know, than worrying about what will happen next."

Pol stopped to look at a shop window selling women's clothes. The shop was closed. "See what the fashions are like in Baccusol?" Even Pol could tell the style was different from anything he had seen before.

Shira laughed. "Empire styles are much better than what we saw in Bossom, aren't they?"

"That's my opinion, but then I'm biased." Pol smiled and led her away.

"It is freer than Shinkya," Shira said.

Pol pointed to a bench in front of a closed store. The sun was going down and shadows bathed one side of the street. "Free is a relative term, I'm afraid," he said. "Some of the countries in the Baccusol Empire are freer than others. I don't think I'd like to live in North Salvan right now. The Duke of Lawster stole Demeron from me. But no country in the Empire is as lawless as South Parsimol or Botarra."

"Not to mention The Shards," Shira said, obviously thinking about the Magician Circle's influence in the nation of islands and pirates.

"Teriland and Gekelmar were free, but they were among the poorest nations on the continent," Pol said.

He took a deep breath and looked across the street. "If I were the Emperor, I don't think I'd change a thing."

"If I were the Queen of Shinkya, I'm not so sure what I'd do.

Shinkya owes its stability to an overweening bureaucracy that's more like Bossom, the more I think about it, but I don't like to do that. My fate is tied to Shinkya's."

Pol squeezed her hand. "I wish my fate were tied to you."

Shira put her head on his shoulder. "If life could only be more simple."

"It's not for either of us, I'm afraid."

The villages began to merge into one long stretch of buildings by the side of the road with occasional breaks for a few fields as the carriage approached Yastan. Pol's stomach began to churn with nervousness.

Malden and Farthia had exhausted all of their questions earlier in the morning. Pol couldn't conceive of giving Farthia enough information to fill her thick notebook, but she finally had to pull out another before they finished. He hoped they had saved days of interrogation in Yastan.

The carriage made a final rest stop.

"I'll ride the horse, if you don't mind," Pol said. "I want to see everything when we reach Yastan." He rummaged around for his conical hat and put it on, smiling.

"No one will notice your fashion statement. Yastan is just another city," Farthia said. "Maybe it is a bit bigger." She smiled at him. "Go on. We'll keep Ako and Shira company."

He missed Shira riding at his side, but Yastan didn't hold the same meaning for her that it did for him. He wouldn't have objected to her riding when they entered Tishiko, but then they would all be riding through Shinkya.

Pol smiled when he thought of Demeron waiting for him in Deftnis. He had to quell his excitement, though. They had reached the outskirts of Yastan.

He didn't know what Farthia meant when she said Yastan was like any other city. If Bastiz was a city of spires, Yastan sprouted towers. He could see them rise stories above the city in the distance. Squat towers, square towers, round towers, and multisided towers. Some had spires, some had flat roofs, and others were gabled.

The buildings at the side of the road began to rise taller as the road widened. The carriage passed a large swath of grass hundreds of paces long that must have circled Yastan's center. They stopped at a huge set of gates embedded in the tallest wall Pol had ever seen. The line to enter the center of Yastan broke into six guard stations.

Malden stepped out of the carriage and pulled out a document of some sort. They were waved ahead without an inspection. Once through, Yastan now looked like any other city, only because Pol's vision was limited to streets lined with buildings.

His heart beat faster when he thought of riding the streets of the Imperial capital. People walking the streets looked no different. There was no guard escort for a single carriage among hundreds of others plying the streets of the capital. Pol smiled at the anonymity, even though their carriage carried a Shinkyan princess and the next Instrument of the Emperor.

He noticed a few curious glances at his hat, but Pol didn't mind. The citizens of Yastan were probably used to seeing a few odd things every day.

Like every other city he had been in, the buildings became more ornate and the people better dressed as they drew closer to the city center. Pol looked up and saw the Imperial Tower. He had seen sketches of it in books. It was hexagonal and made of white stone. At the top, a gilded statue of the first emperor stood with a raised hand looking towards the rising sun.

The tower was so tall that a large platform carried people and things to the upper floors by a series of winches and pulleys pulled by horses in a lower level. The tower stood ten floors high, at least one hundred feet. It might be the tallest building on the continent.

Everyone thought the Emperor lived inside the tower, but he didn't. Inside the palace grounds, the Emperor lived in a fortress-like three story three-sided building with a large triangular courtyard inside, so Farthia had told him.

They passed a smaller grass ring around the palace complex and Malden only needed to show his face to be waved inside.

Pol was sure it wasn't real, but he felt the heavy weight of history and majesty as he rode through an entrance the size of Borstall's city gate. Banners of all colors fluttered along the palace wall. From the outside, the compound appeared to be more like a castle until he got inside and found that Missibes' Inner Ring was closer to the fact. The colorful ramparts hid a smaller city in its own right.

Fadden seemed to know where to go. Pol hadn't expected to stay at the palace, since they had already passed a few inns and restaurants. The crowds had obviously thinned as they rode on the smoothly paved road. Malden poked his head out the window and gave Fadden instructions. Soon they passed through a carved wooden gate into a large courtyard.

Pol dismounted when Malden helped Farthia, Ako, and Shira out of the carriage.

"We're here, Pol," Malden said.

"Where is 'here'? Pol asked.

"The Instrument's headquarters. We even have our own inn."

"Seekers coming in and out?"

Malden nodded. "Farthia and I have quarters elsewhere in the Imperial Compound."

"Now I know what to call it," Paki said. "This is as big as the Inner Ring at Missibes." He shivered. "I didn't like that place at all."

"I had the same thoughts," Pol said. "So we can stay here for now?"

Farthia nodded. "I'll go get Father."

She disappeared into the largest structure on the north side of the courtyard. All the buildings seemed to be connected.

"Imagine two Sisters at the heart of the Empire," Ako said.

Pol wondered what went through her mind. The Shinkyans would already know all about the Imperial Compound, as Malden called it, but now Shira's country would have even more perspective.

Ranno Wissingbel walked out to greet them, with Farthia's arm threaded through his. He looked to be the same nondescript man with a ruddy face and gray, thinning hair. He always wore an expression somewhere between jovial and sardonic. He hadn't changed during the past few years since Pol had met him.

"I'm glad to see you made it to Yastan intact," he said.

"So are we," Pol said. "This is Shira and Ako, both Shinkyan Sisters, and I don't know if you met Pakkingail Horstel of Borstall when you were there with the Emperor."

Ranno shook his head and put out his hand. "Glad to meet you. Do you picture yourself as Seeker material?"

Paki shook his head. "I'm more of a scout, I think," he said.

"I won't hold it against you," Ranno said, winking at Pol's friend. He turned to Ako. "You worked in Alsador?"

"For three years. They were interesting."

"If you don't mind, I'd like a chat with you. Shinkya and the Empire aren't enemies, so perhaps we can have a pleasant conversation."

"I'd look forward to it," Ako said, bowing with her hands folded over her stomach.

"Fadden, I know. Glad to have you back." Finally, he took Shira's hands in his. "You're the one who's been taking care of the Emperor's Pet."

"Who?" Shira said.

"Pol. Poldon Fairfield. Pol Cissert. Aron Morfess. Nater Grainell. Your boyfriend is in there somewhere."

Shira blinked her eyes and smiled. "Pol Cissert, if you don't mind."

"I don't. Who knows what it will be next," Ranno said. He always seemed to be one or two steps ahead of everyone else.

Pol furrowed his brow and looked at Malden, mouthing 'Emperor's Pet?'

"We'll talk about that later. Malden, you know where they are to be settled?"

"I do," the magician said.

~ ~ ~

Chapter Twelve

~

THE ROOM WASN'T THE BEST POL HAD STAYED IN since he left Deftnis, but it was clean and decent-sized with a table and chairs, a dresser, a bed, and a small, empty fireplace. His window looked over a dirt field. Pol guessed it was a practice area of some sort.

He stood when someone knocked on his door.

"There you are," Ranno said. "We need to do a little talking. Come with me to my office."

"I haven't washed up, yet."

"Do you think I care? Come on, boy." Ranno had already begun walking down the hall. "I had a few words with Fadden. He'll take care of your friend Paki and the two Shinkyan ladies while we go over a few things."

What did Ranno have to say to him that couldn't be said in front of his friends? He walked a few paces behind the Emperor's Instrument as they walked up a few steps into another building and soon Ranno walked into a large alcove filled with desks.

"That's my office, and that is Malden's," he said, pointing to two offices with facing doors. A bank of windows ran the length of the outside wall between them. On the other side of the windows, Pol noted a lush courtyard.

Most of the desks were occupied, and only a few of the occupants looked up as Pol passed. He followed Ranno into his office. The Instrument closed the door softly behind him.

"Sit," Ranno said, pointing to a plush chair in front of an expansive desk. His office was paneled in polished wood. Books, scrolls, and knickknacks filled the shelves of floor to ceiling shelves. A carpet covered the floor, but rugs of various patterns were placed on top. The ceiling was coffered with an intricate design, but Pol liked the many-paned window looking out onto the lush courtyard best of all.

Pol struggled to keep from leaning back into the cushiony softness of the back.

"I don't beat around the bush, as you might remember. Reports of your adventures in South Salvan and in Volia have reached our ears. Malden might have told you that we have your account and Namion Threshell's. They weren't quite the same."

"I didn't expect them to be," Pol said.

"Even that impressed the Emperor."

"Does My Emperor know everything?"

"Enough."

"What is the Emperor's Pet?"

Ranno laughed. "That confuses you, doesn't it? You are, you're the Emperor's Pet. It's a designation that hasn't been used before you came along, but Hazett has been calling you his pet since he first met you in Borstall."

Pol gripped the arms of the chair. "I don't understand."

"You'll be meeting the Emperor in a few minutes."

Pol jumped to his feet. "Here? I'm still wearing my dusty traveling clothes."

Ranno motioned for Pol to sit down. "That even adds to your cachet. He is going to welcome you to Yastan, personally. It is a great honor, but one Hazett likes to bestow regularly. He has quite a sense of humor and enjoys catching people off guard. I suppose you already know that."

Pol could only nod.

They chatted about the condition of the roads from Dasalt to Yastan. Ranno even made notes while they talked. Suddenly the door flew open and Emperor Hazett III, supreme ruler of the Baccusol Empire stood at the door.

Pol felt like bolting from the room, but Hazett only laughed. "Sit, sit. My, how you've grown, Pol. You're fine with me calling you Pol, aren't you?"

Pol nodded yet again.

Hazett sat down in the matching chair, but he leaned back and breathed in deeply and exhaled, looking up at the ceiling. "I've always liked your office, Ranno."

"It is yours if you desire, Hazett."

"So you always tell me. Maybe I'll surprise you one day and take you up on your offer."

Pol felt that their conversation sounded more like a ritual between old friends.

"I hear your horse has caused some problems for the Empire."

Pol felt himself blush. "Malden said that Demeron returned with two hundred Shinkyan horses. Are we now at war with Shinkya?"

That made Hazett laugh. "It will take more than that for the Shinkyans to invade. I imagine we would win a war with our neighbors now, but what's the point? Their culture will not easily mesh into the Empire."

Pol nodded. "I agree. I have some perspective on that."

"Princess Shira? I'll bet you do. She is very pretty. I think you two look very nice together, for a teenage couple. What are your plans?"

Pol sighed, even though he knew he shouldn't have in front of the Emperor. "I will take her home to Tishiko and say goodbye."

"A forever goodbye?"

Pol nodded yet again. This time he didn't want to betray his emotions. He cleared his throat. "We have been together for nearly a year."

"Namion said you two had intimate relations. Is that correct?"

Pol shook his head. "No, not at all. We've kept to appropriate boundaries."

Hazett waved Pol's comment off with his hand. "I thought you were smarter than how Threshell portrayed.

"May I ask you a question?"

Hazett looked at his fingernails. "Ask away."

"What is an Emperor's Pet?"

Hazett laughed and Ranno smiled. "My personal pet is someone who I have been watching from afar for a few years. I saw how vilely you were treated in Borstall. You probably know I loosely rule the Empire until forced to become more involved. I worried that you wouldn't survive through the trials that you were given, and that includes your poor health. You took your own short life and made it into a future. I was very impressed."

"I had to."

"No, you didn't. You could have given up. I know you nearly did, but you picked yourself up and found Searl Hogton, and then utterly without any help, you took care of a boil on the Empire's behind in removing Bythia Hairo from the throne before I had a chance to do it myself."

"I only did it because I couldn't stand to see my brother duped and my mother's former kingdom ruined."

"Yes, you had to," Hazett smiled. "Then I sent you on a perilous mission to Tesna."

"Valiso Gasibli was going to pick someone else."

Hazett straightened out his index finger and waved it from side to side. "Only if you weren't available."

"You personally ordered me to go?"

The Emperor feigned a surprised look. Ranno only smiled, a little too knowingly.

"Me? Didn't Gasibli tell you that you went on an Imperial mission for the Emperor?"

"He did, but I thought he was talking in the general sense."

"In the general and in the specific. I'm sorry your vacation wasn't quite what you expected it to be. I didn't expect Namion to show his true colors quite so soon. Fadden stepped in at the right time, but I expected you would have proceeded well enough without him."

"I don't know about that," Pol said.

"I do," Hazett replied. "So on your own, you saved your brother's kingdom a second time. He must be very glad you showed up."

Pol pressed his lips together. He felt extremely embarrassed. "I'm sure you were ready to lance the boil yourself."

"I considered it. Ranno reports that you performed adequately in Alsador for a second time."

Pol grimaced. "I hope that I did."

Hazett nodded and steepled his fingers. "So, I can't think of a better pet than you. A faithful pet. One who does as he is told yet possesses a high, high degree of initiative."

"I'm just a teenager. Someone else would have done what I had to do."

Ranno finally chimed in. "For some of it, yes. But your Volian trip would have ended up as a disaster a number of times had it not been for you. Searl would still be in a minweed stupor, right?"

Pol nodded.

The Emperor chuckled. "I have enjoyed having you frolic around in the Empire and beyond. Therefore, I can call you my pet. There is a reward you deserve for being my pet, you know."

Pol shook his head. "I don't need any rewards or any recognition."

"Need and deserve are not the same words, are they? I am giving you a little advanced notice. I will be adopting you into my family while you are at Yastan."

Pol jumped to his feet. "What? No! I'm not worthy. I don't..."

"You don't what? You refuse an honor that happened last when I was adopted into the Imperial family?"

"You?"

Hazett nodded. "I was much younger. So young I don't remember. My family had been loyal subjects. My real father was a duke, by the way. A dreadful carriage accident and I became an orphan. The Emperor took me in after testing me in quite a different way than you, and here I am."

"But you have children."

"I do, don't I?" Hazett looked evenly at Pol. "You will join them as the second oldest. However, since you are my pet, your Imperial duties will be quite different. You will work for the Instrument."

"But Deftnis needs me."

"Does it?" Hazett pursed his lips. "I heard that they didn't know what to do about a teenage Black."

"I'm a Gray."

"No, they gave you the ranking of a Gray, because they couldn't bring themselves to make you a Black. You've only proved your true rank through your exploits."

Pol felt panicked. "My life will change."

"Indeed it will, once your 'pethood' is announced." The Emperor chuckled for a moment. "Are you uncomfortable with my little moniker?"

Ranno glanced over at Pol with a smile on his face and that made Pol uneasy. "Has anyone else ever been called a pet?"

Hazett laughed. He really seemed amused by it all. "Of course not. It's an expression of affection and admiration. I like my little jokes." He glanced at Ranno. "Don't I?"

"Do you ever, My Emperor," Ranno said with a wry look on his face.

"Your new name will be Pol Cissert Pastelle, your Cissert last name is more appropriate as a first or middle name, isn't it? You can carry the noble title of Duke rather than Imperial Prince, although you will be able to employ that title, as well. That is easy enough since Queen Isa and I confirmed your ducal title while you were gone."

What didn't the Emperor know? It looked like Hazett wouldn't be very surprised when he found out the detailed story from Farthia's notes.

"Who has been told?"

Hazett frowned and counted on his fingers. "Queen Isa, Malden, Farthia, Ranno, myself, of course, and my wife. You will meet your adoptive mother at an intimate dinner tonight. Wear your traveling clothes." Hazett winked at Pol. "I must be off. I'll be seeing you later, son."

Ranno watched the Emperor leave and then he shook his head. "He is quite a jokester, but he is serious in this case. I'm sure you'd like to be alone for a bit to absorb your elevation."

Pol leaned back. "This is all a prank, isn't it?"

Ranno's face turned solemn. "It is not. The Emperor's son might not be suited to the throne."

"You mean I'm to be Emperor?"

Ranno laughed. "You're not that thick, are you? Of course, you're the son of a king. You've been tutored by one of the finest political minds in the Empire, my beloved daughter. You will become the finest magician the Empire has ever seen. You've proven yourself to be astute in dealing with foreign governments and have shown extraordinary courage."

"But I'm only sixteen."

Ranno couldn't hold back his grin. "Did the Emperor say you'll be crowned tonight?"

"No. I figure I'm a backup to his real son."

"Go ahead and think of it that way. I'm already behind in my work." He flicked his hand, shooing Pol out of his office. "Brush your clothes and make them presentable. Fadden will show you where you can get a little food and drink in you. Do you need help finding the route back to your room?"

Pol shook his head. "I remember the way."

"I know you can," Ranno said. "Remember, you work for me, now. You are dismissed."

"Naming you the Emperor's Pet means you are now in his family?" Shira said.

Pol shrugged. He put his finger to her lips. "Don't tell anyone. I still don't believe it. The Emperor has a reputation as a trickster. Perhaps this is an elaborate hoax."

"You'll know in a few hours, then. It looks like just the two of us are invited to dinner with the Emperor."

"If his family is there, then I don't know what to do. How can I be an heir to the Imperial Throne? It's not what I want."

Shira took his hand. "What do you want?"

Pol scowled. "I don't know, but it's not what I'm getting. I thought I wouldn't have to make a decision on anything until I returned to Deftnis after escorting you to Shinkya. You know, get acquainted with my ducal estate."

"What has changed?" Shira said, pressing her lips together in thought. "The monks don't know what to do with you. If you truly are the Emperor's Pet, or if that's changed so you are adopted into his family, why would it be worse? At least you are working for Ranno Wissingbel. No one can force you to be a Seeker. I think if you have a choice that you should work with the Shardian."

"Akonai?" Pol winced. "I forgot. We still have to tell him the bad news."

"I don't think we will be the first," Shira said and then sighed. "While you were with the Emperor being adopted, Malden had a meeting about our trip with his staff and I think I saw a Shardian in the halls."

"It gets worse and worse. Now I think coming to Yastan was a bad idea."

"Your Emperor commanded you to come to Yastan. It wasn't really your choice. You are a citizen of the Empire, not of Borstall or Deftnis. You are his to command."

Pol nodded and played with his hands before speaking. "I am. This is going to take more courage than fighting the Pontifer's Hounds."

She put her hands on his shoulders. "I support you."

Pol snorted. "Isn't that treasonous? A Shinkyan princess consorting with an Imperial Prince, no longer disinherited?"

"No longer disinherited. That's part of your problem, isn't it?"

"What?"

"You've been hiding behind being disinherited. It is your shield to keep others out."

"It didn't keep you out."

"Maybe the shield is to keep you in. Maybe it's a defense that you created to cushion the disappointment you felt for all of that pain and neglect growing up."

Pol shut his eyes tight. He didn't want to hear that, not from Shira. "I want to be alone."

"I'll leave you alone for now, but you won't get rid of me so easily. I'll be at that dinner sitting alongside you."

Pol thanked the servant for escorting him to the Emperor's private dining room in his triangular residence. He entered and saw Shira standing by a well-dressed woman standing by a bank of windows looking out at the lush vegetation in the building's interior courtyard.

The Empress looked to be his mother's age. Pol's hope that the Emperor had played a prank died with the woman's welcoming smile.

"Pol?"

She held out her hand. Pol had no choice but to cross the rug that separated them. He felt like he was approaching the gallows and the woman's hand held a noose that would soon be around his neck. Shira gave him a dirty look out of the Empress's sight. That took Pol out of his reverie. He took a deep breath and crossed the deep divide and within a few interminable steps stood in front of the woman and took her hand. He melted under the warm gaze and friendly eyes of the woman.

"I am Jarrann, Hazett's wife. I have heard so much about you for the past few years. Hazett was thoroughly taken by you when he stopped at Borstall during his Procession. Our children will be here soon. Hazett will join us when he has finished with a matter that has just come up."

"It is my humble pleasure to meet you, My Empress." Pol stepped back and bowed deeply to the woman and gave a lesser bow to Shira. "I see you've met Shira."

"Princess Shira?" Jarrann smiled.

Shira rolled her eyes, still out of the Empress's sight. "You may address me simply as Shira."

"I am impressed with your companion. I feel I have nearly heard as much about her as I have about you."

Shira bowed her head. "I am flattered, Empress Jarrann. We have been good for each other while Pol has been separated from his friends and from the Empire."

"Farthia visited me this morning and described your adventures. I had no idea Hazett sent you on such a hazardous vacation. He enjoys testing his subjects a little too much for my taste."

Pol smiled. "The world can be a dangerous place."

"You should know. Truth be told, Hazett does, too, but he has such a way about him so that it seems like he has everything under control."

Pol thought about what Jarrann said. He could see what she meant. The Emperor was a shield for his family, but not for his pet. Pol thought of Shira's description of the shield within Pol. He hadn't had enough time to re-assess his own pattern with the surprising insight Shira had shared with him.

The door opened again and four children walked in. The oldest, a youth, looked older than Pol but stood half a head shorter. He looked sickly. Pol realized that he might have looked like that if he hadn't found Searl. The youth might have been sixteen to twenty, but Pol couldn't tell.

"These are my children. This is Handor, our eldest, followed by Barya, Glenna, and Corran, the baby."

"I am not a baby," the young boy said. He might have been eight.

Barya looked to be fifteen or sixteen and Glenna was just into adolescence. Pol guessed she might have been twelve. All of them were handsome children, even if Handor was thin.

"Children, this is Pol Cissert."

"Daddy's Pet," Corran said. He took Pol's hand. "You're going to be our new brother."

The heat of a blush crept up Pol's neck. He lowered himself to Corran's level. "Someone told me that today." He smiled at the boy and got a beaming grin in return.

Shira tapped him on the shoulder and nodded. Pol knew what the tap meant and his heart dropped. His life, free and undefined, was about to make a drastic change.

"Why don't we sit down and get acquainted?" Jarrann said.

For the next hour, Pol found it easy to like the Emperor's family. He would have thought the children would be mean and rude, like three of his four Fairfield siblings, but these children were open and talked to one another. Handor might resent his physical condition, but he didn't show it as he laughed and joined in with the rest while Pol and Shira gave a very condensed, very positive version of their trials in Volia.

The Emperor finally slipped in quietly while Pol told his story about how he bonded with Demeron.

"I'd like to see him," Handor said.

"Me, too!" Corran piped up. He noticed his father standing by the door. "Father!" Corran stood, and then the others did, followed by

Pol and Shira. Jarrann remained seated.

"We waited for you to begin our dinner, dear," Jarrann said.

Hazett walked over to his wife and bent over to kiss her forehead. He looked about the room. "Have you all gotten along?"

The Imperial children all nodded, even Handor. "You can make the announcement, although, I'm afraid the word got out," Jarrann said. "Corran already declared Pol to be his new brother."

Hazett smiled ruefully. "There is no use keeping secrets around here." He stood behind his chair at the head of the table. "I am here to formally announce to all of you that the Emperor's Pet will be adopted into our family tomorrow. Is that acceptable?"

Hazett's children and his wife nodded and clapped.

"It's time for a little speech, Pol Cissert Pastelle," the Emperor said.

Pol rose. He felt a lump in his throat. It was unfair of the Emperor to present him to such friendly children. Pol shook his head and took a drink of watered wine.

"I didn't grow up with happy brothers and sisters. Well, one of my sisters was okay." He smiled. "I can see that is not the case with my new family. Thank you for being so friendly." He lost his breath a bit when he said 'new family'. "I hope you can accept me for who I am, faults and all. I do make mistakes and can be somewhat of a know-it-all—"

"Among other things," Shira muttered. All of them heard the remark and laughed.

"I look forward to knowing you all better." He gave them a tight smile and sat down.

The Emperor cleared his throat to grab the attention of those at the table. "Pol will not be living at the Imperial residence quite yet. Something came up today and he will be working with Ranno for a few weeks and then will escort Princess Shira to Tishiko. When he returns, then he will join us."

There were sounds of disappointment at the table.

"May I speak?" Pol said.

"Certainly. You may speak whenever you wish," Hazett said.

Pol pulled out the little green frog that Lord Wibon had given him. "I was given this by a South Salvan in Alsador. In appreciation of the honor that you have given me, may I give you this token of something that I believe might be precious to you someday." He set the Shinkyan carving in front of Hazett.

"Oh, is this a Shinkyan carving? I don't believe we have anything like this, do we Jarrann?"

The Empress shook her head. "No, it is so exotic. It is real isn't it, Shira?"

"They sell those in Tishiko. If you could look at the carving through magical eyes, you would see a highly skilled magician tweaked the grain of the wood to match the carving."

"How interesting," Hazett said.

Jarrann took the piece and squinted at it. "I see what you mean. How delightful."

Pol and Shira glanced at each other. Jarrann was a magician. What a revelation! If it were common knowledge, certainly Farthia would have said something.

Hazett took his wife's hand and cleared his throat. "It is a family secret that Jarrann has some well-developed talents."

Pol bit his lip. Shira had already found something intimate about the Imperial family that Shinkya might not know. He couldn't immediately see anything wrong with Jarrann having talent, but Pol still had much to learn about what was important and what was not. That was another reminder of his inadequacy to be a member of Hazett's family. At least he wouldn't have to face living with them for months.

"You two are free to share meals with us at any time," Hazett said. Obviously, the Emperor had no reservations about including Shira.

The children left after dinner along with their mother. Shira asked to depart, leaving Pol alone with his new adopted father.

"What is wrong with Handor?" Pol asked.

"His condition is somewhat the same as yours. I suppose that is what attracted me to you in Borstall. Luckily, he didn't have to put up with the antagonism that you did."

Pol had an idea. "Why don't I take him to Deftnis. Searl Hogton, the monk who healed me, should take a look at him."

"Really? The best physicians and healers in Yastan have told me time and again, there is nothing they can do."

Pol smiled. "But there is something Searl can do. It's a painful process, but I went through it and thrived. At least it gives Handor a chance to recover his health." Pol also knew a healthy oldest son would keep Pol farther from the Imperial throne.

"He's lived twenty years that way. I think he'll jump at the chance. Why don't you suggest that to him? If he's willing to go, I fully support him." Hazett took a sip of wine. "See? Already you are bringing benefits to your new family."

"I don't know what ails Handor, so I can't guarantee anything."

"At least he can get out and visit Demeron. He's known about your horse since I prepared the Imperial bill of sale. It would do him good to spend some time out of Yastan."

"Good. When I leave, then."

Hazett put his hand on Pol's wrist. "I have a mission for you. There has been a murder in the Imperial Library. Ranno and I would like you to solve it. There are…complications."

"What complications?"

Hazett yawned dramatically. "See Ranno tomorrow morning. I'm tired. It's time both of us went to bed."

Pol rose and both of them left the dining room. Hazett walked to the right and Pol was shown to the left by a servant.

After sitting at the table in his room, fiddling with his bundle of metal slivers, Pol rose when he heard a knock at the door. Fadden and Shira walked in.

"Some startling news," Fadden said. He had a grin on his face. "Remember when I said you were meant for bigger things?"

Pol didn't agree. "I'm going to do what I can to promote Handor. That will include taking him to Deftnis where Searl can perform his magic on him. He'd like to see Demeron, anyway."

"See? The Emperor isn't going to keep you cooped up in the Imperial residence," Shira said. "I don't see much difference between now and after he makes you part of his family."

"Bowing and scraping," Pol said. "I'll be getting a lot of unwanted attention. I got used to being unknown."

"Less unknown than you think." His smile vanished. "You left a path of people knowing you for who you really are from Port Molla to Ducharl in Volia."

"But now I'll require a retinue."

"Who says?" Shira said. "A few trusted souls should be sufficient. It's been that way since we first met. I'm trusted, aren't I?" She twisted her hair around a finger.

If she wanted Pol to smile, she succeeded.

"I can still disguise myself, I guess," Pol said.

Fadden nodded. "That's better. I heard there was a murder and Ranno wants you in on the investigation."

"A Seeker opportunity?" Pol said.

"One more suited to your taste and mine." Fadden smiled once more.

"We get to find out in the morning." Pol peered at Fadden. "Do you want a short-term job? I think the new Imperial Prince is going to require an aide. I'll talk to my new father. We can both be assigned to Ranno, I hope."

"I can't think of anything I'd like better."

"Why can't I be your aide," Shira said.

Pol took her hand. "For a season, you'll be another kind of aide. Will that be all right?"

She nodded and smiled at both of them.

~ ~ ~

Chapter Thirteen

~

AFTER A SLEEP-DEPRIVED NIGHT STRUGGLING with his new status, Pol was ready when Fadden called for him. They walked from the inn building to the Instrument's administration offices and into a conference room. This one was considerably different from Wilf Yarrow's in Alsador. Books and maps lined one of the walls. The table was polished, but like Wilf's, it showed the use of supporting quite a few conferences.

"It is good to see you again," Valiso Gasibli said.

Pol managed a smile and a nod. "Quite a bit has happened since we parted company in North Salvan."

"Malden filled me in. Your life has become a little too exciting, I guess. You toured my homeland."

"Fistyra or Botarra?" Pol said. Valiso's origins had never come up in all the time he worked with the Seeker.

Valiso chuckled and showed an uncharacteristic genuine smile. "Fistyra. I grew up looking across the border into Botarra."

Ranno rushed in with Malden.

"I won't spend much time on this," Ranno said. He threw a set of plans down on the table. "A distinguished scholar was killed at the Imperial library. The Emperor wants the murder solved as soon as possible. There are political considerations. The victim was visiting from Barna researching boundary documents between his country and Vento. It appears that both countries are spoiling for an outright war." Ranno looked at Pol and Shira. "For those new to the Emperor's policy, border disputes and skirmishes are fair game, but invasions are not."

"I already knew that," Pol said.

Ranno ground his teeth, showing a different side to the man. "There are subtleties of which you are still unaware. Regardless, you will be leading the investigation at the Emperor's request. Fadden will assist you. Gasibli has just come from their border and has the background."

"What if we need to travel to the two countries?" Pol said.

"Val is your resource, as I said. There will be no need."

Pol understood when he was being dressed down. "Yes, sir."

Ranno broke into a smile. "Ranno still works. Malden will be your direct contact and knows the particulars. Val knows more than you do about the murder." He looked at those in the room. "Pol leads the investigation. That's Hazett's order. You'll know why later in the day."

Pol noticed Fadden looking over at Val. He never knew the details behind Val and Fadden's conflict, but he couldn't let that disrupt the investigation.

"Any other questions?" Ranno said. "Then I will leave you to it. Malden?" Ranno nodded and rushed out of the room.

Everyone looked at Pol, who turned to Malden. "Please tell us what you know."

The magician chuckled. "Let's get one thing out of the way. We all know each other. I suggest that we all relax. I know of the history between you two," Malden looked at Fadden and Val. "This shouldn't be a situation where the Empire's laws are stretched. Pol has been put into this position as a test, and I'd like us all to work together in order to make that test successful."

Fadden put out his hand to Val. "I'm up for it. I think a certain someone might have made our situation worse," he said.

Val took it and looked intently at Fadden. "I believe you're right. Perhaps we can more properly have a history discussion sooner rather than later."

Pol took a deep breath. "Okay. Malden."

Nothing ever seemed to ruffle the magician, who always seemed to take things in stride. He unrolled the plans.

"This is the Imperial Library. The basement levels hold agreements and treaties between kingdoms and dukedoms. The second basement was where the scholar was killed. Right here."

"Is this a copy?" Pol asked.

"No. You'll have to make one from these. We have thin paper in that cabinet."

Pol looked at Shira. "How are your drawing skills?"

"Am I going to be the scribe again?" she said.

"You get a better view of the overall pattern that way, right?" Pol said. "Sorry, for interrupting."

Malden raised his eyebrows. "No, not at all. It's enjoyable to see how you work, both of you."

Pol didn't know if that was a compliment or not, so he didn't say anything more.

Malden continued. "He left his work in disarray in the second basement level. The papers were found after sundown when the library closed."

"What was missing?" Val said.

"Nothing that we can determine." Malden looked down at the map. "That level has been cleared out."

"What about the body?" Pol couldn't see anyone letting the body stay.

"That is the problem. There was no body left in the library."

Fadden shook his head. "Then how do you know it's a murder?"

"All of the library exits are monitored by a librarian and a guard, at a minimum. No one saw the scholar leave or anyone carrying his body."

"Could he have been disguised?" Shira said.

"The scholar was definitely dead. I've seen the body. It was dumped in a little alley in the Imperial Compound."

"So we do have a body. You think someone killed the scholar in the library and dragged him out without anyone noticing?" Pol said. He looked around and no one had any answers.

"What do we do?" Fadden asked Pol.

"Go to the library and view the scene while Shira copies the plans unless there is a person here that can do the job."

Malden smiled. "You only have to ask."

"Ah," Pol said. "This is something of a test. The murder is real?"

The magician nodded. "I assure you it is, and the facts are as I described."

"Why didn't we get this assignment last night?" Fadden asked.

"Two reasons. Val arrived late last night from Vento and did some preliminary work before retiring, and the Emperor wanted Pol to get a little more used to his new status."

"Status?" Val said.

"I am the Emperor's Pet," Pol said.

"What does that mean?" Val looked at Malden.

"Pol is no longer the Emperor's Pet. That's what Hazett has been calling Pol privately ever since he met him in Borstall. Pol is now Pol Cissert Pastelle, an adopted son of the Emperor."

"No longer disinherited, eh?" Val observed.

"From North Salvan, I am," Pol said.

Val smiled in his own mirthless way. "As expected, you've come up in the world. I thought you would if you continued to live."

"I'm still breathing, for now." Pol demonstrated.

"And you survived your trip through Volia, even with Namion as your guide."

"Fadden took over, and that probably preserved my life," Pol said.

Malden looked at Val. "I'll fill you in on his trip. Pol is probably sick of recounting the events. I'll get someone onto copying this map."

Val just nodded and gave Pol an appraising look.

Paki had been given other duties by Ranno. They had something to do with the Women's Academy for Seekers. Pol thought that might suit his friend more. Ako joined them on their walk to the Imperial Library.

The building itself went up four stories, which would have been impressive enough, but the length and breadth of the building made it seem much shorter than it was.

"How many levels to the basement?" Pol asked.

"Four," Malden said. "It's nearly full. The first Emperor Hazett had the library built one hundred years ago. I've read the histories recounting his critics' complaints about that it would never be filled."

Pol nodded. He hoped Handor would be the Emperor to build another. He looked back at Ako and Shira quietly talking to each other. Shinkya would be picking up a lot of information.

Pol looked up at the edifice. "Do you see?" He gazed with magical eyes and found faint, wispy wards clinging to the stone framework around the doors.

"What am I supposed to see?" Val said.

Ako and Shira stopped. Pol heard Shira take in her breath.

"What do these do?" Pol asked.

"I wish I knew what you are talking about." Val turned to look at the two Shinkyans right behind. "Do you two know anything?"

Malden halted and looked back to see the four of them. "Why did you stop?" He walked back.

"Look at the portal with your magic," Pol said.

"Oh." Malden ran up to the doorframe and examined the wards closely. "Is this your work, Ako? What do these wards do?"

The Shinkyan Sister bowed to Malden. "These have been in place for some time," she said.

The magician laughed and shook his head. "And I said we don't do wards, didn't I?" His eyes returned to Ako. "What do these wards do?"

"Maybe they improve one's ability to think," Shira said. "You walk through the door and your mind sharpens a little. Maybe you don't go to sleep quite so fast when you are reading boring books."

Ako shrugged. "It is very hard to determine exactly what a ward does if you aren't the maker. What better way to prove that Pol can detect wards than to put such a ward on a library."

Malden shook his head. "We will talk of this later. I assume one of you ladies can remove this?"

Pol held up his hand. "Perhaps the ward might help us think in the basement, then I can remove them."

"Of course. You are much more experienced with these things

than I," Malden said, with a smile on his face.

"I don't know how to create a ward, but I am practiced at manipulating them. Just treat them like elements of a pattern, for that is what they are. To remove a ward, you tweak it away," Pol said as he walked through the door.

He put his hand to his head and staggered a few steps past the door. He fell on his knees as he sensed a stirring of the alien essence in his mind. Pol didn't hear a voice but received impressions of how wards were constructed. The knowledge flooded into his mind all at once.

Shira ran to his side and helped him up. "What happened? The wards are harmless."

"To you, maybe."

Ako looked shocked, and Shira's eyes watered. "I didn't mean."

All of them walked through the door.

"We can speak of what happened later." Pol waved his hand and tweaked the wards with his new knowledge. They disappeared.

"How did you do that?" Ako said, amazement in her voice. "Those were expertly woven."

Pol shook his head and rose to his feet with Shira's help. "I tried something new." That was correct, but none of the others knew the whole truth.

Malden put his hand to the doorframe. "Whatever you did, succeeded. The wards are gone."

The new knowledge scared Pol, but he couldn't show it. That particular ward interacted with the Demron essence. Pol had been thinking about wards when he walked through the door. Perhaps that had something to do with his sudden infusion of knowledge. The connection added a little more to the elusive pattern Pol was constructing.

"The rest of you continue. I'll just sit for a bit and follow in a few moments," Pol said, finding a bench in the library lobby.

Malden spoke to the attending librarian and pointed out Pol. Shira walked back and sat with Pol.

"What really happened?" Shira said.

Pol watched the others walk through an archway to the library beyond. He took a deep breath. "It was the connection to the alien, again."

"Again?"

"The last time was Manda's truth spell. I haven't been very good at them, but with Manda trying to control us all, somehow it came out strong. I've never cast one so perfect before."

Shira threaded her arm through his. "I noticed, but I just thought you were being very good like you usually are."

Pol pursed his lips. "You know I have strengths and weaknesses like every other magician."

"With a lot more strengths than weaknesses," Shira said.

"I was thinking about wards when I walked beneath the doorway and somehow the wards stirred up the alien essence that still lurks inside of me. All of a sudden I knew more about wards. If I knew what I do now, we could have easily escaped from the Magicians Circle fortress." Pol put his hands to his head. "What have I become?"

"The Emperor's Pet," Shira said, squeezing his arm gently. "My pet."

"I've already told Malden about my encounter with the alien intelligence."

Shira frowned. "Did you hear voices, this time?"

"No," Pol said, shaking his head, "No voices just an infusion of knowledge. The only time I've heard a voice was in the Demron cave. The essence doesn't seem to have a personality. It's more like a pool of knowledge that erupts from time to time. I just had more strength with Manda. I don't get tired like I used to either."

"Fadden and I noticed that after we left Teriland. With your friend inside, Pol Cissert has become rated more than Black," Shira said.

Pol took a deep breath and stood up. "Pol Cissert Pastelle," he muttered angrily to himself. "Let's catch up to the others."

The pair reached Malden as he stood at the top of a wide stairway leading down. "Are you all right?"

"My Demron friend decided to play a trick on me," Pol said, quietly.

"He speaks and has a personality?" Malden said, quite alarmed.

Pol shook his head. "No. As I told you it's more of an essence. I think the library's wards triggered it to enhance my thinking. I suddenly comprehend wards better, something lacking in my magical education.

I don't lack so much now, but I'm still no expert."

"You instantly learned to make the wards vanish?"

"He removed them before, but not so casually," Shira said. "It's amazing, isn't it?"

"More than amazing." Malden pointed down the stairs. "I will follow you."

Pol started down the stairs and paused to look back. Malden had a worried look on his face. He took Shira's hand and hurried to catch up with the others assembling at the bottom of the second level of the basement.

A guard barred the way until Malden appeared behind Pol and Shira.

"Minister," the guard said, allowing Malden to pass.

"They are all with me."

The guard nodded and let them through into the second level.

"Minister?" Pol asked.

"I needed a title since I work underneath Ranno, and Vice-Instrument or Assistant Minister or Second Instrument never did sound right, so I am Minister of the Instrument's Office." Malden shrugged. "That's better, but still not quite right. I'm sure you all agree."

"I do," Pol said, smiling. Malden seemed a little embarrassed, but like the even-tempered person Pol knew, the magician took it in stride.

Malden walked to a table with books and document folders littering the surface. "This is where the scholar last sat."

"How do we know that?" Val said as he looked over the space.

"These are documents relating to the agreements and history of Barna and Vento. They were as you see them now, open with the scholar's notes scattered on the table," Malden said.

Pol knew what Val was getting at. "How do we know this isn't a misdirection on the part of the murderer?"

"What?" Malden said.

Ako stepped up. "Do we know for sure that the scholar was even in the library?"

Malden furrowed his brow and put his hands on the back of a chair. He laughed. "Of course, you are all Seekers, aren't you? Well, I'm not trained. No wonder Ranno let you come along," Malden said to

Ako. "I felt like I was under attack for a moment. All of you are trying to expand the pattern past the obvious, of course."

"Of course," Shira said.

Pol looked at her. She gave him a sheepish look, despite her positive comment. "So we have a few options to pursue. The scholar never came into the library, but someone else signed in. The scholar came into the library and found a way to leave without being detected. The scholar was killed," Pol looked at the wooden floor. "Bloodlessly, here at the table, and then someone bundled the body up and cleaned everything."

Fadden walked the length of the room, looking down. "No blood and the place hasn't been cleaned recently."

"It was a bloodless death," Val said. "I looked at the body."

Pol examined the papers. "Are any papers missing?" he asked.

"Two treaties and the latest detailed mapping of the boundary." Val leaned against a bookcase and folded his arms. It was obvious to Pol that he was observing more than participating.

"Are there any copies of the documents?" Pol said after a moment where everyone else in the room was silent.

Val looked at Malden.

"Of course there are," Malden said.

Shira moved next to Pol. "So we can solve this by looking at the copies."

"Not solve," Pol said. He sighed. The Emperor had structured this as another test. "Fill out the pattern a bit more. We will at least be able to solidify a few facts, and they might not lead us to any useful information." He looked at Malden. "Are the copies here?"

The magician shook his head. "Will we get access to them?"

"Only one of you."

Pol looked at Val. "You know the situation between Vento and Barna best. Can you look them over?"

Val smirked. "Am I looking for anything specific?"

"Motives. What are triggers that might make one party's position stronger. Make notes," Pol looked at Malden. "Val can jot down notes, can't he?"

Malden nodded.

"Make note of what provisions of the documents benefit which kingdom. It might not be a kingdom we're looking for but a lesser domain or a faction within either of the kingdoms. Sketch out the boundary map as best you can, so we can compare it to the previous boundary drawing that is in the library."

"I did this last night," Val said. "That's why we could delay to this morning."

"What else was worked on last night?" Pol said. He looked at Fadden, Val, and Malden, feeling exasperated that the urgent problems was really a test just for him.

Ako raised her hand feebly. "I put up the wards. They aren't ancient at all."

"Who told you to?" Pol said.

"The Instrument," she said.

Pol covered his face with a hand. "Is this a real crime?"

Malden smiled. "It is, I assure you."

"Then the body truly exists?" Pol said.

"It does." Malden folded his arms. He smiled, but for a change, there wasn't any mirth in his eyes.

Pol looked over the documents on the table through magical eyes and spotted a faint ward on a portfolio. He used a book to slide the portfolio to sit by itself. He examined the ward and looked at it using his new knowledge of wards.

"This document is warded." He didn't understand styles yet, but this didn't look like the wards in Volia, nor the wards used by the Tesnan Abbot. The ward seemed to shimmer and looked more metallic to his eye. The others were colorful and looked more solid. "You didn't make this, Ako?"

She shook her head.

His knowledge didn't tell him what the ward did, but Pol thought it was important to know. "What do you suppose this ward is for?"

All of the Seekers plus Malden peered at the document.

"There is a ward there?" Ako said. "Maybe I see a trace of something."

Shira shook her head. "You see something?"

Pol nodded and looked at the men who signified that they

couldn't. Pol didn't know if they were honest with him or not. He fleetingly thought of applying a truth spell but rejected the idea since everyone in the room was some kind of friend.

"Would one of you touch this document?"

"An experiment?" Malden said with one corner of his mouth turned up.

"Perhaps. I want to see if anything happens when you touch this. I'm sure you've gone over these documents before."

Val nodded. He leaned over and picked up the portfolio.

Pol couldn't see a difference, but then he didn't look quite hard enough.

"Someone else?"

Pol closed his eyes and used his locator sense. The portfolio was visible as an orange smudge among the others in the room. Val's dot had tinges of orange on it. Pol looked around the room and noticed other smudges here and there among the stacks.

"The Abbot was able to link with his wards. Perhaps the person who warded this document can do the same," Pol said when he opened his eyes. "There are other warded documents in this chamber."

"Give me your hand," he said to Val.

Pol could see the barest glimmer on Val's hand.

"What do you see?" Malden said.

"A trace of the ward rubs off onto whoever touches this." Pol waved his hand over Val's. "It's gone now," he said.

"So whoever created this ward will know who touched the document?" Val picked up the portfolio and untied the thong that tied it closed. "Interesting. I like the concept."

Pol nodded. "But who placed the ward?"

"Maybe we can detect the pattern by seeing what's inside," Val said. He looked at Fadden. "Help me read this carefully."

Val spread the document out. It was the two feet long and Hazett I's seal and signature were at the bottom. "An eighty-year-old treaty. It talks about water rights in Vento, but I can't see anything that links this document to Barna."

"So the portfolio wouldn't be applicable to the current dispute?" Pol asked.

Val shook his head. "Not at all."

The ward didn't extend to the surface of the paper, only to the portfolio cover. "Is there a way to determine how old this ward is?"

Ako bent over and looked at the cover. "As I said, I can barely see the ward. It is old. Unmistakably old."

"So someone warded this before any of us were born. This warding technique isn't currently used in the Empire?" Pol asked.

Malden shook his head. "I would know. Detecting the ward on the portfolio is definitely not part of the test."

"To my knowledge, this technique is not used in Shinkya," Ako said. Pol didn't know if he could believe her or not.

"It probably looked different when first applied," Fadden said, "But then I can't see wards at all."

"Then why say it looked different?" Val said.

Fadden frowned but kept his mouth shut.

"I can say that, Val," Malden said and looked closer with his nose nearly touching the cover. He nodded. "It's barely there. A wisp. You can see this and Ako might. Mind if I test you?"

Pol closed his eyes and shrugged his shoulders. He had no idea what they were doing here, so he would just go along.

"Shira and I will use one finger to touch the portfolio while you turn your back. You tell us which finger did the touching."

"I can do that," Pol said and then turned around.

"It's testing time," Malden said.

Pol turned around and looked at Shira and Malden's hands. He closed his eyes and noticed an orange smudge on Shira's dot, but when he opened his eyes all four hands were clear. Pol shook his head smiling. "Turn your hands over."

Shira's knuckle on her middle finger shimmered. Pol pointed to her smudge. "Can any of you see it?"

Val, Malden, and Ako examined Shira's hand but none could see the transferred ward.

"Rub your knuckle on your sleeve," Pol said to Shira.

He could see faint evidence of the ward on the cloth and her finger looked just as clear to him as before. "It can't be rubbed off all at once, but evidence of the ward is on your sleeve, Shira." Pol waved his hand over it and the ward seemed to evaporate.

Malden grinned. "Now I get to look through journals to see if this technique is mentioned anywhere."

"The date on the treaty can limit your search," Pol said.

"Of course, Seeker," Malden said, giving Pol a good-natured bow.

That made Pol blush. He had to restrain his comments so he wouldn't keep bringing up the obvious. Everyone in the room was competent. He would have had a pinch from the old Shira, but this time she just patted his arm.

"So, let's go look at the body to see if the scholar ever touched this document. Even if we don't know why Hazett I had an Imperial magician place the ward, we still can use it to fill out the pattern."

"I agree," Val said. His smile seemed a bit more genuine than usual. "Follow me."

They left the library and went to the Imperial Infirmary. Pol had never seen so many healers in one place before. The Seeker led them down into the basement. The temperature dropped.

"A spell," Pol said, "like the Shardian magicians use."

"That is likely where we got it," Malden said. "It helps us preserve corpses."

Pol shuddered. Human bodies kept fresh just like the meat destined to feed the Magicians Circle.

"It still doesn't smell lovely," Val said.

"I don't suppose it does," Shira said.

They came upon a healer who held the door open for them to the morgue.

Val walked to a table. A sheet covered a body. "He is naked," Val said to Ako and Shira.

Shira colored and turned away. "Perhaps Ako and I can wait outside."

From the look on Ako's face, both women didn't relish looking at the scholar's body.

Val threw back the sheet before the women had even left the room. Pol heard a gasp from Ako, but before he turned to the door, both of them had disappeared. The scholar's neck was bluer than the rest of the corpse indicating he died by strangulation.

Pol examined the scholar's hands, using the shroud to keep from touching the corpse. "Nothing. This man never touched the portfolio. It was on the table when the basement was searched?"

Val nodded. "No tricks this time. None of us would have detected the ward."

Pol threw the shroud over the body and shivered in the cold room. "I'd like the sun on my face," he said.

~ ~ ~

Chapter Fourteen

~

BACK IN RANNO'S CONFERENCE ROOM, Shira found an oversized paper in a flat file and laid it on the conference table. "Shall we start?"

"We still don't have a motive," Fadden said. "If the scholar never entered the library yesterday, then anyone could have killed him."

"Not really," Pol said. If he were being tested, then he'd let them suffer through his obvious deductions. "The killer knew the scholar and what he was researching at the library. That indicates a definite motive, though. Perhaps Val should let us know the details of the conflict so we can see who would gain the most from the scholar's death. Whoever it is went to great lengths to cover his or her involvement in the scholar's death."

Val launched into a recitation of the situation between the two countries. Shira wrote small on the lower right-hand corner of the paper. When he finished no one said anything.

"Let's go over what we know from last night. Where was the scholar's body found?" Then Pol had an idea. "Where are the scholar's clothes?"

"Why?" Shira asked.

"If the clothes are tainted with the ward, then we will know if the murder happened before or after the murderer spread the documents on the table," Val said. He smiled and nodded. "I'll retrieve them. They are being stored in the infirmary."

"And with the ward liable to be spread anywhere, we should also look at the scholar's lodgings."

They found no taint after examining the scholar's clothes and going through his lodgings. The evidence pointed toward someone killing the man before the documents had been spread out, so that ruled out the scholar's lodgings.

Shira documented their findings on the paper. "We now have information to begin to look other places," she said. "Who last saw the scholar, so where did he eat and what did he do when he wasn't researching?"

Pol agreed. His stomach was grumbling since they missed their midday meal.

"I'm hungry. Is anyone else?" Pol said. "Why don't we all do some thinking and eating and then come back here?"

"There is a refectory in the building on the other side of the offices. We can take the paper with us and commandeer a private room," Malden grinned. "I've found myself rather adept at commandeering."

Pol helped Shira roll the paper up, and then all of them walked through the offices of the Instrument and entered a good-sized refectory. It rivaled Deftnis Monastery in size. Malden found an empty room, but they had to push tables together to get an adequate surface.

"I'll take care of getting some food delivered," Fadden said.

Pol looked down at the paper. "We need a spot for the scholar and one for the scholar's murderer to start. Then we need a section for Vento and Barna, so we can list the high points of the political situation. What are we missing?"

"Why not list the possible motives?" Fadden said. "We did that in Alsador."

Shira kept the lists wide apart.

Val looked down at the paper. "This works, does it? I've never seen such a thing before."

"Regent Tamio taught Wilf how to do it. It certainly keeps

everyone viewing the same pattern."

Val folded his arms. "If you're too rigid you can miss when the actual pattern veers from what you desire."

"There is that," Pol said. "But I thought it helped us more than hindered our investigation there."

"You'll have to tell me more about it," Val said.

"You'll get how it works as we go," Shira said. She finally finished. She stood up and stretched. The food finally arrived, so they folded the paper in two and ate.

Pol noticed some herb in the meat sauce that seemed unfamiliar, but other than that, the food seemed like everything else he had eaten in the Empire. He wondered if Imperial cuisine had gone stale over the centuries.

He sat back and unfolded the paper.

Paki opened the door. "Ah, here you are. I've been running around Yastan for the past day learning a lot I never wanted to know. By the way, I brought along some guests."

Kell and Loa walked in followed by Farthia and a tall, fit-looking, young woman.

"Kell!" Pol said, getting out of his seat.

Shira hugged Loa. Malden merely motioned Farthia over for a kiss. The young woman stood awkwardly amongst the greeting. She looked familiar to Pol.

Where had he seen her before? It finally dawned on him. "You are Oak's daughter," Pol said. "You've changed. Deena, right?"

Deena's face became radiant when she smiled. She had gone from pretty to stunning. Pol glanced at Shira who didn't look very friendly, staring at the girl.

"Mistress Farthia took me in as a result of your letter. I sneaked out of a class to say thank you for your letter. It is changing my life."

"What letter?" Shira asked. "Oh, her." She must have remembered the one time Pol mentioned her in Volia.

Pol took a deep breath and introduced Deena to everyone, Shira last of all. "We were in a bit of difficulty in Lawster two years ago. Deena's father, Oak Moss, was the innkeeper where we stayed. He gave us critical advice so I could reclaim Demeron, In exchange, I wrote a letter asking Ranno to provide Deena with a magical education in Yastan."

"She's in the Seeker college," Malden said. "I hear she is progressing quickly in all phases of her training."

Deena blushed, which made her even more pretty. Pol walked over to Shira and stood next to her. He didn't know what else he could do. Shira hadn't liked his comment about helping Deena while they traveled in Volia.

Paki grinned. "I'll escort Deena back to her studies and return."

Farthia nodded and the two of them left. Pol felt the tension lower in the room, but he wasn't sure if the unease that he felt was just in his head. "Paki will be disappointed Deena is on a tight training schedule."

Pol noticed Shira exhale. He hadn't noticed her holding her breath.

"There was nothing between you?" she said almost silently through her teeth.

"Nothing." Pol said, he was happy to say truthfully. He unfolded the paper to bring Kell, Loa, and Farthia up to date.

"Do you have anything to add to the political situation in Barna and Vento?" Malden asked Farthia.

She leaned over to read Shira's work. "There are three major political factions in Barna. Do we know the scholar's loyalty?"

Val's eyebrows rose. "Good point. He was a Resurrectionist. I ran over and talked to the librarian just after we found the body. The man was researching lineages to find relatives from the old dynasty."

"Why would he do that?" Kell said. "Farthia said this was a border dispute."

"We'll have to find out, won't we?" the Seeker said.

Kell colored and stood up. "It was good meeting you all. I have to help Loa prepare to enter the Women's Magician College tomorrow. We just arrived earlier today and I'm sure she's tired."

Loa put a hand to her forehead. "I am, actually. We will get together again before you leave for Shinkya?" she said to Shira.

"I look forward to it."

Kell and Loa left them.

"A well performed strategic retreat, don't you think, dear?" Farthia said.

"I agree. So that's Kell. It looks like they are a pair," Malden said. "We'll make sure they aren't neglected in Yastan."

"Thank you," Pol said. "So what about these three political parties in Barna? Are they strident enough to kill?"

"Only the Resurrectionists and that was the scholar's party."

Pol thought their task was only getting more complex. "I think we should split up the line of inquiries like we did in Alsador."

"What direction should each of us take?" Val said, letting Pol lead.

Pol had to think. He looked down at the sketchiness of the information. "Well, we should split up to accommodate our strengths. That means Val and Farthia trace the Barna factions. The Imperial Compound monitors who comes in and out?"

Malden nodded his head.

"Ako and Fadden can trace the movements of the scholar for the past few days. Malden, Shira and I will cover the research angle again. I want to look at the warded books. The ward must eventually wear off, so I will want to test the librarians. We'll also look into who came in and out of the library. We can meet again in the conference room as evening falls."

"Any further questions?"

A messenger entered the room and presented a note to Malden.

"The Emperor has postponed a certain announcement until our investigation progresses to where we can take an afternoon off," Malden said.

Pol had completely forgotten about his adoption announcement. He would rather it be postponed indefinitely, but at least he had a moment's respite.

"Let's go, Farthia," Val said. "We can start poring through log books. Maybe Shira can join us." Val raised his eyebrows at Pol, a sign that he wanted permission.

"That's a good idea. Is that acceptable?" Pol said to Shira.

"It is. I can get to know your tutor better."

"Tutors," Val said, cracking his humorless smile.

After examining the hands of all the librarians, Pol and Malden found seven of them with the taint of the wards, but some had faded

GUY ANTIBES | Page 137

to the point that the smudges eluded Malden's detection. Pol removed the taint.

Both of them spent an hour walking through the library locating warded papers. A librarian followed them and painted a yellow dot on each infected volume. Most of them resided in the basement and all were warded during Hazett I's reign and addressed treaties and agreements with differing countries in the Empire.

Malden sat at the table where the scholar's books were. "The murderer, if he knows about the ward, could easily come up with an excuse."

"But even the librarians didn't know about the wards, did they?" Pol said.

"No one knew. I've walked through these stacks many times and I never thought to look for wards."

"I don't know how effective the ward would be for storing books, but maybe they were applied during the negotiation process to see who had read the documents."

"We may never know," Malden said. He made a face. "It's time to check all the logs."

Pol smiled. "Ah, the more exciting part of Seeking."

Evening came and the group assembled in Ranno's conference room less Farthia. Shira had already spread out the paper and had already made some notations.

"There aren't that many Barnan's in the compound," Val said. "We found five who declared citizenship and three who Farthia and I identified by their names. None were Resurrectionists and all but two had alibis."

"Two more than we knew about this morning," Pol said. "Fadden?"

"The scholar was a bit of an introvert which made it easier to pattern his movements. He left early for the library and showed up for his midday meal at the inn he stayed, just outside the Imperial Compound."

Pol thought. "Did the scholar's name show up in the records you looked at?" He looked at Farthia.

"He entered every day an hour after sunrise and left before sunset except for his last day alive. All the entries matched, entrances and exits."

"Where was the body found, again?"

Val looked at him. "I never told you exactly where we found it. He was discovered in a little alley adjacent to the courtyard of the Instrument's headquarters."

"So someone killed the scholar by strangulation. That's why there wasn't any blood. Then they carried a body in daylight to the Seeker's building and dumped him?"

"We haven't gotten to that part of your little chart," Val said.

The Seeker was playing with them. "We didn't find anything odd with the logbooks in the library, so there is still a record of the missing scholar. If it was one person they would have had to enter as the scholar, sneak out without being noticed, and then re-enter as himself after taking the documents the scholar was working on," Fadden said.

"So our murderer or part of the murderer's cabal is either a great thief or a magician who knows concealing spells," Pol said. "That is what Seekers are trained in. Do you catalog the abilities of present and former Seekers?"

Malden glanced at Val and Fadden. "We do."

"That gives us a place to look if we expand the pattern to accept a hired killer. Someone who can conceal spells or work with disguises."

Val lifted up the corner of his mouth in a near-sneer. "Why do you think of Seekers?"

"The best Seekers are magicians who know how to take care of themselves."

"You mean kill?" Val said.

Pol nodded. He didn't understand why Val was pressing him. "Like yourself?"

Val's question took Pol's breath away. It was something he had discussed with Shira and Fadden but no one else. "I don't like to kill."

"But you have."

"We wouldn't have made it across Volia without defeating our enemies," Pol said. He took a deep breath. "I once wanted to be a Seeker, but after watching Namion, that desire died."

"Namion Threshell." Val spat out the name as a curse. He

narrowed his eyes. "Namion is adept at camouflage spells, similar to Shira. He could have done it."

"Don't a lot of Seekers know how to use such a spell?" Shira asked.

Malden shook his head. "Val can't."

Pol looked at Val.

"You must have discovered by now that when you get to advanced spells, every magician has different abilities," Val said. "I am best at disguises but am a mediocre pattern-master. Namion can't wield a sword much better than any other man."

"Or woman," Ako said.

Val smiled and nodded his acknowledgment. "But he is very good at concealment. One of the best." He looked at Pol. "No one that I know of can make themselves invisible for as long as you can and there are only a few Seekers who can stay invisible for more than a moment."

"A person would only need a moment to get through the door," Malden said. "We shouldn't restrict ourselves to Seekers, but that gives us an additional focus."

"Can Fadden and Val look through your files to find a present or former Seeker that fits the right profile?" Pol asked Malden. "Is Namion currently a Seeker?"

Malden paused for a moment and looked at Val. The look told Pol Malden's answer.

"He has been suspended, and I don't doubt that the suspension will turn into termination. Your story and his were materially different in parts," Malden said. He looked at Fadden and Val. "Can you two work together?"

Fadden rubbed his chin. "I don't have an answer to that."

"Yes we can," Val said.

The Seeker's confidence in his answer surprised Pol. Fadden definitely didn't like Val or Namion.

"A little talk in the hallway," Val said. He led Fadden out.

In a few minutes, both of them returned. Fadden looked a bit shaken.

"I can work with Gasibli," he said. Fadden looked at Pol. "Sometimes the reality isn't what you see." He shook his head to ward off any follow-up.

"Then find us a list of Seekers to talk to. Go back to the gate records and find those identified as magicians. If the murderer is a magician, we should be able to narrow down the possible murderers." Malden went to the map drawer and pulled out a regular-sized paper. It had printing on it, so it must have been official stationary. He scribbled something and gave the document to Fadden. "Here is your authorization. I'll want the results at breakfast. I'll arrange for us to eat in the conference room, this time." Malden looked at Pol. "No work for you tomorrow afternoon. The Emperor is anxious to get the announcement over."

Fadden nodded. "We'll be done before then," he said, and the pair of Seekers left.

"I think we've had enough togetherness for today," Malden said. "That doesn't prevent you from thinking more on your own. Good night."

Pol looked at the two Shinkyans. He rubbed his hair. "I'm tired."

"I'm leaving you," Ako said. "Have a few words together before you part."

Pol watched Ako leave. "That was nice of her."

"It was a royal command, actually." Shira smiled slyly. "I spoke to her as a princess."

"Let's get something to eat and then find a nice place to talk."

Shira narrowed her eyes. "About your project?"

"Among other things."

They walked to the refectory and took a table in one of the many alcoves in the dining hall. Pol guessed that lots of secrets were passed over meals, so whoever designed the place provided a lot of private spaces.

A server took their order and left them alone.

"We went through a lot of information today," Shira said. "You must be exhausted."

"I'm sure both of us are," Pol said. "I never would have thought that the Emperor would keep wards to himself."

"He doesn't," Shira said. "It just seems that way. Remember the Abbot at Tesna? He was an expert."

Pol nodded. "Maybe they just don't teach them or use them at

Deftnis. Malden knew all about them, so I wonder if he picked that knowledge up here in Yastan."

"Does it matter?"

Pol thought for a bit and shook his head. "I guess not. Now I know more than I ever wanted to."

"What is it like to get flooded with information?"

"I suppose it's like chugging down a pitcher of ale. Not that I've done it, but I imagine you are bogged down at first, and over time the feeling goes away. The information is still swimming around in my mind, but I haven't had time to use it."

"Then why don't we do that after dinner. We can go out in the courtyard and I can watch you practice. I do know how to weave wards a bit."

Pol laughed. "How many wards have you made?"

"Maybe ten," Shira said sheepishly, "and they were all in classes. But I was the best in my class."

"I'm sure you were."

Neither of them talked about their journey south, but if Shira felt like Pol, she wouldn't want to bring up the painful subject. They ended up speculating what Val and Fadden talked about until dinner came. A door opened directly out onto the courtyard and they found a sheltered spot.

"Did the essence provide any insights into wards?" Shira said as they sat own on a bench.

"Tweaks are manipulations of patterns. Wards are not. Wards are created to respond to a disruption in their own pattern. Compulsion spells are more like wards. Mind control films are more like tweaks. The wards at the library were inactive until someone passed through them. A human has disturbed the ward, so the ward responds with a stored tweak. Does that make sense?"

"That is how I learned it in Tishiko," Shira said.

"I couldn't create a ward because I looked at wards as tweaks. I can make them go away and tweak the ward, but now that I understand a bit more of what they can do, I can make a ward. Like a tweak, it's an expression of the magician's will."

"You could teach this."

Pol laughed. "I've never tried. I wouldn't want to teach without experience."

"So start. Create a ward that glows if someone steps on it."

Pol concentrated on a steppingstone in front of them and thought of a stationary tweak. When he willed it into existence, a flat blue ward appeared on the stone.

"Step on it," Pol said.

Shira put out her foot and tapped the ward. It flared with a red light and broke apart.

"Why did it do that?" Pol asked. He pulled the knowledge from his head. "Oh, that's why wards have to be woven. My ward had a single purpose."

"Not so simple as you thought?"

Pol shook his head. "That must be why the wards at the Magicians Circle fortress had knobs and spikes. Those were their equivalent of weaves."

Shira nodded. "I don't think I could make anything that looked like that, but that might be an explanation for all of the projections."

"So I had no idea that weaves were more sophisticated than a ward without a weave. Pol looked at the stone, now without the ward. He sighed. "Enough of that. Tomorrow, I'll be adopted."

Shira smiled. "Am I supposed to be impressed?"

Pol shook his head. "No, not at all. I'll be the same person before and after. I'm sad I can't tell people I'm no longer a disinherited prince, though."

She took his hand. "That's become part of your identity."

"It has," Pol said, "but I think I can get over it. I don't like the notoriety, but we'll get this murder solved and be on our way to Deftnis."

"Deftnis. I'm looking forward to see where all my friends were trained."

"Do you include Namion Threshell?"

She looked away. "I don't like that man. He's never been a friend to anyone as far as I can tell."

She threaded her arm through his and laid her head on his shoulder. "Let's just sit and not say anything." She sighed and closed her eyes.

Pol looked down at the top of her head, disappointed that his elevation might end up destroying their relationship as much as her return. Life continued to be unfair to him.

~ ~ ~

Chapter Fifteen

~

EVERYONE HAD ALREADY ENTERED THE CONFERENCE
ROOM by the time Pol walked in. He had not slept well anticipating the big change in his life and worrying about its implications.

"We have news," Fadden said as he entered.

"You found the murderer?"

"We have a strong suspect. Namion Threshell."

Pol stopped before he had sat down. "Couldn't be."

"He's certainly fast at getting the wrong kind of work," Malden said, "if he's the one."

Val stepped up to the large sheet of paper. "Namion entered the Imperial Compound not long after the scholar did using his own name. He used one of his aliases to get access into the Imperial Library and exited signing under the same name twenty minutes later. Rather than leaving immediately, it took him another twenty minutes before he left the Imperial Compound. He didn't sign into the Seeker's quarters, and as far as we can tell, didn't meet with anyone else. Our investigation is not finished, but he has got to be the prime suspect."

Pol knew Val well enough that he wouldn't present Namion as the killer unless he was pretty certain. "Do we arrest him?"

"The warrant is already out. With his suspension, he lost his wages, so his motive could be purely monetary."

"So we still need to apprehend the people who hired him," Pol said.

"Now you are all caught up," Malden said.

"And that gets us back to motive," Pol said. "Namion is the equivalent of a sell-sword, and someone hired him."

Shira looked at her work. "Do we know what the scholar's position was on the dispute?"

Val spoke up. "If he found evidence that didn't support his party's point of view, then that might be enough."

"Catching Namion is the quickest way to find out," Pol said. "Do we know where he is staying?"

Malden nodded. "You aren't the only one who doesn't trust him." Malden pulled a folded document from his coat. "He is, or was, staying at The Morning Arms."

"If he is anywhere around the inn, I'll be able to locate him if he hasn't been able to remove the tainted ward," Pol said.

"Then let's go," Malden said.

"Val, Shira and I will go, disguised of course," Pol said.

Pol disguised himself using the facial pattern of Paki's father. He didn't know who Val or Shira had used. They walked past The Morning Arms and sat down on a bench in front of an adjacent feed store.

After crossing his arms, he leaned back and feigned sleep while Val spoke quietly with Shira getting some first-hand answers to his questions about their trip to Volia. He scanned from the inn and outward. As he spread out the location range he spotted a location dot with the bright tinge of the ward, too strong for a contaminated hand, but an actual document. He opened his eyes and looked at a restaurant across the street.

"There are two people over there," Pol said.

"The restaurant?"

Pol nodded. "Can you go in a back way? Shira can stay in front and freeze him if he bolts past me," Pol said.

He looked at Shira. "Can you do that?"

"Is it all right for you to handle him on your own?" she said.

"I'm not on my own. If I get into trouble, both of you converge."

"Let's get this over with," Val said.

Pol and Shira waited to give Val some time to get in position.

"Ready?" Pol asked.

Shira nodded. "Don't do anything stupid."

"I'll try not to," Pol said, getting up.

They both walked across the street to the restaurant. Pol checked to see if the dots with the taint remained. They did. He sauntered in the establishment and spotted one person with the taint.

He looked at Val who stood by the kitchen door. Pol walked up to the person, but it wasn't Namion. This person wore no disguise, yet his hands were bright with the taint and the man had a warded document in his coat.

Pol sat down. "Where is Namion Threshell?"

"I don't know what you mean?" the man said. He looked too afraid to be innocent.

"He gave you a document from the Imperial Library."

Pol took a deep breath and called Val over.

"Is this a Barnan you recognize?"

Val shook his head.

"Come with us. We are on Imperial business," Val said.

A burly man stood up and threw off a padded cloak. "And I'm not," the man said.

Pol detected an orange smudge on the man's hands and recognized the voice. "Namion!"

Now that Pol was closer, he could see the ward's shimmer on Namion's hands. Namion pushed a surprised Val aside and flew out the front door. Shira lay collapsed on the wooden sidewalk. Pol checked her quickly and she was evidently under a sleep spell. She must have forgotten to shield herself.

He continued after Namion, who was half a block ahead. Undeterred by the distance, Pol used sips of magic to run faster and eventually caught up to Namion, who stopped suddenly and took off down an alley. Pol pulled out a metal splinter and shot it at Namion, but somehow, the Seeker had come up with a shield that worked against Pol's teleportation.

Namion came to a busy street and began putting everyone in Pol's path to sleep. A carthorse dropped in front of him and the carter fell off his conveyance, sliding past something that opened up a long gash in his upper arm. Blood quickly soaked the man's shirt.

Pol looked ahead as Namion disappeared into the crowd. He couldn't run after Namion with this man in critical condition. Pol sighed and went to work on connecting severed blood vessels and repairing his wound.

The horse neighed as it lay on its side struggling to stand. Pol took a deep breath and used his magic to move the horse into a standing position.

A crowd formed around the cart and the wounded man. They applauded when he moved the horse. Pol thought he would collapse, but he just felt weary. This time he thanked the alien essence for giving him the strength to help these two, even though Namion escaped.

Pol smiled and nodded to the crowd acknowledging their appreciation. He quickly left and ran back up the alley. He stopped to pick up his metal sliver and then rushed to the other street to check on Shira. Val had put Namion's accomplice to sleep beside Shira and knelt over her.

She stirred just before Pol reached them.

"Namion got away. He upset a cart and I had to save a carter before he bled out," Pol said.

"And you paused to make sure Shira was alive," Val said. He stated it in an accusing way.

"I don't regret my actions. I nearly caught up to him, but…" Pol paused for a bit. "I guess I am more sensitive to others' plight."

"You're too sensitive," Val said. "Are you sure you want to be a Seeker?"

Pol shook his head. "No, I'm not. I'll never be like Namion. I suppose I won't be like you either," Pol said, feeling irritated.

"You cost apprehending Namion because of your foolishness," Val said.

Pol looked at Val evenly. This was the Val that Fadden didn't like, he was certain. "Without me, you wouldn't have caught the person who hired Namion." He looked down at the slumbering man.

Pol bent over and pulled out the portfolio. He opened it up and wasn't surprised to see that it contained the documents that Val had identified as missing from the library. "This is what the scholar died for."

"Can you see the ward?" Pol looked at Shira who looked shocked when he brought her out of the sleep spell.

"Barely," Val admitted.

"There!" Pol threw the document at Val's feet. "Pick it up. Don't worry Shira or I can remove the ward." He bent over and helped Shira to her feet.

"I'll leave it to you to get this man transported to the Imperial Compound."

Pol tried to calm down but didn't succeed. He took Shira by her wrist and stalked off.

Taking a deep breath, Pol tried to remain calm as four guards carried in the man Val had put to sleep. Val, Shira, and Pol had cast off their disguises. They put him in a chair and tied his wrists to the chair's arms.

Ranno walked in with the Emperor. All stood in the room as Hazett entered.

"What do we have here?" Hazett said.

"You are going to find out along with us, My Emperor," Malden said as he woke the man up.

"What is your name?" Val said.

The man struggled with his bonds until he spotted the Emperor.

"A truth spell, if you please," Hazett said, looking at Malden.

The magician nodded and complied.

"What is your name?" Malden said, gentler than Val had.

"Izabod Mikel," the prisoner said.

"Where are you from?"

"Pentawiss in Barna."

Val folded his arms and stood in front of the man. "You are a Resurrectionist?"

The man nodded and looked back at the Emperor.

"How did you find Namion Threshell?"

The man gave Val a puzzled look.

"The man who escaped from the restaurant is the one who you contracted to kill the scholar and retrieve the old treaty. Is that correct?"

"He didn't go by that name. I didn't want the scholar killed," the man said.

Hazett stepped forward. "Is the man still under the spell?"

Malden nodded. "But you hired him to retrieve the treaty."

"I did."

Pol looked at the bright taint of the ward on the man's hands.

"So Namion can't see wards," Pol said. "The trace of taint on the portfolio was unavoidable. What concerns me is that he somehow learned to create a shield that protects him from my splinters."

"Splinters?" Val said.

"Pol can send a sliver of metal into a man's heart, killing him nearly instantly," Fadden said.

Val looked at Pol with astonishment. "And you tried to stop Namion with one of these splinters?"

Pol nodded.

Val sighed. "I take back what I said about you and Seeking. It's a poor apology, but that's as good as I can manage."

Fadden's eyebrows rose along with Malden's.

"I'll accept it even if it is poor," Pol said. "But what do we do with him?"

Hazett took a deep breath. "It's not something you need to deal with at this juncture. The man hired Threshell, who murdered the scholar. Perhaps something went wrong or Threshell decided to silence the man forever. He is a party to the crime that is now solved. Threshell is wanted for murder and has probably already fled Yastan."

Ranno nodded and rubbed his hands. "And I am ready for lunch. Does anyone want to join me?"

Malden smiled. "Can I come?"

"Not you, son-in-law. You have more interrogating to do and then a report to write up. Make sure it is detailed enough to include the contributions of all those present," Ranno said. "Oh, and make sure Namion isn't in Yastan, would you?"

The magician sighed. "As you wish, Instrument."

Hazett waved his hand. "Not so fast, Malden. You have my permission to delay your work until after my announcement." A clock tower rang. "I invite all of you to the throne room in one hour." The Emperor winked at Pol and turned to leave the conference room.

Pol smiled weakly at Hazett's back. He was glad he wore a disguise in the city street when he healed the cart's driver and moved the horse. Perhaps some other person could get the credit.

He left the room with Shira and walked with her towards their rooms.

"You didn't tell them about your adventure while I slept on the sidewalk," Shira said.

"It's part of the episode that doesn't need to be told," Pol said.

"But you were so noble about caring for the cart driver."

Pol gave her half a smile. "I had a choice to make. Catch Namion or save a man's life. Val wasn't too impressed that I chose to save a life," he said.

"I'm impressed. What more do you need?" She grinned and bumped into him.

"Nothing, but I'm afraid I'm going to get more than I ever wanted."

"Adoption?"

Pol shook his head. "What do you think? There is a lot I owe the Emperor, so I promise I won't run away."

"I never thought you would. It's your duty."

"That's how I'm looking at it," Pol said. He sighed and took her hand. "I have a sliver of time to remain free, but I'll bet there are clothes waiting for me in my rooms."

They walked hand-in-hand. A woman stood in front of Shira's room.

"There you are, Mistress. There are seamstresses inside."

"The sliver of time is over," Shira said. She gave Pol a pouty frown and followed the woman into her room.

Pol met with the same thing. He walked through the door and another man stood by his bed. Court clothes were laid out.

"All black?" Pol said.

"As a reminder that you are a magician rated Black by your monastery."

Pol knit his eyebrows. "I left as a Gray."

"It looks like you get promoted twice today," the servant said. His eyebrows rose and he put his hand to his mouth. "Forgive me. We aren't supposed to talk about your second promotion until My Emperor's announcement."

That brought a smile to Pol's lips. "I don't suppose it is a well-kept secret?"

"Nothing is in the Imperial Compound."

Pol wondered if his good deed would remain a secret.

~ ~ ~

Chapter Sixteen

~

THE SIZE OF THE IMPERIAL THRONE ROOM STAGGERED POL. He looked out across the sea of people as he stood on steps leading down to the vast floor. He had been so intent on solving Hazett's mystery that he hadn't noticed anything else going on in the Imperial Compound.

His escort, two guards in dress uniforms, led him through the crowd. They parted at the urging of the two men in front of him. He arrived at the foot of another set of seven steps leading up to the Imperial Throne, painted in white and gold.

"His Imperial Highness, Hazett III and Empress Jarrann."

The pair of the walked in followed by their four children. All of them smiled at Pol, including Handor.

Pol stood among his fellow travelers at the foot of the steps as Hazett took the throne. Jarrann stood on one side and the four children lined up by age on the other, with Handor at his father's side. Pol felt out of place. He looked up and felt he didn't deserve to stand in that line of siblings.

Hazett rose and the audience quieted down. "This won't take long, but I will make sure you are treated to the Empire's best food after what we do here this afternoon."

Pol looked at the sides of the room, and through the crowds, saw tables covered with cloths. His stomach growled, reminding him he hadn't eaten since earlier in the morning. He looked up at Hazett, who beamed with that chronic mischievous look in his eyes.

"Most of you may be aware of a bit of nuisance we had to the east of here in North Salvan. We have the Disinherited Prince with us today."

Pol groaned at Hazett's use of his status as a title.

"As you may know, he was instrumental in discovering King Astor's plot to take over our Empire. He recently spent a few seasons in Volia making friends and a few worthy enemies. What you might not know is he recently discovered a plot to overthrow his brother's throne in Listya and soon after he arrived in Yastan, he led a select group of Seekers in solving a murder perpetrated right here in the Imperial Compound."

The crowd began to murmur, so Hazett put up his hands to quiet them down.

"Poldon Fairfield, who goes by the name Pol Cissert, is only sixteen years old." Hazett chuckled. "Nearly seventeen. He is an orphan as a result of the events after his disinheritance, but he has proven a worthy lad. In keeping with precedent, I have elected to adopt Pol into my family. From this day forward, he will be known as Pol Cissert Pastelle and will stand with us by the throne."

Hazett motioned to Pol to join him. The Emperor put his hand on Pol's shoulder. "You will note that he wears black clothes. I wanted to let you all know that he came to us from Deftnis, where he truly earned the highest magician rating they offer, Black."

That brought more murmuring, which Hazett stopped by clapping. "Let us celebrate my new son."

The court erupted in even more applause. Pol looked out at the audience and could see those who were excited by the news and others who demonstrated more reserve. He noticed Malden, Ranno, and Farthia standing next to Shira and Paki. They all were supporting him and that was all that Pol needed.

"Now it's time to fill our gullets with Yastan's finest food and wine," Hazett said. He turned to Pol and embraced him. "Pol, you truly deserve every accolade I could possibly give. I learned of your adventure today and I couldn't be more proud of the choice that you made. I know that in other circumstances you might have chosen differently, and that doesn't make the decision wrong. Now, hug your mother and siblings. We are a hugging family."

Hazett broke the embrace and stepped down to join the crowds. Jarrann beamed at Pol. "I can't say how proud we are of you. You will always have us as your family."

Pol noticed the tears in her eyes and that made his water a little. She really meant what she said. Pol just couldn't believe that the Imperial family could accept him so readily.

His new older brother shook Pol's hand and leaned closer to him. "I'm not so enamored of all the hugging," he said, smiling. "Now that you've passed Father's test, we can leave for Deftnis!" Handor pumped his fist with excitement.

Pol felt like the older brother as he talked to Handor. "I look forward to it."

The other three children gave Pol hugs and genuine welcomes except for Corran who eyed the food. "Welcome," he said, and then he hustled down the steps and nearly ran towards a dessert table.

Pol found himself standing next to Empress Jarrann.

"I can't believe this is happening to me."

She chuckled and then turned serious. "You will, but maybe not so much until you come back from Shinkya. That's another test, you know. Hazett can push you like he can't Handor. Take care of my eldest on the way to Deftnis. Leave him in good hands."

Pol nodded. "Just about all the hands in the monastery are good. I will make sure Searl Hogton examines him."

She took Pol's arm, her eyes a bit damp. "Please do. Excuse me, Hazett calls."

Pol watched her descend the steps. He wanted her to remind him of his own mother, but Jarrann was a stronger woman. He liked it that she was no less a loving mother.

Shira beckoned him down from the Imperial dais. Pol suddenly realized he stood alone at the top, but no one noticed him, so he laughed to himself as he walked down the steps. As soon as he did, a crowd of well-wishers converged. He took Shira's hand and did what he could to act the prince that he was…again.

Pol stood in front of the Emperor's study. The doorway impressed him with its opulence. He didn't see Hazett as the kind of man to seek after so much gilt on so many surfaces, but some former Emperor was.

The door opened and Ranno stepped out with Malden. Both of them gave Pol a little bow. They had never done that before.

"I'm not—" Pol said.

"Yes, you are," Ranno replied with a smile on his face. "Enjoy your time off while you take your new brother to Deftnis and return Shira to Shinkya." He patted Pol on the shoulder as he passed.

Malden merely gave Pol a sympathetic smile. "We need to talk before we leave tomorrow. The Emperor has given me permission to have dinner with you."

Pol didn't like the sound of his new father having to give someone authorization to talk to him. He walked into a expansive room much more to his liking. Instead of gold and white, Hazett's personal study was furnished in grays with accents of red. Pol wondered if that was how the Emperor viewed his responsibilities, grave with occasional light-hearted moments.

"Come in, Pol." Hazett stood and motioned for Pol to sit in one of the dark, gray suede, upholstered chairs. "We need a few minutes alone before you leave us."

The cushioning on the chairs was surprisingly firm. Pol hoped that was intentional. He sat and pressed his lips together. He had been royalty before, but now he was a member of the Empire's ruling family. The thought made Pol uneasy.

"I wish circumstances were different," the Emperor said as he sat down. "I'd like to have you here in the palace for a season or two before sending you out." He sighed. "But even an Emperor can't do everything that he wants."

Pol knew that was certainly true for kings. "I wish I could get to know my new brothers and sisters better, too." Pol said and found that he meant it. That thought's only consolation was Handor joining him on the way to Deftnis. "I'll get to know Handor better."

Hazett rubbed his hands together. "Right. I'm not expecting him to turn into you, but he has led a more protective life than you have and he, uh, doesn't have your level of ability with magic."

If Handor didn't possess extraordinary magical talent, then his physical state might not be handed down from the Demrons. "It's very possible that Searl can't cure him," Pol said. "Magic works well for wounds, but less so for illness."

Hazett smiled and waved his hand. He obviously knew all that. "Just make sure he has an opportunity to ride your horse, Demeron. It's time for him to be away from his mother for a good length of time. Just make yourself into a friend."

Pol nodded. "I can do that."

The Emperor fiddled with his hands for a bit. That indicated he was uncertain about what he would be saying. Pol prepared himself.

"Shinkya is an odd place. They are a different race as you know better than probably anyone else. I've been to Tishiko once in my life and I never felt safe the entire time, even though I was surrounded by Seekers and magicians. You are going with Fadden. I would send Valiso, but he is needed elsewhere. Take your friend Paki."

"Do I need to fear for my life?"

"You've always had to do that. Get in, meet with the Queen, if possible, and get out. They will likely ask you to return the Shinkyan horses that Demeron brought to Deftnis." Hazett grinned and shook his head. "Imagine what that horse did. Don't agree to send them back. They won't go to war over horses. In fact, they won't go to war unless we invade them. I'm sure of that."

Pol had to agree with the Emperor. He couldn't see Shinkyans looking with anything but disdain at Imperial lands.

"Am I your representative?" Pol asked.

Hazett shook his head. "You are on a personal mission. I've already sent birds to the Shinkyan Queen and our ambassador stating that you are returning Shira to Tishiko due to your relationship with her. That doesn't mean you close your eyes and ears. Malden and Akonai Haleaku will be expecting a great deal of information when you return to Yastan. I don't want you returning to Deftnis. Travel straight back here. That is an Imperial command from your Emperor. Come back safe is a command from your new father." He flashed Pol a smile.

"May I ask you one more question before I leave?"

Hazett put steepled his hands and sat back, smiling like a satiated cat.

"What is my true standing in the Empire? I'm a citizen, I was that before, but what am I in addition to your adopted son?"

The smile didn't leave Hazett's face. "I wanted you to ask that question. You are an Imperial Prince. Handor is not physically fit to rule, but you are. I'm sure you can do the cogitation necessary to understand that you are essentially next in line to my throne. For Handor's dignity, I have named him Crown Prince, but there it is." He casually waved his hand. "I intend on living for another thirty or forty years, so don't fret. I don't need you by my side for another decade or so. Live your life the way you want until you are needed, as long as you realize that you are my true heir."

"I'm still the Emperor's Pet?" Pol said.

Hazett pointed to the green Shinkyan frog carving on his desk. "That is now the Emperor's Pet." The Emperor picked up the carving and ran his fingers over its surface. "You are something more, much more." He sighed and stood up. "I have an Empire to hold together. I won't be seeing you off."

Pol stood as Hazett came around the desk and shook Pol's hand. He put his arm around Pol's shoulder as he escorted him out.

"We'll do some things to get to know each other better when you return from Tishiko," Hazett said.

"I look forward to that," Pol said.

~~~

Chapter Seventeen

~

POL LOOKED AT THE LONG TRAIN OF SOLDIERS AND MAGICIANS behind him. He had gotten the impression that they would travel to Deftnis with a small group similar to those who would accompany Pol and Shira to Tishiko, but the Emperor never mentioned a large contingent going from Yastan to Deftnis.

He had tucked the fact that he was the heir to the Empire to the back of his brain to mingle with his Demron essence. He hoped they would be happy together. Pol smiled at the thought.

He looked up ahead and saw Malden riding with Akonai and Handor. After Pol's meeting with the Emperor, Shira and he had told their personal story to Akonai over dinner. Malden had arranged the affair. Akonai had heard most of the events from Fadden. Pol had expected tears and worse, but Akonai was more of a support to them than they were to him. The Shardian moved quickly on to pulling information about the state of Volia that the Emperor could use.

Pol liked both Malden and Akonai. He trusted both men and knew they gave solid support to the Emperor. Learning all about Imperial politics would be something he would concentrate on once he returned to Yastan. Despite Hazett's claim that Pol could begin learning all about the Empire in a decade, Pol knew that anything could happen at any time.

"We'll be passing through Rocky Ridge on our way?" Paki said

Pol laughed. "We aren't two hours away from Yastan and you ask me that?"

Paki blushed. "Well, I wanted something to look forward to."

"Why don't we stay at the same inn? Darrol and Kell aren't with us, but I'm sure you can overcome that. There won't be a festival, this time."

Paki grinned. "I don't need a festival," he said.

Shira called from behind them. "What's this about a festival?" She left Ako and trotted up.

"I'll tell you the whole story," Pol said.

Paki turned red and waved to them. "Feel free, I'm going back to ride with Fadden."

Ako trailed behind Shira and Pol as he related the story of Kell's abduction and the strange doings at the Rocky Ridge version of 'Summer's Come', the first of summer celebration Hinkeyites celebrated in the middle of Spring every year.

Ako traveled close enough that Pol could hear her laugh when he described Paki's antics. "I've never heard of a Shinkyan horse working so closely with their master," Ako said.

"You'll meet Demeron and come away impressed," Pol said. "It is rumored he picked up a lot more tricks on his journey through Shinkya."

"More than tricks," the Shinkyan Sister said behind them. "He brought a few hundred Shinkyan horses with him."

Pol couldn't detect any animosity in Ako's statement. "I think it will be good for you to see them on Deftnis Isle. I am certain they are well-treated."

Malden and Akonai led the column through Baccusol and into Galistya. They traveled on roads that did not take them through the Galistyan capital. One night they put up at a small village's only inn. Most of the column slept out in the open on the far side of the village, but Pol's group ate at a table in the common room.

Handor had initially been reserved, but with a few tankards of ale, his personality changed. He slapped Pol's shoulder.

"Am I ever glad you came along," he said with a slur. "Now I have nooo pressure."

"Pressure?" Pol asked. He never did like to drink very much, so he nursed his first mug of ale.

"Mother wants me to be a mirror image of Father, but I can't measure up."

Pol looked at Malden and Akonai. Fadden entertained Shira, Ako, and Paki at another table. No one else should have heard what Handor had to say.

"Sure you can," Pol said. "Farthia Wissingbel, Ranno's daughter, relentlessly made me study. Right, Malden?"

Pol could see that Malden mirrored his discomfort. Akonai merely looked amused.

"She'll be on your back soon enough, trying to make you something you're not." Handor waggled his finger at Pol. "Just you wait and see." Handor drained his mug and put his head down on the table. He began snoring.

Malden sighed. "Hazett has a more realistic view of his son than Jarrann does," he said. "She has been pushing Handor to improve, but the boy can only go so far."

"What does she think of me?"

Akonai laughed. "The Empress let her son go to Deftnis after resisting ever since he was fifteen. I think she respects her adopted son enough to relax a bit. You have satisfied both of them well enough."

"But have I satisfied myself?" Pol said. "I didn't ask to do this."

Akonai looked Pol in the eye. "I was taken to Yastan and drafted into Ranno's organization. I didn't have a say, but it has worked out. Hasn't it, Malden?"

"Most of the time we have to make the best of situations that we don't control. You've had to do that for most of your life, Pol. Handor has a few more challenges than you do, but he would step into his father's role if prodded. Now it's up to you to do whatever is right for the Empire."

"Is this common knowledge?" Pol said. "Am I going to be looked at as the Emperor's heir or will people still think of me as his pet?"

Akonai nodded his head. "A bit of both is the truth, I suspect."

Malden smiled. "It is true. With a nudge from Ranno, the Emperor spotted you in Borstall. I think at the time he wondered if Handor could overcome his challenges as you have, but even though Handor has survived, he isn't you. He is over three years older, but you have acquired as much experience as a normal person could hope to gain in a decade or more."

Pol wanted to dispute that, but he kept quiet. "Let's get him to bed."

Malden and Akonai rose from the table and the three of them escorted the Emperor's eldest to his room. They both decided to retire as well, so Pol slipped back downstairs. He needed some air, so he stepped outside.

"It's stuffy in there," Shira said as she joined him in the darkness.

Pol put his hands on a hitching rack and leaned on it. "You could say that."

"I just did," she said as she put her arms around him giving him a back hug. "Shall we go for a walk now that we are truly alone?"

Pol nodded. "The village isn't very large. Our escort is camped that way," Pol pointed to his left, "So we will walk this way."

He took her hand and they strolled to their right. Neither of them spoke for a bit until they were nearly out of the village.

"Has the Emperor cast aside his oldest son?" Shira said.

There was no reason to cover up his elevation so Pol nodded. "I think I am unofficially the heir. You can guess how I feel about it."

"Your opinion hasn't changed?"

Pol shook his head.

Shira's laughter lightly filled the silence that surrounded them. "Tishiko is different. What we experienced in Alsador and Yastan is nothing compared to chronically boiling politics in Tishiko. It may look placid on the surface, but the plotting and maneuvering never ends."

"Are you sure you want to return to that?"

Shira made a soft grunting sound. "Have you forgotten about Ako? She is with us to make sure I do. She is friendly enough and I quite like her, but if it's between my staying or returning, she will kidnap me if she has to."

Pol stopped her. "I'll miss you when we part." He didn't know what else to say.

Shira just stood and grabbed hold of him. "I wish I could poke you again. You were my punching bag when I fought off so many demons when we traveled in Volia."

"Why did you stop?"

Shira laughed without humor. "Ako quite rightly told me that my behavior was out of line for a Shinkyan Princess and for a girl with her boyfriend. I took advantage of you and because you endured my tiny tortures so well, I never stopped."

Pol smiled, but he doubted she could see that in the darkness. "Blame it all on me."

"I wish I could," Shira said. Pol thought she might be on the verge of tears.

"You can hit me now and I won't mind."

Shira pounded her fist on Pol's chest, but the anger that had punctuated her blows in Volia were soft and she finally collapsed and held him close while she sobbed.

"I don't want to be without you, but there is no way."

"I could become the prophet that Ako called me."

"The Great Ancestor?" Shira giggled through her tears. "You fit well enough. All you'd have to do is enter Tishiko in your Demron guise and that might be enough. I never told you but we have drawings in sacred places of what the Demrons really looked like."

"You never told me."

"Sacred places," Shira said, putting a finger to her lips. "I've only heard about them."

"I'm tempted, but who knows how your people would react. I'm not one for adoration and look at me now."

"I'm more than willing to look at you now," Shira said. She tilted her head and closed her eyes, but shouts from the village ended their interlude.

"Trouble," Pol said. He touched his trousers, feeling the bundle of splinters that he always carried. Their walk was so spur-of-the-moment that he had no other arms other than a Shinkyan throwing knife in his boot.

Shira leaned over and came up with a more standard knife and began to run towards the inn.

"Go get our escort," Pol said as they came up to the inn. He could see the flickering of flames inside and stopped up short as he made sure Shira continued to move towards the other end of the village.

Pol manipulated the pattern to extinguish the flames, but they started up again. He looked around and saw a magician standing in the shadows on the other side of the street. He didn't hesitate to pull a splinter out of his pocket and take care of the attacker.

The flames died down since they were only at the front of the inn. He stepped inside, wishing he held his Shinkyan sword and spotted Fadden fighting a swordsman. He used another splinter and found he had only four left.

"Where is Handor?" Pol asked.

Fadden shrugged. Pol raced upstairs to find two magicians battling with Akonai and Malden. Now he was down to two splinters and still had no sword.

"Are you all right?"

Malden shook his head. "I'm about out of power. What about you, Akonai?"

The Shardian nodded his head, breathing heavily. "The same. There are others up here."

Pol stepped into the open door to Handor's room. The Emperor's son was on his bed waving a sword weakly at an intruder. Pol used another splinter and put it in the man's thigh. He went down immediately, so Pol put him to sleep. They needed someone to interrogate.

Handor moaned on the bed. Pol leaned over to attend to him when another assailant broke the window and began to climb in. Pol used his last splinter on that man before he had a chance to climb all the way through and the intruder fell back to the ground below. He picked up Handor's sword and laid it on the bed and returned to stopping the bleeding as best he could. Pol helped him to the corridor outside and put him between Malden and Akonai, resting against a wall. "Are either of you proficient with this?" Pol held out Handor's sword.

Akonai raised his hand. "I'm no pattern-master, but I'm better than he is," he said looking at Malden.

Pol just nodded and ran back into Handor's room to grab the attacker's sword. He sealed the door shut by joining wood to wood and passed all three on his way back downstairs.

Fadden had gone to join Paki and Ako. They faced four attackers, but with Pol by their sides, the men were subdued quickly.

"Go upstairs and join Akonai and Malden. Handor is injured, but he's out of immediate danger." Pol stepped over more bodies in the inn. He sealed the back door shut after he let some of the staff out who had taken refuge in a closet.

Imperial Soldiers and magicians began to pour into the inn. Shira followed, gasping.

"Send some men to patrol around the village," Pol said. He ran back upstairs. Akonai stood with a sword in his hand as Malden now administered to the Emperor's son.

Opening the door by removing the sealed joints, Pol walked in, finding the assailant moaning in his sleep on the floor. Shira joined Pol in the room.

"Let's tie him up," Pol said, looking around for something to do so. Shira ripped sheets into strips using her magic and the man now sat bound on the floor.

Pol removed the sliver and took the bloody strip of metal and cleaned it on the man's pants before putting it in his own pocket.

"Malden?" Pol called. "Are you done with Handor?"

"For now," he said. "You said you knew how to heal, but I didn't realized how much you've learned."

"We can talk of that later," Pol said, knowing he was too curt with his mentor. "It's time to wake this man up."

Malden brought the man from pattern-induced sleep, and Pol administered a truth spell.

"Who hired you?" Pol asked.

The assailant shrugged. "My boss dealt with him."

"You are part of a gang?"

"Mercenaries. Three magicians and the rest are swordsmen."

"Who were you attacking?"

"Dignitaries. Two young men. Probably you and the other one who I fought."

"Were you supposed to kill them?"

The man nodded his head.

"Where do you operate?" Malden said.

"We work in Terrafin along the Imperial road from Yastan to the Spines, mostly."

Malden nodded. "They are robbers if they don't have a contract."

Pol figured as much. "How did you know we stayed in this inn?"

"We didn't, but when you didn't camp with the soldiers and magicians outside the village, it was easy to figure you were at the only inn in town, so we took the opportunity." He eyed Pol and Malden. "We didn't figure you would put up a fight. We thought you'd all be like the other boy."

The man meant Handor.

"You're the only one left alive. Stand up."

"I can't without help."

The man was being truthful. The leader of the escort, a seasoned soldier put his head through the door. "The village is secure, My Prince."

Suppressing a wince at the honorific, Pol said. "Help me with this man. He is probably the only survivor."

"No there is one more. The other Seeker is tending him."

Pol grimaced but looked forward to getting more information. "Have him taken downstairs. He'll likely be heading back to Yastan to Ranno Wissingbel."

The soldier saluted and left. By the time Pol and Malden stood, a magician and a soldier took the attacker down the stairs.

"How are you?" Pol asked Handor.

The Emperor's son looked up at Pol from his sitting position with an eager expression on his face. "You are amazing. Thank you for saving my life!"

"You are welcome. Excuse me. We have another person to talk to," Pol said. He ran down the stairs and found Fadden bent over a body.

"Is he alive?" Pol said.

"Ako had to put him to sleep," Fadden said, shaking his head. "The man certainly knows how to curse."

"Docs anyone need healing?" Pol said, now that he could put

aside his concern for questioning another attacker.

Shira trudged up to him. "Can you do anything for someone who is still out of breath?" she said.

"No, but you can sit down and rest. All the attackers are identified," Pol said.

"Paki and I could use some help and so could our sleeping enemy," Fadden said showing him a cut on his other shoulder.

Pol spent the next few minutes repairing his friends' injuries until Malden arrived.

"I have Akonai sitting with Handor. What do we have here?"

Ako nudged the attacker with her foot. "He might be their leader. Watch out when you wake him. He is on the vicious side."

Once the man was bound, Malden woke him up. Pol and Shira stood at the side. Ako and Paki had gone to keep curious villagers out of the inn.

The assailant shook his head and began a string of swearing that included a few actual words. "What do you want with me?" he finally said glaring at Malden.

Pol sensed something wrong with the man and put his hand on his head. Mind control.

"He's been ensorcelled," Pol said as he removed the spell.

The attacker blinked his eyes. They still glared, but much of the anger seemed to be replaced by wariness.

"Who slapped mind control on you?" Malden asked after he patterned a truth spell.

"Mind control?" the attacker's eyes were gaining a little more rationality.

"Did you lead the attack on the inn?"

The man nodded. "I did. It's my job."

"What is your job?" Shira said.

"To kill two princes," he said.

Malden looked at Pol and then at Shira. "Who hired you?"

The criminal laughed. "I never know. All our jobs are from anonymous sources. We prefer it that way, so do our customers."

"What kind of jobs do you usually take?" Malden asked.

"Murder, mayhem. Sometimes we warn people, sometimes we

don't bother to warn." The man shrugged.

"That didn't answer my question."

The attacker looked up and squinted his eyes. "Just what is your question?"

Malden snorted. He was a better magician than he was an interrogator.

"Where do you base your group?" Pol said.

"The Dukedom of Asfall, but we were working a job in Galistya when we were contacted."

"Who contacted you?" Pol shook his head. There was an individual who fit the pattern.

The man struggled with the truth, but then he said, "A Seeker."

"With the name of?" Pol said.

"He didn't give me his name," the man said. A smile returned to his face. "Everything is anonymous."

"Describe him," Malden said.

The description matched Namion Threshell perfectly. It seemed that Namion was getting some revenge.

"I have an idea," Shira said.

~~~

Chapter Eighteen

~

MALDEN, AKONAI, AND THE ESCORT LEFT THE VILLAGE in the morning after buying a rickety carriage to carry two coffins ostensibly holding the dead Imperial princes. They really held the two sleeping mercenaries.

Pol and Handor had left in the middle of the night and would travel on their own to Deftnis with Pol now wearing the face of one of the fallen attackers. Shira had turned Handor's hair to black to match Pol's new hair color and Ako hacked at Handor's hair creating an unsightly mop. No one would notice either of them except for the fine swords at their waists and the long bar concealed by a leather covering tied to Pol's horse.

The villagers all wailed at the deaths of such noble personages in their village. Not a single attacker remained to contradict what the villagers thought they knew to be true.

Ako and Shira, now disguised, rode off with Paki and Fadden just after Malden left. Pol knew she truly felt as bad as he that a precious week together would be sacrificed for the deception.

In a day and a half, Pol saw the first sign of the Wild Spines. He had been over the pass before and didn't worry about anyone accosting a shabbily dressed man and his son.

If Hazett wanted to give Handor some real life experience, he would be thrilled with the two young men riding by themselves in the countryside.

"Can you teach me some of your magic?" Handor asked as their horses plodded down the pass into the Dukedom of Sand.

Pol shook his head. "I don't want to spoil your education," he said. "Malden pushed me at Boxall, but I never learned the basics. I did pick up a few good spells, enough to save my life a few times. When I first arrived at Deftnis, I had lots of power, but my health wouldn't let me use it. The monks put me in with a couple of Reds, but I embarrassed myself time and again because I never had a good foundation. We'll get you healthy and then the experts at Deftnis will be thrilled to teach you."

Handor looked disappointed.

"I'll make you a gift when we spend the night at Rocky Ridge. It's a town on the way. We won't make it there tonight, but we'll arrive around midday tomorrow, if my memory is correct, and spend the rest of the day."

"Rocky Ridge, eh?"

"I liked the inn we stayed at before. The innkeeper is a good person, but she won't recognize me."

Handor laughed. "I don't recognize you. I hardly recognize myself!"

Pol joined in the mirth. He never had a brother he could relax around. Even though he had reconciled with Landon, his older brother wasn't a companion like Handor proved to be.

Handor pointed out a fancy inn as they rode into Rocky Ridge. "Is that it?"

Pol smiled and shook his head. "That's called The Dainty Lady and it's not for us."

"We can afford it," Handor said. "I'll bet it's comfortable inside."

"Not for me. I've been in it before. It's the town's brothel." Pol noticed a gaudily dressed woman standing at the open doorway looking out at the road.

"Oh," Handor said and then broke out laughing. "Mother would be shocked."

"Yes," Pol said, "Mother would be." He thought of Empress Jarrann. He wondered how surprised she would be, knowing that Pol and Handor rode past such a place by themselves. His stepbrother seemed to be soaking it all in like a more innocent Paki.

They rode along for a few moments and turned into the stable yard of the inn Pol had stayed at over a year ago. So much had happened since he had last spent a night in the inn.

The same woman ran the place and welcomed them in.

"Have you stayed here before?"

Pol smiled and said, "I have some time ago. I stayed during a 'Summer's Come' festival. The town was lively. This is my son, Handy. My name's Cissert."

"No festival this time," she said, "but Rocky Ridge still has its charms."

"Handy noticed The Dainty Lady and asked if we could stay at that inn."

She laughed. "It's a better establishment now than if you visited it on your last trip, but it still serves the same clientele. Where are you headed?"

"Port Mancus," Pol said. "I have a good friend that's waiting for me there."

"Your wife?"

"No. He's a big dark guy. I grew up a bit with him."

"Well, it's a nice time of year to travel."

Pol put some Imperial coinage on the counter. "I can't remember how much I paid the last time."

She looked down at the coins. "Did you come from Yastan?"

"Handy and I left our family there. It's time he got around a bit. Right, son?"

Handor coughed and nodded his head.

"Is your kitchen open?"

The innkeeper nodded after taking a silver coin and leaving the rest. "Room and board that includes three meals. This," she held up the coin, "will get you baths as well."

Handor brightened up. "Good."

"My son likes to be clean. Me, not so much," Pol smiled and tried to look embarrassed.

Pol took their key and let Handor follow him up the stairs.

"Can you show me the staff? I've been meaning to ask."

"Part of this will be your gift." Pol slipped off the leather cover.

"It's just a metal rod?" It looked like Handor had expected more.

"Not just a metal rod, Handor. Beings who appeared on Phairoon a few thousand years ago created this. This metal was made by my ancestors."

"You haven't mentioned the rod before."

"I didn't see the point," Pol said. "Let's get some food in us and then get to work."

They walked downstairs and ate in the half-full common room. The food tasted good to Pol after camping the night before.

"Does it suit your palate?" Pol said.

Handor nodded with his mouth full. He ate faster than Pol and urged him up the stairs.

"First, a trip to the stable," Pol said.

Handor followed him out into the stable yard.

Pol stopped a stable boy. "I need some leather strips. My sword grip has worn out. Do you have any along with a length of good wood?"

The boy looked dubiously at them until Pol pulled out a few coins. "Something for your trouble."

"I'll be right back."

Pol inspected the wood and the grain looked straight enough. The leather was strapping and appeared to be in very good shape. They walked up stairs, and Pol shut the door and locked it.

"I don't want anyone walking in on us."

Handor just nodded. He seemed much younger to Pol, but that only made Pol like him better.

He pulled out his long knife. "This will take a little time and a considerable amount of magical energy. I've never worked with this metal before."

Pol laid the knife on his lap and looked through the grip with his magical eyes, checking out the pattern of the entire blade. He'd done it before, but Pol wanted a fresh pattern to duplicate.

Handor looked on, but Pol ceased to notice him as he went to work drawing out a long knife out of the bar. He stopped. Handor had gone to sleep on the other bed. Pol shook his head at how long he must have worked. It was time for dinner.

The alien steel took a lot longer to work. The knife looked exquisite. The surface looked polished like a mirror with just a hint of the yellowish look of his amulet. Shaping the pommel and the wood handle took minutes.

Before he woke up Handor, he finished making the knife. The blade was very sharp, but the balance wasn't quite right, probably because the metal was lighter than steel. He unwrapped the handle and added a bit more metal to the tang. In a few more minutes the knife was finished. He would fashion a suitable sheath from the rod's original leather covering later.

He still had enough for a sword and knife of his own. He shook Handor awake. "This is yours to keep. It's a memento of our trip to Deftnis. It's sharp, so watch the blade."

"You were totally immersed when you made this. I can see why."

Pol smiled at the excitement in his brother's face. Handor worked the blade with his wrist. He might be sickly, but he had obviously had a lot of training with weapons.

"It's a Shinkyan pattern?"

Pol nodded and picked up this Shinkyan long knife. "This is a real Shinkyan knife that I used for the pattern. I'm going to make a sword and knife just like that for me," he said. "But first I'm really hungry. Manipulating the pattern of that metal was not easy."

Handor nodded. "It needs a sheath."

"I'll make one after dinner."

The meal tasted even better than the one at midday. Pol ate all he could. His strength hadn't been affected, but his appetite was large as usual after a lot of magic. Handor packed his dinner in. How could he be so slight if he ate like that in Yastan?

Handor yawned. "I'd like to watch you, but I'm tired."

"Go ahead and lay down." Pol locked the door and merged it to the frame in a few places to give them privacy. He didn't like losing track of time when he had worked on Handor's gift.

Handor soon began to breathe evenly, while Pol lit a magician's light, coloring it to look like a candle, and went to work.

This time he decided to work start with the sword. If it looked good, he would give his Shinkyan blades to Jonness. The former Seeker would appreciate them. Pol put the sword on his lap and began to draw the metal. He stopped to make sure he had enough to make both.

Pol focused his attention on drawing the metal. Something made his sight waver, and then the Demron essence gave him a new pattern. He became lost in his work and finally blinked his way out of some kind of trance.

His new sword lay on his lap, but it wasn't a duplicate of his old one. This sword looked nothing like he had ever seen before. The tip wasn't rounded but came to a point. The curve of the blade only appeared on the cutting edge. The top of the blade had a thick triangular ridge. Along the cutting edge, small ovals lined it in a row.

Just underneath the sword was a companion piece, a long knife of similar design. Was this the style of blade the aliens used? Pol never noticed swords in the pictures at the Demron cave.

He rubbed his head and walked over to the washstand to throw water on his face. He finished off the hilts. With a simple leather wrapping and oval guard, the weapons would look just serviceable until someone drew the blade.

He yawned and completed sheaths for the knives and a scabbard for the sword. He disguised them to hide their unique shape. Pol laid Handor's knife by his brother's bed and leaned his in a corner before collapsing onto the mattress. Thoughts of the disturbing assistance by the Demron essence ran through his head for a moment or two, but Pol was so tired he quickly joined Handor in slumber.

Handor shook Pol. "It's morning."

Pol opened his eyes, surprisingly alert after a night of magical work. "I believe you're right, brother." He noticed Handor's knife at his waist. "Do you like it?"

"I do. The scabbard isn't very fancy, but then neither is the knife."

Pol nodded. "It's not meant to be. Let the weapon do the talking, not a fancy scabbard and a jeweled pommel."

Handor nodded enthusiastically. "That sounds like something Ranno would say or even Father."

"It's something your younger brother says." Pol stretched and retrieved his weapons. "I was going to make duplicates of my Shinkyan weapons, but something came over me and I'm afraid I was a bit creative."

"Yours looks simple like mine."

"Not quite so simple," Pol said as he drew his sword. "Have you seen anything like this before?"

Handor's mouth dropped open. "I'm speechless," he said.

"No you're not," Pol replied, smiling. "The sword nearly designed itself. It is a multipurpose blade, now that I look at it. There is a cutting edge with oval depressions spaced along the edge. I don't know what they are there for, but it looks good. The top is reinforced with a triangular bar running from the hilt until just before the tip. If I wanted to break rather than cut, I would use the blunt top of this sword to do it."

Pol swung the sword for the first time. "The balance is superb. Do you want to try it?"

Handor's eyes grew as he took the sword. "This is marvelous. Father will be jealous."

"I can make him one out of steel since I'm afraid there isn't any Demron metal left." Pol accepted his new sword from Handor and put it back in the scabbard.

"You hide it in there."

Pol grinned. "So it will always be a surprise to my enemies."

"Spoken like a pattern-master."

Pol shrugged. He grabbed his matching knife. "And here is its little brother." The long knife looked more menacing. Pol noticed that the top edge was taller and there was a sharp double ridge on each side of the top bar. He had no idea what that was for, but it gave the blade a complicated look. The top would inflict its own kind of damage.

"Precious," Handor said. "I like my knife better."

"Good, since I'm not giving this up." He clapped Handor on the back. "Ready for breakfast?"

"I am."

He was about to go downstairs. "It wouldn't do to wear your new knife to eat."

"Oh," Handor said. His face lit up with understanding. "Of course." He grinned and set his weapon on the bed.

They had both slept in and the common room was nearly empty. The innkeeper walked in.

"I thought you had left."

Pol shook his head. "I had something to do last night in our room."

"Read? Are you a traveling scholar?"

"Us?" Pol said. "No. That wouldn't describe us that way, at all."

Handor sat down with Pol and waited for some fresh eggs, bacon, and fried bread.

A group of travelers walked into the inn.

"This is it!" Paki said grinning. "I have some good memories."

Shira stared at Pol. "You were supposed to be far ahead of us," she said.

"I promised something for Handor that delayed us. I didn't think you would catch up."

Ako made a disgusted sound. "Paki convinced Fadden to forge ahead under the bright moon. He wants to spend the day here."

"And night, I would imagine," Pol said.

Paki blushed a little. "Deny a traveler's reunion?"

The innkeeper walked in. "You, I remember," she said looking at Paki. "I hope you're not looking for the wench you serviced the last time you rode through."

Paki turned even more red.

"She's married and is waddling around with a firstborn in her belly."

"Oh," Paki said, rather quietly.

"Oh. 'Summer's Come' is a time we all put aside once the festival is over. Understand? She's my cousin's daughter besides."

Paki nodded.

"You know these people?" the innkeeper said to Pol.

"I have a passing acquaintance with them."

"Passing is right," Shira said smiling.

"Perhaps we can travel together. There is a village further down the road where we can all spend the night," Pol said. "First, join us for breakfast. It looks really good."

Fadden sat next to Handor. "You don't have to ask twice," he said.

"None of us know how to cook that well on the road."

Pol looked at Shira, who shrugged, but then she smiled and sat down next to him. "I hope you don't mind me sitting next to you, old man. My name is Shira."

"I'm Cissert and this is Handy, my son."

Paki coughed. "Your son, eh?"

"Yes."

After a hearty breakfast, Pol and Handor joined up with the others. They maintained their disguises and soon left Rocky Ridge behind.

Fadden joined Shira and Pol as they rode in the coolish morning. "What did you do in Rocky Ridge? Paki wondered if he should stop to ask for you in that brothel we passed."

"I went in there with Darrol Netherfield, looking for Kell." He told Fadden of their adventure in Rocky Ridge.

Fadden laughed. "Paki gave us a different version."

Shira giggled. "He really did."

Pol pulled out his new sword. "I made this last night. The Demron essence provided the pattern."

Ako gasped behind him, as she looked at the blade. "You shouldn't have one of those!" she said. "Is it out of the metal bar?"

Pol nodded. "What's wrong with it." He looked back at Ako and turned back to Shira.

"There is a picture of the Great Ancestor deep in the basement of the Royal Palace," Ako said.

"I know, Shira told me."

"An Ancestor is holding a sword identical to that one."

Pol looked at the blade. "An ancient pattern. Let's hope I don't have to draw it in Tishiko." He sheathed it and pulled out his knife. "Is this a little less of problem?"

"A little," Shira said. "Can I hold it?"

Pol gave it to her.

"You used your magic to make this? I can see wards inside if I look closely," Shira said.

Pol yanked out the sword again and looked closely. "A very

intricate weave. I don't even know what the wards will do."

After shivering a bit, Shira gave the knife back to Pol. "It would be best not to find out."

Pol said nothing. Now he had to play with the knife to see what the wards did. He couldn't let Shira's challenge go unmet, but that was only a fleeting thought. Pol was quite disturbed by the re-emergence of the Demron essence.

He didn't feel that the intelligence had taken over his mind, but he wondered what had happened the previous night. Pol hadn't fought the essence and maybe the time had come to do that.

In his own mind, the sword looked brutal and aggressive, quite unlike the lithe lines of his Shinkyan blade, but the balance was even better than his old sword. It felt light and perfect in his hand.

"Put it away," Ako said. "The sword makes me shiver."

Pol could hear a bit of anxiety in her voice. Maybe he would ask Shira to take him to the picture of the Demron in Tishiko.

~ ~ ~

Chapter Nineteen

~

A WHIFF OF THE SEA DANCED ALONG THE INCOMING BREEZE, bringing a smile to Pol's face. They were close to Mancus Port and Deftnis Isle. Demeron waited for him on the other side of the monastery and he looked forward to their reunion. Shira and he had eliminated their disguises that morning, and Pol enjoyed looking like himself again.

"The boat ride is really rough?" Handor asked Paki, just after Shira returned his hair color to normal.

Paki's smile faded. "I've never been so sick in my life. Wait, I take that back. I'm always sick on the ocean."

"I'll put you to sleep for the duration of the ride," Shira said from behind. She rode with Ako like she always did when she wasn't at Pol's side.

The Shinkyan Sister had seemed to avoid Pol when she could, ever since he showed off his new sword. Pol viewed the new blades as a barrier and wrapped them up. He took to wearing his Shinkyan weapons and she began to warm up to him again.

Fadden rode up ahead and held up his hand at the top of a hill. Pol joined him.

"Port Mancus," Fadden said. "Look further out."

Pol couldn't help but grin. "Deftnis Isle. It's been a long time."

Shira came up to his side. "That's it?" she said looking at the large island not far from the shore. "It reminds me of The Shards," she said.

"It's not like The Shards at all. The monastery is a fortress, but it has no wards," Fadden said. "I haven't been here for years and it still sends a thrill through me."

Paki moaned. "All I can see is that stretch of ocean."

Handor just looked and smiled. Ako viewed the town and the island with an impassive gaze.

Fadden picked up the pace and before Pol knew it, Paki slumbered in the boat while the rest rode the calm sea across to Deftnis.

Paki sputtered when Shira woke him, but once he realized he was on Deftnis Isle, he jumped up and picked up the little pile of his belongings. The rest of their possessions would come over with the horse barge.

Pol tried to communicate with Demeron, but they were out of range on the small dock. He grabbed his saddlebag along with the Demron weapons and walked to the Deftnis stable in the port where they would get transport to the Monastery.

Fadden found a driver and soon they all tumbled into the back of a wagon, heading up the twisting road towards Deftnis.

Midway up the road, Pol tried to communicate with Demeron again.

Pol? Is that really you?

He could pick up the excitement in Demeron's thoughts.

"It is me," Pol said out loud, unused to the silent communication. Shira looked at him oddly. "Of course," she said.

"Demeron is speaking."

"I didn't think he could talk," Ako said, giving Pol a wry smile.

"Communicating?" Pol said. He thought, *How have you been?*

I'm fine. I'll meet you at the back of the monastery. Hurry! I've waited a long time to see you!

Pol had to grin, but then as he reviewed Demeron's thoughts, he picked up something different. Could the horse have changed? Had Pol changed? He wondered until Shira picked up his hand.

"Are women allowed at the monastery?"

Pol didn't know, but Fadden, who rode with the driver, turned to Shira. "Yes. We have a small section in the administration basement that can be used by women. It has all of the necessary facilities in two apartments."

"I didn't know that," Paki said.

"Are you a woman?" Fadden smiled when Paki vigorously shook his hand. "I thought not. The apartments are used by visitors who can't be put up in the monk's cells."

"I never made it to a monk's cell," Pol said. "I always stayed in the dormitory."

Fadden nodded. "I doubt you'll be staying there this time. Maybe Abbot Pleagor will put Handor and you in one apartment and the ladies in the other."

Shira leaned forward to Fadden. "I'm amenable to that."

"I'll bet you are," the ex-Seeker said.

The talking died down as they approached the dark stone walls of Deftnis.

"Is that the Deftnis symbol?" Shira said, looking at the sword and flame encircled by a chain wreath device above the gate.

"It is," Paki said. "I'm glad to see it again."

Pol nodded, a bit afraid at what awaited him in the monastery. He thought there was a high likelihood that he wouldn't be a monastery member for very long.

"Are you excited?" Pol said to Handor.

The prince nodded with a pensive smile. Handor had enjoyed the trip, Pol thought, and now he would be entering a new environment away from Yastan and the rest of his family. "I have much to look forward to," Handor said.

They stopped in the courtyard. By the time their bags were unloaded, the Abbot, Vactor, his magic tutor, Searl, the healer, and Jonness, the Seeker instructor, stood in a row with Darrol behind.

Pol went right to Darrol and hugged him. "It's so good to see you again," he said.

"My Prince," Darrol said and when to a knee. The others did as well.

"Welcome to Deftnis, Imperial Princes," Abbot Pleagor said.

Pol went to the Abbot and lifted him back up. "We are two acolytes seeking entrance into Deftnis."

"Two acolytes? Paki and Prince Handor? You, Prince Pol, are no acolyte."

Pol scoffed and then stood back. "I'm sorry. I'm so excited to be back that I forgot to introduce my traveling companions. This is Prince Handor, Princess Shira, Sister Ako Injira. You might remember Fadden and you certainly know Paki."

His companions nodded to the monks, and then Pol introduced the monks to his friends. "I won't be here for long. Princess Shira joined me on all my travels and Fadden joined us in Volia. We picked up Ako in Alsador."

"I suppose Akonai and Malden were thrilled to discuss your activities," Abbot Pleagor said. "We finally received a report on your actions last week. Malden thought it would make for good reading in our archives. I keep up on the activities of Deftnis graduates."

"There is a bit more to tell," Fadden said. "But maybe after getting us settled down and over a meal?"

The Abbot nodded. "Of course, of course. We have cells for Paki and Fadden—"

"A cell for me?"

"Of course. Shira and Ako will use one of our visitor apartments and so will the princes until we have formally evaluated Prince Handor." The Abbot turned to Pol's step-brother. "If you are accepted you'll be in the dormitory with the rest of the acolytes."

Handor grinned. "My trip to Deftnis has gotten me used to living in more mundane circumstances."

"Good. Jonness will take you—"

Pol heard a whinny and saw Demeron's head poking around the edge of the administration building.

"Excuse me," Pol said. He took off towards Demeron who pranced from his hiding place.

Pol! Pol! Demeron said as he settled down enough to nuzzle his master.

"I have so much to tell you," Pol said out loud.

And I you. Who are the others? Two are Shinkyans. You know that, don't you?

"I do. They are my friends," he said as he put his arms around Demeron's neck. "Come over and meet them."

Demeron nuzzled Pol's shoulder as he walked back over to his friends.

"Up to your old tricks?" Jonness said to Demeron.

"What tricks?" Pol asked.

The monk laughed. "He has a mind of his own and quite a mind it is. Did you know that he's learned to communicate with others?"

"You have?"

Demeron nodded his head. *Introduce me.*

Pol made the introductions while the Deftnis monks waited.

"You can get reacquainted later," Abbot Pleagor said. "For now, let our visitors get settled."

I will, Abbot, Demeron said. *I'll go tell the others the good news. Bye, Pol.*

Pol saw that the Abbot heard correctly. He wondered what other things Demeron had learned.

"Let's take you to your rooms," the Abbot said.

Jonness took Paki and Fadden to one of the buildings holding monk cells.

Vactor and Searl took some of the women's bags and they all followed the Abbot into the administration building.

Pol followed, pausing to look up at the administration building. It felt good to be back at Deftnis. He smiled at his quick reunion with Demeron. He knew they would only be staying for a brief time, but Demeron and he would have plenty of time together on the ride to Tishiko.

The Abbot bowed to them at the stairway that led down into the building's basement. He stopped Pol.

"We will talk later. Malden mentioned an episode you had in Volia. Vactor and I would like to talk to you about it and test you. With your permission, of course."

"I'll look forward to it. I have something to show you, as well."

"After dinner, perhaps. You'll want to head out to the plain, of course. That's where Demeron spends most of his time."

Pol nodded and caught up to the others. He had never been down here. There were two three-bedroom apartments. Ako and Shira were already in theirs and Handor and Pol took the other. There was a large sitting room and two doors on each side. One of the doors led to a lavatory and bath.

The furnishings were simple but well-made. The wood looked polished throughout, even the paneled walls. A line of windows were at the top, presumably at ground level.

"A few birds announced your coming, so we had these rooms cleaned and freshened," Searl said. He looked at Handor taking his bags into his own room. "Do you think his condition matches yours?"

Pol shook his head. "He has some talent, but nothing extraordinary."

Searl snorted. "Ordinary to you might be extraordinary in someone else. I'll take a look at him before he gets admitted as an acolyte."

"The Emperor will appreciate anything you can do."

"Your father, you mean?" Vactor said.

Pol shook his head. "I'm still Pol Cissert," he said.

Vactor laughed. "You missed your last name, Pastelle."

"It's still hard to get used to. Handor is a good brother. He's been sheltered because of his health and because of his protective mother. Our trip has helped him get a better perspective," Pol said. "The time he spends at Deftnis will do the same."

"I think I'll take a nap," Handor said as he walked back into the sitting room. "I guess all of the travel has finally caught up with me."

Searl smiled. "Let me do a quick check on you and then I'll be on my way."

"I'll go see Demeron, then," Pol said. "He'll be here until I leave. I'll make sure you get a chance to ride."

"I look forward to it," Handor said walking with Searl back into his room.

Pol dropped his things in the other bedroom and called Vactor in. He pulled out his Demron sword.

"I'm was going to wait to show this to the Abbot and you, but look at this. I made this sword from a bar of alien metal I brought with me from Volia."

"From the Sleeping God's cave?" Vactor said.

"Something else happened in there. This is a Demron design. Look at it closely."

"Wards? You made this? Where did you learn all the patterns?"

"Shaping metal is just an extension of tweaking, you know that. The wards came from somewhere else." Pol gave him his knife. "This is the companion piece. I'll let you experiment with it."

Vactor pulled out the knife. "Same basic design. I've never seen anything like it."

"Neither have I," Pol said. "I'm heading out to see Demeron. I'll want that knife back."

He entered the hallway just as Shira and Ako opened the door.

"Do you want to meet Demeron, again?" Pol asked Shira.

"Can I come along?" Ako said. "I've never seen such a large Shinkyan stallion.

Pol grinned, looking forward to seeing the whole herd of the horses. Let's go.

The monastery seemed exactly the same. Pol recognized monks and acolytes as he walked through the grounds. Escorting the two pretty women certainly upset the normal routine of Deftnis.

They reached the gate that led to the plain. It was half open and Pol took a deep breath and opened it wider. The woods obscured the view of the plain and Pol wanted to run through the little forest, but he walked, listening to the two women speak in Shinkyan. Pol knew much of what they had to say but stayed silent to give them some privacy.

He turned a corner in the woods and saw his first glimpse of the plain. He called out to Demeron. Suddenly, the horses in the plain ran into a formation and walked towards Pol.

Demeron emerged from behind with two other horses and led them to stand in front of Pol.

These are all my friends. Demeron said. *I see you brought the Shinkyans.*

A golden-colored mare standing next to Demeron stepped forward and bent her head towards Shira.

Shira put her hand on the mare's nose and blinked a few times. "I think I've bonded to you," she said.

The horse said something to Shira, but Pol couldn't hear the mare's thoughts.

Her name is Amble. She and I became friends in Shinkya. She helped me get here, Demeron said. *I'm surprised she bonded so quickly with the Shinkyan. She has spurned a number of tries by the monks.*

Ako looked surprised at Shira's interaction with Amble. "You bonded so quickly."

"I think I know why," Shira said, looking at Pol. "She has a bond with Demeron. I don't understand what that is, but she sensed my own feelings about Pol."

"Impossible," Ako said. "They are just horses, after all."

"You wouldn't say that if you knew Demeron," Pol said.

Shinkyan horses are more than horses, Demeron said.

"I heard him," Ako said, with a shocked look on her face.

Pol smiled. "See?" He looked at the assembled horses. "Can I walk among your friends?" Pol asked Demeron, who nodded.

Pol took Shira's hand and they all walked among the horses, who parted for them. Demeron and Amble walked behind the three humans.

Tears came to Shira's eyes. "Amble has been telling me of the treatment many of these horses had." She touched the muzzles of the horses as they walked among them. "They love their new home, Ako. I support their freedom. Shinkya has plenty of the brothers and sisters of these beasts. It's time to give them a chance at their own life."

Ako paused, her hand pausing over a dark brown mare. "Oh. This one talks to me," she said. "She said she is willing to return to Shinkya with me if I will keep her. Sisters aren't allowed to bond, but what shall I do?"

"Take her to Shinkya. We will both return these two horses, who will be proof of this herd's love for their new home."

Amble nuzzled Shira. "Amble approves," she said, "as long as Demeron escorts her to Tishiko."

Amble will leave? Demeron said.

Pol watched Amble and his horse look each other in the eye. They moved their heads as they communicated.

It is settled, Demeron said. *I will go with you to Tishiko and I will say goodbye to Amble at the same time you say farewell to Shira. I will miss Amble, but she really wants a good Mistress more than she wants to stay here.*

"Why?" Pol said.

Pol could detect amusement in Demeron's thoughts. *Horses' relationships are different than humans. Amble is a very good friend and that is unusual for horses. I will be sad to see her go, but that is what she wants.*

"I guess that works out well," Pol finally said. "Can we go on a ride tomorrow?"

Demeron nodded his head. That was sufficient for him.

"Maybe all of us can go," Ako said. "Sunflower hasn't ever had a human ride her, but she's willing learn."

Pol let Demeron get back to the herd with Amble. Sunflower pranced off in a different direction.

The three of them walked back to the monastery.

"I am thrilled to know Amble," Shira said. She took Pol's arm. "She said she will be sad to leave Deftnis."

"Demeron said he'd be sad, too." Pol shrugged. Let's get back. It's close enough for dinner. I'm sure you two will be the center of attention at the refectory."

"Are we the only women in the monastery?" Ako said.

Pol smiled. "No, thank goodness. Acolytes do a lot of the housekeeping, just like Tesna, but we have plenty of female servants so you won't feel quite so alone."

~~~

Chapter Twenty

~

POL'S WORDS WERE TRUTHFULLY SPOKEN. Monks of all ages stared at Shira and Ako. Pol thought they would be stared at as much for being Shinkyans as being female guests.

As they left to go back to their apartments after dinner, Vactor took Pol aside. "Let's have a talk tonight in my classroom. I'll give your knife back."

His former instructor accompanied them to the administration building. Pol left Vactor while he retrieved his Demron sword.

Vactor had assembled fabric, wood, and metal items.

"The knife first," he said. Vactor took it out of the sheath and examined the blade. "I think the wards keep the blade sharp. Let's test for that now."

It seemed that Vactor was right. He ground the edge against a steel bar before and after cutting a sliver of wood. "No difference, but you can see how deep the blade cut into the steel. That means the steel is softer than the metal." He went to a chest in the room and removed a shiny sword and rubbed the sword's edge on Pol's sword. The degradation of the cutting edge of the steel sword was visible to Pol.

"That's enough. Now go over your experience in the same detail that you did with Malden Gastoria. He asked me to get the story directly from you."

Pol looked around to see if anyone lurked in the shadows and he quickly used his locator sense to verify that no one was in earshot before he described everything in detail, including all of Pol's experiences with the Demron essence.

"No voices?"

Pol shook his head. "Impressions, definitely those, but no communications like I have with Demeron."

"No possession, then. That's a good thing, not that we'd know what to do if something like that occurred," Vactor said looking a Pol's sword. "You didn't get that pattern from Volia or Eastril? I have no idea what weapons look like on Daera."

Pol chuckled. "Neither do I."

"Change into the Demron," Vactor said.

Pol took a deep breath and took on the features of the Demron. It was a near-painless change into the disguise this time. Could that also have been due to the alien essence?

"Definitely not human." Vactor felt the planes of Pol's face. "The skull is not much different. The aliens in the drawings looked human except for their faces? You know, I can't even detect that you are wearing a disguise. Is that something that the essence has done?"

"Maybe. The drawings in the cave looked a little different, but not many images were close up. I did see the face of the Sleeping God up close. She looked pretty much like I do now," Pol said.

He waited a bit while Vactor thought. The monk sighed. "I can't help you any more than just observing your magic. Now, show me what else you've learned."

Pol started with teleporting his shards. They put a block of wood against the wall. Pol teleported a splinter into it.

"Nasty," Vactor said. "I doubt if more than a handful of magicians in the Empire can do that. I certainly can't. The essence gives you strength?"

"Not physical or magical strength, actually, but I have more magical endurance. I still get hungry, but I don't feel the physical drain like I did before."

"Interesting," Vactor said. "It's all interesting. Now wards. I can do a few simple ones. I'll put them on this board and you tell me what you see."

Vactor's wards were all different colors. "I can't tell what they can do, just that they are there. This one is a pink block. This one is like strands of hair bunched together but not in a weave." Pol pointed to another one. "This one looks like frozen dark blue smoke."

Vactor told Pol what they did and asked him to remove them. Pol waved his hand casually over them and they all faded away. Vactor just stared at the board.

"It would take me minutes of concentration to remove what you did. I definitely see the wards differently than you do," Vactor said.

"I found that out in The Shards. People see wards differently except for the black wards at the guard station in Missibes. Shira and I saw black weaves, like a woven curtain."

"Our understanding of wards isn't particularly good. That's because they exist outside of a pattern and if you trained as a Black, you would learn that wards are not practiced by us."

Pol nodded. "Let me try to create wards. The essence gave me some insight, but I still feel I'm missing something." Pol relaxed and created the ward that would flash a bright light. Another would emit a shrieking sound, or so Pol intended. The last of the three was a tight weave created to stop Pol's blade. That was a personal experiment that Pol had been thinking about ever since they left Yastan.

"They won't hurt you, but you can use the steel sword to activate them. Look away from the first."

Vactor tripped the first two wards. Neither of them lasted more than three effects. Pol could see that more weaves would have made the wards work longer from the shock of knowledge he received at the library in Yastan. For the last ward, Vactor struck the weave with the steel sword and the wood below remained undamaged.

Pol took his Demron sword and slammed into the board. The wood dented, but the edge of the sword still didn't penetrate the ward.

"I have one more thing to do," Pol said. He took out a steel sliver and teleported it into the board. The sliver struck the ward and fell to the floor.

"That's similar to what Namion used."

"Namion? Namion Threshell?"

Pol told Vactor about the scholar's murder in Yastan. Malden sent the documents on Pol to Deftnis before they had solved the murder.

"I wondered how someone could deflect my slivers. Namion wore a warded coat."

"Light armor."

Pol retrieved the Shardian warded cloak. "These are wards. It's hard for me not to see the colored wards. I thought they were splotches of color on the coat, but to Fadden, the colors aren't there. It just looks dirty.

"Those are wards?"

Pol nodded. "Flat and tightly woven, just like this. I fought a Shardian pattern-master with this coat on. He would have taken off my shoulder if I hadn't worn this. I still bruised from the stroke. It performs the same function as a well-made magicial shield, but it is constant protection."

Vactor looked closely at the wards. "Tiny and tightly woven, like you said. Can you duplicate this?"

Pol looked down at the board. "I think I just did. The weaves can be smaller and that will make the ward flatter. Someone could wear this instead of armor."

"Not a full substitute, but in a number of ways, better," Vactor said. "There are more magicians who have the potential to manipulate wards than can teleport your little splinters."

Pol had a question for Vactor. "What did the Imperial Magicians do to eliminate the compulsion on the South Salvan soldiers?"

"They developed a tweak that eliminated mind control. It took a large number of magicians spread apart to do it, but it worked. The tweak to safely remove compulsion never worked. So they used an ancient tweak, originally used to eliminate a truth spell that wiped the brain clean of any spell. The thing was, the compelled soldiers all died if they had any significant magical ability."

Pol shivered. Darrol and Val would have been killed on the battlefield if Pol hadn't found them first. "Do you know how many men died?"

"Not so many as you might think. Maybe fifty or a hundred out of thousands, but with all the fighting, who knows how many."

Pol sighed. It had to be done if nothing else than for self-defense, he thought.

"I think I've had enough for tonight," Pol said.

That brought a yawn from Vactor. "It's after midnight. That was a good session. I still have tests, but they can wait for a day or two. Searl is going to do a deep examination of Handor, tomorrow. Why don't you attend?"

Pol nodded. "I will."

An acolyte stopped Pol as he walked to the infirmary.

"Pol Cissert?"

Pol looked into a very familiar face. Nater Grainell looked significantly more fit than the last time he met him.

"I never knew how much of a reputation you had at Deftnis. When I tell people I knew you, they stop and listen."

Pol smiled. Nater's tone had changed a lot in the last year. "How do you like Deftnis?"

"It's okay. I'll be spending another year and then return to my father's estate. It's been good for me to get away." He wore an orange cord around his robe.

"Thanks for letting me borrow your face. I found it useful more than once."

Nater batted Pol's comment away. "I heard about what you did last year. I might have been dead in North Salvan if it wasn't for you."

"I nearly was dead in North Salvan, so I'll take that as a compliment," Pol grinned, very happy to see the change in the youth. "I have to head to the infirmary."

"Oh," Nater turned a bit red. "Of course."

Pol had forgotten about the fact that Nater might have gone to Tesna if Val hadn't intervened. At least Nater might have been another life saved as a result of his mission. The youth might not have heard of Pol's elevation yet, and that was a good thing in his mind.

The infirmary didn't look any different from the last time Pol visited. He had escorted Handor to the front desk. Searl showed up with the same two healers who often helped Pol with the illness that Searl had eventually cured.

"Come this way," Searl said.

"Are you a proud grandpa?" Pol asked as they walked down the corridor.

Searl turned and gleamed. "I am. A fine baby boy. You'll have to meet him before you leave. My Anna has just started her nunnery in Mancus Port. You can go over and see my new grandson and show Shira how we teach healing and magic to the Empire's women."

"I'll do that." Pol said as the healers in front led Handor into a familiar examination room.

Pol helped Handor onto the high, thinly padded bed. "I spent a lot of time on this thing," he said. Pol walked around so that the four of them surrounded Handor.

"Have you kept up your healing studies?" Searl asked.

Pol nodded. "Battle healing only, I'm afraid."

Searl looked at the other two healers. "Having Pol with us gives us another who can look deeply into Handor's body. This is instruction for him, so forgive me for being a bit chattier than usual."

The other two healers nodded towards Searl. "It is always instruction for us, Master Healer," one of them said.

Searl nodded and closed his eyes. "He is now asleep." As he worked he told them where he was looking. Pol could see that Handor's heart was strong and worked well. The source of his illness was, as suspected, different from his own.

"I've already been over the defective organ structure that plagued Pol when Handor first came, but I will show you so when he needs further treatment, you can benefit from my diagnosis."

Pol smiled at the confidence in Searl's words. He had saved this man from a life of dissipation under the influence of the natural drug, minweed.

"Ah," Searl said. "Look at the growth gland," Searl said.

"Where?" Pol asked.

"At the base of the brain. It's small. You might see it as a purplish gray lump about the size of the tip of your little finger or a large pea," Searl said.

Pol found it. "It's covered with bone?"

"It is," one of the healers said.

Pol looked closer. "There are tiny nodules inside. Is that normal?"

Searl shook his head. "It is not. That is Handor's problem. I can fix that but it will take months, one little nodule at a time. If I removed them all at once, the growth gland might cease to function or there might be unpredictable side effects. That gland does a lot of things for the body and I have only seen this once before and I went too fast, then. I won't risk Handor's well-being by being hasty."

Pol thought back to the time he removed the compulsion spell too fast from Val's brain. Now he knew that long lasting spells were more like wards than tweaks. "I really do understand."

"You do?"

Pol nodded. "I learned to removed compulsion spells. Experimenting is not a good thing to do when under duress."

Searl smiled and leaned over the bed to pat Pol on the shoulder. "Don't forget that." He turned back to Handor. "We might as well start today. Observe."

Pol concentrated on the gland while Searl tweaked out one of the tiny nodules. Handor flinched in his sleep.

"I don't know if he feels pain, but we will let him settle down for a week," Searl said. "What else can we give him?"

The healers began a conversation on the relative merits of herb mixtures. Pol knew most of the herbs, but when they talked about combinations, he just stood and let them talk without bothering to understand.

Their knowledge set them apart as true healers and Pol knew that took years of study and practice. He felt inadequate.

"Don't look so down, Pol. We are the only four in the monastery who can see that little gland in action. Those nodules are called cysts and we will be looking more closely into Handor's body for more in his organs. Handor's treatment will take time, so he's in the right place."

"Will it affect his magic?" Pol said.

Searl shrugged. "We still don't know what makes a person more able to tweak than another. He's in the right place to evaluate that as well. Deftnis will be a refuge for him so he can return to Yastan in a year or two in much better health."

And Akonai Haleaku's visits could keep Handor informed about the state of the Empire. Pol smiled, no longer thinking about his inability to heal illnesses. He felt good about helping his brother.

Paki declined to accompany Searl, and Pol's Shinkyan friends to Port Mancus, having just eaten. Pol, Ako, and Shira changed their appearance on the way across the water, still wary of showing themselves in Port Mancus.

Searl led them to a walled estate at the edge of the port. "Garylle Handson, the mayor of Deftnis Port, found this for us. The monastery is putting up the funds for the nunnery. It will be called Mancus Abbey."

He sounded very proud of the place as they walked through a gate. The large house had new decorative iron coverings over the windows. That brought a smile to Pol's face. Anna Lassler, Searl's daughter, had a husband who was a wrought iron master.

Anna and a few other women spilled out the front door to greet them.

"Father, who have you brought?"

Pol shed his disguise, as did Shira and Ako.

"Pol! I wondered if you would ever return to Deftnis. Welcome to the Abbey. You brought two Shinkyans with you. Welcome to you, too. Please come in."

Anna led them into a hallway, and then the group moved to a large sitting room.

"We are just getting started here," Anna said. She looked at Ako. "I'm sure you do things differently in Shinkya, but we separate men and women for training in the Empire. Mancus Abbey will be devoted to the healing arts and magic. Any of our acolytes who wish to train with weapons will be sent to Yastan. It's part of our charter with the Emperor."

Ako leaned forward. "We separate men and women, but for slightly different reasons," she said.

Pol knew that powerful Shinkyan males rarely made it past Handor's age, so the curse that the Demrons had afflicted on male magicians forced some of Shinkyan training decisions.

"Do you know how to heal as well as your father?" Shira said to Anna, but she glanced and smiled at Searl.

"I do my part," Anna said. "No one can look into a person's body as well as Father."

"With the exception of Pol," Searl said. "He was able to spot the tiny cysts in Handor's body." He cleared his throat. "Of course, I was able to see them as well."

Pol smiled. That was quite a compliment coming for Searl.

He sat back and let the conversation flow around him. Ako seemed especially interested in Anna's efforts.

"Perhaps I could come here for some training," Ako said. "I am a Sister, but I'm a little tired of spying all the time and living in a disguise."

Her admission startled Pol. He wondered if the Shinkyan Queen would let one of their Sisters mingle with Imperials. Ako had spent three years in Alsador and perhaps in other cities earlier.

"You are interested in healer training?" Anna said, leaning forward. She didn't disguise her interest in Ako's offer.

"Maybe I could provide some magic training in exchange," Ako said.

One of the nuns brought in a baby. It wasn't newborn, but young enough not to be walking.

Searl's eyes lit up. "My boy!" He held out his arms for the woman to give the baby to his grandfather.

Anna stood. "Why don't I show you our vision for the nunnery while a doting grandfather spoils his only grandchild." She smiled at Searl.

They walked out of the room, still listening to Searl make unintelligible noises.

Anna showed them the second level. "We will start out small. As you know, nuns are not celibate at most abbeys in the Empire, but we do insist on keeping men out of the premises except for servants. Married nuns will live in Port Mancus."

Ako nodded her head with a smile. "That's much more sensible, don't you think, Shira?"

"It is," Shira said, disengaging from holding Pol's hand.

"You didn't tell me Sisters were celibate."

Shira cleared her throat and blushed. "They are when they are in Tishiko, but Sisters don't stay in Tishiko."

"For a reason, Pol," Ako said.

Shira took his hand again and squeezed. She whispered. "You are a reason." She smiled.

Anna showed Ako a large bedroom. "This could be yours." They walked in while Shira and Pol stayed in the corridor.

Shira looked at Pol and narrowed her eyes. "Did you talk to her about staying?"

Pol shook his head. "I'm as surprised as you are. I've never heard of a Shinkyan nun before."

"She might be the first. I think I'm a bad influence," Shira said.

"A good influence, in my mind."

Shira put her head on Pol's shoulder. "A good influence, then." She looked up with damp eyes. "I'll miss you and I'll miss the Empire." She clamped her lips together. "There, I said it."

"Aren't Imperials not much better than dogs or sheep?"

Shira looked away. "I never said you were."

Pol circled her with his arms. "I think I know how you think of me."

She hugged him back. "You do, and that will give me problems back in Tishiko."

"Don't let it. I'll be with you when we get there."

She pulled away. "You can't fight centuries of culture."

"I'm the Great Ancestor, right? Aren't I supposed to bring change?"

"Great Ancestor, my foot. I've known you for a year and wouldn't I know if you were the Great Ancestor or not?"

"My sword…"

Shira's eyebrows shot up. "Don't mention that!" She rubbed her arms, fending off a shiver. "There are plenty of people in Tishiko who will do anything to keep the Great Ancestor from appearing, ever."

Pol nodded. "Then we will have to be circumspect."

"Don't claim to be someone you're not," Shira said.

"I won't. Tishiko isn't Fassin," Pol said.
"That's for sure."

~ ~ ~

Chapter Twenty-One

~

"DEMERON HAS SOMETHING TO TELL YOU," Vactor said. "He didn't want me to let you know."

"Demeron?" Pol said, surprised, but then he relaxed. "Oh, I forgot he can talk to other humans. What did he have to say?"

"Go for a ride with him, by yourself."

Pol nodded and called Demeron to the stable.

"How are Amble and Ako's horse getting along?"

We are a close group, Demeron said. *The rest of the herd will be sad to see them go, but then we all look forward to bonding with humans who we get to choose.*

Pol smiled. "That's right. You didn't choose me," he said.

I didn't have to bond with you, but I liked you from the start. Amble likes Shira, a lot. I think both of them had a hard time in Shinkya.

Pol patted Demeron on the back while he stood on a stool while he saddled the horse. "You've been through a lot," Pol said running his hand along the bumps that the scars made from Demeron's clashes with wolves.

So have you, Demeron said. *It's just that you've been damaged inside. You have a different feel since we were together before.*

Pol told him about his personal experience in the cave.

I knew something was different. It isn't a taint, Demeron said. *But I know something has been added to my feel for you.*

"And what is different about you? I thought it was because I forgot how you feel, but you've changed, too. Is that what Vactor said you wanted to discuss?"

Demeron dipped his head. *It is. I have gained the ability to tweak.*

"As in tweak the pattern? Work magic?" Pol said.

I gained the ability in Tishiko. An Elder, one of their senior magicians, said she was a Scorpion. That is a political faction in Shinkya. She tried to force herself into my mind and make me stay in Tishiko, but something happened. I resisted and absorbed her magic. Did I do something wrong?

"Wrong? How can a horse acquiring magic be wrong? I don't understand how something like that could happen, but I'd say it's admirable. More than admirable, it's amazing," Pol said. "Did she give you any inkling about why you reacted as you did?"

I'm not sure I understood it at the time, but Vactor said it has something to do with our bond. When we were together, some of your abilities rubbed off. Enough so I could absorb her power. I remembered enough about listening to you talking to your friends along the way to fiddle with the pattern. Pol could sense Demeron's version of a shrug

"What can you do?"

I can't teleport like you can, although that would be very useful for a four-legged creature, but I can nudge small things and give a strong enough push to knock a mounted human to the ground. I can resist shields and create shields of my own. If a person with a sword wishes to slash at me, I can create a shield good enough to turn a blade. Vactor verified that. He said with a little training, I might be as powerful as a Blue magician.

Pol couldn't help but grin as he leaped onto the saddle. "Shall we go into Deftnis Port? I'm sure I can persuade the stable master at the monastery stable at the port to give you a bucketful of grain."

Demeron pranced a bit. *I'd like that!*

They rode out the open gate and down to the little town by the sea. Pol loved to ride with Shira, but sometimes, like the present, he enjoyed the companionable silence Demeron and he shared as they traveled to the port.

Pol stopped by an open field and used location to see if anyone was near. He wondered. "Can you locate?"

Demeron whinnied. *I can. Humans show up as faint dots, but I can detect horses and know their emotions by the color. Horses don't have the emotional range that humans do.*

"Bend the grass by the road," Pol said.

Demeron pointed his head where Pol pointed and the stalks bent to the right. That brought a grin to Pol's face. "We will find some uses for your magic." He leaned over and patted Demron on the neck. "I'm very glad we are together again."

You like me better than Shira? Demeron said.

"I like you both, but in different ways," Pol smiled at his horse's comment.

You like her in a human way, and I can tell that you are sad that she will leave you.

"I am, but now that I have you back, you'll help lessen the pain."

I'm not sure I can, but together, we will try.

They proceeded down to the port and decided to make the same trip every day. Demeron suggested that Pol invite Ako and Shira, but asked to go alone from time to time.

And so they did. One day after attending to Handor's third treatment and after two weeks at Deftnis, Shira and Pol rode their Shinkyan horses down to the port. Ako and Fadden begged off, claiming they needed to organize supplies for the trip to Tishiko.

"Demeron still tries to teach magic to interested horses, but none of them have any talent other than being able to communicate with someone they've bonded," Pol said.

"Amble is a bit disappointed, but she now has the faith that I can protect her," Shira said.

Pol didn't want to contradict. After talking to Demeron about Tishiko a number of times, Pol didn't trust anyone in that city. Shira always laughed the factions off, and Ako stayed quiet on the subject.

He looked to his right as they made their way down the road and noticed a ship sailing towards the port. Pol took a glance to the left and saw another sailing on the other side of the isle.

"Do you see those ships?" Pol said.

"What?" Shira said. She must have been having a conversation with Amble. "Ships to our right and left?" Shira paused. "Oh. You think it's an invasion? Those aren't Shinkyan ships."

"Namion or Grostin." Pol said.

"Or both!" She turned Amble up the hill. "I'll warn the monastery." She paused. "And Amble will assemble the herd."

Pol nodded. There were monks and guards living in Deftnis Port, but not enough to stop two shipfuls of any competent enemy.

He yelled back to Shira. "Don't forget. Everyone gets shielded. Even the horses!"

She nodded and waved back before taking off up the hill.

"We don't have much time, Demeron," Pol said.

The Shinkyan stallion began to move and then took small sips of magic like Pol had taught him to speed up. He moved faster than anything else on the ground.

Pol stopped at Garylle Handson's house and threw open the unlocked gate.

Garylle stomped out of his house.

"Two ships converging on the port. We need to be prepared," Pol said.

"Shira and I might be the targets or it might be Handor and me, again, or all three."

Garylle nodded. "Go to the docks, I'll be there presently." He ran inside his house.

Pol proceeded directly to the town's docking square and stopped at the dock master's shed. "Do you expect any ships in today? There are two ships heading to Deftnis from each side of the island."

The dock master stood up. "Nothing that big until next week. You're not thinking it's an invasion?"

Pol nodded. "I didn't think Deftnis has ever been attacked."

"Not in either of our lifetimes. I'll call the guard and wait for Garylle."

The man began to ring a bell that hung outside his shack. Guards and residents ran to the docks. Garylle finally arrived, now decked in armor. He began to issue instructions.

"Not yet," Pol said. He put a shield on every person's mind before he raced up the right-hand road to follow the ship into port.

There was only one other landing point on the right side of the island. Monks found evidence that South Salvans had landed when Pol previously lived at the monastery. Pol and Demeron stopped at the cliff above the little shingle and watched the ship sail by. Pol located and found one hundred men inside the ship.

"It is an invasion," he told Demeron.

Seven horses. None of them are Shinkyan.

"Pol leaned over and gave a gentle tug to Demeron's mane. "We make a good team, you and I."

Demeron shook his head and reared up on his hindquarters before sprinting back to the port.

By the time Pol arrived, fifty monks lined up on the docks. Monk Edgebare did most of the talking. Just as Pol showed up, the men disbursed, leaving Edgebare, Jonness and Garylle talking to the dock master.

"One of the ships holds about one hundred men and seven horses," Pol said.

"Seven?" Jonness said. A white horse nudged the monk in the back. "Demron located them, right?"

Pol nodded. "He did. I suspect about the same in the other ship. They should be in sight soon. We sighted the one coming from the right of the port."

"Where is Shira?" Jonness said.

"Getting my weapons." Pol looked out to approaching vessels.

"We've drilled for this often enough, although I don't think we ever did while you were at Deftnis. There are monks at the monastery and acolytes are all over the Isle in twos making sure there aren't any flanking attacks. The docks are the best place to land an invading force, by far."

Pol nodded. He paced around while Demeron stood next to the Jonness' Shinkyan stallion. They looked like friends, but Pol had no idea what relationship Demeron had with the rest of the herd. Demeron had told him that the white horse was the former leader of the herd.

He heard hoofbeats coming up from behind and looked as Shira and Amble drew up. Fadden and Ako accompanied them. They looked ready to fight. Shira dismounted and untied Pol's magician's cloak wrapping up a chainmail shirt, a tunic, his Demron sword and knife, as well as a small sack. She had even included Pol's conical hat. He shrugged and put it on. It might stop something.

"Thank you," Pol said as he peeked inside the small bag to find an assortment of Shinkyan throwing knives and a generous supply of metal splinters. He began to buckle up and distribute the knives and splinters around his body.

"I'm ready." He didn't ask for permission and boosted everyone's shields around him. He nodded to Shira.

"I've already done that," Garylle said.

Pol nodded. Still, a bit of reinforcement wouldn't hurt.

He heard a horn blowing off in the distance off to his left.

"One of the ships is coming," the dock master said.

They saw it round the edge of the harbor, and then another horn announcing the second ship. Pol looked between them and yet a third ship, and then a fourth approached taking up the middle.

The dock master chuckled. "Four ships for two docks. This will be fun to watch."

"Not if they begin shooting arrows," Garylle said.

A contingent of guards arrived along with a cartful of shields.

The gruff mayor of Port Deftnis pulled out two shields. "One for you and one for me," he said, extending one to the port master.

"This is madness," Fadden said.

"Something is not right, here," Pol said. "Do they have a secret weapon?"

A forest of ladders appeared on the ships.

Jonness looked on in disbelief. "Those are siege ladders. They can use them to get off those boats and then lug them up to the monastery."

"And that's why our dock master isn't laughing right now," Garylle looked at the man who backed up a step.

"Where are the ships from?" Pol said. They looked like ships from the Empire, but the Emperor wouldn't need to invade Deftnis to retrieve his son.

"Why are they here?" Shira asked.

Pol had a sinking feeling. "They are after Handor and me," he said. He heard the flapping of wings as ten birds flew to the north over their heads. A flight of arrows emerged from the ships, but only a few birds plummeted into the sea. "Less arrows to use on us."

"But why now?"

"Because we were more protected in Yastan. Maybe they think the monks at Deftnis are inept. If it were me, I'd wait until we were in southern Finster, where there are fewer people."

"Not Shinkya?" Ako said. Pol could tell she tested him.

"The Shinkyans know we are headed their way. They would wait for us to come to them and some factions might well be doing that," Pol said. "We will leave Deftnis as soon as we take care of the attackers."

"That's spoken with confidence," Jonness said. "Are you so sure of yourself?"

Pol smiled. "I've lived at Deftnis long enough to know the monastery has teeth and claws." The sound of many hooves made them turn around and watched Shinkyan horses filling the square and separating into groups, just as if they were an army. "And hooves," Pol said.

I don't need to send anyone to the monastery to retrieve the herd, Demeron said.

"You won't like the arrows," Pol looked back at the ships.

They won't like big horses who know how to fight together, Demeron said. *But you have a point.*

"So do the arrows," Pol said out loud.

The horses trotted out of the square, splitting into two major groups. They looked like well-drilled soldiers to Pol.

"Tell them to get close to the backs of buildings that face the harbor so they are protected from any arrows that fall." The horses would be exposed if they didn't seek cover. When the invaders landed, then the horses could attack. Pol knew the arrows would come again and within moments another hail of arrows flew to the left and the right before another flight headed straight towards them.

Pol put up a shield around the tight group that watched.

"We have three hundred more men and women ready to flood the square as soon as they set foot on the isle," Garryle said.

"And over one hundred horses who know how to fight without

riders," Jonness said. "Lightning has gone back to lead the herd that is protecting the monastery."

The ships glided into the edge of the harbor. None of them even tried to dock at the two piers. The front ladders slapped down onto the pavement and others splashed into the water. Men scurried down to line up on the pier.

"No arrows?" Pol said.

"Not yet." Jonness raised his arm, but a shock of mind control hit them.

"They have magicians on board," Garryle said holding his head.

"We can't have this," Pol climbed up on Demeron. "There's no time to parley." He didn't wait for the others and charged into the soldiers. The two units of horses emerged from the side streets and began to fight the enemy troops.

Pol checked his shields and located a group of magicians on leftmost ship. "They are yours to command. Don't worry about me," Pol said to Demeron as he tweaked a blast of air, widening a gap in the invaders' line. He jumped off Demeron and ran up a ladder, fighting soldiers on the ship's deck using every pattern-master technique he could.

His Demron sword had never been in combat but it certainly proved up to the task. The sword made deep cuts into the edges of enemy blades. It clove through chainmail as if they were made of twine.

The cloak turned blades and the cloak, the tunic, and the chainmail shirt kept the battering to a barely tolerable level, while he fought through the soldiers and confronted the magicians who, with fear in their eyes, began to concentrate on Pol. They were attacking him with a compulsion spell. His eyes began to water as he struggled to retain his concentration. He pulled out his splinters and teleported, but they fell harmless to the ground.

That wouldn't do, he thought. He used more than a sip of magic and thrust his warded blade through the shields and into the first magician. The magicians' protection lessened just a bit and Pol capitalized on it.

He didn't like slaughtering others, but compulsion deserved a death sentence. As he rained destruction on the magicians, all remnants of the shield burst into nothingness. The last magician ran, but Pol killed him with a thrown Shinkyan knife.

He found himself surrounded by soldiers and realized he had gone too far as the first enemy arrow thudded into his shield. Pol teleported himself to the railing and jumped into the water, clutching onto his sword and his hat.

He swam further to the left where there weren't any ships and climbed up the ladder on the opposite side of the empty pier. He had used that ladder many times before and was glad it was there. The swim had taken away most of his physical strength.

The fighting continued on the dock, but the horses and monks, probably mostly pattern-masters were killing or disabling most of the enemy soldiers.

Pol recognized a face in the enemy. He waded into the battle and put one of the enemy leaders to sleep, and then he began to do the same to as many as he could.

When the other monks saw Pol's actions, they began to slow their fighting and sought to put the invaders to sleep whenever they could.

Finally, when the fighting ebbed in the square, monks began to flood up the ladders and into the ships.

After less than an hour of heavy fighting, Port Deftnis had withstood the attack.

"Make sure Handor is safe," Pol said to Shira and Ako. "I have a lot of work to remove compulsion here."

Pol went to the first man he put to sleep and put his hand on the man's head. He knew Jamey Carter had no magical ability and the compulsion quickly turned into mist. The effort to put the enemy asleep saved over one hundred lives.

Healers from the monastery took over from the swordsmen, administering to fellow monks and the citizens of Deftnis port, as well as the enemy. Their efforts included the fighting horses.

Pol was surprised that only ten of Demeron's herd died in the battle. The attacker's horses never did make it to shore.

As he walked through the sleeping attackers, he recognized more faces from Borstall.

"You look disturbed or afraid. What is it?" Fadden said.

"A lot of these men are from Borstall. All of them have been under compulsion."

"What?"

Pol nodded. "These might not have been after Handor at all."

Paki showed up and looked as stricken as Pol felt. "These soldiers are from home," he said.

"I'll bet birds went out to North Salvan before Lord Wibon left for Volia," Fadden said.

"I can see the pattern would still be consistent if Wibon diverted his ship to North Salvan and headed straight to Borstall." Pol didn't want to believe Grostin could sink so low, so fast, but the pattern was obvious.

Paki got up from one of the men. "Do you think this was a suicide mission?"

"We can ask," Fadden said, waving his hand over the lines of sleeping attackers.

Pol nodded. "The magicians didn't get off the ship, nor did the sailors. Luckily, their planning didn't include a herd of Shinkyan horses—"

"Or your ability to defeat the magicians and eliminate their spells," Fadden said.

The Abbot rode down from the monastery with Vactor. "Not a pretty sight. We found four groups of assassins. None of them made it inside Deftnis and the few who were coherent enough to answer questions only mentioned they were after you."

"Are they all dead?" Paki asked.

"About half. We put the rest to sleep when they refused to surrender. It looks like you did the same. One of the healers recognized the compulsion spells. He removed them. Two of the survivors died when the healer lifted the spell."

"Magicians," Pol said.

The Abbot sighed. "Waste of talent."

Pol made another pass through the survivors and found two magicians among them, but they weren't powerful, so he cleaned them in one long go.

"The Emperor needs to be told."

Abbot Pleagor patted Pol on the shoulder. "Don't worry. Birds will go out in an hour or so to follow-up with the ones we sent at the invasion's start."

"Jamey is waking up," Paki said.

Pol rushed over.

"Pol! You're alive."

"No thanks to you," Pol said with a smile. "What happened?"

Jamey sat up and looked around. "Grostin and the remnants of the Tesnan magicians. Grostin called a meeting of my guards, where his magicians put the compulsion spell on us. Everything is pretty hazy after that. I remember they loaded us onto ships. We set sail for Deftnis some weeks ago."

"Right after we left for Yastan from Alsador," Fadden said. "Wibon must have sent birds to North Salvan as he left the Listyan capital. He must have arranged for someone to track you to Deftnis."

"Grostin, I refuse to call him king of anything, has his fingers in all kinds of subterfuge in the Empire. Lord Wibon is a close ally and passed us just south of Shinkya." Jamey said. "That's where I heard about Manda. Lord Wibon doesn't like you, but I do." The man managed a grin.

"What about Queen Isa?"

"She will eventually be swallowed up with the rest if the Emperor doesn't act. Grostin can just bottle South Salvan up and gobble her up at his leisure. He's worse than King Astor ever was."

Pol had his doubts about that.

"Amonna?"

Jamey smiled. "She'll be in Yastan about now," he said, but then he winced and put a hand to his forehead. "I have an awful headache."

"So will the others who survived."

"One of Grostin's new magicians said you'd never survive a circle of Tesnan monks," Jamey smiled. "They boasted about a shield that stops your little metal pieces, but I guess they failed."

"They succeeded, but there are other ways around their shield." Pol said and didn't elaborate.

"None of you can go back to Borstall, now," Paki said.

"Yes we can," Jamey said. "I'll convince the survivors to head north to join the Imperial Army. I'm sure they will be making a return to North Salvan."

Fadden shook his head. "Not if Grostin has stirred up enough trouble to keep Hazett occupied."

The other invaders began to wake up. None of them attacked the monks once they woke.

"I don't remember much about the fight, but did I see horses fighting as a group?" Jamey said.

"Shinkyan horses," Paki said. "Demeron leads them."

"Who's Demeron?" Jamey wrinkled his brow.

"My Shinkyan horse. The one who ran away at the Tesnan monastery."

"You found him! Lucky us. You might be dead if it weren't for them."

Pol didn't bother to contradict his friend, but Jamey and his fellow North Salvans would all be dead if it wasn't for Pol and Demeron working together. He had no doubts the monks would have prevailed.

"There were assassin teams amongst us," Jamey said.

"How many?" Pol asked.

"Five. Three of them were led by magicians. They were under orders to kill the Shinkyan girl and you."

"Five!" Pol felt a shiver go through him. Shira was up at the monastery. He looked around for Demeron and called to him. In a few moments, Demeron showed up, bleeding from shallow wounds.

"We have to return to the monastery. There is another assassin team to find. This one is led by a magician, too."

On the way to the monastery, Pol wondered how many magicians survived the Emperor's army. Evidently, more than he thought. And now Shira was exposed.

"Instruct the horses to protect Shira."

I already have, Demeron said. *Time to use a little magic.* Suddenly, Demeron sped up.

The doors to the monastery were still closed, but they opened when Pol yelled to have it opened.

Edgebare yelled down at him from the wall. "What is the matter?"

"There are five assassin teams. The one we haven't found yet has a magician. Do you know where Shira is?"

"In the basement of the administration building protecting Handor."

Pol nodded and Demeron disgorged him at the entrance. Pol ran up the steps to find the front door locked. That door hadn't been locked the entire time Pol had been at Deftnis. He drew his blade and tweaked the lock. He pushed it open into an empty lobby.

Making himself invisible, Pol walked silently through the lobby. He spotted two monks. One was too injured to help, but Pol healed the worst of the other's life-threatening injuries. Their wounds were fresh. How could the team have slipped inside the monastery unseen? He located a group of people in the basement. The assassins had reached one of their targets.

He slipped down the stairs, hearing voices at the bottom. Pol vaguely remembered one of them.

He peeked around a corner and saw Shira, Ako, and Handor on their knees. They folded their hands behind their backs. He saw no recognition in their eyes. For some reason, Pol's shield hadn't protected them.

Pol reinforced his shield as strongly as he could.

One of the men turned and Pol recognized Sakwill's face. That didn't make sense. He never thought of Sakwill as being particularly strong. Perhaps his lack of ability was an act? Pol shook his head at the thought until he spied a second magician. This was his father's Court Magician at Borstall. The man had fooled them all.

Pol thought he detected a film of mind control, but then so did most of the Tesnan monks. Pol wondered if the Court Magician was responsible for the easy entry into Borstall Castle by the South Salvans. Perhaps he had ensorcelled Seen, the captured soldier and others to open the Borstall Castle gates wide open.

Pol took a sliver and sent it into the magician. The man turned around when he heard the tinkling sound of the sliver sliding off the magician's shield.

Pol sent a sliver into the rest of the assassin group in quick succession. All the men dropped except for Sakwill and the Court Magician.

Sakwill cried out and looked afraid, but the other man was unfazed and turned towards Pol's direction. "We've spread the secret of protecting us from your little shards of metal," he turned but his gaze showed he didn't know exactly where Pol stood.

The man's gloating sickened Pol. He looked back at the three on their knees. They began to rise, so Pol put them to sleep and Sakwill sunk to the floor with them. The Court Magician remained standing.

"I can kill them with a snap of my fingers," the man said.

"You are Tesna-trained?"

He turned with a sneering smile, still not knowing exactly where Pol stood. "Of course. You stopped most of the monks, but there are still many ex-Tesnans out in the world."

"There will be one less."

The man squinted and the Shinkyans and Handor began to moan in their sleep.

Pol threw a thick shield around them and they stopped. The magician's eyes widened. "You can protect them from a distance?"

Pol materialized and nodded, facing the magician with his Demron sword.

The magician looked at Pol's weapon. "Brutal looking, but I'm sure it's all for show. Grostin told me how you've tricked everyone into thinking you are more powerful than you are."

"You've seen my power," Pol said.

"Lifting people? Removing mind control? You think that's power?"

"Teleporting weapons, Disguises. Can just any magician do that? Locating? Defeating a circle of magicians on the ship? I just did that with my all-for-show sword."

Pol's retort removed the magician's smile.

"Do you see the wards on my coat? You obviously don't see the wards embedded in my sword."

The magician made an unpleasant face. "Wards aren't important. Compulsion is the way to power."

"Compulsion is a ward. Haven't you figured that out?"

"It is?"

Pol advanced on the magician. The man bathed Pol in fire, but Pol's shields held. He put out his sword and pushed into the magician's shield. He wiggled the blade and it began to work its way through the magician's defense.

The magician backed up against the wall. "You aren't supposed to be able to do that."

"Is it because I'm too weak, or am I just acting, you know, for show?"

Pol continued to push the blade all the way through the shield. The magician grabbed the sword with his hand, but the blade bit through his skin. The man screamed in pain. Pol quickly put an end to him.

He threw the sword aside and went to Shira. She was fast asleep. Handor was the weakest magician, and it only took Pol a few minutes to unpeel the purple patch of compulsion on his stepbrother's mind.

Sakwill wasn't even under mind control. Pol would let the monastery judge him.

He lugged both Shira and Ako into their rooms and laid them on their beds.

The Abbot rushed in. "You've taken care of the assassins?"

"One is still alive," Pol said, "Sakwill. He's asleep. He wasn't even under mind control. I won't tell you what he deserves."

The Abbot's face hardened, and he gave Pol a curt nod.

"Ako and Shira both have been compelled. The layers are thick, and it will take some time to remove the wards. I'm convinced compulsion is a ward. The Tesnan's didn't even know it. Perhaps Onkar or Abbot Festor did." Pol nodded "I'm sure Festor would have known, but it wasn't presented that way in the Tesnan texts." Pol shook his head.

"Handor's compulsion is gone. I suggest taking him up to the infirmary. I'll be down here for a few days with Shira and Ako, anyway."

The Abbot left. Paki and Fadden clomped down the stairs.

"Pleagor told us that Shira and Ako are ensorcelled. We'll head back up and keep everyone away from you. The monks will be busy interrogating each and every survivor. If there are evidences of thick compulsion, they said they will keep the men asleep until you are through with the Shinkyans," Fadden said. He looked long at Ako and shook his head. "Will they be all right?"

"Did Val seem any different when you worked with him in Yastan?"

Fadden shook his head, but then he figured out what Pol had meant and left.

Pol began on Shira, who had the thickest patch of compulsion. It was worse than Val's. He worked for quite awhile, taking off slice after slice before he had to stop.

Paki brought down a tray filled with food. "The Abbot thought you would need to eat a lot."

"I do, but there is enough here for both of us to share."

Paki sat down across from Pol in the table in the women's apartment.

"Did you see who the magician was?"

Paki nodded. "I helped carry him all the way up the stairs. I guess he was probably as much to blame for the fall of Borstall Castle as anyone, right?"

Pol nodded. "He probably continued Bythia's work of controlling the royal family. He deserved a slower death, but," Pol shrugged. He was tired of revenge. He felt a little better that the man was dead, but if Grostin was willing to throw the Court Magician away, he wondered who stood by Grostin's side now? That was a question for another time. At least it couldn't be Namion, who never would have had the chance to make it all the way to Borstall since Pol had returned.

Whoever developed the ward that stopped his splinters was a master magician, most likely technically superior to Pol, although that wouldn't take much considering Pol's magic was all about power rather than technique.

"You're not talking," Paki said.

"No, I'm thinking. We are leaving Deftnis as soon as I get these two on their feet. You can choose to stay or come. It will be dangerous to leave Deftnis with us. We will be riding hard and fast. No comforts until we reach Shinkya, but then I have no idea what their perception of comfort is."

"I'm with you. Kell is in Yastan. Fadden and I will come. Darrol was severely injured fighting an assassin team or he'd be coming, too."

Pol hadn't had the opportunity to interact with Darrol very much while he escorted Shira around Deftnis. Pol nodded and wiped his mouth. "I'm finished," he said. "Leave the rest when you are done."

Paki continued to eat while Pol started on Ako. He sliced off layer after layer. Her patch was a little smaller than Val's but thicker than Darrol's, which came off easily when he removed his in South Salvan. Darrol's was more like Handor's compulsion. It was an indicator that Handor's magic was limited.

Shira lost a few more layers before Pol was exhausted. His strength from the Demron essence probably helped him a bit, but it didn't eliminate exhaustion.

He sat in one of the overstuffed armchairs, sinking into the cushion. He wondered who had the expertise to create the ward that repelled his slivers. Pol kept thinking about it until his head fell off his arm.

He woke up in the dark. After lighting a candle, Pol worked on both women again. The rest had done a lot to allow his strength to return. He realized that his removing compulsion was at the tail end of a succession of tweaking earlier in the day and his magic had worn down. With renewed ability, he finished off the ward on Ako and finally got to the point of starting on the tendrils that sunk into Shira's brain.

He plopped into the easy chair after finishing off the tray of cold food that Paki had left.

The sun pierced the high windows in the sitting room. Pol woke again and stretched while rubbing his eyes. He took a drink of water from a pitcher that someone had left after replenishing the food in the room while he slept.

He stood over a slumbering Shira. How many more times would he see her sleeping? He sighed. Their time together was drawing to a close. He wished he was older since he couldn't bear to think about marriage. Perhaps he shouldn't marry his first love, for Shira was certainly that, and he, most likely, was hers.

He kissed her cheek and spent the rest of the morning delicately removing the remaining shreds of the spell. He thought he'd be days, but he was glad he overestimated.

Pol brought them both out of the sleeping spell at the same time.

"Pol! I thought your father's magician would kill you! He boasted of having knowing special spell," Shira said.

"It wasn't special enough. It was the same thing that Namion used, and the magicians had on the ship. You were under compulsion, so it took awhile to remove it. I think that they used compulsion to keep you docile until you were killed. He never had the chance to try it on me."

"Thank you," Ako said quietly.

Pol smiled. "I'm going into my apartment to wash up. I suggest you take the time to do the same."

~ ~ ~

Chapter Twenty-Two

~

FADDEN STOOD WHEN POL MADE HIS WAY OVER to him with a tray piled with food.

"I imagine I wasn't needed to heal the wounded?" Pol said.

"You were. Shira and Ako count as wounded. You fixed them up, I imagine?"

Pol nodded as he set the tray down. "They are back to normal. I worked through the night. I want to leave first thing tomorrow. Are you ready to go?"

"Ako is all right?" Fadden asked.

"Both of them are," Pol said.

"I'm ready enough. Who else is coming?"

"Paki. Just the five of us will be traveling fast and mostly cross country."

Pol noticed Handor gazing over the monks and acolytes. He spotted Pol and hurried to their table.

"I heard you might be leaving us," Handor said.

"Word gets around."

"I talked to Shira. She said you want to leave tomorrow?"

Pol smiled. "The sooner I leave, the safer the monastery will be. The invaders came after Shira and me."

"Not the Crown Prince?" Handor said. He looked a little crestfallen.

"Grostin, my middle brother," he paused, "from my Fairfield family. The men were from North Salvan under compulsion spells."

"So I really didn't have anything to worry about?"

"With an invading force of compelled men, I think we all had something to worry about. Horses and men died to keep the attackers at bay."

Handor's eyes lost focus for a moment "To save me, too," he said quietly. "I understand my father a little more."

"You do?" Fadden said.

The prince nodded. "He says that he has to sacrifice to protect the Empire and that means regrettable deaths, as he calls them. We had regrettable deaths yesterday."

Pol put his hand on Handor's shoulder. "We did. You lived through it. There are always conflicts from time to time in the Empire like this. The Emperor lets most of them just happen. I'm sure he regrets having to do that, but the strategy has worked so far."

"Loose reins," Handor said. "I've heard him use that term before, too."

Fadden took a morsel from Pol's tray. "You'll see a lot more of that, Handor. You'll be staying in Deftnis for a while before returning to Yastan, My Prince?" he said to Handor.

"I want to be here for at least a year, maybe two. Being out of Yastan has already given me more perspective than I would have ever dreamed. I can learn magic at home, but I can't learn about life first hand, boxed up in the Imperial Compound."

"You learned about life and death, already. I wish you well," Pol said. "I'll tell you all about Shinkya when I return."

Handor grinned. "Do that. Bring me back a little carved animal like you gave Father."

"If I can. No promises, but I'll try."

"I have to go back to the infirmary. The healers said they can use helpers."

Pol watched Handor leave. His vacation from Yastan would help turn him into a man.

Shira and Ako walked in together and soon the four of them sat discussing the final leg of Shira's trip around the world.

"Where is Paki?" Shira said.

"He'll be busy for a while yet, helping interrogate the invaders. Jonness and his Seeker instructors have the job of separating willing and unwilling participants. The Borstall captain—"

"Jamey Carter," Pol said.

Fadden nodded. "Yes, he is going to be taking over the questioning from Paki when he leaves. He will have a good idea of who will ally with Grostin, and who will fight for the Empire."

Pol finished his food before Shira and Ako returned with their meals.

"I'll be saying some goodbyes," Pol said and left for the infirmary.

He saw Handor helping some monks. Pol found Searl washing his hands after working on an injured man.

"I won't be seeing you until I return to Deftnis, whenever that will be," Pol said. "I feel that this isn't my home anymore."

Searl gave Pol a half-smile. "I don't suppose it is. You don't fit in as a monk. Find an excellent technically-strong magician in Yastan and learn more of what you don't know. Malden Gastoria can help you there. Even now there are a lot of tweaks you just aren't aware of." He chuckled. "You've made a lot out of what you do know. I would appreciate it if you would promote the Mancus Abbey to the Emperor when you make it back there. The Abbey will help Deftnis and Port Mancus. There is always a shortage of healers."

Pol nodded. "That's an area where I don't know as much as I should."

"You know more than most healers about saving a man from injuries and combat. That might be enough. The rest requires a lot of time and dedication."

Pol knew what Searl meant. "I don't have much of either, right now. Maybe later."

The healer chuckled again. "There is always later, isn't there?"

Changing the subject, Pol said. "How is Handor doing?"

"It's early in his treatment. So far so good. He has another six to nine months of it. I'm taking it slow at a lesion or two a week. I am encouraged so far, but time will tell how much strength he gains. He's probably been ill for most of his life and he's years past adolescence, so I don't know how he will respond to a properly functioning growth gland. He will get healthier and stronger, but those might be relative terms in describing his recovery. Will he ever be strong enough to lift a horse?" Searl shook his head, "no. But he will be able to live a longer life."

"That still makes his treatment worth it," Pol said.

"Just being here in Deftnis rather than being smothered by a loving mother makes it worth it." Searl correctly diagnosed Handor's major problem.

"I have to find Darrol. Is he here?"

"He is. He had an arrow pierce his stomach and other things. He'll be in the infirmary for a few weeks, it was that bad. You won't be able to say goodbye. We are keeping him under for a few more days."

"So he won't be coming with me." That disappointed Pol, but he'd rather have a healthy Darrol waiting for him to return.

"Have a safe trip. I hope to see you again on your way back to Yastan."

"I afraid that won't happen unless I sail back from Shinkya. The Emperor wants me to go directly to Yastan. Keep watch on Darrol and Handor."

"I will," Searl said

Pol left the infirmary in a sad mood and walked to the back of the monastery. Jonness's large classroom had become a dormitory for the attackers.

Jamey Carter and one of Jonness's seekers were each interrogating invaders. Both of them gave a brief wave to Pol as he made his way over to Jonness who was at a table, writing.

"I came to say goodbye. I'll be leaving early in the morning."

Jonness looked up. "I wish you could stay longer. Are you ever going to come back as a monk?" After he looked at Pol's face, he quickly said, "I thought so. Still, don't be a stranger. We get ex-monks visiting Deftnis all the time. Make sure that you are one of them. Demeron is going to want to check on his herd."

Pol smiled. "Already he is complaining about horses leaving Deftnis."

"What he doesn't tell you is how many colts those horses produced last spring. I think we will have a net increase in the herd once everything gets stabilized. There aren't that many monks who can bond with a Shinkyan, anyway. I'm glad I'm one of them. Lightning's very happy to stay put at Deftnis. His choice and I'm glad he made it."

"Good. Take care." Pol could see that Jonness had a lot of paperwork as a result of the temporary influx of residents on the Isle. "I wish you well, Jamey. Perhaps we will see each other in Yastan."

"I'll count on it," the ex-guard said.

His next goodbye wasn't far away. He found Edgebare talking to one of the instructors.

Edgebare put out his lip in a bit of a pout. "You didn't bring either of your swords."

"Isn't it safe to walk around unarmed?"

The old swordsman shook his head. "You are armed well enough even when you're wearing nothing but nature's clothes with that magic of yours."

"Magic is why I'm a pattern-master."

"Keep working on it. There are plenty to be found in Yastan. Malden or Ranno can get you set up with practice partners. There are always better techniques to learn."

Pol believed that. He had the advantage of magical strength and good swords, but even now, he felt that Regent Tamio would still defeat him in a duel. There must be others as proficient in the Emperor's employ.

"I'll do that, but I've got to get to Shinkya and back, first."

"You're heading cross country?"

Pol smiled. "Maybe."

"Use a crooked route, not a straight line. There could be bands of the enemy all along the way."

"Good advice. I might keep it," Pol said.

Edgebare winked at him. "Stay safe." He waved Pol away. "How is Darrol? I understand he'll be missing for a few weeks."

Pol repeated the diagnosis that he got from Searl.

"Be off with you, but make sure you visit when you return."

"I will," Pol said.

On the way back to the administration building, Demeron called to Pol. He walked over to the stable. The stable master had set up a long line of buckets. Demeron and a few Shinkyan horses fed while Pol walked up.

"What's this?"

We can come and eat grain whenever we want and that comes with a good firm brushing. Now, what can the horses do for the trip?

"Eat well. Make sure you are all in good shape. If there are wounds where saddles and saddlebags will sit, make sure you get them treated today."

Already done. I've got a mare who is homesick for Shinkya. Paki or Fadden can ride her to Shinkya.

"As much as I like Paki, let Fadden ride her. I suspect Fadden will be riding with Ako more than he will with Paki. We will be loading up early, so if you can spend the night in the stable, that would be wonderful."

I'm looking forward to the ride, but not for a return to Shinkya. Will you give me magic lessons along the way?

"We can do something, but there is still a lot I don't know."

Pol had to wait a quarter hour before Vactor concluded his tutoring.

"Come in. Sorry about the wait."

Pol grinned. "I've done it before. This is goodbye."

Vactor put out a chair for Pol and sat on the table that he used for instruction. "I'll be there tomorrow morning."

"I wanted a more private discussion," Pol said. "Take care of Handor. He may get homesick. If that is the case—"

"Don't worry about Handor. You're acting like his mother."

"I'm his step-brother."

Vactor held up his hand. "You have a point, but we deal with homesick acolytes all the time. Handor is the same age as our typical acolytes, so he will do fine. I've talked to him and he is anxious to learn. This is all a new experience for him."

Pol nodded. "Do you want a report on the wards of the Demron blade?"

Vactor narrowed his eyes. "I do. What did you notice?"

"It cuts through shields. Whoever is advising Grostin on matters of magic has something that protects from teleported projectiles."

"Like Namion?"

"Just like Namion. It has got to be a ward like the one we created together. My little splinters, that can kill, just bounced off."

"Ah, then you used the sword to puncture the ward?"

Pol grimaced. "I did. I don't like slicing a person up, but that was the only way to save Shira. It was like piercing leather or something. I had to work the sword in and use physical strength to push. The other magicians on the ship used the same kind of ward, but I was too caught up in the fight to think much about it and just reacted to overcome them."

Vactor peered at Pol. "So Namion might have learned to use the ward in Yastan. That means Grostin's reach goes all the way to the capital."

"Grostin or perhaps someone in Yastan is working with Grostin," Pol said.

"Oh. You don't know who's in charge?"

"Yes. I'll have the Abbot send a message to Yastan with my suspicions, but I'm going to be out of communication for weeks, while I escort Shira back to Shinkya."

"The culprit wouldn't be a Shinkyan?"

Pol shook his head. "They don't want to run the Empire."

"That's right." Vactor knew about Shira's comment in the cave where Shinkyans generally perceived Imperials as sub-human.

They talked about magic and learning at Yastan for a bit. Students knocked on Vactor's door.

"Time to go," Pol said.

He walked to the Abbot's office and was let right in.

Abbot Pleagor stood up and directed Pol to a chair.

"I heard you've been walking around, making your goodbyes. We will be sad to see you go. Will you be coming back?"

The Abbot certainly came to the point quickly enough.

"I intend to, but just to visit. Demeron has an interest in the preservation of the Shinkyan herd. Lightning used to be their leader and can do the same again. Besides, I still have a box of my possessions in your care."

"Jonness reports the horses are happy at Deftnis. Has your new father given you any responsibilities?"

"No. Handor didn't have any either, as far as I can tell."

"You aren't Handor."

"No, I'm Hazett's pet."

Pleagor chuckled. "We all are to some extent. You might have a shorter leash than the rest of us. I'm sure the Emperor will be interested in any observations you make in Shinkya. The only place you haven't been is Daera, right?"

"As well as most of the countries of the Empire," Pol said. "I still have a lot to learn."

"I think you've learned more than most of us, including me." He smiled and rose to look out his window. "I know that Shira and you drew the invaders to Deftnis's doorstep, but I'm glad you were here to fend them off. I regret the loss of life, but the exercise had its benefits. We will learn much from the invasion."

"I didn't mean to bring such destruction."

"Destruction? What was destroyed? Deftnis now has four ships, in various stages of repair. What other monastery can boast of a fleet? Garryle already is working on designs for new piers. We will find something to do with them."

"I need to find out where they were from."

"Leave that to Jonness. Imperial Seekers will be combing through the vessels and interrogating the attackers all over again. Ranno Wissingbel knows his business."

"And you know yours," Pol said.

"Flattery, flattery," the Abbot said. "Although you probably won't need it again, here is your black cord. You've earned it a few times over." The Abbot sat back down and took out a thick black cord from a desk drawer. Small silver symbols of Deftnis hung on from silver caps at each end." The Abbot waved an end at Pol. "A recent decoration, and for you, a remembrance. I enjoyed working with you."

"I'll be back sooner than later," Pol said.

"And knowing Hazett and Ranno, that will be turned into later rather than sooner."

Pol thought of one more loose end. "I've invited another acolyte to Deftnis. He is Lord Greenhill of Alsador's son. I would appreciate your admitting him."

"It's already been taken care of," the Abbot said. "Be off with you. Prepare for your trip and put that cord in your saddlebag for luck."

Pol smiled as he stood and bowed to the Abbot. "Thank you for putting up with me. I haven't been entirely easy."

"I'd skip the 'entirely'," he returned Pol's smile. "Certainly entertaining and amazing." He waved Pol out the door.

Pol stood between the desks that guarded the Abbot's door and took a deep breath. Saying goodbye to the Abbot was definitely a tough experience for him. He looked at the black cord for a moment and headed down to his apartment. He might never sleep in a monk's cell at Deftnis.

Handor walked in on Pol making more throwing knives and splinters out of two old swords he begged off of Edgeware on a return trip to the back of the monastery.

"Dinner?"

"I had mine," Pol said.

"Do you mind if we talked while you pack things up?"

"I've already bundled up most of it. Fadden's taking care of a packhorse with supplies. You can watch me tweak some small weapons," Pol said.

"Like your sword?"

"Not quite like my Demron weapons." Pol had already separated some of the first blade and tweaked into the thick sheet about two inches square. He concentrated and the splinters broke off on their own accord, each one about a quarter of an inch wide. When he was done he gave one to Handor.

"This is a weapon?"

"When I teleport it into a man's heart, it can kill him."

"You could put it anywhere, even in a brain." Handor said.

Pol wondered why he had never tried. "I don't know where it

would stop a person as quickly as a heart." It wasn't the kind of thing conducive to experimentation.

He tweaked another flat sheet and pulled off another eight splinters. That would be enough for now.

"What's next?"

Pol pulled out one of his Shinkyan throwing knives. "I can make about five of these. I'll give you one, too. I can't carry on a conversation and make one at the same time," Pol said.

"Don't mind me. I'm seeing something extraordinary."

"I don't know, but I might be the only person who can do this."

Pol concentrated on finding the right amount of steel in the old sword and tweaked a Shinkyan-style knife. He looked at it closely and saw the same ward woven into the knife as he had done on the Demron steel.

He grabbed a splinter and didn't see the same ward. Perhaps he might be able to defeat the barrier that stopped the splinters. He concentrated, and with a tweak technique he didn't remember, he warded the splinter. The essence had placed the ward's pattern in his mind. He did the same to the other splinters and rounded the tips to tell them from his unwarded ones.

"What did you do?"

"I placed wards on these." Pol held up a warded splinter. "I don't know if they will work any better or not, but I will save these for anyone with one of those ward barriers the Borstall magician created."

He made another warded knife and gave it to Handor. "A souvenir."

Handor handled the flat Shinkyan throwing knife as if it were made out of gold rather than an old sword ready for the scrap heap.

"Take that to Jonness, he will teach you how to throw it," Pol said. "It's meant to hide flat on your body."

A look of alarm filled Handor's face. "This is an assassin's weapon?"

"Probably. Use it as a defensive one, but it takes practice to learn how to throw it."

"I will," Handor said. "I'm moving to the dormitory tomorrow after you leave. I'll like that. It makes me feel like a normal person."

Pol laughed. "You'll get a good taste of independence, then.

Deftnis is a good place to learn how to fend for yourself. Most of the servants are your fellow acolytes and you'll be joining them."

"I look forward to it." Handor yawned. "I think I'll lie down for awhile."

"You do that," Pol said.

He finished using the last of the steel long after Handor began snoring in the other bedroom.

Pol sat back and looked out the high window. Here he sat, his last night at Deftnis after wanting so desperately to return. What would he really become? Pol sought out a pattern that didn't include the Imperial Throne and had a difficult time finding one.

Handor was such a meek young man. He liked his new brother but feared he wouldn't last long on the Imperial Throne. As much as Pol tried to think otherwise, Pol had the upbringing and the experience as well as the strength to lead. He certainly didn't covet Handor's position as Crown Prince, but Hazett wouldn't have let Handor learn at Deftnis if he didn't have an alternative to his firstborn son.

Could his journey to Tishiko be a final test to determine if Pol was competent to rule? He shook his head. Pol realized he was getting way ahead of himself. He had to get Shira back home and make it back to Yastan while Grostin was out to kill him. Pol thought that he should concentrate on staying alive more than thinking about what Hazett had up his sleeve.

~ ~ ~

Chapter Twenty-Three

POL'S EYES OPENED IN THE DIM LIGHT OF DAWN. He got up and put on traveling clothes. Handor looked sound asleep, so Pol didn't wake him.

He had mostly packed the night before and lugged his things out into the hallway. Ako and Shira had already left their apartment since the door was wide open. He trudged up the stairs and out of the silent administration building.

Magic lights illuminated the stable.

"Demeron?"

Ready to go. You are the last since Fadden made sure Paki would be up and ready before you.

Pol smiled at being the final member of their party. He walked into the stable to find everything ready to go. He slapped his saddlebags over Demeron's flank.

"Let's go," he said. "I hope the ocean is calm." With no wind, it looked likely. "I'll have breakfast on the mainland."

"So will we," Paki said.

Shira yawned. Pol moved to help her mount on Amble. The Shinkyan horse wasn't as big as Demeron, but the mare was still larger than any horse he'd seen Shira ride.

Ako shooed Fadden aside and jumped on her own Shinkyan mare.

Finally, they said goodbye to Vactor and the bleary-eyed acolyte who acted as stableboy and left a still-sleeping monastery.

By the time they reached the port, the sky was beginning to color. Garylle Handson met them by the barge.

"Couldn't sleep. I wish you all well." The mayor of Port Deftnis stepped aside as they rode their mounts aboard the barge. The air was still and the dawn light reflected off the ocean that showed gentle swells.

Four men manned the sweeps. Paki and Pol joined them. They pushed off and with a final wave to Garylle, they slid off into the beginning of the final leg of Shira's journey. Paki began to feel uncomfortable, even with the gentle sea. Fadden put him to sleep and took over the large oar.

All were wrapped up in their own thoughts for the trip. At last, they reached Mancus and put in at the Deftnis pier.

Anna Lassler and Searl greeted them.

"I spent the night with my grandson," Searl said. "The added benefit is to see you off. Be careful, all of you. Who knows what traps your Borstall brother has set in your way."

Ako hugged Anna. "I will see you again," Ako said.

Her words surprised Pol. She didn't sound like she'd be in Tishiko for very long. He wondered if the Shinkyans had strict rules about Sisters leaving their order and living in the Empire.

Searl gave him a hug. "Come back, Pol. I didn't go to all the trouble to fix you up to have you gone before your time. The Empire needs you and I want to see you again."

"Take care of my brother," Pol said.

"The Emperor's firstborn? Don't worry."

The five of them mounted and trotted out of Mancus passing the few villagers that trickled out of their houses and onto the town's streets to start their day.

"North," Fadden said, "and then we will head east and go through the Dukedom of Crimple into Finster."

"Aren't we going to eat?" Paki asked.

"In an hour or two," Fadden said. He urged his horse into a gallop as soon as they were out of Mancus.

Pol sighed. He was on his way to Tishiko. No more stops.

Crimple didn't excite Pol. The dukedom was flat and the people were totally normal. Maybe that was a good thing. Crimple was a remarkably stable place. The Duke of Crimple had a large extended family, and they were all content to live happily together.

Pol, Shira, and Ako wore disguises. Ako and Shira were males and had changed into loose men's styles the previous morning. Pol took on Nater's visage again. He made sure they talked Shinkyan as much as possible while they traveled alone. They stopped at a small village inn for the midday meal.

"Heading east?" the innkeeper said.

"Boxall," Pol said. "I heard their king is building up his army."

"He is. The rumors have made it all the way down here. You aren't the first to come through our little village, nor will you be the last."

Pol wanted to know more about the rumors but knew that the less said the better.

They ate their meal, saying little and continued on their way.

"Boxall," Fadden said. "I hope the king is replacing men lost in the South Salvan war."

Pol wondered if Grostin was expanding his influence, looking west to Boxall, which shared a boundary with Baccusol to the north.

"It's not something we should worry about," Fadden continued. "Hazett probably has Seekers everywhere after receiving news of Grostin's attack."

"There was no proof it was Grostin. Only the claims of a few of the attackers like Jamey Carter," Paki said.

"Do you think Hazett is concerned about legal proof? Grostin's magician? Borstall men manning the ships? No, he'll be looking towards the East," Fadden said.

Pol had to agree. If Hazett lost sight of what was going on, Ranno certainly wouldn't. Pol had made sure he explained the possible threat in the ten tiny messages sent to Yastan along with other messages on the Monastery's birds.

When they resumed their travels, Pol settled down for a lengthy conversation with Demeron about magic. They thought in Shinkyan. Pol found that they shared the same limited vocabulary.

They crossed into Finster and began to ride in a zigzag fashion heading northeast, then southeast. Sometimes they headed west when they passed a village in the distance to ride in from the opposite direction they were headed.

They kept off main roads except to cross them unless they were stopped by a large walled or fenced area. That meant a noble's estate.

Fadden consulted a map at noon one day and looked north and south. "It's time to bolt for Shinkya," he said. "We've gone far enough east to miss—"

"The swampland," Ako said. "I noticed." She gave Fadden a tight smile and took his hand. "Soon we will be in Shinkya and Shira and I will do the leading. I will miss the freedom of the Empire," she said. Her eyes were focused on Fadden. Evidently, their relationship had grown close at Deftnis. Pol was so wrapped up in himself that he hadn't even noticed.

Shira poked him with her riding crop. "Did you hear?" She looked grim.

"I did. Do you feel the same as Ako?"

"No. I won't miss Fadden, I'll be devastated when you head back north."

"Save me the grief," Paki said, with his hand over his face. He took off south.

Fadden and Ako laughed and followed.

Pol got off his horse. Shira dismounted as well and they hugged each other for a few long moments before they galloped to catch up with the rest.

The land began to change after an extended range of low hills.

Do you remember this land? Demeron said.

"I do. We rode along the north side of these hills on our way to South Salvan. What is on the southern side?"

Shinkya, Demeron said. Pol could sense the sadness in his horse's thoughts. *I would have been happy never to return.*

"We won't be in Shinkya very long," Pol said. "Deliver Shira, poke around for a week to take in the culture, and then it's back to the Empire and Yastan."

And you would be happy never to return to the Imperial capital. I can sense that in your thoughts.

Pol couldn't help but agree. He wondered if duty was enough to make him go back. Pol really didn't know if he had enough to offer the Empire. Perhaps as some kind of Seeker, but he tried to tuck the thoughts into the back of his mind, along with the Demron essence that hadn't shown itself during their journey to Tishiko.

He lost himself into their final run into Shira's country. Fadden kept up the pace for three days before they stopped short.

Ten men rode towards them from the southwest. Their luck at evading Grostin's men had run out.

They stopped at the top of one of the rolling hills and waiting for the group of men to approach. The horses took deep shuddering breaths.

Get off, Demeron said. *Take the supplies off the packhorse.*

Pol wondered what Demeron had in mind, but within moments they stood with their belongings at their feet. Demeron and Amble stood in the middle of a line of six horses.

Eleven to ten, Demeron said.

Pol smiled at the confidence in Demeron's thoughts. The men rode close enough and stopped a hundred paces in front of them. Two riders continued closer, while Pol put five Shinkyan throwing knives in his gloved hand. If he had to kill a horse, he was afraid a splinter wouldn't do.

"Have you seen a boy and girl come through here?" One of the men said.

He didn't look like a warrior. Pol asked Demeron to have Amble ask Shira if the man looked like a magician to her. He looked towards her and Shira nodded. Pol loosened his Demron sword and took the sheathed long knife out of its sheath.

"It's just been us heading south to the border and then directly east to South Salvan.

"The border with South Salvan is closed," the other man said.

"Why is that?" Pol asked.

"Perhaps that is none of your business," the other man said.

"Perhaps it is. I have property there," Pol said.

"Not for long," the magician said. He squinted at Shira and Ako. "For you anyway. I can see your friends are wearing disguises."

"Not for long," Pol said as he shed the disguise and returned his hair color. "I'll give you a chance. You are outnumbered."

The magician laughed. "Five against ten?"

"No Eleven against ten," Fadden said.

"Do you think a few trained horses are any match for us?"

"Last chance," Pol said.

"No chance."

Pol fingered one of his warded slivers and sent it into the man's heart. It didn't make it all the way but stuck in the man's chest.

"You can't do that!" the magician said.

Pol was sick of continuing to hear that phrase.

The magician took a deep breath and pulled the bloody splinter out and tossed it to the ground. The man's confidence looked a bit ragged.

Pol took out a Shinkyan knife and used as much power as he could. Blood blossomed on the magician's chest just before he fell off his horse. Evidently his warded blades could defeat the new defense the magicians had devised if more magical force was used.

"Who is next?" Fadden said.

The bandits charged. The men converged on Pol and Shira. Ako and Fadden grouped around Shira and Paki stepped up to Pol's side.

Before they closed, Demeron and his horses began to rear up and knock the men riding in the back off their horses. The enemy's mounts ran off, leaving the attackers exposed to iron-shod hooves.

Pol blew a man off his horse and Ako did the same.

"You'll have to teach me that," Pol could hear Shira say to the Sister.

He stood with his Demron sword and slashed at the next man's thighs with a boot knife as the longer blade held off the attacker's slashes. Pol had no time to play around throwing splinters and knives in the close fight.

A slash got through Pol's guard from one of the other men, but it bounced off Pol's warded coat. The thick tunic beneath the chainmail shirt helped, but Pol shuddered from the blow. He stepped back into Paki, knocking him down.

Three men advanced on Pol, their horses snorting, their flanks flecked with sweat. They raised their blades. Pol didn't have any alternative than to push Paki with a hip.

"Run away," he said. "Get out of my way and help Shira."

After he was sure Paki was out of the way, Pol turned invisible and began to twist and weave his way through the blades, catching the men on their wrists and legs and feet, by keeping low.

He gasped in pain when he stood up. How did a blade make it through to crack a rib? Pol would never know. His frenzy was just that. He struck out at his foes and gave himself up to reacting as fast as he could as he cut, and cut, and cut.

His cuts weren't lethal, but he kept at it until the men's legs were covered in blood. Only moments passed before Demeron and Amble and the other Shinkya horse raised up behind the men and struck their horses with their forelegs. The horses shied and moved to evade the pain.

Given a little time by the diversion caused by the horses, Pol pulled out slivers and took care of them. He stood alone. Paki, Fadden, Ako and Shira sat on the ground heaving, out of breath. Pol put his hands on his knees and bent over to catch his own breath as well.

Their assailants' bodies were scattered among them. None of them seemed to be alive.

Pol staggered to his friends. Not all the blood on his friends' clothes were from the enemy. His back and arms felt like a blacksmith had worked him over. Despite the cloak's protection from a bare edge, the chainmail and tunic didn't keep bruises at bay.

Demeron and Amble stood with the rest of the horses. Pol would have to treat some of the attackers' mounts. He shuffled over to the others and began to close up their wounds. None were life threatening now that all the wounds were closed.

Galloping all the way to Shinkya wouldn't be comfortable for any of them.

"I say bury them," Fadden said. "We'll take the horses with us. Let the rest of the assassins wonder what happened."

Pol agreed. "I'll need some time to rest."

"We can eat, then," Ako said.

Two hours later, they walked the horses south. All but Paki worked to eliminate their tracks. They didn't come across another group until they stopped as the sun descended from the sky.

Ako said, "We are probably in Shinkya."

"Do you think the border means anything to them?" Pol felt irritable and ached all over. Since they made it to Shinkya, he colored his hair as black as a Shinkyan's.

"No," Ako said, "but we aren't in the Empire anymore. I thought all of you would like to know.

"Sorry," Pol said. "Are there any towns or villages close by?"

Ako laughed. "I don't know northern Shinkya that well. There aren't a lot of villages until we are farther south. You'll notice the ground is rocky and the vegetation sparse. It's the most arid part of our country."

"Is she right?" Paki asked Shira.

She shrugged. "As far as I know. I've never been to the northern edge except to the west where it's swampy."

Pol asked Demeron if the terrain looked familiar.

It all looks familiar to me. We crossed over into Finster close to here. He went silent for a moment. *The other horses don't know any more than Ako.*

"It isn't much of a mystery, we just have to head south," Fadden said. "We'll run into someone who can tell us where we are." He looked at a map and showed it to the rest of them. "We could be anywhere." He circled a large portion of the map.

"I suppose we can spend the night, right here," Shira said. "Amble says there is sufficient forage, but we will have to look for some water in the morning."

Once the horses were unloaded, Ako and Fadden went to work on their dinner, using magic to cook. Fires would be spotted from quite a distance.

Pol walked the perimeter of the camp by himself. He located a person closing in on him.

"Care to walk with a friend?" Shira said.

"Just the person I was thinking of," Pol said. "We could be intercepted by a Shinkyan patrol at any time. Then our relationship changes."

"It does. Are you wondering if I will take you captive?"

Pol smiled, "You already have." He felt a flush move up his neck. What a sappy thing to say, but he meant it.

She laughed and hugged him. "Whatever happens I am glad we spent this year together. It is the highlight of my short life."

"I hope your life is long," Pol said. "It's a pity I won't be around to enjoy it with you."

Shira didn't say anything for a moment. "I don't think you'll like Tishiko."

"Did you like Yastan?" Pol said.

"I did, but I have responsibilities to face now that I have returned."

"I know. My life will change again when I leave Shinkya."

"Prince and Princess," she said. "Did we ever think we'd be together even this long when we met at Tesna?"

"Nope," Pol said. "I was surprised you didn't desert once we marched out of the monastery."

"I nearly did, but I had to find out more about the army. By the time I reached Covial, I was hooked on you." She hugged him again.

"I know. Same with me." Pol sighed. "And now…"

"I won't desert you once we get to Tishiko unless I am dragged away."

Pol shook his head. "I'm not so sure that won't happen."

"Ako agrees with you, oddly enough. She will see me safely to Tishiko and then she will have to make a big decision."

"Follow Fadden back to Deftnis?"

Shira nodded in the darkness. "That will be a big risk for her, but I will do what I can to help."

Pol felt Shira's warmth in the cooling evening. "She doesn't have to leave immediately."

"I know. Fadden needs to be out of Shinkya before Ako does

something rash. Make sure that he doesn't push Ako too hard."

"Has he been?"

Shira shook her head and made a sound like a single chuckle. "They have been very circumspect."

Pol didn't bother to contradict Shira. They just held onto each other until Paki called them to dinner. They kissed as if it were their last before they headed back to camp.

Pol didn't taste any of his meal and found a soft spot of ground before he wrapped his blankets around him hoping he could sleep with his painful ribs. He didn't know how long he suffered thinking about the next few days until Fadden kicked his feet.

"Up we've got visitors."

Pol shot to his feet. Not so soon, he thought.

A few poorly dressed Shinkyans stood talking to Shira and Ako. At least they weren't guards and they didn't kneel or anything. Pol had no idea what served as genuflection in Shinkya.

He walked up to them, comprehending most of what they said, but he feigned not understanding their conversation.

"What's going on?" Pol said in Eastrilian.

"We are on their lord's land," Ako said. She looked around. "No signposts or fences, but then the holding is likely vast."

"They will escort us through to the southern side. We will have to spend the night at their lord's manor. They can tell that we are an uncommon group and their lord will be curious."

Fadden looked at the men and nodded. "Are we in danger?"

Ako shook her head. "Probably not. Shinkyans are a curious people."

~ ~ ~

Chapter Twenty-Four

THEIR THREE ESCORTS WERE FRIENDLY ENOUGH, but since Pol still let them think he couldn't understand their language, they spent plenty of time running down the empire.

Shira, who now only rode with Ako, would turn around and glare at the men, who would look repentant until she turned back and then grinned behind her back. Pol had to restrain from speaking in Shinkyan until something important happened.

Mid-afternoon, Pol saw a two-story structure in the distance, perched on one of the taller hills.

"Is that the manor house?" he asked Ako, who relayed his question to their escorts.

The man nodded to Pol and pointed. "Lord Garimora," the man said.

Pol repeated the name back. The escort nodded and smiled. "Right, our Lord's house."

They finally reached the house. A low wall encircled the property midway up the hill. Pol wondered what kind of defense that would give the house.

"Lord Garimora doesn't need to fear attack," Shira said. "Shinkyans don't attack holdings, but if he traveled to Tishiko, the lord would have to be on constant guard. That wall is meant to keep animals out, not Shinkyans."

Shira didn't say humans. He wondered if her perceptions would shift back to how she viewed things before she left. Pol sensed a cultural barrier building up between them. Already Ako and Shira had to behave distant and reserved.

Pol sighed as he rode through the gates of the Lord Garimora's manor house. There were few plants growing in the garden. Gravel, rocks, and stubby trees were arranged artfully.

He looked up at the large two-story house. Each level probably had twelve-foot ceilings. The tiled roof was one large gable that overhung all sides. He recognized concrete walls. Some of the wall was smooth and other parts were textured with indented lines running up and down to an overhang that came out between the floors, looking like the top floor was plopped on top of the first floor's roof. It had the same look as what he had seen in Covial, but this had a feeling of artful intention that the Covial architecture did not.

One of their escorts went to the double doors and knocked on the doorpost. A wizened man poked his head out the door.

He stood too far away to make out all the words, but the escort and the butler, if that's who it was, laughed at the Imperials.

They were finally ushered in.

"You have four Shinkyan horses with you. Humans ride two of them. How can a human bond with a Shinkyan horse?" the butler asked Shira.

Pol looked away. He was disappointed at the disdain the servant portrayed.

"We will discuss such things with Lord Garimora," Ako said.

"Of course, Sister." The butler scuttled away.

"You heard?" Shira said.

Pol nodded. "I can see how much you had to overcome in my behalf."

Shira blushed. "Ako and I can look past the prejudice. I have long shed what I shared with you at the Demron cave," she said. "Whatever I say, do not show alarm. If our hosts find out you can speak Shinkyan, we will lose flexibility."

Pol wondered if losing flexibility included their Imperial lives.

A vigorous man, a bit shorter than Shira strutted into the room and looked them all over. He turned to Ako. "I am Lord Garimora. These are Imperial humans?"

What else would we be? Pol thought.

"They are. May I introduce them to you?" Ako said in Shinkyan. Fadden admitted to knowing only a few words and Paki probably didn't know any. She introduced Paki as a Deftnis monk, Fadden as an Imperial magician and Pol as a Seeker.

"You think these men will protect you all the way to Tishiko?" He smiled and nodded at the Imperial men as he talked.

"Pol Cissert has bonded with the big black Shinkyan stallion. He has other magical talents. Fadden Loria has trained with magic and with sword. Pakkingail Horstel is a companion of Pol Cissert's. I assure you they are seasoned travelers," Shira said.

Lord Garimora put fists on his hips and faced the Imperials. "You are welcome to my home. For my hospitality, I will expect good answers to my questions," he said in heavily accented Eastrilian.

The man didn't look trustworthy to Pol. He wanted Ako's opinion, but that didn't look likely. They were shown to their rooms by female servants, dressed nicely in a style which was unfamiliar to Pol. Most notably there was an absence of buttons, as far as he could see.

They had long black hair braided and piled on top of their heads. He smiled at the thought that Shira had arrived at Tesna with a shaven head. He wondered how much of a sacrifice she had made.

Garimora had the three of them share a room to clean up from their travels. He provided them thin, silk robes in the Shinkyan style to wear at dinner.

They were shown to a dining room. The table was low, with short, carved legs. Pillows were set on the floor in front of each place. They sat on the left side of Lord Garimora and Shira and Ako were dressed like Shinkyan ladies, Pol guessed. Their hair was piled on their heads, although Shira's wasn't close to the length of Ako's.

Lord Garimora entered at the sound of a gong. He went to the head of the table. The gong sounded again and he sat. Then Shira and Ako took their seats. Lord Garimora motioned for the Imperials to follow.

They had sat at low tables before in The Shards, but Paki still had a hard time gracefully sitting so low.

Garimora clapped his hands and serving men delivered Shinkyan food to the table. Bowls of steaming noodles were placed in front of each person along with another bowl of a broth. Three smaller bowls of vegetables were finally delivered along with a small pot and a cup for each diner.

The Lord poured the tea in his cup and nodded, so the rest did the same thing. Pol hoped they followed the protocol well enough. He'd rather make mistakes in front of this rural lord than in front of Tishikan citizens.

They all lifted their cups above their heads.

"We give thanks for our ancestors forbearance and to the Great Ancestor for giving us life and sustenance," the Lord intoned.

Ako and Shira repeated the Lord's words. Pol kept his mouth shut and drank his tea after the Shinkyans did.

"Now you may eat," Lord Garimora said in Eastrilian. He raised his hand and a servant brought a chair without legs and assisted Lord Garimora. Pol guessed that it would be bad manners to sit in the chair before the prayer was made.

The Shinkyans used spoons and two long, thin sticks to eat. Shira had them all practice how to use the sticks at Deftnis. Paki was the best. Fadden struggled, but Pol never got the hang of them. He ended up cheating by using tiny sips of magic to adhere food to the sticks.

Garimora noticed Pol's effort to eat. "You have an unusual way of using eating sticks," he said in Eastrilian.

"It is not a skill that comes easily to me."

Garimora expertly snatched a vegetable with the sticks and smiled. "A Shinkyan child can do better than you. But it looks like you are at least able to put food in your mouth. Are all Eastrilians as unconventional as you, Seeker?"

"I'm afraid not, Lord. I do many unconventional things to the dismay of many whom I encounter."

Pol meant it as a subtle threat, and it looked like Garimora took it that way.

He leaned towards Pol. "Are you out to antagonize your host?"

Pol shook his head. "If I meant to challenge, you would know it. I am just a talented boy who knows more than I should."

"An arrogant pup," Garimora said in Shinkyan to Shira and Ako. "Why did you bring him with you, Sisters?"

"He is here at the request of Emperor Hazett III to see me home. He has unconventional skills, which he alluded to." Shira said.

Lord Garimora bowed to Shira. "I always thought Sisters to be more independent and self-sufficient than to let attack dogs trail after them."

Pol ground his teeth together. Paki and Fadden had no idea what Garimora said and he'd leave it that way until they were well on their way out of the estate.

Shira flicked her eyes at Pol, who lifted his chin and then lowered it.

"Dogs make the best pets," Ako said.

"Pol Cissert is the Emperor's Pet," Shira said. "I am told his bite is vicious and his enemies should beware."

Lord Garimora waved his hands. "We were making with Shinkyan wordplay," he said to the Imperials. "It is a Shinkyan thing. You will find it to be utilized at a very sophisticated level in the capital."

Pol doubted it would be much worse than what he observed, but he suspected the players to participate at much higher stakes. The Shinkyan lord concentrated on his meal and asked harmless questions about the Empire for the rest of the dinner. The fangs had briefly come out and then had retracted.

They went to bed, resting on low beds with a thick mat made of woven reeds as a mattress, covered with silk sheets.

In the morning they rose. Lord Garimora didn't join them for breakfast which was eaten cold. Even the noodles were at room temperature. They walked out the front door. Demeron and Fadden's mount had been replaced by other horses.

"Where is my horse?" Pol said.

Garimora strutted around the corner of his manor. He looked at

Ako. "Dogs don't ride our sacred horses. I won't permit it."

Pol was about to object when Demeron told him to wait for a bit. He and the other Shinkyan horse trotted out and nudged Garimora to the ground.

"My Shinkyan horse does not appreciate your gesture," Pol said.

The lord rose from the ground and dusted himself off. "How did he…?"

"He is as unconventional as his master," Pol said, removing his saddle from Garimora's horse and putting it on Demeron. "I believe he was exercising a great deal of restraint, just now."

"You are bonded?"

"Are we Demeron?"

We are indeed. He shook his mane and nuzzled Pol.

Fadden finished with his horse and they mounted.

"We appreciate your hospitality," Shira said in Shinkyan and gave Garimora a little bow. He returned the bow and presented Shira with a small purse. "Thank you for purchasing the other horses that we brought with us," she said.

Ako and she rode out without a backward glance. The Imperials followed.

The manor disappeared behind a knoll. Shira broke out in laughter. "Demeron. Your timing was perfect. I approve of your actions!"

I was only too happy to show you my respect for our host. He didn't even share his grain with us. Bad manners!

Pol noticed that Fadden, Shira, and Ako laughed along with him. Demeron had spoken to all of them.

Shira rode at Pol's side. "I don't care what my people think," she said as she leaned over and grasped his hand. "You heard everything he said?"

Pol nodded. "Is it really going to be worse in the capital?"

Ako spoke up. "Worse. You'll be getting compliments from one faction and curses from another. You won't know who is lying and who isn't. That includes those who ostensibly curse you."

"Indirect speaking is an art form in Tishiko," Shira said. "You're restraint was admirable. Keep it up as long as you can."

"I will," Pol said. He wondered if he was up to the subterfuge, but if he were to be billed as an Imperial Seeker, he would have to rise to the challenge.

Signposts began to proliferate on the road. Ako and Shira now knew the way. Pol puzzled out the signs and Demeron was able to help him decipher some of the picture writing. They rode through their first actual Shinkyan town.

They entered the stable yard of a Shinkyan inn. Except for Shinkyan architecture, the inn was much like any other Pol had stayed. It had a common room, but in addition, it also had small individual dining rooms for more discreet meals. The setup reminded him of the Seeker commissary in Yastan.

Ako and Shira negotiated the prices and purchased the right to one of the dining rooms along with private sleeping rooms for everyone.

"Lower profile," Shira said as they assembled in the small lobby. Paki looked longingly at the laughter and carousing, going on in the common room. Ako twisted Paki's nose. "That's a good way to have everyone learn who we are and why we are here."

They followed a serving girl to a private dining room. It had room for eight.

Ako looked at Paki, who still had disappointment written all over his face. "The longer we are all a mystery, the longer we have some control over our circumstances. Once people know Shira is a princess, our options shrink. If she arrived at the inn as a princess, the innkeeper would refuse to rent a room."

"Refuse?" Pol said.

Ako spoke up. "Shinkyan nobles don't mix with the common citizen. This inn isn't certified to accept noble customers. We would have to travel farther to find a suitable inn."

Shira nodded. "She's right, but nobles often travel dressed like more common people so they don't have to be so inconvenienced unless they want useless pandering by the inn's staff instead."

"But Lord Garimora treated us like peers," Fadden said.

"He should have, I slipped a very fat purse to his butler. If he thought we were high-ranking nobles, he would have never switched horses. At least we made a little bit back by selling him the bandits' horses," Shira said.

"Sisters aren't noble?" Pol scratched his head, not quite getting the ranking.

"Magicians come from all facets of Shinkyan society. Not all Sisters are noble. I'm not," Ako said. "We stand a bit apart from the rest."

Pol wondered what other facets of Shinkyan life would be revealed. Shira had always been circumspect in regards to herself and life in her country, but Pol learned that there were layers of complexity that he would probably never understand during his short stay in the country.

Shira casually bribed a noble so they could have a decent dinner and a night at his manor. Was Shinkya for sale? If the Shinkyans weren't so culturally reclusive, he imagined there would be vast horse farms supplying Shinkyan horses to the Empire. He wondered how much the political factions were driven by the accumulation of wealth versus political power. He would know soon enough.

Pol was having a hard time shaking his disappointment. He had thought Shinkya to be an exotic country with ancient rules and practices. That seemed to be there, but it appeared Shinkyans lived a life of bribery and deception overlaid on their ancient culture. He suspected life in the capital would be more of the same.

Dinner seemed to be a variation on what Lord Garimora served them. The broth tasted different. This time he noticed that Ako and Shira began their meal by putting some of the vegetables into the steaming soup. Pol followed suit. The combination wasn't very good.

"You better do some tasting before you flavor the ogamuri," Ako said. "I imagine the look on your face is a good indicator about the taste."

"Ogamuri?" Pol said. His Shinkyan vocabulary didn't have words of dishes. There was a word for soup and that wasn't it. "It means?"

"Vegetables in soup," Shira said.

"Romantic," Fadden said.

Paki plopped all the vegetables in his soup and then he tossed in the noodles, making some of the soup spill out onto the table.

"This is great!" he said using his spoon and his eating sticks. He was surprising adept using the Shinkyan utensils.

"It looks like you won't starve in Shinkya," Pol said, grinning at his friend. Actually, Pol wouldn't either. He picked up some noodles and dipped them in the soup and that seemed to be tasty enough.

"No meat?" Paki said.

"Only for the midday meal," Ako said. "Red meat is expensive in Shinkya and it isn't polite to have it for the evening meal."

"No red meat at breakfast, either" Shira said. "Only fish or fowl. Custom says a person can't digest meat properly at night."

Pol shook his head. "You know that's not correct. I've seen you eat meat for dinner and blissfully sleep the night away."

Ako looked up. "I didn't think you two slept together."

Shira laughed. "I was disguised as a male when I first met Pol and we were shoved into the same room. Other than that, we've camped out quite a bit. Right, Pol?"

Fadden nodded instead of Pol. "Paki and I joined them while on the road."

The Sister smiled. "Of course, I forgot. I must admit, I can eat any meat at any meal, but I only consume it in small quantities." She actually batted her eyelashes when she admitted she ate meat.

Pol wondered how ingrown the customs were, yet Ako and Shira were able to easily adapt to Imperial dining habits. Was it because of the uniqueness of the two women or was it because the customs didn't have much of a hold on Shinkyans. He found the Shinkyan culture more frustrating to figure out than the more easily pattern-able cultures and customs on Volia.

The Shinkyan style was something that Shira had been absolutely right about. Everything from eating utensils, crockery, architecture and clothing styles were unique to Pol's existence. Covial's affectation of Shinkyan architecture was a hollow imitation of the real thing.

Dinner was over. Ako and Shira rose first.

"We have to do some shopping," Shira said. "Join us here at daybreak." They left without another word.

Pol didn't want to reveal that he could speak the language, so after a quick walk of the town's main street, getting all kinds of stares from the townspeople, Paki, Pol, and Fadden retired to their rooms.

When Pol returned to his room, someone had sawed the joint he had made. The door was slightly ajar and he could see movement within. Pol pulled out a splinter and held it concealed in his head. He slid the door open.

A woman leaned over bedding that she spread out on the floor.

"What did you do to the door?" she said in Shinkyan. "I had to get Kabo to cut it open." She peered at Pol. "Are you a magician?"

Pol noticed a trace of fear on her face. Pol shrugged and shook his head. "I don't speak Shinkyan," he said in Eastrilian.

She threw up her hands. "Humans shouldn't be allowed in Shinkya," she said and pushed Pol aside as she left.

After checking his belongings, Pol could tell that nothing was disturbed. He lay down on the bedding, just laid out on the bare floor. A mat made with horsehair bound in some kind of springy substance provided padding. This was different from the low beds they slept on at Lord Garimora's manor house.

The room's windows were opaque being made out of waxed paper. Pol breathed in through his nose and took in a distinctive smell. Oddly, it was similar to the lord's manor house. Did the Shinkyans use an aromatic wood in their construction? He smiled as he took in the difference. It was too bad Shinkyans were so hostile to Imperials. It would be a wonderful place to visit, but then most people never traveled very far from their birthplaces in the Empire.

He sighed, fixing the smell in his memory. Pol vowed to take as much as the Shinkyans would allow him to absorb. He wanted memories of Shinkya to join his memories of Shira.

~~~

Chapter Twenty-Five

~

T HEY ATE A COLD BREAKFAST and loaded up their horses. Shira and Ako changed into a different style of clothes. They wore silk blouses covered with a leather vest. The shoulders extended over their actual shoulders giving them a winged appearance. They wore thin leather pantaloons with wide bottoms. Pol had seen split skirts on women riders in the Empire, but these were different. Even their hair was different. Both of them wound up some of their hair into a topknot wrapped with a silk cloth on Ako's part and a pink colored suede on Shira's hair. Both topknots were skewered with a thick silver pin that looked more like a nail.

"Sister attire?" Pol asked.

Shira smiled. "I'm glad you noticed. Now that we will be traveling through more populated areas, our attire will help us avoid any unnecessary delay." She mounted Amble. The others did the same. "We have one more stop in this town."

Shira led them out of the stable yard. People gave them a wide berth, now that Ako and Shira dressed like Sisters. Pol sighed. Her new style left Pol with the feeling that she had started to distance herself from him.

She stopped at a two-story building. This one sported glass panes rather than the waxed paper that most other establishment used.

"We all need official papers," Shira said.

"What are papers?" Paki asked.

"We needed them in Bossom. Remember when we entered from Fistyra and then again in Missibes so we could enter the Inner Circle?" Pol said. "I guess we need them in Shinkya."

They tied their horses up in front of the building and walked inside.

Four men staffed a long counter.

"Follow me," Shira said, as Ako went to one of the men on her own.

"I have three Imperial humans with me," she said in Shinkyan.

Pol nearly winced when she referred to them as humans.

"And you are?"

"Princess Shira Graceful Willow."

Pol thought the Shinkyan pronunciation of her last name was quite nice.

"One moment."

The man looked skeptical, but pulled a thick book from a bookcase full of them. He opened it up to a log in front and ran his finger down a list. He flipped the pages four times until he found the entry he needed. Pol noticed tabs stuck to certain pages. The man found the entry that he looked for.

"Do you have the code?"

"Paper 54302"

The bureaucrat's eyes grew a little larger before he bowed deeply to Shira. "Princess, Shinkya welcomes you back. You would like formal papers for yourself and these humans?"

"I do, and a set of informal papers for myself."

"We will work diligently and quickly to fulfill your royal request." The man gathered to the two idle men and they flew into a frenzy of motion.

"What happens if a common Shinkyan asks for papers?" Pol said.

"You heard, obviously," Shira said. "They might have to wait days until these men got to it. They do actual work when they feel like it. Without papers, anyone, including me, would be incarcerated in

Tishiko and the larger towns. Excuse me."

She drifted over to Ako who was engaged in a heated conversation with the clerk. "I am Shira Graceful Willow of the Queen's family. You may talk to the other clerks to verify my rank and standing. I demand that you quickly work on Ako Injira's papers."

Pol now knew that Injira meant 'white mountain' in Shinkyan. The clerk went pale and bowed deeply.

They still waited for half an hour before being presented with their papers. Pol could make out most of the words. He rolled his traveling certificate in the little leather covering provided and put it in his waistband when he saw Shira do the same thing before they mounted and rode out of town.

"We will have to show our documents at every inn from here on and whenever a patrol stops us which will definitely happen with Imperials. The inns won't be much different, but the service and the price will be much higher. I had to bribe the innkeeper last night to give us rooms without papers."

"How many humans live in Tishiko?" Pol asked Shira in Shinkyan.

Ako turned her head. "You've learned Shinkyan rather well for a human," she said in Shinkyan and then smiled. "Are you learning a lot about us?" she said in Eastrilian.

"I used to treasure every little tidbit that Shira let out about Shinkya, trying to get a pattern of her upbringing. Some of what I knew has been verified, but there have been many surprises," Pol said.

"What is a surprise?"

"I am sure under normal circumstances that both of you have multiple sets of papers. Nobles, who wish to stay at common inns, will have a set that doesn't disclose their status. Those were added to Shira's formal papers, correct?" Pol said.

Ako whistled. "Shira, see how dangerous it is to enter into a relationship with a Seeker?"

Fadden laughed as Pol's suspicion was confirmed and placed firmly in his revised pattern about Shinkya.

Shira said they were about a week away from Tishiko. Every day seemed about the same. Pol spent more time with Shira and Ako on the road speaking Shinkyan. At night he would go over vocabulary and practicing diction in his room. True to Shira's words, the inns were pretty much the same, as they all had private rooms every time, but the service was smothering. Pol had finally gotten used to the Shinkyan architecture. It no longer seemed strange, but part of the country.

Ako explained all the rules to follow in Tishiko. Imperials were treated as curiosities in the towns and two cities that they had passed, but in Tishiko that wasn't the case. 'Humans' were regarded as speaking animals by many higher status Shinkyans.

The tedium of travel ended when they were finally stopped by a Shinkyan patrol. The ten soldiers were dressed with leather scale armor. Pol had seen scale armor before, but in Shinkya, armor was often painted with glossy shellac. These soldiers wore light blue armor. Their trousers were more like what Ako and Shira wore, but out of a thicker leather and were red. Their helmets were painted black and the leather was molded into a deep ribbed design.

They passed them by and then rode back.

"Don't touch your weapons," Shira said.

Pol had already exchanged his Shinkyan sword and knife back at Lord Garimora's manor. The Demron steel blades were wrapped up tightly onto the saddle of Demeron as Shira and Ako had requested.

The soldiers rode slowly past them as Pol's group slowed down to a walk. They eyed each of them closely. Pol started when he noticed that two of the soldiers were women. They were probably magicians.

The column filled the road ahead, forcing them to stop.

"Travel documents please, after you have dismounted," one of the women said.

Pol pulled the rolled up papers and waited while the soldiers spoke with Shira. The conversation turned heated on Shira's part. They stood too far away and spoke too fast for Pol to catch all of the conversation.

"What right do those humans have to ride Shinkyan horses?" the woman said to Shira and then she lifted her chin towards Pol.

Shira parroted her question in Eastrilian.

"Demeron is bonded to me." Pol pulled out his certificate of ownership signed by the Emperor and gave it to Shira. "I have permission from the Emperor of Baccusol."

Shira showed the document to the woman and showed her the emperor's signature.

"Have him tell the horse to turn around," she said. "No speaking."

Demeron didn't wait and turned around and then nuzzled Pol.

"He listens?"

Shira nodded.

"What about the other Imperial human?" the woman said.

I can take care of that, Demeron said.

Fadden's horse turned around and pushed her nose into Fadden's back.

"Tell the humans to behave. As you know there is little tolerance for their barbaric practices."

The soldiers mounted and continued on their way. Pol watched them trot off before remounting.

"Barbaric ways?" he said to Shira.

She shook her head. "She has no idea how Imperials live."

And that was part of the Shinkyan problem, Pol thought. If they continued to ignore how 'humans' in the Empire lived, there could be no reconciliation. Ako and Shira proved that Shinkyans could peacefully co-exist with the rest of the human race. Pol considered Shinkyans a branch equal among humanity, not above it.

"I was just interested in living for the present," Paki said. "Can we go now?"

Shira smiled at him and nodded to Ako, who took off at a gallop. The others followed and soon the unfortunate incident was forgotten as they rode through the Shinkyan countryside.

Pol tried to think of it as a romp, but then he realized their spirited ride only got them to Tishiko that much sooner.

I remember this place, Demeron said. *Amble should too. An old doctor lives in that place. It was the first time I used magic.*

"That's where you were nearly captured?"

Not nearly, but he tried.

Pol looked at the house as they passed and caught a glimpse of an old man in white robes tending to his garden in the back.

"He still lives."

I didn't kill him, you know, Demeron said. *He can hear any Shinkyan horse. I guess that is a rare talent.*

Pol laughed. "It sure is, and one I don't possess. Tishiko is up ahead?"

An hour or two away.

Pol's breath caught at his throat. The end of his relationship was really near. He wanted to ride up and pull Shira off Amble and kiss her, but he couldn't, not among all the Shinkyans on the crowded road into Tishiko.

A few minutes later, one hundred soldiers with gilded leather armor approached them. They all rode white horses, only two of them were Shinkyan and those soldiers appeared to be women.

"Princess Shira, we welcome you to Tishiko. The Queen is anxious to see you," one of the women said.

"Is that you, Anori?"

The soldier turned red. She nodded.

"Congratulations on your graduation."

"It has been more than a year, Shira," the soldier said. "Did you bring back prisoners?"

"Our escorts from Emperor Hazett. Just enough to keep me safe along the way."

"You were attacked?"

"Even the humans have factions, my dear Anori," Shira said.

The way Shira replied told Pol that the soldier wasn't a real friend. He kept his face as impassive as possible as he observed the exchange.

"Should I just kill them now and put them out of their misery?" Anori said with a wicked grin.

Pol gripped the hilt of his Shinkyan sword tighter.

"Don't underestimate them, Anori. They escort me for a reason."

"Two boys and an old man?"

"They are all magicians. Two are what the Imperials call pattern-masters who use magic as they fight."

"No one matches us," Anori said.

"That one saved my life more times than I can count," Shira pointed her chin at Pol. "He's been with me the entire time I've been gone."

"Nonsense. He looks younger than you."

Shira shook her head with irritation. "My mother won't be pleased if we continue to chat in the middle of this road."

That brought the woman to attention. "Of course, Princess Shira." She gave Shira a cocky smile. They moved out with soldiers surrounding Shira and Ako. A row of soldiers separated Shira and Ako from Paki, Fadden, and Pol.

Tishiko had no wall, Pol noticed, as they rode into the outskirts of the city. The proximity of their escort gave him no further chance to talk to Shira, and that made him sad. However as the buildings began to increase in size, Pol's focus was replaced by the excitement of watching Tishiko's architecture grow as they moved towards the center of the city.

Citizens looked surprised by the size of the escort. Pol saw thousands of Shinkyan faces as they moved through the city streets.

The tiered structures that Shinkyans called pagodas began to sprout. First a few stories high and as they moved onward, there were two story structures that dwarfed Lord Garimora's manor. Some of them could have housed over one hundred people.

The residents' dress became more fancy with additional layers of silk robes, vestments, and sashes. The variety of men's hats reminded him of the Magicians Circle fortress in The Shards. These men were too old to be powerful magicians. Women wore gold and jeweled ornaments in their hair.

Pol could appreciate why the South Salvans would pattern some of their buildings after Shinkyan designs. He thought he had acclimated to Shinkyan architecture, but Tishiko's buildings were stunning. Pol wondered what a Shinkyan thought of Yastan.

Pol knew someone who would know but he had never asked her. There were a lot things that Shira and he had never talked about and wouldn't since their lives would part at some point while he stayed in Tishiko. He leaned back in his saddle and absorbed the city. He would forever link Shira to this exotic city.

The center of Tishiko had its own smell. He noticed a lack of the stench of open sewers. Poorly dressed men walked around pushing carts. It reminded him of the Inner Ring in Missibes. Was Tishiko like Missibes? All for show? A bureaucracy could only get more confining at the seat of government.

Pol wondered about the factions. He wanted to stay long enough to understand the distribution of political forces throughout the city.

I've been to that building to your left before, Demeron said.

Three of the large two-story buildings formed a U-shape facing the street. At the end of one of them rose a seven story pagoda.

That is where the Scorpion faction has its headquarters. They took me in and fed me. Karo Nagoya, the Shinkyan at Nater Grainell's estate, lives there, Demeron said.

Scorpions, Pol thought. He remembered the episode from Demeron's description of his time away from Deftnis. Karo Nagoya. Perhaps he would seek the Shinkyan out.

"Pol!" Shira said from ahead of him. "Come up here…please."

He smiled at the pause before the please.

"I want my mother to see you at my side."

"We could have talked while we went through the town," Pol said as he took a position on the other side of Shira from Ako.

"You would have been bored. Anori and I spent the whole time discussing the state of the factions. We will go over them later," she said.

'Later' encouraged Pol. She didn't intend to just dump him at the palace steps and order him to return to Yastan.

"Sit up straight. You are the Emperor's emissary," Ako said, leaning forward to speak around Shira.

Pol thought he sat up straight, but he stretched his neck to sit taller in the saddle.

"That's better," Shira said. "You need to show my mother that you are proud of your station in life."

Pol smiled. "And what is my station? The Emperor's Pet?"

"Prince of the Empire and definitely not the Princess's Pet. Not in Tishiko."

Pol got the message. Having her treat him as a peer was better than casting him aside as a 'human'. Not that he expected Shira to do such a thing, but those around her would, if the pattern that he continued to build held.

A huge gate opened and swallowed the procession. They rode through a tunnel made out of concrete, so long that magician lights were spread out to illuminate their way. When they popped out into a square, Pol had to squint to make out those arrayed to greet them.

Ahead of them five pagodas, four of them were eight stories high. The center structure was twelve stories high. They had seen the tops of the pagodas from the street, but this close they seemed to reach up into the sky.

To their right, rows of soldiers in brightly colored leather armor vests stood at attention. A strange fanfare of drums, scratchy string instruments, and flutes assaulted Pol's ears. Shinkyan music was another item Pol had never discussed with Shira. He suppressed a sigh.

Opposite the soldiers stood groups of nobles. There might have been ten or fifteen individuals in each group. These must be the formal factions in Tishiko. He wondered how many unofficial factions there might be. In front of them was a line of mostly women. The queen would be among them, but if she was, she didn't dress any differently from the rest of her ruling group.

Another fanfare grew in intensity as a palanquin entered the square. Ten men on each side carried the conveyance on their shoulders. Women dressed in silk hooded robes swung incense back and forth in the same rhythm. They both preceded and followed the procession.

The palanquin slowly lowered to the ground and a vigorous looking woman with white hair stepped out after one of the robed women pulled back a cloth of gold curtain.

"Dismount!" a loud male voice cried out in Shinkyan. Pol didn't respond, but all the Shinkyans did, leaving the Imperials still sitting on their mounts.

"He said to dismount. This is a ceremony to greet the queen and to welcome me back. I didn't expect this," Shira said in Eastrilian. Pol noticed the trace of a worried look on her face.

Pol, Paki, and Fadden joined the rest.

"Bow to the Queen!"

Everyone went down on their knees and put their hands in front of them and touched their heads to their hands three times.

The Imperials bowed from their waists while the others paid

homage to the Queen, just as Shira had told them to do that morning. It seemed like an age ago to Pol. A messenger had arrived after breakfasting in one of those private rooms in an inn with a message that there would be a welcoming ceremony, but after riding through Tishiko, this show of obeisance was unsettling. Even in all the courts that Pol had visited, nothing compared to this moment.

The Queen approached Shira who remained bent over. "Rise, my daughter," the Queen said.

Shira stood, and then the others rose. Pol straightened up. He looked back to see Paki still bowing.

"Time to rise," Pol said.

Paki grinned and nodded. It looked like he was enjoying the pomp. Pol turned back to find the Queen's eyes on him.

"You are my daughter's protector?" she said in accented Eastrilian.

"I am," Pol said. "My name is—"

"I didn't ask you for your name, Pol Cissert. Or should I say Pol Cissert Pastelle?"

Evidently, the Queen was well informed. Pol bowed in response. The Emperor's Pet had officially arrived in Tishiko.

"Come with me," the Queen said to Shira.

They entered the palanquin, and as quickly as that, Shira was gone. Ako stood next to him as they observed the conveyance lifted into the air and carried back the way it came.

"Now what?" Pol asked.

"I don't know. We will wait here until told otherwise." Ako's last word was nearly drowned out by a different fanfare after which the foot soldiers marched out of the square, followed by their mounted escort leaving through the tunnel, then most of the factions disappeared into various palace buildings. Soon they stood in the middle of the square holding onto the reins of their horses.

A few soldiers remained, overlooking the square.

"We still wait," Ako said, but it appeared they didn't need to stand in formation. She led her horse to Fadden and they began to talk in low tones. Pol didn't join them but beckoned to Paki.

"Wasn't that impressive?" Paki said. "Weird music, though. I've never heard anything like it. Scratchy."

"It is." Pol would have used a different word. Even in the Shards, the music was more melodious, always accompanied with vocal elements. "What do you think of these buildings?"

"Everything is so strange. I thought spires with balls poked on them were different. Here the people don't even dress like us."

Fadden chuckled. "What about the Shards?"

"We were on the run so much that I didn't care," Paki said.

"Just soak it in. Few Imperials ever visit here," Fadden said.

A short, stocky Imperial man dressed as a Shinkyan approached them.

"You are the Seekers the Emperor sent? Pol Pastelle, Fadden Loria, and Pakkingail Horstel. Come with me." He turned and walked towards one of the buildings facing the square. "Bring your horses," he called back without turning around.

Fadden and Pol looked at each other and shrugged. "What else are we going to do?" Fadden said.

"Don't worry about me," Ako said. "I have a place to stay outside the palace."

They followed him out the square and between buildings. The man led them on a twisting path until they came to a compound within the palace walls. A four-story pagoda was framed between two two-story houses.

The man led them inside a simple wrought iron gate. Six Shinkyan servants rushed out and lined up.

"Take care of their horses and take their things into the Green building," the man said in Shinkyan. He turned to the Imperials. "I am the Emperor's envoy. Welcome to Tishiko. Treat this embassy as your home. You will be safest within its walls, for now." He put an arm across his stomach and bowed.

~~~

Chapter Twenty-Six

~

THE AMBASSADOR INTRODUCED HIMSELF. "I am Barian Woodcut of Hentz. Ranno Wissingbel and I spent some time in a monastery in Solisya together. I was in need of a job and Shinkya was in need of an Imperial ambassador. I've been here for seven years. And yes, I am the only Imperial in the compound, until today."

He showed them all into a modest dining room. The food was already laid out on the table Imperial style.

"This is my Imperial dining room when I'm not in a mood to eat sitting on a pillow," Barian said. He looked at Pol. "I was the one who had to wrestle with the Queen and her bureaucracy to allow you to possess your black Shinkyan stallion. Now the horse has made my life difficult. We still haven't come to an agreement on the horses he took with him to Deftnis Monastery. You may begin. We can eat while we talk."

Pol smiled. "They won't be returning. You know that and the Queen must know that."

Barian looked a little angry. "There must be some way to compromise."

"Fadden's horse wanted to return to Shinkya. We will be leaving her in Tishiko. Deftnis is not a horse prison and any of the horses will verify that none of them had a current Shinkyan owner except Amble, who is now bonded to Princess Shira."

"Ah. The golden horse had a successful bond. That might help, especially if Princess Shira is in favor."

"As far as we know, she is," Fadden said.

The ex-Seeker slipped a glance Pol's way. Fadden must have felt the edge to Barian's questions. He didn't speak comfortably. Pol looked the envoy's way again and realized the man wore a disguise. He had to be a she. She did speak very good Eastrilian, but Shinkya probably had no shortage of Sisters who had spent time in the Empire. He wondered if Barian still lived.

Pol took a deep breath. "So what faction do you belong to?" he said.

Barian sputtered. "Faction?" She said in a higher-pitched voice.

"Yes, you are at least a Master, maybe a Grand Master. I doubt a Shinkyan Elder would debase herself to mingle with 'human' Imperials. And we are the lowest, males," Pol said. Shira had told him that Shinkyans perceived boldness as strength, except around the Queen.

The ambassador changed appearance with a grunt. "So it's true about you. Only a Grand Master or Elder can detect disguises."

Pol nodded. "I have done so a number of times. You can ask Shira."

"Princess Shira," the woman corrected. "I am Grand Master Horani of the Lake Faction, if you must know. Did the Princess describe all the factions to you?"

Fadden shook his head. "No. Just that they exist. Ako said that it would take a while to learn the good points and bad points about each faction."

"A wise approach, for now," she said.

"What about Barian?" Pol asked.

"He will be joining you tomorrow. The human is unharmed and will resume his duties. For the rest of today and tonight, I am your hostess," she said. "What would you like to know?"

"Are we prisoners?" Paki said. From his expression, it looked like she would enjoy holding them.

"No, but you must still behave yourselves. Tomorrow, there will be a formal welcome in the Princess's honor. You will all attend. The Queen wanted me to make clear that you will respect Princess Shira's responsibilities."

"And what are they?" Pol asked. "She was thrown to the Tesnan wolves a year ago. We have been through quite a bit together," Pol said.

"That was a time for instruction and seasoning."

"So now it's time for Pol to lose his savor?" Fadden said.

Horani laughed softly. "Aptly put. It is."

Pol felt disappointment, but this was what he expected and what Shira had explained would happen.

"You three are curiosities. The Queen will have an audience with you three together or with Pol separately. After that, you will be given quarters close to the palace, but you will leave the Imperial enclave. That will be in two or three days. You may leave Tishiko as soon as you wish after that."

"I will be taking Demeron with me," Pol said.

"Do you really think you have any bargaining power within the palace grounds?"

"I have power." Pol said.

"So we understand. An Elder's power, according to Shira. That is unique in our country. Men with power do not grow old in our country."

"I had a similar affliction," Pol said.

One of Horani's eyebrows rose. "You did? How were you cured?"

"A great healer at Deftnis Monastery remade my organs."

"And if you had children, would they still carry the curse?"

Pol nodded. "I suppose so. There are patterns with the cells of the body that determine how we grow. Searl did not change those."

"Cells, you say?"

"Your Ancestors were able to put the curse in those cells. Have you heard of the legend of the Great Ancestor?"

"Of course," Horani snorted. "Why do you bring him up?"

"The Great Ancestor is a male, then." Pol knew that, but he wanted to impress that fact on the woman.

"I have seen a Great Ancestor in the city of Fassin in Gekelmar."

"We know of the Sleeping God. It is a sham."

"Is it? Shira knows what we saw. She was with me." The adventure in the cave wasn't something Pol felt he could reveal unless forced and definitely not to this woman.

"What did he look like?"

"She. It was the preserved body of a dead pregnant Ancestor. She had angular features and white hair." Pol was tempted to assume the alien's face, but he would save that for another time.

"You give us much to think about. Let us change the subject."

"Where did you get the idea for your architecture?" Paki asked. "It's different than any other I've seen."

Horani relaxed. "The basic structural concept came from Daera. They have small pagodas on that continent. We took those ideas from long ago and made them our own."

Pol could believe that since he saw no evidence of the Shinkyan architectural style in the few buildings pictured in the cave. What surprised him was a civilization on Daera and that Shinkyans would borrow such distinctive architecture from mere humans.

"We were told civilization does not exist on the Daeran continent."

"Something I know that you don't?"

Pol didn't appreciate the woman's sarcasm

She nodded her head. "Most of the continent is barbaric. I honestly think they are anti-civilization, content to live idle, non-productive lives. However, inside Daera there are two somewhat civilized countries, Kiria and Zasos. Kiria, superficially looks like Shinkya, Zasos covers the most arid part of the continent. They are bandits and thieves. They think the world revolves around them."

"Like Shinkya?" Fadden said.

Horani raised her chin. "Shinkya is above the simple dealings of humans. As the world revolves, Shinkya stays anchored above."

Pol nearly broke out laughing. Did this woman really believe what she said? Certainly, Tishiko was a striking city, but Pol lived with Shira for a year and had spent a few months with Ako. They were no more or no less human that anyone else Pol knew.

"Are you uncomfortable eating Imperial style?" Pol asked.

"Actually, I prefer it," Horani said. "As one gets older, knees don't bend as they should." She smiled.

Pol let her eat before asking her any more questions. The food tasted no better than the Shinkyan food that had already eaten so far. This time they ate with forks, knives, and spoons like Imperials.

"Tell me about Deftnis," Horani said.

Paki rubbed his hands and began to talk. Pol watched the woman absorb the information Paki gave her.

"No factions?"

Paki looked at Pol.

"No. Deftnis graduates typically serve the Empire if they are pattern-masters and often open up their own healing establishments if they are healers," Fadden said. He'd been eating and observing the woman while Pol bantered with her. "There are factions in Yastan, the capital, but they don't organize into overt groups like here. Factions operate in secret."

Horani laughed at that. "Don't think everything is out in the open in the capital. There have often been armed clashes between our factions, just not in the city."

"Does the Lake faction align with the Queen?" Fadden asked.

Horani nodded. "For the most part. There is no faction that is strictly the Queen's. The royal family is its own faction."

"I heard of another faction, the Scorpions."

Horani's face hardened. "They do not sponsor the Queen."

"If they don't support the Queen, then who do they sponsor?"

"It is complicated. They are very interested in the legend of the Great Ancestor. As if such a person would ever return. The Queen doesn't accept the legend," Horani said.

Neither did the Lake faction by the way Horani spoke. "So do many factions split about the return of the Great Ancestor?"

She waved her hand, a little too casually. "We have other issues that divide us. How we treat the Bureaucracy, the Merchant Class, the Soldier Class, and the Trades are different between the factions."

"What about the Farmers?" Pol asked.

"No one cares about the farmers. Most food production is through noble-owned estates."

Pol suspected that there was an underclass of Shinkyans that

Horani preferred not to talk about. "Do the factions have members in all of the classes?"

"Of course," Horani said, "even among our priests."

"Priests? Shira never mentioned anything about a religion."

"We don't worship a god if that's what you mean, but we have our Musings. They are an accumulation of wisdom that guides our culture. There are musings about the return of our Ancestors."

"The Great Ancestor legend is part of your Musings?"

Horani nodded. She narrowed her eyes. "I think you are getting the best of me. I seem to be answering more questions than I should."

"You don't need us to learn about the Empire. There are Sisters in every major city in the Empire and they are sprinkled throughout Volia as well," Pol said. "I would think Barian can provide you with anything you need to know."

Horani didn't try to deny it.

"What is Emperor Hazett III like?" she said.

Pol smiled. "He is a crafty character, but smart and he has continued a practice of loose rule among the kingdoms and dukedoms that make up the Baccusol Empire."

"What do you think about being proclaimed a Prince of the Empire?"

"I would rather it didn't happen," Pol said.

Horani raised her eyebrows and leaned forward. "Why?"

"I enjoy my freedom. I've been a prince once and that was enough."

"Barian knows the story better than I. He read it in a dispatch. The Disinherited Prince."

Pol nodded, surprised the woman was on such easy speaking terms with the man she impersonated. "I'm no longer disinherited. The Emperor had me take on an investigation in Yastan before he adopted me. I suppose I'm not through with his 'seasoning' and that included escorting Shira back home."

"But you have so much power. I thought you would take over the throne."

"Why?" Pol asked.

Horani sputtered a bit. "Because you can do things with your magic that most other magicians can't."

Pol thought the woman was too well informed about him. "Have you ever seen a person burdened by rule?"

She shook her head.

"You become a slave to the people. My brother is the King of Listya. He spends most of his time dealing with disputes and crimes and deciding water rights and boundaries. It's not a life I want to live."

That brought a laugh from Horani. "That's what the Bureaucracy is for. They do all the work and all the Queen has to do is produce children and get them trained."

Pol didn't see the Queen as Shinkya's tool. Pol could see the mantle of authority on her when she strode so confidently out of the palanquin when they first arrived.

Everyone's plate was empty. Horani rose from her chair. "It is time for you to retire. A servant will show each of you to your room." She left them without another word.

Three men filed into the dining room and pointed to the person they were to escort. Pol left last and followed the servant to the other building. They walked through a maze of sliding doors and up a wide stairway to a set of doors with carvings of a design primarily of flowers. It was well done and would be valuable if offered for sale in the Empire. Kell would likely go wild calculating what kinds of Shinkyan products he could trade.

The servant opened the door, bowing as he did so and ushered Pol inside. This wasn't a bedroom but a study. A tall spare man from the Empire sat at an expansive desk. "Did you have a pleasant time conversing with my wife?"

Pol looked into the pale blue eyes of Barian Woodcut.

"Horani is your wife? She said we would meet tomorrow."

"Hori is quite headstrong as are most Shinkyan Grand Masters," Barian said. "She wanted to grill you humans to see what you are made of."

"So she could enlist us into the Lake faction?"

Barian waved his index finger. "You are the Seeker Ranno said you'd be. Yes, indeed. I will find out tonight what she thinks. I suppose you extracted more information from her than she did from you?"

Pol thought for a moment. "I don't know what her expectations were. How did you persuade a Shinkyan to marry you?"

"I possess a bit of magic. In Deftnis terms, maybe a Purple. I can't do disguises, but I did learn a good bit of pattern magic. Ranno warned me not to flaunt my capabilities in Tishiko, but a male magician of decent capabilities is an attraction to a Shinkyan female magician."

Was that why Ako was attracted to Fadden or Shira to me? Pol thought.

Barian continued. "There has to be a mutual attraction, but the magic doesn't hurt. We've been together for five years. Horani is a widow, her noble husband died of a wasting disease. Healing isn't quite to Imperial standards in Shinkya."

"How do you get birds down here? You are a week and a half away from the border."

"Ranno taught me how to tweak a bird to seek out a certain coop in Yastan. He has a magician do the same thing with birds heading in our direction. It's quite convenient."

Pol learned something new that had been left out of his education. That was why the monastery could let so many birds fly north to Yastan. It brought a smile to his face.

"You didn't know that did you?" Barian laughed. "Good for you. Now to business." He rubbed his hands. "What do you intend to do about the Princess?"

"Nothing," Pol said. "She is home. Our relationship ends and we both will have cherished memories of our time together."

Barian looked at Pol with shrewd eyes. "You love her?"

Pol could feel his face blush. "What is love when you're not quite seventeen? Infatuation? I feel deeply for her and wish her the best." He felt uncomfortable talking about his relationship.

"You could take over Shinkya, you know. Ranno told me about your ability to take on the image of an Ancestor. I wouldn't dare tell my wife that, by the way. Many of the factions might jump at the chance to proclaim you ruler."

"Not me," Pol said. "I don't want to rule anything. That would bring great disappointment to my new father."

"Hazett?" Barian nodded. "You're right. Why bother with Shinkya when the entire Empire will be yours if everything works to your advantage."

"I don't want to rule," Pol said.

"With Shira by your side, you could bring Shinkya into the Empire."

Pol shook his head. "And would that be a good thing? A bit more trade would be useful for both sides, but Shinkya wants to be insular. They refuse to think of themselves as members of the human race."

"You're right. Sometimes Hori thinks of me as her pet, even though she spent a decade and a half in the Empire as a Sister."

"The Emperor feels that way about me," Pol said, "being his pet."

"I'm sure in a different way," Barian said chuckling.

Pol felt embarrassed again. "Yes, in a different way. Is what your wife said about our audience with the Queen and then being able to stay in Tishiko for a week or two correct?"

Barian nodded his head. "I'm sure once you leave the palace grounds, the factions will be vying for your attention."

Barian confirmed that the factions didn't just break down into anti-Queen or pro-Queen, but split with each other on a myriad of positions and interests. Barian must have learned early on that he wouldn't be able to ally with any of the factions other than his wife's. Pol didn't learn anything specific, other than he and his friends would have to watch their steps. They talked about factions in general until Pol yawned.

"I will bring up the Shinkyan stallions at Deftnis," Pol said changing the subject of their conversation.

"That is a touchy subject. Your horse hasn't made my job an easy one. I am reminded often of the fact that Shinkyan horses are a state treasure."

"Not all of them are treated as such," Pol said. "Amble, Shira's horse, was beaten by her master. Demeron rescued her. She wasn't treated like a treasure and Amble isn't the only example of mistreatment. The Queen can interrogate Demeron and Amble through Shira. The herd is treated very well at Deftnis. Shinkyan horses, especially, are thinking beings. They don't have the emotional range that humans and Shinkyans do, but they are thinking beings," Pol said.

Barian physically reacted when Pol said 'humans and Shinkyans'.

He knew how the Shinkyans felt about Imperials. "You may not get very far," the ambassador said.

"The horses aren't in Shinkya. Shinkya will not go to war with the Empire over the horses. The Emperor has no desire to do so. Hasn't Ranno communicated this position to you?"

Barian looked away. Pol was uncomfortable scolding an older man, but he wanted to see what position the ambassador took, and Barian didn't seem to support the Emperor.

"I'm just warning you about the Shinkyan position."

Pol took that as an evasive answer. He let it go. Now he suspected that Barian could not be counted on for support.

Their conversation stopped with a knock on the door. A servant entered with Barian's permission. "The mistress suggested it is time for the Imperial to be shown his room," the servant said.

"He'll be out presently," Barian said in poorly pronounced Shinkyan.

Pol was more fluent than Barian appeared to be. He felt it was prudent to be cautious about the man. Barian seemed a bit more Shinkyan in his behavior than Imperial.

~ ~ ~

Chapter Twenty-Seven

ALTHOUGH THEY HAD BEEN PROVIDED WITH SHINKYAN CLOTHES, Paki, Fadden, and Pol elected to wear their best Imperial wear. He strapped on his Shinkyan swords and made sure he had knives and steel splinters readily available. He also changed his hair color to its original goldish white.

By the looks on their faces, Barian and Horani were surprised by his hair color change, but they didn't comment as they proceeded to lead them out of the Imperial embassy through a different maze of pathways into the pagoda complex. At the bottom of the tallest, a large open space acted as the royal throne room.

They all faced an empty silver bench framed with red cushions on the seat and sides. A silver and black screen rose up about six feet behind. Above the screen hung a deep blue disk with a gold irregular star in the center, the same shape as the amulet Pol wore around his neck.

Pol looked up at it. For all the time he wore it, Shira had never mentioned the resemblance between the Shinkyan symbol and his amulet. He knew where the blue disk came from. He faced the original blue disk, which was the portal from the alien's world to Phairoon. Pol wondered if Shira knew what the circle was before she entered the Demron cave in the Penchappy Mountains on Volia. He didn't know if he felt disappointed in her or angry. What other secrets had she withheld from him? She hadn't admitted she knew about the pictures of the Demrons or the weapons they held until Pol had crafted his Demron weapons. He looked around the room and didn't see her anywhere. Ako wasn't among the many people in the throne room either.

Horani told them to stand in silence. Pol listened to the murmuring about the color of his hair. The throne room rose up three or more stories within the pagoda. A ring of stairs enabled people to climb further up into the many-leveled building. At each story, a ring of stairs circled the inside. Square windows, glazed with the ubiquitous waxed paper, lit up the massive room.

Pol remained impassive while the crowd continued to talk until some long horns blew their mournful tones from above. To Pol's ear, the tones weren't harmonized but sounded discordant.

"The Queen!" Five men shouted at the same time. Drums sounded out a slow cadence.

Tall doors opened from behind the throne, casting sunlight into the room. Six women dressed in purple and white silk robes entered at a slow pace, matching the drum strokes. They carried golden spears with silver shafts. Their hair was tied up into topknots with purple and white ribbons descending down their backs. Pol recognized Ako among the escort.

Four women wearing red robes with elaborate embroidery in silver and black preceded the Queen. Their hair and faces were powdered white with red lips. False eyebrows were painted an inch above normal. Pol could barely make out Shira through the elaborate makeup.

The Queen strode behind them all. She wore an elaborate white wig, festooned with jeweled gold ornaments. Her face was made up, but nothing more fancy than what Pol had seen most court ladies wear within the Empire.

He wondered if such pomp was normal. He wanted to ask Barian, but no one spoke as the Queen entered. Pol's eyes stayed on Shira as she took a place among the Queen's closest escorts. He caught her eyes for a moment, but then she looked away, the expression on her face unreadable through the white makeup.

Once the Queen sat on her throne, flanked on each side by two of the white-faced escorts, the crowd began to murmur again. Pol tugged on Barian's sleeve.

"Is this normal?"

Barian turned to Pol. "No. Shira has just been elevated to one of the four Crown Princesses. She is now formally in line to the throne. Similar to your predicament. If you thought you lost her when she entered Tishiko that is now confirmed. The Queen will never let Princess Shira abdicate her position."

Pol caught at the word predicament. "She can't become a disinherited princess?" He made the comment more to himself than to Barian.

"No," the ambassador said.

"What about the purple and white escorts?"

"One has to be a Sister to participate, but they often rotate. It is an honor to be selected," Horani said.

"Who does the selecting?" Fadden looked at Ako as he asked his question.

"The Queen and the Crown Princesses," she replied.

Pol expected that Shira had selected Ako. His mind tumbled with questions and doubts about Shira's feelings. Had she already set their relationship aside? Why not? Pol thought as he kept his eyes on Shira.

Everyone stopped talking as the Queen rose from her seat.

"As most of you noticed, I have finally replaced Nira as our fourth Crown Princess. Shira has been on the outside for a year learning about human customs and practices and has finally returned."

The Queen clapped her hands in a rhythm, which was followed by the crowd. It certainly wasn't spontaneous applause, but Pol clapped along with the Shinkyans, the only one among the Imperials who did.

The Queen sat back down. "Crown Princess Shira's escort from the Baccusol Empire will approach."

Pol kept still until Horani told them to stand in front of the low banister that ran a few paces in front of the throne.

Shira's eyes finally locked onto Pol's. He could now recognize the pain in her face. It was awful to see, but it reassured Pol that she hadn't cast him off.

"Your hair color has changed, I see," the Queen said in her accented Eastrilian.

"The time for disguise, as mild as it was, had ended when we finally delivered your daughter to you."

"Address her as Crown Princess Shira, Pol Pastelle."

"I will if you will address me as Imperial Prince Pol," he said, feeling a little angry at the Queen's condescension.

The Queen glared at him. "Very well. I give you leave to refer to the Crown Princess in any way you wish except as my daughter. I have many, but few are Crown Princesses."

Pol gave the Queen a slight bow. "I appreciate your understanding."

The Queen pursed her lips and narrowed her eyes. "You and I will talk later, in private."

He bowed to the Queen again.

"In gratitude for safely returning the Crown Princess, I will grant you small chests of gold and silver. You may buy anything you like and are permitted to take what you purchase back to the Empire," the Queen said.

Paki bowed deeply, but Fadden and Pol remained standing impassive. Pol bowed again so Paki wouldn't look so foolish. Pol didn't want a reward for giving up something as precious as Shira. However, he would purchase souvenirs for his new family and for some of his friends at Deftnis and Yastan.

"These humans are to be treated like Shinkyans for the time they are among us," the Queen said in Shinkyan. "You are now excused," She said in Eastrilian and waved them back.

Horani and Barian walked forward. "The audience for us has ended," Barian said as he gently took Pol's arm while Horani took Paki's to lead them out of the throne room.

"I've never seen anything so exotic before," Paki said after they left the room. "The costumes were weird. Shira didn't even look like herself."

"Ako didn't either," Fadden said. "I never realized how foreign Shinkyans were until now."

Pol shook his head. "Those traditions never existed when they left Volia. I am sure of that. There were no pictures of such pomp in

Teriland. They are trying to overcompensate for their status under the Demrons. Even Queen Anira wears a white wig. It's easy to see why."

"Teriland?" Horani said. She had been listening in and Pol regretted being so loose with his words.

"That's where the Shinkyans originated on Phairoon. Your Great Ancestors came from another world through a blue disk, a magic portal. They brought you with them," Pol said. "We have seen pictures in an ancient cave. None of them showed the ceremony we have just witnessed."

He would be surprised if Barian didn't roughly know what they did in Volia, so telling Horani a detail or two wouldn't expose them too much.

She didn't look very happy and didn't say another word while they walked back to the embassy.

They were shown to a Shinkyan-style dining room, somewhat larger than the one they had used for dinner and breakfast. The food was presented Shinkyan style and Pol knew that was a deliberate insult on Horani's part. They would be pummeled with subtle and not so subtle messages as long as they stayed in the embassy and likely their entire time in Tishiko.

She remained silent as they sat down on light blue cushions.

"Is that your real hair color? If it isn't you have deeply insulted Shinkya," Horani said.

"Now, Hori, speak less harshly to the Imperial Prince."

Horani scowled. "He's not my prince." She glared at Pol. "Answer me!"

Pol didn't like being cowed by the woman, but he took a deep breath. "This is my natural hair color. Ask Paki or Fadden. If you don't want the words of an Imperial, talk to Crown Princess Shira or Ako Injira. They have seen me as I truly am."

"I know what you truly are, an imposter!" she stood, shaken, and left the room.

"You will forgive, Hori," Barian said it as an apology. "Your presence unsettles many Shinkyans."

"My presence?" Pol said.

"The legend of the Great Ancestor. Many think you fulfill the prospect of the return of the Ancestors."

Pol pulled on his hair. "If you ever traveled to Teriland on Volia, you would see many people with this hair color."

"It's not just that, My Prince. You are a powerful male magician who has overcome the curse. That fact has been spread around by the Scorpion faction. They have a member, who met you in the Empire and was deeply impressed by you."

Pol thought back. "Karo Nagoya? Nater Grainell's tutor?"

"I don't know who Nater Grainell is, but Nagoya is the very one."

Pol laughed and looked away in disbelief. "I spent a few days at his lord's estate. How can he expect me to step into the shoes of the Great Ancestor? I don't believe it myself."

"Surely, you've thought of it," Barian said. "Please eat." He took a bite with his eating sticks.

Pol retreated into the mechanics of eating for a few moments. "Ako told me a bit about the Great Ancestor, but Shira never mentioned it."

"It is a mystery shared to those of noble birth after they have achieved maturity, which in Shinkya is twenty years old. I'm sure Princess Shira was exposed to the legend, but not the details. It is an uncomfortable prophecy for Shinkyans."

"What is it specifically?" Fadden asked. "One of your Musings?"

Barian nodded. "At a time of great prosperity, when Shinkyans will claim they own the sun itself, a Great Ancestor will arise who will cast them down into their former status as servants to the Ancestors. He will arrive in Tishiko with long white hair streaming down his back, riding a black horse and wielding a magic sword. All who fight against him will perish and he will rise from the ashes of Tishiko as the undisputed ruler of Shinkya. I think that sums it up well enough. I'm not big on legends, but Shinkyans are sensitive about their beginnings, as I am sure you know."

Pol nodded. He knew more than Barian did about the origins of the Shinkyans, but he imagined few Shinkyans knew the significance of the blue disk or the star.

"I am not the embodiment of any prophecy," Pol said. "I have had plenty of opportunities to die in my travels. Fadden and Paki know that well enough."

"He has," Paki said. "We just managed to escape from Borstall last year."

"But you did and you are sitting here within the palace grounds," Barian said. "Maybe my wife is right, Shinkya has something to fear."

"Not from me," Pol said. "I don't have long hair, anyway. Let's talk about something else." He began to eat.

A servant intruded and gave some intricately folded papers to their host. Barian read them and handed them to Pol. "You can't read these, but five factions have formally invited you to stay at their compounds in Shinkya while you visit."

Pol quickly scanned the messages. He understood most of what he read. "Which factions?"

"Fox, Scorpion, Lake, my wife's if you recall, Fearless, and Blue. It is not likely others will come."

"Do you have any suggestions?"

"Not the Lake Faction. They are too closely aligned with the Queen. If anything they want less to do with the Empire. It has led to arguments," Barian said. "Any faction will seek to control you, but my wife's will only seek your silence."

The ambassador's advice would be followed on that one.

"Fox?" Fadden said.

"Too new and too weak. They have a few Grand Masters and no Elder in their ranks. Everyone is looking towards the day when they get gobbled up by the Lakes or the Blues. The Blues are a middle-road group with notable members, but no notable accomplishments or positions."

"So what about the other two?" Pol asked. "Is staying at an inn a viable option?"

"You have no protection at an inn. If you were travelers without influence, that might be advisable, but you know the Queen, the new Crown Princess, and represent the Emperor every bit as much as I do. The Scorpions are open to change in Shinkya and have challenged the Queen's rulings. They whine about the moribund bureaucracy, but no one in their faction has run anything. Bureaucracies do not respond well to external threats. The Fearless faction is the most interesting of all. They are not a particularly political faction but focus on Sisters and soldiers. They support the Queen, but have shown the ability to ignore orders that were not to the benefit of Shinkya."

"A military faction, then?" Fadden said.

"The Fearless would appeal to Ranno, that is for sure."

Pol thought for a minute. "You said there might not be any more invitations?"

Barian shook his head. "Highly unlikely. Other factions would have been consulted before the invitations were extended."

"Could you set up interviews with all five?" Pol said. "Politically, we can demonstrate fairness and there is a possibility that we might learn more about Shinkya and Tishikan politics. You are invited to sit in, but I'd rather Horani only attend her own faction's interview."

That brought a frown to Barian. "Do you have a predisposition?"

Pol didn't care what Barian thought. He guessed that Horani would not be happy, but that was the ambassador's problem. He looked at Fadden.

"Scorpion or Fearless," Fadden said. "But we should be willing to keep an open mind."

"I will arrange for a series of interviews this afternoon."

~ ~ ~

Chapter Twenty-Eight

~

THE BLUE FACTION BROUGHT A GROUP OF FOUR GRAND MASTERS. According to Barian, the lack of an Elder in the group meant they weren't serious about taking in Pol's group. The offer was strictly for show.

Barian made the introductions. He knew two of the Grand Masters. Horani watched them carefully as they entered the Imperial style dining room, now set up with eight chairs at the table.

"We would like you to live at our compound while you are in Tishiko. You plan on staying for a week or two?" One of the Grand Masters said in Shinkyan. Barian translated.

Fadden nodded. He would be doing the talking for this faction. "We do. Our needs are minimal. I will need to procure a horse for my trip back to the Empire. I do not require a Shinkyan. All three of us will be interested in bringing back a few souvenirs. The Queen has graciously provided us with the material means to do so."

The oldest woman of the group nodded before Barian could translate.

"What is your intent politically?" she said in heavily accented Eastrilian.

Pol thought that was getting right to the key question.

"We have no political agenda that we are pursuing in Tishiko," Fadden said.

Pol raised his hand to speak. "We do wish to ensure the freedom of the Shinkyan horses that currently reside on Deftnis Isle. They came to us on their own free will as thinking beings. They want to stay and the Emperor wants them to remain."

"What do you intend to do about your relationship with Crown Princess Shira?" another Grand Master said, looking directly at Pol.

"I don't think that is any of the Blue Faction's business. It is my opinion that any relationship that I have had with Shira is likely over, don't you? That appears to be the Queen's policy."

The elder Grand Master straightened her silk robe. "I don't think that is any of the Blue Faction's business, either. I am not sure it is in your best interest to accept our offer of assistance." She looked intently at Pol and spoke in Eastrilian. "Be wary of the Queen. She does not have your best interest at heart."

"I am already well aware of that, but thank you for your confirming the fact to me." Pol nodded.

At the woman's nod, the delegation rose, and after mutual bows exited the room.

Pol walked into the hallway. Horani spoke in Shinkyan to another woman. She wasn't dressed like a servant.

"The Blues made their visit and left. They actually warned the Imperial Prince to watch out for the Queen." She sniffed, looked at Pol, and then back at her friend. "The prince's insolent gaze is insulting, is it not?"

Pol turned away, biting his tongue. He slipped back into the interview room.

"Horani hears everything we say," Pol said into Barian's ear.

The ambassador just nodded. "I expected as much. Now you are warned."

Pol thought it odd that the ambassador was so free with his speech after she left. Horani obviously listened to their entire breakfast conversation, and the pattern supported the fact that Barian's behavior in the interviews was a performance for Pol's benefit.

The next group came from the Fearless Faction. The Elder needed help getting through the door and into her seat. Two armored men, probably Sisters with disguises, accompanied her.

Pol let them sit first and then sat down. "Ladies," Pol said as he nodded to each one.

Barian introduced the Elder, but not the Sisters.

"We are here to offer our protection," the Elder said. "You will not find a more neutral place to spend your time in Tishiko. We have no ax to grind with the Queen, even though we don't always seek the same path."

"Do you have any questions to ask us?" Pol said.

"None. Our offer is an open one, even if your first choice is not satisfactory," the elder spoke in flawless Eastrilian. "We would like to talk to you about your various views, of course, but that is up to you."

The Elder struggled to her feet and the women walked out.

"No conditions, no questions," Barian said. "That offer will be hard to pass up."

"Are they playing games?" Fadden asked.

Barian had a faint smile on his face. "I don't think so. Their power rests in military force, both magical and physical."

"But two of them wore disguises. Pol caught them out."

"Nothing to worry about. That is the normal escort for that Elder. The Fearless flaunt their Sisters. I'm sure they were relieved to see Pol expose their disguises. They have firsthand evidence that Pol has power."

They waited an extra half an hour for the Lake Faction to arrive. All four men discussed what questions to pose. Fadden volunteered to be the spokesman, now that they had decided how to manage the Lakes' visit.

Horani led two women in. Despite their youthful look, Barian's wife introduced them as Elders. Barian shook his head, out of view of the three women. So they weren't Elders.

"We have rooms prepared for you," one of the 'Elders' said. "You may get your things together and we will escort you to our compound. It is only a few steps away from the palace."

"Why should we take advantage of your hospitality?" Fadden said.

"Because we are the Lakes. We are closest to the Queen in both the location of our compound and in our feelings for the royal family."

"Pol would like to visit Crown Princess Shira a few times before we leave. Could you arrange that with the Queen?" Fadden said.

"What? Preposterous. The Crown Princess cannot sully herself with Imperial contact."

"Really?" Fadden said, leaning forward and looking at Horani. "Yet you have sullied yourself marrying Barian. Why?"

Horani sputtered. "I love my husband."

"Even though he is a mere human?"

She blushed. "What do you mean?"

Fadden stood up. "This interview is at an end. We will take another offer. It appears that you introduce women as Elders who aren't and were late to meet us. The Imperial Prince is not used to such treatment."

Pol looked into Horani's eyes.

"It is clear that the Imperials are not civilized enough to be gracious," Horani said in Shinkyan.

Barian winced and looked at Pol, who stayed as impassive as he could as he stood. "Thank you for providing an offer. I am sure the Emperor will be pleased at your condescension." He bowed and leaned over to talk quietly into Fadden's ear. "Arrogance is never pretty," he said.

Fadden nodded in return.

The women got to their feet and left, while Barian rubbed his hands. "You two are good at this. I am enjoying myself seeing men negotiate with women so eloquently."

Pol doubted if the word Barian really meant was eloquent, but his wife was probably back at her listening post.

The Fox faction had been chased off by the Lakes. They left a message for Barian stating circumstances had changed, proving that Barian's assessment seemed to be accurate.

Paki sat back and moaned, "Why do we have to interview these people? It seems a lot of trouble to go through."

"I've enjoyed it," Fadden said. "There is only one faction I would say 'yes' to." He looked at Pol and then caught himself and said to Barian, "What did the Lake women say at the end?"

"Imperials are too barbaric to see a good thing. Something like that," Barian said.

They waited for a few moments before Horani entered.

"The Scorpions are here," she said. "They even brought two men with them."

Pol wondered what was wrong with two men?

Barian stood and introduced an Elder, a Grand Master, a male Master. He didn't look much older than Pol, but Pol might look much younger with his cure. Barian obviously didn't know the last person to enter. He put his hand across the table.

"Karo Nagoya. It is good to see a familiar face in Tishiko. We met at Lord Grainell's estate in Boxall. I am surprised that they let a Competent come, but I'm glad they did." Nagoya's eyebrows rose when Pol inferred his Competent rank.

Pol bowed to the Scorpions. The young Master scowled a bit. He wasn't a happy magician.

"We will make this brief. I wanted to greet you all in person," the Elder said in barely accented Eastrilian. "We hear the Fearless Faction offered you shelter while in Tishiko. We think that is the best place for you."

That was unexpected, thought Pol.

"I would be pleased if you spent some time with us, during daylight hours. Nights can be trying for Imperials." She looked at Barian, who nodded.

"Demeron thanks you for the food when he was a stranger at your gates," Pol said.

"No stranger," Karo said. "We were happy to provide it."

The young Master glared at him. He acted so immature and was quite easy to read. Pol must have been like that at Borstall before Farthia finally began teaching him the proper way to behave.

"Make sure you take that horse away from Tishiko. We had an interesting exchange, but he is better suited in the Empire," the Elder said.

"Oh, it was you."

The Elder nodded. "Quite unprecedented. I am sure that you had something to do with his 'awakening'. I would like to converse with you about it." She held up her hand. "I am not upset at the encounter, but I would like to get a measure of what kind of magician bonded so well with his horse."

Pol smiled. "I would be happy to talk to you about that and other things. I surmise that you are on tolerable terms with the Fearless Faction?"

The Elder looked at Barian. "Tolerable is a good way of putting it. We will let you communicate your decision to the faction that has gained your trust today. Bear in mind, our invitation has been withdrawn." The woman stood. "I look forward to another meeting or more." Her smile seemed genuine to Pol, more genuine than the young Master or the perfunctory nod given to them by the Grand Master. He wondered if that woman spoke Eastrilian.

Karo came around the table and shook each of their hands. "No one can be fully trusted in Tishiko. You realize that don't you?" he said quietly.

"We do," Pol said. "That applies to us as well."

Karo blinked at Pol's statement but nodded enthusiastically.

"It is time to depart," the Elder said as she walked out the door.

"Later, then," Karo said.

"Later for sure," Pol said and meant it. The Scorpions intrigued him. They could have captured Demeron, or tried anyway, but they ended up helping him. Perhaps Pol and his group would be too much of a burden or would make them more of a target.

"Those Scorpions," Barian said. "They like to mix things up and do the unexpected. Today was no different."

Pol nodded. "They are a group I definitely want to talk to."

"I'll not stop you. I suppose you are staying with the Fearless Faction."

Fadden stood and stretched. "An interesting exercise. The pattern all five showed us is pretty clear-cut."

Paki blinked his eyes with confusion. "How could you build a pattern with only four interviews?"

"And the canceled one contributes as well," Pol said. "There are four basic stances: Pro-Queen, Anti-Queen, Pro-Tishiko/bureaucracy, and Anti-Tishiko/bureaucracy."

"You got that from our interviews?" Barian said.

"I'll admit that Fadden and I did talk to Ako about the various factions. Shira isn't quite an objective party," Pol said. "Fox and Lake are Pro-Pro. I would bet they will eventually merge or Fox will officially subordinate to Lake. Blue is Anti-Queen and likely Pro-Tishiko. They were unhappy about the Shinkyan horses, which I consider a bureaucratic issue, although I may be wrong about that. The bureaucracy would be more upset with our presence than the Queen if it wasn't for Shira."

Barian smiled and nodded. "You are correct but for the wrong reason. The Shinkyan horse issue is more related to the fear of Imperial magicians in the battlefield riding Shinkyan horses. As you probably know, Shinkyan horses can communicate over a mile."

"Communications," Pol said. I never thought about that."

"I did," Fadden said. "Did I think of something you haven't?"

"Then the Fearless Faction will not be happy about Demeron."

"You will have to ask them that. I'm sure the issue will come up, but to them, it is less of an issue than being told by untrained faction leaders how to conduct their business," Barian said.

"So they are actually more neutral than anything else. That still fits my pattern. The Scorpions are anti-everything since they think they are smarter than all the other factions," Pol said. "They will respect you if you are smart and have something unique to offer."

"But Karo isn't that great of a magician. They even said so," Paki said. "He wasn't treated very well."

"He is one of the few Shinkyan males who have traveled in the Empire. Men have a different perspective about things, and vice versa," Fadden said. "Shinkyans get all their intelligence from Sisters."

Paki put his hands to his head. "My brain is spinning," he said.

"Slow it down. We will be going to Fearless. I want to spend a good chunk of time with the Scorpions. I think I will learn by what they say and what they don't say."

"You are making a mistake," Horani said, entering the room. "You will be safest with the Lake faction."

"Perhaps safer," Pol said, 'but we won't learn as much."

"What do you possibly hope to learn? My husband has been the ambassador to Shinkya for years. He knows us as well as anyone."

"Did we say we were going to ignore him?" Fadden said.

"No," she said.

"I would be happy to visit the Lake faction," Pol said. "I'm not sure they would be comfortable to talk to the Great Ancestor for any length of time." He smiled.

Horani snorted. "Your joking doesn't affect me."

Pol made his face look like an alien. "Do I look more like the Great Ancestor now?"

Horani screamed and ran out of the room. Pol turned back into his normal self.

"I've never seen her so horrified," Barian said, laughing. "I hope it did her some good, but I'm not so sure about you."

"She knows all about disguises. When she realizes that's all I did, she will settle down," Pol said.

"I wouldn't be too sure. She is probably heading over to the Lake compound to describe what she saw. She'll be telling them that you looked like the Great Ancestor." Barian laughed. "Even I was a little shaken by the transformation. I'm glad it wasn't a real representation."

"But it was," Pol said.

Chapter Twenty-Nine

~

AS POL, PAKI, AND FADDEN PREPARED TO LEAVE THE EMBASSY, a woman arrived at the front door with a letter addressed to Pol. She remained at the Embassy.

"The Queen wants an audience this morning," Pol said to Barian. "I am to be escorted by the woman who delivered the message."

"That's no ordinary messenger. She is one of Shira's half-sisters."

"A Crown Princess?" Pol asked.

"No. She isn't strong enough magically. Her name is Moruko. I'll have to greet her."

They walked to the embassy foyer.

"Princess Moruko. Thank you for coming all the way to deliver this. I'm sure Prince Pol is honored by your presence," Barian said in Shinkyan.

She didn't even rise at first. She ignored Barian and peered at Pol from her seat. "This is the human my sister fell for?" Maruko said in Shinkyan. She snorted and then stood. "Come with me," she said in nearly unintelligible Eastrilian and opened the door herself, leaving Pol behind to follow.

"You don't like me?" Pol said in Shinkyan.

Maruko stopped and looked back at him. "You speak Shinkyan?"

"Is that a crime? Barian speaks Shinkyan, although his diction isn't polished," Pol said, finding the right Shinkyan word. He figured that Maruko was far down on the pecking order if she was the one to fetch him, so he doubted she would tattle on him about speaking Shinkyan, assuming Shira hadn't already done so.

"No," Maruko said. "I thought Shira told me nothing but lies about you."

"Lies?"

"No one believes that you are as powerful as she claims or that you are so smart."

Pol laughed. "I've done plenty of dumb things in my short life."

Maruko turned one side of her lip up. "Short is right. You're due to die soon, aren't you? That is what the Lakes told Mother."

He ran around Maruko. "Do I look frail? I was once, but I was cured."

"Cured. I don't believe it."

Pol smiled. "If you have any doubts, let one of your healers examine me. I'm in good health and should live as long as any other normal male human."

"Show me your magic."

"Something harmless?"

Maruko nodded.

Pol picked up a pebble. "See that wall over there?"

He pointed to one of those concrete walls. Pol held out his palm with the pebble.

"Watch the pebble and the wall."

He stood next to Maruko, who, he noticed, was much shorter than Shira. He concentrated on the wall and sent the pebble to slam against the wall. There was a pop and a puff of dust came off the wall.

"Shall we go see?" Pol said grinning.

Maruko ran to the wall and put her finger into a hole twice as big as the pebble. "You could have killed someone with that pebble."

"I could, but why would I?"

Maruko stared at Pol. "Because you have power."

"A person's real strength is to use his or her power with the utmost control. Watch."

He picked up another pebble and held out his palm like he did before at the building on the other side of the pathway. He teleported the pebble to just before the wall and then moved just enough to click against the concrete before it fell to the ground.

They walked to the wall. The pebble left a small mark on the concrete. Maruko picked up the tiny rock.

"Can I keep this?" she said.

"This is your mother's compound. It's her rock."

She smiled this time and put the tiny stone in her pocket. "I didn't think I'd be learning anything from you on the way to my Mother, but I did. Thank you." She walked ahead of him with an energetic gait.

Had Pol made a friend? He didn't think so, but if he gave Maruko something to think about, enduring her initial rudeness was worth it.

They walked past the central pagoda and slipped into the next one over. She took him past a set of four uniformed women, who nodded simultaneously as Maruko led him through a pair of low barriers. They walked through another guarded barrier and up a set of wide stairs.

Pol didn't see a single male face as they traveled along a long corridor. None of the women wore the ornate costumes from the formal court experience.

Maruko nodded to two more guards. These were large men for Shinkyans. She knocked and opened the door.

"I won't be following you in," Maruko said as she gave Pol a little nod, "Prince Pol."

He didn't know if she gave him the honorific due to being in possible earshot of her mother or because of the chance that Pol impressed her.

"Prince Pol Cissert Pastelle, you may approach the Queen," a woman said from around the corner of the door.

Pol twisted his head around to see a desk in the corner. The woman stood when she announced him. Pol looked at the Queen in front of a low desk. She sat on a thick cushion on a wide bench reminiscent of the throne, but made from highly polished wood.

Pol stood as the Queen's eyes drifted up from a portfolio spread out in front of her. There were two stacks of portfolios on either side of her. Pol guessed one side was for unread documents and the other for those the Queen had seen. Barian was totally wrong about the Queen. Pol expected she had her hand wrapped around the Shinkyan bureaucracy's throat.

"You are staying with the Fearless Faction while you are in Tishiko?" the Queen said in poorly accented Eastrilian.

"Yes. We talked to a few factions and found it most appropriate to take the Fearless up on their request. They seemed to be the most neutral of those who were willing to take us in."

The Queen nodded as if she didn't care about what Pol said in reply. She looked at her secretary. "When will Shira be joining me? I don't care to speak in the Empire's barbaric tongue any longer," she said in Shinkyan.

"There is no need for a translator," Pol said in Shinkyan. "I might not know some words, but I am a quick learner of languages as is Shira."

The Queen's eyes widened and then narrowed. "Why did you keep this from me?"

Pol thought the woman certainly didn't mince words. "I didn't keep anything from you. Shira knows I speak your language. She's been teaching me Shinkyan ever since we landed on Eastril."

After a snort, the Queen lifted a finger.

"Yes, Queen."

"Summon the new Crown Princess. She doesn't have to rush."

The Queen's eyes swiveled up to Pol. "What am I to do with you?"

"Nothing. My friends and I will be spending a few weeks in Tishiko before we head back to the Empire if that is acceptable to you. Excuse me, what is the appropriate honorific?"

"You may call me... Queen Anira if I can call you Pol. That seems to be the name Shira uses for you," the Queen said, not quite so imperiously as she had in the throne room.

"Thank you, Queen Anira." Pol bowed. He still stood, waiting for her to speak.

"Shira still has feelings for you and that will not do. What are you going to do about it?"

Pol didn't like the snappish tone in the Queen's voice. He expected disdain, but she spoke with repressed anger. Pol bit the inside of his lip.

He worried that Shira had dropped her regard for him and in some ways he had hoped she had relegated him to her memories, but Anira admitted their relationship hadn't ended when Shira set foot in Tishiko.

"I have feelings for her, but I understand that makes for difficulties."

Anira snorted. "Difficulties, indeed! Even if marriage was an option, both of you are too young. Marriage is illegal in Shinkya before the age of twenty."

"And why wouldn't marriage be an option?" Pol asked. "I am not a Shinkyan, but other than that, is there an objection, Queen Anira?"

Anira tugged on her robes to straighten them. "The Queen of Shinkya must take on many partners and have many daughters. I know Shira well enough to know she would only want you and that makes you a liability to Shinkya."

"Does that mean that you are like a Queen bee?"

Anira didn't look like she understood him.

"A Queen bee gives birth to the hive. She selects her successor from any number of eligible worker bees who are females."

"That is too apt of a simile, Pol, and it is mostly accurate. Shira through her experience and prior training is too accomplished to step aside from a possible destiny as Queen of Shinkya. You would have to be someone special in order to upset Shinkyan Royal protocol."

"I am the Great Ancestor," Pol said. "Isn't that special enough?"

Shira stood at the door and gasped. "Don't, Pol!"

He turned around and walked to her side. Pol took her hand and squeezed it as he escorted her back to stand in front of Anira's desk.

The Queen snapped her fingers and directed the secretary out of her study with a move of her hand. She pursed her lips in evident disapproval.

Pol looked over to see Shira's eyes getting moist.

"I will not tolerate a union between the two of you. Get used to it. I am Queen of Shinkya and my word is law."

Pol looked at Anira and realized the woman was lying.

"You work with the bureaucracy as you both rule Shinkya," Pol said, relying on a sudden understanding of the Shinkyan pattern. "You are more than a figurehead, but your word is not final law."

"It is as far as Shinkyan customs and traditions are concerned."

"And I am the Great Ancestor."

Queen Anira laughed. "You dare to tell me that twice?"

Pol pulled out his amulet. "Does this look familiar? My mother gave me one similar to this. I know what it is and Shira does too. It appears on the symbol in your throne room. Do you know what it is?"

Anira looked towards Pol, but couldn't take her eyes off the amulet. "Shira told me of that."

"Did she tell you that we also know of the portal? That is the blue disk that is the background of this star in your throne room. I have spoken to the Ancestor who lived, if you want to call it that, in the portal."

"You didn't tell me this," Anira said, glaring at her daughter.

"Would you have believed me?"

The Queen looked away and sought composure in silence. "You are both too young for marriage, anyway. I will pretend I did not hear any claims about Pol being the Great Ancestor. The very idea is preposterous. I don't accept it."

"May I ask one thing of you?" Pol said.

"What would that be?"

"I would like to visit your daughter or have her visit me a few times before we leave. I promise to leave Shinkya and Shira when the time comes."

"You'll not make a claim to be the Great Ancestor?"

Pol looked at Shira and squeezed her hand. "I will not if you just let my friends and me spend a pleasant week or two in Tishiko. We will leave, just as we intended to."

"What about the hand of my daughter?"

Pol took a deep breath, aware that Shira looked at him from his side. "I never intended to ask you for her hand. I agree that we are too young."

He heard Shira sigh.

"Shira?" her mother said. "It's not as if he isn't worthy of you. An Imperial Prince, and if what you say is true, he does have Ancestor blood, even if he isn't the Great Ancestor."

"He was a disinherited prince until we visited Yastan," Shira said, "but I agree with Pol. We are too young, even without Shinkya's rules."

Pol felt her grip weaken. "I would like to continue to communicate with him until I am married," she said with some conviction.

"Don't get ahead of your hopes, daughter. I will permit correspondence, but only to maintain a parallel channel to the Emperor."

Could that mean that the Queen might not trust Barian? Did the Queen suspect his connection to the Lake faction? If she did, the Queen didn't hold Horani's faction in the high esteem the Lake faction thought or intimated.

"I will accept that," Shira said.

The Queen snorted. "I am so pleased you deign to do so."

Pol wondered why the Queen made Shira a Crown Princess if she looked on her with so much disdain.

"Is there anything else that you wish me to do or communicate to the Emperor through my parallel channel?"

"Does Hazett intend to keep the Shinkyan horses at Deftnis Monastery?" the Queen asked.

"It isn't what the Emperor thinks, but what the horses have in mind. We brought two horses that wanted to return to Shinkya. Ako Injira has bonded with one of them. The Deftnis monks intend to do the same with any horses. They have no desire to convince other Shinkyan horses to leave their homeland."

The Queen grunted most un-regal-like. "Then what is done is done." She sighed.

Pol hadn't expected so many gestures. It made Anira seem coarse. Most queens in the Empire would generally behave with more comportment, but then this was Shinkya and it looked like Anira had no desire to impress anyone. Her response to his statement about the Shinkyan horses confirmed Pol's suspicion that the bureaucracy was more affronted than the Queen.

"That is all for now. Shira, see the boy out."

She nearly pulled Pol out of the study. "This way," Shira said.

They walked up two stories into the pagoda. Everything was designed around the stairway that always wound around the outside of the pagoda, bringing light into the corridors.

She opened a door and led Pol inside. The room was a study of some kind. She locked the door and put her arms around him.

"I'm sorry," Shira said burying her face in his shoulder, speaking Eastrilian.

"For what?" Pol hugged her tightly and then gently pushed her away. "We knew our relationship would end in Tishiko."

"I refuse to believe that," she said. "Mother wants me to bow to her every whim, but none of us do. We have more power as Crown Princesses than she admits. I can choose my husbands."

"So am I to be part of your stable of men to sire powerful daughters for Shinkya?"

Shira slapped him on the shoulder, not too hard, Pol thought. "If we are married, I will refuse to share you. Queens and Crown Princesses have men come and go. Their marriages may only last weeks or months. The Queen had twenty-three. She has none now that she is past childbearing."

Pol laughed. "I called her a Queen bee."

Shira giggled and took his hand. "Did you really? That is as good a description as any."

"I know," Pol said. He squeezed. "I missed your input to the factions that paraded into Barian's embassy."

"The Queen was quite interested in your choice."

Pol gave her a detailed review of the entire process.

"You made the right choice. Mother would not have tolerated you staying at the Scorpion compound. They are too overtly against the government and the crown, to use an Imperial term."

"Karo Nagoya is a Scorpion."

"I know. I checked on him when I had a moment, remembering that he met you. It looks like he was instrumental in getting their highest Elder to meet you."

"Demeron had more to do with that. The Elder treated Karo like a little boy. Are Competents held in such low regard?"

Shira nodded. "It's part of our culture." She hugged him tight. "Your continuing to take on the role of the Great Ancestor would not be wise."

"I understand. The only people who would applaud that might be the Scorpions, but somehow I think their Elder is smarter than that. I think she realizes that the Great Ancestor has the potential to destroy Shinkyan culture."

Shira nodded. "If you upset the wrong people, you will become a target, and I'm not so sure you can rely on the Fearless faction to protect you."

"I won't fight anyone unless pressed," Pol said. "If we are safe while in Tishiko, then no one has any reason to be anxious. We will just leave and correspond. I'll make sure Barian has enough funds to have a large coven of birds for our messages."

Shira smiled and hugged him again. "I will allow one kiss."

"Allow?"

She nodded. "That is a restriction on myself. We can't spend too much time together, but I'll arrange a meeting every few days." She lifted her chin up and Pol kissed her.

He felt sad their relationship was about to be cut off, but Pol still retained the stark sensibilities of a royal child. One had to succumb to duty when duty demanded sacrifice.

"Who is Maruko?"

Shira's face lightened up. "You impressed a girl who just isn't impressed. The fact that you took the time to show her control rather than just force astounded her. She thought the Imperials were all bluster."

"Enough are," Pol said.

Shira nodded. "She may not be a friend, but she is not an enemy. Perhaps I can talk her into being a go-between."

"What about Ako?"

"She has already left the palace grounds and you'll see her often enough at the Fearless compound. Fadden will be thrilled."

~~~

Chapter Thirty

~

THE FEARLESS FACTION HAD TWO PAGODAS IN THEIR COMPOUND, a four-story structure, and a five-story, wider, building. Their hosts gave them the third level of the taller pagoda to themselves.

Each of them had their own bedroom and Ako showed up to occupy the fourth during their stay in Tishiko. In this pagoda, the stairs wound up in a square of two flights per floor around a center atrium. Pol could look up to see a latticework roof covered with a translucent covering that acted as a skylight.

The bedrooms took up two of the sides with a study area with four desks facing a food preparation and eating section. A bathroom with water magically pumped up from the compound's well finished their space.

Pol didn't quite get used to people going up and down the stairs that were open to their area, but Ako didn't mind and neither did the intruders. Paki, on the other hand, liked to do a bit of casual people watching.

A man walked onto their floor. "Prince Pol, the Elder would like to talk to you."

Fadden rose from a couch. The man held out his hand. "Just the Prince."

Pol shrugged and patted Fadden's shoulder. Ako was gone for the moment, and Fadden looked like a person with unwanted time on his hands.

Pol patted himself to make sure he was adequately armed and followed his escort down the stairway. The man didn't say anything while he led Pol to one of the larger two-story gabled buildings. This one had more carvings on the columns and in the overhangs.

The escort led Pol into a large conference room on the main floor. The old Elder greeted him without standing up.

"Welcome to the Fearless," she said.

"I thank you for your hospitality." Pol replied bowing.

"No need for any of that. You are using us and we are using you. That is the way of Tishiko," the woman said.

Pol knew the Fearless were mostly pragmatic and the woman's comments proved it. "I can use you and be appreciative at the same time."

"I suppose one can," the Elder said. She lifted up one side of her mouth in a sort of smile. "How did your meeting the Queen Anira go?"

"Our discussion dealt mostly with my relationship with her daughter. I did verify that the Queen will accept a Shinkyan herd at Deftnis. That was one of my goals after delivering Shira safely."

"Not all will be happy to hear that a herd of our precious horses are gone. The general who ran after them is part of our faction. She looks forward to reacquainting herself with Demeron. That's his name, isn't it?"

Pol nodded. "Does she hold a grudge?"

"No, but her pride was battered about for a bit when she returned with empty hands. The Fearless have no official position on the matter, nor will we. You have nothing to worry about as far as your horse is concerned," she said. "Make yourself comfortable in your quarters. Those are for visiting faction members. Many of our people live outside of Tishiko."

"I trust we are not inconveniencing you," Pol said.

The Elder smiled. "Not at all. I would like a magic demonstration."

"What would you like to see?"

"Something novel."

Pol turned himself invisible and moved to another part of the room and re-appeared. "Is that sufficient?"

The Elder coughed. "Sufficient doesn't describe it," she said. "We have camouflage spells but nothing like that. I heard rumors that you can locate."

Pol looked about. "There are three people behind that wall in a small room. Two guards each at the two doors, not to mention that person over there, blending in with the curtain."

That brought the Elder's eyebrows up. "Locating is not an ability that Shinkyans possess. Detecting an expertly camouflaged person is rare, very rare." She snapped her fingers and pointed to a door. The camouflaged woman ended her tweak, bowed, and left the room.

"Ako and Shira were unable to learn how to do it, no matter how much I tried to teach them."

"Are you adept at wards?"

Pol shook his head. "I can see wards and deactivate them. I'm not adept at creating them, so I have a lot to learn about making them do what I want them to do."

"We just guess," the Elder said. "I'll admit it since you are so free with your information."

"I did learn that people see wards differently. Different colors, different shapes, different textures. I have had experience in trying to avoid them. The compulsion spell that the South Salvans developed is really a ward. I see it as a purple patch with tentacles reaching down into the afflicted person's brain."

"You are quite a prodigy. I expect you've been told that before."

"I have," Pol said. "I'm still young enough that I'll be told that many more times."

That brought a low chuckle from the woman.

"And you are perfectly healthy."

"Now I am."

"Ako has verified that. You are easily Elder rank, Prince Pol Cissert Pastelle. There are many in Tishiko who are frightened of you."

Pol nodded. "Are you one of them?"

"To be honest, I can't help but feel a little anxiety about a man who can tweak and understand patterns as well as you. There aren't many like you, even in the Empire. I know, since many of the Sisters working in the Empire are Fearless. You can detect disguises?"

Pol nodded. "The two men who escorted you to the Imperial embassy were women."

"Ha! I told them you would find them out. They didn't believe me and were shocked when you called them ladies!" She looked at Pol appraisingly. "When you leave me go to the desk you passed when you entered the building. I want you and your friends to always be accompanied with an escort. It has two purposes—"

"To protect us and to send a message to others to stay away. In addition, your status as a faction will rise with distinguished foreigners choosing Fearless over the other factions."

The woman clapped her hands once and grinned. "Precisely!"

Pol and Paki walked the streets of Tishiko flanked by two armed Sisters wearing Fearless colors. There were no markets in the city. All goods were sold out of shops. The only carts on the streets were food vendors.

Pol stopped by a window and spotted something he wanted. "I want to buy a few of those carved animals," Pol said. "They are small enough to pack, yet unique to Shinkya."

"I think that's a great idea," Paki said.

They walked in and saw a number of decorative items displayed on the shelves. Pol went right to a locked cabinet filled with the little animals.

"Are these made in the city?"

"Most people think of these as Shinkyan carvings, but they are actually from Daera."

"Daera?" Pol said. "Even a couple of Shinkyans thought these were made in Shinkya."

"I wish," the shopkeeper said. "Then they wouldn't cost as much, and I could sell more." He sighed and unlocked the cabinet. "Most Tishikans just think they are made outside the city."

Pol picked one up. He could see the grain of the wood match

the carvings. "These are made with magic. I didn't think they had any magic on Daera."

"Who told you that? You are the Imperial Prince, aren't you? You speak our language very well."

Pol smiled. "The magic?" He reminded the shopkeeper.

"Daerans have magicians, but I'm told their magic is different than ours." He raised his hands defensively. "I don't have a bit of magic in me, so I have to accept what my supplier says."

"Daeran. I gave a frog to the Emperor thinking it came from Tishiko." Pol barked out a laugh. "All of us were fooled."

He looked at the carvings and found a few animals that he would present to his new brothers and sisters.

"Your papers," the shopkeeper said, "I am required to document all purchases."

Pol bought a cat for Amonna. Pol would make sure she received it since he didn't want to forget his Borstall sister or have her forget him. He also bought a carving for Shira.

The purchases took care of all the money Pol had on him.

Paki said, "I'll buy some of this wooden jewelry. It looks exotic enough. Ask the shopkeeper if these came from Daera, too."

Pol asked the clerk and received a negative reply.

"Those are made in Shinkya, and they don't look like anything in the Empire," Pol said, translating the shopkeeper's words. "They are cheap enough that you can buy a number of pieces and give them out to the girls you want to impress."

Paki grinned. "That's what I was thinking." His money went a lot further than Pol's.

They walked out into the sunny day and bought some meat on a stick for themselves and for their escorts. Pol looked across the street and noticed Ako and Fadden walking arm in arm. It looked like Fadden would have a personal escort when he went out. No wonder he let Pol and his friend go on without him.

Paki bought a simple silk robe in the Shinkyan style for his mother. She had left North Salvan during their trip to Volia, but he didn't know where she ended up.

Pol's mood darkened as he thought what kind of country Grostin was creating. He never wanted to return as much as Grostin didn't want him to ever show up. As an Imperial Prince, he would be officially protected from Grostin slapping him into a jail cell, but that didn't stop his brother from hiring assassins and ensorcelling others to kill him. He shook his head at the cost and effort Grostin went through to attack Shira and him. At least Shira was now out of his reach.

He had forgotten about all that with his attention focused on the events in Tishiko. The Empire and Shinkya were two different worlds. He snapped out of his thoughts as Paki poked him.

"Isn't that the Shinkyan you know?" Paki pointed to Karo Nagoya speaking to a couple of men in front of a large faction compound. The compounds were easy to spot with their large two-story buildings and at least one pagoda surrounding a large open area. Some had walls and some didn't. If Karo stood in front of the Scorpion compound, it didn't have a wall. Was that an expression of confidence?

They walked over to the Shinkyan.

"I see the Fearless faction let you out," Karo said in Eastrilian.

"With babysitters," Paki said.

That made Karo smile. Pol glanced at their escorts. At least one of them showed that she understood the Imperial language by the tightening of her expression.

"Do you have some time? I think our High Elder would enjoy talking to you," Karo said.

Pol expected that bringing him to her would enhance his standing. Mediocre male magicians weren't held in very high regard in Tishiko. Pol wondered if the concentration of male magicians was higher outside of the capital.

"Do you mind Paki?"

He shrugged.

"Why don't you take my packages and our escorts back to the compound. I can take care of myself."

"Yes, you can!" Paki said. He looked at the prettiest of the pair and smiled. She was the one who knew at least a bit of Eastrilian and returned his smile with a look of interest, surprisingly. Pol watched Paki take the arms of both women as they headed back towards the Fearless compound.

"This way," Karo said.

Evidently, the Elder wasn't as free as Karo indicated, but after an hour's wait, Pol was ushered into a cozy study. The Elder sat on a normal chair at a desk as high as any in the Empire.

"I can see you eyeing my office," she said. "I like sitting on chairs rather than sitting on my creaky legs." Her eyes crinkled in a smile. Her good humor seemed to be genuine. "You are in danger, you know."

"That's why I was walking with two escorts."

"A lot of good they will do if you are attacked."

Pol pursed his lips. "I've been attacked before."

"But not by people used to attacking other magicians. Tishiko is different than Yastan."

Pol sat back in his simple chair. "You've been to Yastan?"

She smiled. "Years ago. I was a Sister there. It is so easy for us to blend in when all your cities and towns have markets. I like the Empire, but I don't want to live there and I don't want the Empire to seep into Shinkya."

And that spoke to Shinkya's isolation.

"Surely a little more trade and exchange with the Empire would be good for your country."

"For my country, yes, but not for our culture."

"What will you do when the Great Ancestor returns?"

"Are you really the one?"

Pol wondered himself. "I don't feel like a Great Ancestor."

"Yet you told the Queen you were the one."

Pol thought it interesting that the Scorpions could listen into conversations in the Queen's own study. He kept the observation to himself.

"She didn't believe me any more than you do."

"I think you are right," the woman said. "We both think you may be the Great Ancestor, but you are too young to be taken seriously."

There it was again. Pol was too young. Too young to marry Shira, too young to become the Great Ancestor, and likely too young to rule the Empire. He didn't want to do any of those things right now, but Pol only wanted the option to do anything he wanted and those options didn't currently exist.

He had to admit that he had needed Fadden and even Namion to escort them through Volia. Pol realized that he had relied on Fadden to lead on the way to Shinkya. He had needed mentors all along and for the first time thinking about it, the concept chafed at him. Could he feel comfortable striking out on his own? Pol didn't know.

"I suppose when you are nearly seventeen, that is just the way it is."

A man put his head through the door. "Jumio has collapsed, again!"

"It is the young Master who accompanied us the other day. Come with me."

The Elder walked swiftly through the corridors of the building but slowly took the stairs up to the second level.

A few people stood outside a door. The Elder ignored them as she strode into the apartment. The young Master rested on a bed. His eyes were closed and his breathing was shallow.

"They get progressively worse," the Elder said. "I was told you know how to heal. What can you tell me about his illness?"

Pol panicked for a moment. He couldn't duplicate what Searl did, but then he took a deep breath and realized that the Elder only looked for a diagnosis. Pol could do that much.

He put his hand on the young man's chest and looked into his heart. Pol had done the same a few times when Searl and he practiced on the streets of Alsador and again a few times at the monastery before Val dragged him away to Tesna.

Pol never knew what his own heart looked like before, but Jumio's was a mess. It looked misshapen compared to the others Pol had seen. He could see a blockage in the main artery and was able to cut away some of the tissue, careful to make sure there were no large particles left to block Jumio's circulation elsewhere.

The youth's lungs weren't much better. The tissues seemed thick. Did that mean they weren't doing the job? Pol wondered if that was what he saw. Repairing anything other than what was obvious exceeded Pol's knowledge. It showed Pol how lucky he was to have found Searl to remake his organs. He also understood why it took weeks to repair.

Jumio's breathing deepened a bit and he opened his eyes. He gave them a weak smile. "I am still alive. I thought that was my last attack," he said. The young Master looked at Pol. "What are you doing here?"

"Giving you what little comfort I can," Pol said. "I know a bit of healing. I found something to ease your circulation for a bit. You need to rest." He wanted to say he had been healed, but Pol didn't want to give Jumio false hope. If the Shinkyans couldn't even do what Pol did, what hope was there?

The young Master nodded and closed his eyes.

"What did you do?" the Elder asked as they returned to her office.

"I cleared out a blockage in his main artery."

"You can see into his chest?"

Pol nodded. "I found I could see into a number of things. It's part of comprehending patterns. When I was fourteen, Paki, you met him at the embassy, convinced me to steal an apple and the constable caught us. I found that I could see into a lock and tweak the insides. It only took a little practice and I could do the same thing with a human body." Pol by implication classified Jumio as human. "I'm not experienced, except at healing injuries. His insides are not pretty and not normal. If I hadn't cleared out a blockage, I'm not sure the Master would have woken up."

The Elder sighed. "It's only a matter of time. Jumio has been with us since he first was identified as having a strong talent for magic, about six years ago. He comes from a common family."

"Why do you take him in if he's going to die so young?"

"We train him so he doesn't hurt himself or others. All the factions do unless the boy is noble, and then the Royal Academy will take him in. Most of the Grand Masters and Elders are graduates of that institution or one of its affiliates."

"And Sisters?"

"You are referring to the new Crown Princess?"

Pol nodded.

"She went to the Royal Academy. They have a Sister program. The Queen objected to her doing so but eventually relented. Anira wasn't happy about her daughter going on a dangerous mission, but Shira showed exceptional power."

"It only became more so as we traveled. Shira has had a little more seasoning than the Queen desired, I'm sure," Pol said.

"And you did the seasoning?"

That question made Pol blush. "I decline to answer that."

The Elder smiled. "That is perfectly acceptable." She looked at Pol intently. "I like you Pol Cissert Pastelle. It's a shame you weren't born a Shinkyan." She raised a hand to forestall a comment from Pol. "Don't give me any Great Ancestor talk. I'm aware of your lineage, your power, and your intelligence. Watch yourself. I still consider Tishiko to be an unsafe place for you and that you make Tishiko unsafe." She stood up. "Thank you for your time."

Pol walked back to the Fearless faction compound wearing a Shinkyan face. He trudged up the three stories to their level and sat on the sofa. Fadden and Paki weren't around.

"Excuse me, you have a visitor," a woman said, poking her head above the floor on the stairs.

The face of Shro, Shira's male alter ego walked up. She dressed as a male, but now that she was a bit older, it was more apparent that she was a woman. "Is Pol Castelle here?" she asked in Shinkyan.

"Shira!" he said.

"Pol? I only have a few moments!"

Pol turned his face back into himself.

"You're getting too good with disguises. I couldn't tell you wore a disguise."

Pol laughed. "Is that possible?"

"It is with you." She changed her face and sat next to him. Neither of them spoke for a bit.

"I saw how my insides must have looked to Searl, today. What a mess!"

"The Scorpion Master? Did you visit them?"

Pol nodded. "I did. No wonder I was so sickly." He balled one of his fists. "What the Demrons did to the Shinkyans and Terilanders was abominable."

"You just realized that?"

Pol smiled and shook his head. He took her hand and kissed it. "I was mad about it long ago. I just had no one to blame before my mother told me about my father. What have you been doing as a Crown Princess?"

"I get more access to the palace compound. I came here today to look at your Demron swords again."

"Why?"

I was shown the Ancestor archives this morning. There are closely held secrets there, but just as Ako said, there is nothing we don't already know. They have some picture plates similar to what we saw in the cave. None of them show Shinkyans preparing 'food' for the Demrons, but I did see a few armed Demrons. One of my sisters sneaked a drawing of the sword out of the archive before I left for Tesna, so I recognized your sword when you showed it to me and today I verified that the one you made is an accurate copy."

Pol went to his room and came out with his Demron weapons. "Did they look like these?"

Shira nodded. "It still gives me goosebumps to see those. If my mother knew you had swords in the same pattern as the pictures, she would be very, very nervous about the legend of the Great Ancestor. We don't have any real religion in Shinkya, but that legend is as close as it comes." She rubbed her arms as if she was cold.

Pol put his arm around her. "The Scorpion Elder said I was too young to present myself as the Great Ancestor, and I agree. I'm too young for everything. You and I have talked about this before."

Shira leaned against him. "I know. I'm too young to be a Crown Princess, but my mother moved quickly in defense against you. My title keeps me in Tishiko. It turns out that I am now too junior to go out into the world."

"The world being the Empire?"

She nodded. "I will wait," she said. "Three more years when you are twenty. Then I want you to take me away from Tishiko. We can live in your dukedom in South Salvan."

Pol squeezed her. "That's a goal. I don't know what kind of restrictions Hazett will place on me as Imperial Prince, but I'd rather think of myself with you in South Salvan than sitting around Yastan as the second heir."

She grinned. "Good. Now I'll be able to endure the palace better. That means we will be together before Winter's Day after you are twenty."

"We will." Pol put the weapons back into his bedroom and returned with a black horse carving. "Did you know these are made in Daera?"

"Really? I always thought they were Shinkyan. Even the Queen has a collection."

"Daeran and not cheap." He put it in Shira's hand. "The shopkeeper said they have magicians in Daera. From what the captain on the Bossomian ship said, they are a backward people."

"Not so backward," Shira said. "They have a couple of civilized countries on Daera, but both of them are inland."

"You never mentioned it," Pol said.

"It's supposed to be a secret." She shrugged. "But if you know," she beamed, "then we can talk about it. There is a tribal society that roams in vast arid lands similar to Shinkya and another culture that is deeply religious, worshipping their ancestors like the people of the Shards. I don't know much more than that. The carved animals are probably from the religious ones." She looked closely at her gift. "This is genuine."

"They all are. I checked. Think of Demeron when you look at that, and then of me."

Shira smiled. "I'll think of you first and then, maybe, I'll think of your horse," she said, standing. She turned back into Shro. "I only had a few minutes, but I'm glad you were here rather than wandering in Tishiko." She gave Pol a quick kiss and hurried down the stairs.

Pol leaned over the railing and watched her disappear from view. A stolen moment was certainly better than none. He wondered about their pledge. Could either of them keep it? He would do his part. Maybe in three years, he'd have to return as the Great Ancestor to take Shira away, but if that meant getting back together, he'd do it.

He sighed as he thought of her and of the many things that could impede their future reunion. Perhaps she would find another. Maybe he might do the same, but he doubted it. He put his head back on the couch and closed his eyes.

~ ~ ~

Chapter Thirty-One

~

"WAKE UP," PAKI SAID. The pretty escort stood at Paki's side. "Nirano speaks great Eastrilian!"

Pol noticed she stood rather close to Paki. Evidently, despite Paki's rudeness in the shop, she either succumbed to his friend's charms or she was ordered to become friendly. Pol had no idea what the truth was. Paki didn't have much trouble attracting members of the opposite sex.

After stretching, Pol stood. "What time is it?"

"Time to get something to eat," Fadden said, walking out of his bedroom. "Ako will be back in a few minutes to show us to the common room. "I see you've made a friend." Fadden looked at Paki and gave Nirano a little bow.

"Maybe Shira can afford a little time," Paki said.

"She's already visited and had to get back to the palace."

Ako called from below. "Come on down." She stood on the second-floor landing.

"Can you eat with us?" Paki asked Nirano.

"If you don't mind," she said in accented Eastrilian. It was obvious she had never been a Sister in the Empire.

Pol went to his room and splashed some water on his face. "That's better," he said, patting his cheeks. "Let's go."

Ako and Nirano chatted in Shinkyan ahead of Paki and Fadden. Pol brought up the rear so he couldn't hear what the two women said. They took them to a single story building in the rear. The ceiling opened up to the rafters, but banners with stylized designs hung down, effectively lowering the ceiling.

"Those are various army units the Fearless have served," Ako said, urging them to get into a food line. "You should like this kind of food. It is a much better version than what is served out in the field. More meat covered with more sauces. We have to hide the taste somewhat when we train."

"Who do you fight?" Paki asked.

"Mostly ourselves," Nirano said. "Factions go to war with each other. They are forbidden to fight in the city, so we do it outside Tishiko. Factions have affiliates in the major cities and towns."

"But you would win every time, wouldn't you?" Fadden said as he examined the choices.

"With magicians, every faction must struggle, except for a faction like the Fox. They are new. No one expects them to be independent for long."

Pol nodded. "That's what Barian said."

"Barian?" Nirano asked.

"The Imperial ambassador," Paki said, obviously glad to impart some knowledge to the young woman.

She nodded. "Oh."

Pol waited until they were seated. He tasted some of his selections. "We've been told that Tishiko is dangerous."

"It is," Ako said, "but you won't see a pitched battle. There are forays that test the factions' defenses quite often."

"Assassins?" Pol said.

"Sometimes. Most factions have wards that protect their compounds," Ako looked at Nirano, who nodded in agreement.

"I didn't notice any," Pol said.

"Grand Masters apply them fresh every evening. Come out after dark, you'll see." Ako said.

Pol ate while each couple spent most of the time talking to each other. Now Pol knew how Paki felt on their trip to Shinkya. He didn't mind. Pol had enough to think about after his short time with Shira earlier in the afternoon.

He actually felt comfortable about waiting for three years. Pol thought he would lose Shira at the end of the trip to Tishiko, but her visit reassured them that that might not be the case. Of course, he had to admit that anything could happen in the more than three years that they would be apart. She might be forced to marry as soon as she reached twenty. Pol, actually, might be 'encouraged' to do the same in Yastan. He had no idea what the Emperor's thoughts were on the subject. He could only hope that Searl performed a miracle on Handor as he had on him.

Pol left early for their apartment, wondering about the pictures that Shira had seen. He poked around in the living area and then when no one showed up, he carefully hid his Demron weapons between the walls of his room. Pol wouldn't get them out until they left Tishiko.

He wandered around the compound at dusk, and then made his way to the front of the compound and watched five women dressed as Grand Masters placing wards on the front. These looked more like the wards that the Tesnan Abbot used than what he observed in The Shards.

He stepped closer and asked what the wards did.

"They set up an alarm if they are tripped. We have a watch in the main building that is alert all night long," a woman said. "You have seen wards before?"

Pol nodded. "In Tesna and in the Shards. Wards are used in the Empire, but sparingly." He didn't know how sparingly they were used, but if they didn't teach them openly at Deftnis, that meant they weren't in common use. "Can't someone just disable the wards?" Shira knew how to defeat them.

"Few know how," she said. "It is a rare talent. It is easier to create wards than defeat them."

Pol waved his hand and defeated a six-foot section of wards. "Like that?"

The woman's jaw dropped.

"It's easier for me to eliminate wards than make wards," Pol said.

"Show me how you do it and I'll repair the section I destroyed."

The women and Pol spent the rest of the time as dusk turned into evening putting up wards. Pol learned how to patch the wards that he destroyed. It took more effort to join the patch, but he now had more practical knowledge about wards that he had lacked when the essence flooded him with insight.

Pol tried to teach the Grand Masters how to defeat them, but while they did learn how to eliminate a string within the weave like Shira did, the women had no ability to quickly dissipate an entire ward.

What the Demron essence wasn't able to convey was embedding the element of intent into a ward. The women showed Pol that it was a mental tweak. He perceived it as a coating on top of the ward's strands. The compulsion wards that the Tesnan's used were crude but effective compared to the elegant weaves he learned working with the Fearless Grand Masters. Each strand had an instruction, a coating that did the actual work of the ward. He now realized that there were two parts to every ward, the trigger and the effect that destroying the ward started.

The Fearless Grand Master said they tweaked their wards to last all night. A single strand was set to dissipate at dawn. With it, the entire ward would follow suit. Pol thought of it like a fire spreading. Wards could have military applications if they didn't require so much magical power to create.

The women were tired out at the end of their task. The wards glowed faintly, with strands of yellow, green and red. The discharging ward pulsed white, but dimly among the colored strands.

Now Pol knew how to tie off wards without disabling them and repair any hole that might be made. As a Seeker, that would be a very useful tool in situations where wards actually existed.

"The Prince learns quickly," one woman said to her four companions. "He is every bit as powerful as the rumors foretold."

"I would hope we all learned from each other," Pol said. He accepted some offered water and left for his apartments.

"Where were you?" Paki asked. Nirano wasn't there.

"I helped out with the wards," Pol said.

Ako walked out from her bedroom. "You did what?"

"I worked with the Grand Masters on the wards. I taught one of them how to defeat a ward and she taught me some basics on tweaking instructions onto the wards. I eliminated a section in progress and, with her help, I repaired it." Pol smiled. "It was fun."

"Those wards are supposed to be a faction secret," she said.

"The Grand Masters didn't stop me from working with them. In fact, they treated me like I was part of their group. It was one of my more pleasant experiences in Tishiko," Pol said.

"You aren't allowed to defeat Fearless faction wards."

Pol took a deep breath. "I am very good at eliminating wards, aren't I Paki?"

Paki grinned. "Pol is very good, just as he says." He laughed. "Shira knows that even better than I do."

Ako narrowed her eyes. "Wards are not meant to be blocked easily."

"I'm sorry, Ako. The Grand Masters didn't seem as upset as you are."

She put fists on her hips. "I can only hope you aren't summoned to Elder Furima. She is very, very strict." She walked back into her bedroom. Paki and Pol shrugged their shoulders together and then laughed.

A half an hour later, two women entered their apartment. "You are summoned to speak to Elder Furima."

Pol followed the women down the stairs and back into the administration building. He thought Elder Furima was the woman he had met twice before, but she was a different person. This one was younger, thinner, and appeared to lack a sense of humor. Pol could instantly tell the woman didn't fit in with the rest of the Fearless he'd met.

The five Grand Masters stood in a line with heads bowed and hands folded at their stomachs. The one Pol had befriended lifted her head enough to give Pol a worried glance.

"You are responsible for disturbing the work of my warders?"

"I wouldn't put it that way, Elder," Pol said. "I wished to view the wards in the dark and walked out to see them. I engaged one of your Grand Masters in conversation. We talked and I showed her that I could untangle the wards. I showed her how to do that, and then she showed me how to build up your wards. The other Grand Masters were able to observe our time together. I ended up helping them finish up. I am not aware that I disturbed their work in any way and we probably finished up a few minutes faster with my help."

"That is beside the point," the Elder said.

"It is precisely the point," Pol countered. "These women did nothing wrong, yet you are parading them in front of me as they hang their heads in shame. They have nothing to be ashamed about." The whole scene made Pol upset. "Is this the way you treat your guests? I thought the Fearless were above such a petty thing."

The Elder harrumphed and looked at the Grand Masters. "Has he described the situation accurately?"

"Yes, Elder," they nearly said in unison.

"I was told differently."

"From whom?" Pol asked.

The woman refused to answer. That was fine with Pol. He was a guest anyway. "Did you ask these women what happened?"

"Why should I?" the Elder said.

"Because they were there. A good Seeker makes sure he or she has the right information before jumping to conclusions." The woman didn't want to let it go.

"Are you accusing me of not being a good Seeker?"

"Have you ever been a Sister?" Pol asked

"No. I'm too powerful." The Elder was insufferable.

"Am I excused to return to my apartment?" Pol asked.

"Begone, all of you," the woman said shooing them all out of her office.

"I am sorry," one of the Grand Masters said after they left the woman's study. "One doesn't want to run afoul of Furima. She can be a little...strong."

Pol knew the woman would have liked to have used a stronger word or phrase. "I didn't expect you to get into trouble," he said, as they walked out into the night air.

"It isn't the first time."

"Or the last," another said.

"I thought Grand Masters were to be treated with respect," Pol said. He chuckled. "I certainly respect you."

They all bowed their heads. "That means a lot coming from you. That woman is a very strong magician and she used connections to join the Fearless, but...I won't say more."

"Don't," Pol said. "Thank you for an illuminating evening." He smiled and bowed back.

They walked to another building and Pol stood in the middle of the compound trying to fit Furima into the Fearless. It seemed that politics could ruin an honorable faction like the Fearless.

~ ~ ~

Chapter Thirty-Two

POL WAS SUMMONED TO THE ELDER who was his prime contact, just after breakfast.

"I heard you had a run-in with Furima last night. Word travels quickly in the compound."

"Do I need to describe what happened?"

The Elder shook her head. "I have a good idea. She probably saw you working with the warders and couldn't countenance a man working with wards. She is a strict fundamentalist."

"Did I do something wrong?"

The Elder smiled and shook her head. "I've been trying to find a way to expel Furima."

"She belongs with the Lakes," Pol said.

The Elder's eyes brightened. "My exact thought! I don't trust her, but she is probably the most powerful magician in the compound." She stared at Pol. "After you, that is. You impressed the ladies. They have never seen someone with such a mastery that you could wave your hand and eliminate their wards. Furima couldn't do that."

"The wards weren't active yet. If they were, I would have had to be more careful."

The Elder nodded her head. "You even know that aspect. Who taught you?"

"It helps to be a powerful magician, but I had a few teachers. Shira introduced me to wards when we first met." Pol purposely remained silent about the Demron essence.

The Elder peered at Pol but waved away the subject with her hand. "The Grand Masters were over it by the time I found out. You impressed them with your willingness to help."

"I'll even help you if you have something I can do."

"Just stay alive," she said. "Keep alert. Furima is not one to forget...anything."

Pol went back to his apartment. Paki, Fadden, and Ako were gone by the time he returned. That brought a smile to his face. He dug out his Shinkyan language books and began to fill in the blanks that became more apparent with every conversation.

"Are you there?"

Pol jumped up at the sound of Shira's voice. "I am. Just brushing up on my Shinkyan. I heard a lot of new words yesterday."

"My mother received a report that you overstepped your bounds yesterday."

"I was asked to take a look at the Scorpion Master."

"No, not that. Working with the Grand Masters last night."

"Furima?"

"Elder Furima went right over to Mother's secretary and told her that you were teaching women how to extinguish wards."

"Are there no real secrets in Tishiko?" Pol said. "You were the first person who told me that was possible."

Shira pursed her lips. "Grand Masters are permitted to know such things, but Furima is an enemy in your midst. Be careful around her."

"They should remove her from the Fearless faction."

"She was put here by the Queen. It would present difficulties to expel such a person."

"I think the Fearless tolerate her, but she had the Grand Masters cowed. They were shaking."

"All for show, between you and me. They have to present a suitably submissive appearance to her," Shira said.

Pol wondered how many other infiltrators made their way into the factions. Was that the norm? Did the Queen exercise that much power? Pol didn't know, but if Anira was so powerful, he was very, very exposed in Shinkya and the talk of factions glossed over the fact that they might be more closely controlled by the Queen than Ako or Shira had let on.

Perhaps they would cut their visit short. Pol wanted to protect Paki and Fadden, and that meant limiting their time in Tishiko. He walked to the palace grounds and entered the embassy.

No one was around, so Pol tweaked invisibility and went further into the building. He heard voices in the Shinkyan dining room and heard Barian and Horani speaking in Shinkyan. Barian's Shinkyan was now much, much better than when he spoke it in front of Pol.

They spoke about their activities during the day until Horani changed the subject. A servant walked past Pol and paused, but continued. Perhaps Pol smelled. He rolled his eyes and tweaked clearer hearing.

"The prince has been stirring up the factions. It's embarrassing. His departure will solve all our problems," Horani said. "Using a healer to rescue a dying Master from the curse is heretical."

"Let's not talk about religion. I know you don't like the Great Ancestor rumors that are running rampant in Tishiko. I am more concerned about the stability of the city. I agree that without the Prince's presence, the restlessness will die down. Furima made it clear that she will not tolerate him living in the Fearless compound. Even the Elders in the more moderate factions feel the same."

"Then all we have to do is convince the Queen to banish the boy sooner on some pretext or another so we can continue to live in peace," Horani said.

"I disagree with that thinking," Barian said. "If he still lives, he might return to claim the Crown Princess at some later date. If you arrange his death, we won't have to worry about future problems."

"You don't think there will be ramifications with the Emperor?"

Barian said, "Hazett sent him to Tishiko as a test. If Pol Pastelle dies, the boy failed. What else is there to say? The Emperor won't lift a finger. I'm here to protect Shinkya from any actions from the Empire, so don't worry."

Pol had heard enough, so he withdrew. He had intruded and that wasn't polite, but then talking about his assassination was worth any guilty discomfort. He quietly slipped out the front door and walked, still invisible until he had left the palace compound.

He couldn't believe that Barian so casually plotted his death. But then, if he sought out a pattern, it all made sense. Barian looked at his ambassadorship as a lifetime appointment. He had a house on the palace grounds and a Shinkyan wife to keep him tuned into all the juicy political developments. Then Pol comes and threatens his way of life. Pol could understand, but he didn't have to accept it.

He wanted one more meeting with Shira, but that might not happen. He had to convince Paki and Fadden to leave immediately. Tonight would not be soon enough.

The apartment was empty, of course. Pol paced the floor wondering what to do next when a woman appeared at the stairwell.

"A man from the Scorpion faction is at the front of the compound," she said.

Pol grabbed his Shinkyan weapons and rushed down the stairs and out towards the street. Karo Nagoya stood with the Scorpion Elder by his side.

"This is no time for niceties," she said. "We just received word that you will soon be expelled from the Fearless compound and are not to be taken in by any of the factions. Your friends were kidnapped and taken outside the city. We rescued them, but you'll have to make your way to the border."

"Why have you done this?"

"To save your life, you dolt," the Elder said. "It will be touch and go as it is. Take your horses. You can't bring much with you or it will be apparent that you are fleeing. There are those who want you to stay and those who want you dead. Don't give them the opportunity to make the choice. Karo knows the way well enough to where your friends are being held. He will be your guide. He will be across the street when you exit the compound and can ride one of the horses. It will look less conspicuous leaving Tishiko that way."

Pol didn't like being rushed into action and if he hadn't overheard Barian and his wife talk, he would refuse the offer and fight if he had to. But Paki and Fadden were gone. If they were truly kidnapped, the decision was thrust upon him.

"It won't take me long," Pol said. He turned around and wanted to run back to the pagoda, but he schooled calmness and walked slowly, thinking furiously about what he would take. They still had Shinkyan money, so they could buy supplies along the way. Their papers must still be valid.

It didn't take Pol long. He carried two saddlebags out of the pagoda, and had assumed a Shinkyan disguise. He would wear the travel clothes that he had changed into. He didn't have the time to open the wall and take the Demron weapons, but he knew they would be safely hidden in the pagoda until his eventual return.

He slipped on his warded coat with his Shinkyan weapons buckled on beneath. He would have to leave his conical hat behind. The carved animals didn't take up much space. Pol grabbed the little money chests in each room and poured them into the other side of his saddlebag along with a change in clothes and anything else that he thought his friends would need. Perhaps the decent Fearless would send the rest of their belongings to Deftnis.

His breath was short and his palms were wet with perspiration as he walked down the stairs and to the back where the stables were.

"We are departing," Pol told Demeron. "Eat up. I will need to steal a horse for Fadden. Which one should I take?"

A Shinkyan?

"No! We are in trouble enough." Pol went on to describe all that happened while he saddled the three horses. He tossed the saddlebags on the horses and led them out into the compound and into the street.

Karo walked towards the curb after recognizing Demeron and mounted one of the horses. "It is past time," he said as he urged his horse forward. Pol held tightly to the other horse as they trotted through the central part of Tishiko, heading south.

In less than an hour, they emerged from the city. Pol looked back, aching for Shira, but he would have to wait for another day. He would also have to find an alternative way to get messages to Shira. He didn't see how he could trust Barian.

They rode for another hour until Karo turned off on a track that

GUY ANTIBES | Page 317

led to a small manor house. There were horses tied up on railings.

"It looks like your friends have arrived," Karo said.

Pol took a deep breath. Everything was happening too quickly. "Friends? Are they here? You said they were kidnapped." Pol looked around. "Why did we head south?"

Karo looked at him, but Pol didn't like the nervousness in the man's face. "To throw any pursuit off," he said. "We used a number of our people to rescue your friends," he admitted.

That sounded reasonable, but there must be a pursuit right behind them to make Karo so nervous. Pol dismounted and helped tie up the horses. There were a number of dots inside the house. He doubted if Paki and Fadden would have left without a fight if they thought they were being kidnapped. He rushed in.

Paki and Fadden were in the foyer on the ground. He ran to their sides. Both of them were unconscious. He looked at the people surrounding his friends.

"Thank you for saving them." A few nodded.

Pol knelt down to assess their injuries. He felt relief that there were none.

"At least they are unharmed," Pol said just before someone struck him in the head. His last thought was that of betrayal as he sank to the floor to join his friends on the floor.

~ ~ ~

Chapter Thirty-Three

~

Demeron

~

DEMERON DIDN'T LIKE THE SITUATION ANY BETTER THAN POL. He never did trust Karo Nagoya and the man exuded nervousness to him. He didn't detect any malice towards Pol, so he stayed silent. The horse knew that Pol's mind was roiling as he rode. Demeron wouldn't enter Pol's mind unbidden. The bond wasn't like that, but he wished he had that power now.

They rode out of the city and then south for a while until they turned down a road to a tiny manor house. Pol tied him up to the railing. That didn't happen very often. He must have been very nervous and it showed when he looked at Karo.

Demeron had a bad feeling about the whole thing. Pol went through the door and Karo didn't bother to shut it. The horse could see the prone figures of Paki and Fadden. He didn't sense any anger in the people surrounding them. They all appeared as men, but half of them were women.

Pol checked on his friends. Before Demeron had a chance to warn his master, Karo administered a blow to Pol's head. He went down on top of Paki.

"That was easier than I thought," Karo said, his fear beginning to ebb. "We just have to wait for the Elder. She was right, he wore a shield to protect from our playing with his mind, but Pol had no protection from a physical blow."

Demeron considered attacking the men, but with Pol unconscious, there was little he could actually do in this situation, but observe.

Eventually, a Shinkyan carriage arrived. The Elder got out and patted Demeron's flank. "I have a job for you," she said to the horse. "We are going to transport Pol's two friends to a ship on the coast that will take them to Deftnis."

What about Pol? Demeron turned his head to look at her directly.

She smiled. "That's right, you can communicate to me."

Among others, Demeron said. What's going to happen to Pol?

"He would be dead before tomorrow morning if he stayed in Tishiko. The Queen used her influence to turn all the factions against him. We Scorpions took a different path, as we usually do. It would be dangerous for us to let him return to Yastan, so we are sending Pol to Daera."

Pol won't agree to that.

"He won't have a choice and neither will you."

Me? Demeron said.

"You are devoted to Pol and will be his guide on Daera. We will ward Pol's mind with forgetfulness. He won't remember you or Shira. More importantly, he won't be able to remember how to tweak patterns."

I can't nursemaid a mindless man, Demeron said.

"He won't be mindless. The ward is very targeted. It's a secret the Scorpions have held close for a few centuries, using it only under dire circumstances."

What about Fadden and Paki? Will they go with him?

The Elder shook her head. "Deftnis, just like I told you. They will be told that Pol was kidnapped by a different faction and no one knows where he went. To the rest of the world, Pol will just disappear."

Two men carried Pol out with his heels dragging and set him down on the porch. He wore different clothes, but the Shinkyan disguise still remained.

"Ah, the ward has been applied?"

A woman older than the Elder stepped out into the sunlight. "It has. His appearance will remain the same until the ward is broken."

Broken? Demeron said. He might regain his memories?

"We wouldn't cast him off without a chance to succeed. We wouldn't be Scorpions if we did such a thing. A powerful magician of Elder level, with the right expertise, can remove the ward, but the closest magician with that kind of power is five hundred miles from where you two will land on Daera. You will have some money and mundane weapons."

So there is a chance?

"If he regains his memories, tell him that we saved his life. It truly is the safest thing we can do and still preserve the life of Princess Shira. With Pol out of the way, Tishiko will settle down. Pol may never find the right person and have the presence of mind to ask." The elder looked at Demeron more intently. "You might have to help him search for a mighty magician. They do exist over there. If he returns, it will prove he is the Great Ancestor. If that happens have him seek us out. We do this for both his and Shira's protection. I will leave you."

She mounted a horse with some help and trotted back down the little road heading for Tishiko along with the other Elder who created the ward. Demeron watched them go. Pol still breathed, so that might count as a small victory. Tishiko was a den of vipers among other things, he thought.

Karo approached him. "I'll be riding you while on the road to Port Inirata. I'm told it will take a week. The carriage is for your friends."

A covered wagon came around from the back of the manor house, and they put Pol on a pile of blankets, and then Karo put a light cloth over him. Paki and Fadden still lay on the floor of the house when Demeron followed the cart back out onto the road south.

The edge of the sea came into view before the land dipped down revealing Port Inirata. Demeron didn't know much about ports, but this one seemed to be about the size of Mancus. Six ships filled the docks with another waiting in the bay for one to leave.

Pol had been force-fed once each day. Even with that, he looked like he was losing weight. Demeron, on the other hand, was fed grain, but the good fodder didn't make up for his concern for Pol's condition. It had been much too easy for the Scorpions to take his master.

Karo patted Demeron on the side of his neck. "You've been a good boy, but I'll warn you, the voyage won't be pleasant," the magician said.

"I can put you to sleep. It might make it more tolerable to be down in the hold for two weeks at sea. Luckily, Daera is close to Port Inirata."

And Karo thought that was a good thing? Demeron wanted to buck the man off the horse, but the only person who really mattered was Pol, and Demeron could do nothing for Pol until they reached the other continent.

The stallion had to admit the magician did treat him well. Karo made sure he was groomed every night and fed grain. The trip was at a pace that all the horses in their group could handle. Demeron wanted to feel angry, but couldn't muster the emotion. His focus would be to help Pol restore his memories.

They reached the port as the sun set in the west. The men bundled Pol into a palanquin and carried him aboard. Karo followed.

"I'll be joining you on your trip, but will return with the ship to Shinkya," Karo said.

A sailor took Demeron by the bridle. "If you can walk up that plank, you'll make our lives easier,"

Demeron nodded and clopped up the ramp to the deck and down another ramp into the hold. It didn't look too bad. There was lots of straw and Demeron guessed that he could always eat his bedding on the way to Daera.

Karo came down to put a blanket over the horse. "I'm told it can get damp down here. I'll check on you a couple times a day," he said.

Demeron nodded and shook his mane. He felt powerless to do anything else.

They left that night. The ship swayed as it traveled the sea. Demeron could look up through the holes in a hatch cover to see the deep blue sky. He settled into the never-ending tedium of the voyage.

One night the sailor came down and put up a box around Demeron.

"We have some lively weather coming. You won't be battered around so much with these fences, so be patient," a sailor said.

Karo came by, looking nervous. "Bad weather." He held an armful of blankets and put them over the sides of the box. "This will protect you from scraping the edges of the wood." He scurried up the stairs.

Demeron prepared for the worst. He had traveled back and forth to Deftnis Isle enough times to know what bad weather meant. The light darkened and it certainly wasn't nighttime yet. The ship began to roll back and forth and then it changed heading and began to pitch forward and back.

The whole vessel shook and creaked as waves began to batter the sides. The ship began to take on water. Demeron could hear the anxious cries of men trying to make the best of a dire situation on deck.

Karo appeared in the blackness. "I am taking you up on the deck. The captain is worried about making it to Daera. I can't leave you tied down here if something happens to the ship." The man was very afraid.

Demeron couldn't communicate with anyone on the ship, which only made the situation worse. He shuddered as a thundering crash shook the ship.

"That's the mast the captain was worried about," Karo said as he finished up unclipping the fasteners of the box. "Come with me."

Demeron didn't need to be coaxed out of the wet hold. Angry red streaks of a terrible dawn shot through clouds to the east sliding through jagged holes in the sky. A flash of lightning lit up the ship followed by a peal of thunder that shook the ship. Sailors were running to and fro.

"I'm tying you here," A sailor said as Karo clung to a rope strung along the deck. "If you pull on this loop, the knot will fall apart. Do you understand?"

Demeron nodded. He couldn't help but catch some of the fear that permeated the ship.

Two men brought Pol on the deck and put his saddle on Demeron. They tied him to Demeron's back as the wind began to whistle through the rigging and intensified.

"We aren't far from the coast," the magician said. It's that way." Karo pointed towards the south and the west.

Demeron looked at the red sky and spotted the sun. He now had some bearings if the worst happened. Karo slapped a set of saddlebags onto Demeron and tied them securely to the saddle. They stood as the storm swirled around them and the waves punished the ship.

Another brilliant blast of light lit up the deck and the other of the two masts burst apart at the top. The mast leaned over, making the ship waddle in the water. Demeron had seen enough. He tugged on the loop and let the rope drop to the pitching deck. With one final look at the east, Demeron leaped into the water.

He struggled to rise to the surface. Pol had no ability to hold his breath, so it was up to Demeron to save them both. He breached the surface and flailed with his legs until he floated on the waves. He didn't float well but Pol was mostly above the surface of the water.

Demeron began to wheel his legs in powerful strokes. He swam down into troughs and up. When he reached a peak he made sure the sunrise was still on his left flank. On and on he swam. After forever, the sound of the wind was replaced by a rhythmic pounding. They were approaching a shore. At the peak of another wave, he saw the dark line of the Daeran coast approaching.

As he got closer, Demeron realized he was heading for rocks and changed his course towards a strip of lightness in the dawn. He didn't like sand, but they could rest there.

The sea took him closer to the rocks. A surge pushed Demeron against a large rock that appeared suddenly. Before he could generate a shield, it slammed into his side taking his breath away. Demeron sank into the water, suddenly without strength. His hooves found the bottom and he ran with all of his might. Pol was now below water and that wouldn't do.

He could feel his heart thudding in his ears as his head burst through the water. Another surge pushed him closer to the beach. He continued to run until the sand slowed his progress. He took another few steps and collapsed, making sure not to fall on Pol.

Demeron had no idea where they landed and had no idea what to do. His lungs shuddered, catching up to the massive effort he had just made. He heard Pol moan. It was enough. Demeron's last thought before oblivion took him was that they both made it to Daera.

Chapter Thirty Four

~

Pol

~

AFTER OPENING HIS EYES, the youth found himself strapped to the saddle of a horse laying on a beach. While the big black beast slept, the boy untied himself and tried to walk but couldn't take more than a few steps. He sat down, head dizzy and stomach roiling.

The stallion woke and stood, regarding the boy. It seemed that the horse might recognize him. The horse began to write in the sand. P-O-L. Then he drew a crude arrow at the youth.

"Is that my name?" the youth said, amazed that a horse could write.

The horse bobbed his head up and down.

"I know you?"

The head nodded again. Pol, the boy thought. He searched his mind for a different name and couldn't come up with anything. He had lost his memories. Pol looked out at the ocean. They must have come from the sea.

"We were on a sinking ship?" Pol could only come up with that as a reason.

The horse nodded and wrote something else in the sand. It took a while to puzzle out the letters, but Pol could read: D-E-M-E-R-O-N. The horse drew a line toward himself.

"You are Demeron?"

The big black stallion approached Pol and bent down to nuzzle. "We are friends?" the boy asked.

Pol got a vigorous nod. He rubbed the horse's jaw. Pol tried to figure out where his memories had gone, but every thought came up with a blank. He had no idea who he was or where he came from, but he could speak and read. He didn't know where he was because he couldn't remember any country names or even how old he was.

His stomach rumbled again and he had to stagger into the brush where he lost what little he had in his stomach. He returned and removed the saddlebags from the horse. The leather was just beginning to dry and Pol knew enough that the swim to the shore had likely spoiled any food inside.

Pol found a change in clothes and some shoes. That would be great considering he was barefooted. He did find a purse of coins.

"Shinkya. I can read this writing. It's different from what you wrote." Pol said. As his wits returned, he realized that a horse that understood human speech was unique and one that knew more than one language must be remarkable. He let the coins spill out into his hand. There were gold, silver, copper, and iron coins. Was he in Shinkya?

He found nothing in writing as he continued his search. He did pull out a black cord at the bottom of one of the bags. A silver circular device depicting a chain around a sword backed by flames dangled from both ends. It had to mean something, but Pol had no idea what. He found no food, so hopefully they could find a habitation that might accept the Shinkya coins.

"We need some food. Can you carry me?"

Demeron nodded, and Pol climbed up on the big horse. They traveled on the beach for a few hundred yards to the south before Pol spotted a trail that spilled out onto the sand. They plunged into the verdant growth and followed the trail.

After crossing a stream. Pol dismounted and let Demeron drink the water. It looked clear, so Pol hoped it would be potable. He wondered where he had learned that, but after another search of his memories came up with nothing, so he leaned over and took a drink.

That seemed to settle his stomach as they continued to follow the twisting trail. It rose up an incline in the jungle. Pol guessed they were climbing a hill, but he couldn't see very far through the trees and undergrowth. They only stopped to drink a few times at clear streams.

Pol sensed the light dimming and figured it was approaching nightfall. He suddenly stopped and listened. Did he hear peoples' voices? He dismounted and led Demeron towards the sounds. He didn't know if the inhabitants of wherever he was would be friendly or hostile.

They slowly made their way towards the sounds. Pol made a fist. He realized he wanted to hold onto a weapon, but he had nothing to protect himself. A fallen tree at the side of the trail provided Pol a chance to break off a dried branch. He realized if he could break off the branch, it might not do much in a fight, but the thick stick felt better in his hand than nothing.

The light continued to dim as the sounds of people increased. Pol slowly walked ahead, his makeshift weapon pointed in front of him. Demeron continued to walk behind after Pol had draped the reins back across his neck.

Suddenly four men jumped in front of him brandishing knives. Another three emerged from the trail behind Demeron. Pol instinctively dropped his weapon. He knew that in the past he had other resources to fight, but he couldn't remember what they were, and once that realization came to him, he raised his hands in surrender.

"I'm not an attacker," Pol said in his native tongue, whatever that was. The men didn't change their expressions. "I'm not an attacker," he said in Shinkyan, the language on the coins.

One of the men lowered his knife a bit. "Shinkyan?"

Pol had to shrug. He didn't know what a Shinkyan looked like.

"You look Shinkyan," the man said, "but why are you here?"

"Ship sank," Pol said, realizing he didn't know the word for 'shipwreck' in that language.

The man nodded to the others and they lowered their knives. "Come. We will attack if you try to fight."

Pol gave his head a shake and then nodded. He didn't know if the man asked him a question or had made a statement. At least they could communicate.

After following them for a few hundred yards, Pol entered a village or a town. It was larger than he first thought as they threaded their way through many haphazard lanes between dwellings. They all looked the same with whitewashed walls and palm leaves stacked in many layers over lightly sloping gabled roofs. The shacks looked familiar somehow, but Pol's attempts to pull images from his mind failed him again.

His escorts led him to a grass square perhaps a hundred yards on each side. A few larger, two-storied buildings were ahead. Children dressed in loincloths frolicked in the twilight. He couldn't tell if they were male or female. They crossed the field and stopped in front of one of the larger buildings.

A man dressed in a grass cape dyed many colors walked out. He wore a feathered headdress on his head and what looked like soft tan leather pants. His face was decorated with colored paints. They were too brilliant to be tattoos. A picture of a tattooed man flashed in Pol's mind. At least he had a memory for some things.

His captors conversed too quickly for Pol, so he didn't quite understand what they said. He tried to pick out their words but shook his head in frustration when he couldn't pick out enough words.

The gaudily dressed man peered at Pol and pointed his stick at him. Pol's head began to spin until he couldn't resist anymore, and then everything went black.

Pol sat up on the floor of a large room. The walls were whitewashed and above him the ceiling was a frame showing the palm-thatched roof above. The gaudily dressed man looked at another, taller individual who looked down at Pol.

"You really don't have any memories," the taller man said in Shinkyan.

"Could you speak more slowly. I know some of your language, but if you speak it too quickly, I can't understand."

The man nodded. "Naori, our shaman, has never seen anything like it."

The gaudily dressed man nodded his head. "You are unique to my experience."

Pol scratched his head. "How do you know?" Pol struggled to understand them, but he found that he could comprehend what they had to say after asking them to repeat their words. At least he could communicate.

"I put you into a sleep spell and talked to you while you slept. Don't worry, I didn't meddle with your mind. I think it has been meddled with enough."

"Can you fix my memories? Pol said.

Naori shook his head. "I'm the best shaman in the village, but it will take the best shaman on Daera to even attempt to repair your mind."

The taller man spoke. "I am Chief Gonga. We will take you in for awhile, but you'll have to work."

Pol had nothing to help him exist wherever he was, so he nodded. He could work for his living like anyone else. He nodded. "I am willing to do what I can to survive, but I won't give up the horse." Who would think to let a communicating horse go? He wouldn't. Demeron could be a key to retrieving his memories.

"You won't have to, in fact the horse might help you in your new position as an apprentice to Bingi, the village tanner," Chief Gonga said.

"Tanning? I don't know anything about tanning," Pol said. He took a deep breath. At this point he needed to get his bearings and learn as much as he could about his new environment.

"That's why you will be my apprentice," a man said from behind Pol.

Pol barely understood the words and turned around. The man was grizzled, in late middle age. As the tanner approached, Pol nearly shrunk back at the stench emitting from the man.

Gonga made Bingi repeat himself a few times, but the tanner finally spoke slowly. "I will teach you all you need to know. But don't worry, I am a good teacher." He cackled and slapped Pol on his shoulder. "Don't worry about the stink and the heavy work. We will have a wonderful time together." He grinned, showing brown, crooked teeth. Bingi's breath matched the reek on his clothes. "You will become the Tanner's Pet."

~~~~

If you liked *The Emperor's Pet*, be sure to leave a review wherever you purchased the book. An excerpt of *The Misplaced Prince*, the sixth book in the series, follows.

An Excerpt from Book Six

THE MISPLACED PRINCE

Chapter One

~

Pol

~

POL'S STOMACH COMPLAINED AS THE VILLAGE TANNER CLAPPED HIM ON THE BACK. "Does being your apprentice get me some food? I honestly can't tell you the last time I had anything to eat," Pol said, looking Bingi, then at the tall Chief Gonga and Naori, the village shaman.

"That's something we will fix right now," Bingi, the village tanner said. "Let's go. Is everything on your horse?" The tanner's aromatic garb was a put-off, but Pol felt he could persevere as long as he could get something in his stomach quickly.

"It is, although that doesn't mean much. I'm guessing the ship that I rode went down with more of my belongings," Pol said. He figured his Shinkyan coins wouldn't last long, so they would be tucked away in his saddlebags, waiting for the day he left the village. Having lost his memory, he needed some time to determine where he was and what he could do.

Bingi gave the chief a nod. "I'll bring him back tomorrow sometime. I'm sure you'll want to tell him about the apprenticeship rules."

"Rules?" Pol said. Perhaps he made a poor decision in accepting the apprenticeship. He knew what an apprenticeship was, but he couldn't remember if he had ever been an apprentice.

"Tomorrow," Gonga said.

Bingi pulled Pol out of the Chief's hut and waited for him to fetch Demeron. Pol peeked in the saddlebags to see if his money was still there. It was. He took a relieved breath and followed the tanner out of the village leading Demeron.

"We live a fair distance from Soagi, the name of our village. Oddly, no one wants to live around my tannery," Bingi said grinning.

Pol had to ask him about a few of his words, but he caught the gist of what the man said. Where had he learned the language? He didn't remember Shinkya, but they said he looked like a Shinkyan. The writing on the Shinkyan coin was different than scribblings Demeron had made on the beach. If he remembered languages and didn't know all the words of the villagers, that meant he had never been to this land before.

He felt out of control, and that made him uneasy. Pol wanted to take everything in stride and go along with the flow of events, but he just did not have enough information to know who he was. Could the trauma of the ship going down have damaged his mind?

Demeron nudged Pol from behind. That brought a smile to Pol's face. At least the horse had been a friend. What kind of horse could spell and communicate? Pol didn't know. How could his memory be so selective that he could remember languages, but not the countries where the languages originated?

"Do I get paid for being an apprentice?"

Bingi turned around. "Pay? Of course. It isn't much once I deduct for room and board. My wife cooks our meals, so you will have to endure that. There is a decent sized shack for you, although it could stand a little cleaning."

The man mumbled half of his words, so Pol had to ask him to repeat himself, but he was picking up how Bingi spoke. He wondered how much he could learn from the tanner. He didn't have high hopes about that, but Pol would try to get into the village as much as he could to learn about his new country.

After walking for a while, the tanner turned into a little compound. There were some sturdy wooden frames set up on one side of the yard. Half of the frames had hides stretched out. Three wall-less sheds with odd tables that were thick but narrow. Pol looked around and saw a row of wooden vats downslope on the lower edge of the property.

Pol turned his head and saw three whitewashed shacks. The roofing looked a bit disheveled, and the whitewash wasn't white anymore. One was large, and two of them were smaller. He supposed those had to be the living quarters.

Pol didn't know what to think about the place. It all looked foreign to him, but then what did he expect if his memories were locked away in his brain if they even remained?

"You have to make a little corral for your horse. There is a clearing on the other side of the houses," Bingi said. "Put your things in your shack, and then we can get to work."

"What have you got there?" a large woman said as she walked out of the largest shack. "Where did you ever get that horse? It looks like it belongs to a Lord." She gazed up at Demeron.

"The Lord is our new apprentice, Doara. Meet Pol. He washed up on the beach not far from here, and the sea washed out his brain. He can't remember where he's from. Chief Gonga won't take him in, so I got him as an apprentice."

"About time. Maybe we can make some money again," Doara said. She walked up to Pol and peered at his face. "I isn't one of us."

"Naori said he looks like a Shinkyan. He speaks a bit of Shinkyan but not like the Shinkyan's I've ever talked to."

"Poor dear." Doara took Pol's hand and rubbed it. "Not a working man, that's for sure." She looked at Pol. "We'll take care of you while you get your memories back. There's a lot of work here, and soon these hands won't be as soft."

"I know how to work," Pol said. "My name is Pol, and my horse is named Demeron."

"I'm Doara, Bingi's wife, but you probably have got that figured out," she said slowly and loudly.

Pol smiled. She could tell he didn't speak very well and had spoken slowly. "I would appreciate it if we could talk from time to time to improve my language skills."

She nodded. "You're different from the typical riff-raff Bingi brings. They have been the naughty boys in the village. You don't look like one of those." She smiled and stroked his hand again. "There is a nice clearing on the other side of our house for your horse. You'll have to build a corral."

"Demeron doesn't need one, but if you'll feel better about it, I can put something up." Pol said. He didn't exactly know how to make a corral, but he could figure something out.

Doara squeezed his hand and led him to the smallest of the shacks. The place was dirty, and the furniture looked like it would easily. The woman pursed her lips. "You can clean, can't you?"

Pol nodded.

"Then this place is yours. The last two apprentices wanted to live in the main house. I didn't really like that, so this is yours to fix up as you please."

Pol smiled. "Thank you. I think I would like to be alone, anyway. I believe I have a lot to think about."

"Thinking's for another time," Bingi said. "Time to get to work."

The tanner pushed Pol out of the little house, leaving Doara standing by herself.

"I'll give you a quick idea of what we do, and then we'll go harvest bark for tanning."

Pol looked back at Doara standing at the door to his new home. He bowed to her and followed Bingi over to the yard to learn about how to tan leather. It was all new to him. Tanning was a dirty, smelly process. Pol didn't know if he knew how it worked before or not, but he would have to learn.

The hides came from a few cattle farms a day to the west and northwest. The first step was to soak them for a few days in water. They had to be scraped and then put in a lime solution to help take off the hair. The long thin tables were for scraping. The hides had to be scraped again and then put in tanning vats for weeks. After rinsing, the hides were stretched onto frames and beaten to maintain pliability.

Bingi said the hides could be smoked and or oiled depending on the order.

"I don't make fine leather for clothes. My, or should I say our, work is for working uses. Shoes, saddles, belts, straps of all kinds. Durable stuff."

Pol figured out the process and realized that it took a lot of work to make leather and Bingi had been doing it by himself for the last eight months. No wonder Doara said they couldn't make any money.

"Now that you know all of that, follow me," Bingi said. He led Pol past the scraping huts; the tanner showed him to a stream that flowed on the north part of the property. The village was south.

Pol looked at the stream flowing beneath his feet. Someone, Bingi most likely, had built up a high edge on the side of the stream heading towards the tannery. A pipe led from the bank heading back towards the tannery.

"That is my water supply," Bingi said. "I use it for all kinds of things. Tanning takes a lot of washing and a lot of soaking."

Pol now understood that. "Where does the waste water go?"

Bingi grinned. "The stream heads all the way to the ocean. There isn't another village from here to there, so I just dump everything back into the stream on the other side of the vats. It cuts down on the smell. Someone located the tannery here a long time ago for that reason."

Pol couldn't tell. The odor from the tanning processes and the hides couldn't be worse, but he vowed to endure. Doara seemed nice, but he wasn't so sure about Bingi. The place seemed to be refuge enough for Pol's purposes. After another whiff of the vats, it was plain that whoever set up the place put the tannery where it was for a reason other than easy access to the water.

"Come with me," he said, walking into the woods. Bingi pointed out three species of trees. All of them had rough bark. "These are used for my tanning. There is tannin in the bark that takes the rotting parts out of the leather. That's what tanning does. If you leave untanned leather out, it goes bad. We don't want that. You'll have to travel north on the path to a red stake. That's where you can scrape the bark off the trees and bring them back here. You need to spend a day each week doing that."

"Why do I go so far?" Pol asked.

"The trees closer in have all been harvested. This tannery has been in operation for a long, long time. I get help from the village to remove the old trees and plant new ones on a regular basis. We all pitch in to make things work, here."

Pol nodded. He wondered if he already knew this, but his mind didn't give him an answer. He may be learning something once familiar to him, but he just soaked it in. The village working as a cooperative unit seemed something worth contemplating. He guessed some people cooperated more than others, and he expected he'd have the opportunity to test that guess.

After a hard day doing all of the physical work in the tannery, Pol walked into Bingi's house where he ate with the couple. He had little to do the next day, but that still meant checking the vats to make sure the solutions were topped up, so the curing leather didn't dry out. Bingi timed the work so they could get a less intensive day once a week.

Bingi was out in the yard counting hides in the second shack that held Bingi's cured hides. Doara put lamb stew on the table.

"I wish we could raise animals, but the smells affect the animals as much as it does the rest of us," she said. "I have a tiny shack just off the road to the village where I wash and change my clothes." She smiled. "I get better treatment when I shop after I've cleaned up."

Pol hadn't heard of it before, but then he still hadn't found the time to go into the village, and he had spent the last two months learning all about tanning.

"How do I go about whitewashing my shack? It's dismal inside."

Doara brightened up. "We make our own. Bingi's too lazy. You can take Demeron into the village and buy a bag of chalk to mix in with the lime that Bingi gets delivered. Do you want me to go with you?"

"I'd like that. Will Bingi be upset?"

She shook her head. "Not at all. We'll go tomorrow morning."

The next morning, Pol was up and ready. Doara stepped down onto the ground, and they headed to the village. Pol could still hear Bingi snoring even after they reached the road.

"A nice day. Did you bring any money?"

Pol stopped. "I didn't."

"Never mind. We'll spend your pay today."

Pol didn't even know what the local coinage looked like since he left the village for the tannery in the same hour that he arrived.

There was a market set up in the middle of the village. Unfamiliar men wearing a different style of clothes manned the stalls.

"The merchants don't live here?" Pol asked Doara. She looked different, dressed more nicely after she had changed in the shack. At least Pol had thought to bathe in the stream the previous night.

"No. The market men travel from village to village. There is usually two or three of them selling the same things. Competition is good to keep the prices down," Doara said. "Watch me haggle. You'll get a better feeling for what things are worth. We'll buy you a new set of clothes so you can put them in my changing shack. No matter how hard you try, you can't wash the tanning smell from your work clothes."

Pol had gotten so used to the smell, that he didn't even notice, but from the looks of the villagers, they did. He hung back from Doara but listened as she shopped for food and his clothes. Bingi needed more drawing knives, so she haggled for a while with a cutlery merchant.

"Do you need a knife?" she asked Pol.

"For what?"

"A man needs some protection. Pick one out," she said.

Pol looked at both used and new knives. He held various ones and realized that he knew about balance. He wondered what other things he knew but hadn't yet drawn from his mind. After trying a few out, Pol chose a used longish knife with very good balance. He swished it around a bit.

"The lad looks like he knows how to use one of those."

Doara looked at Pol. "Do you?"

"I might," Pol said. He could picture himself using the thing.

"There's no sheath for this," the merchant said.

"I can make one," Pol replied and looked at Doara.

"I like the shiny new ones better," she said.

The merchant chuckled. "The lad has picked the best of the lot. Most people pass that one by, but even though it's older, it's a well made Shinkyan blade."

Shinkya. Pol narrowed his eyes and looked at the knife with its blunt edge and slight curve. Had he used one of these before? He must have.

"I hold a knife throwing contest in two hours. If you are still around, you might want to try. I provide the knives. If you like the one that you throw you can buy it at a large discount, too."

"I'll be back," Pol said. He wondered if he learned to toss knives and figured that if he tried, he would find out.

For the rest of the time in the village, Pol learned the value of the Kirian coinage. He also learned that he lived in Kiria and kept his ears open as he picked up a lot of things as he observed Doara as they walked through the market. They sat down with a purchased lunch at the village's social center, a wall-less building that was a roof covering a concrete floor filled with tables.

He let Doara pick out his clothes and made sure they looked like the clothes other youths wore in the village. She took him to a materials supplier who had a stall, but the marksman didn't sell as much as take orders.

"Two bags of chalk. You can deliver it with our next lime shipment," Doara said.

"Time to repaint those shacks of yours? I didn't think Bingi would ever do such a thing."

"He won't. Our apprentice Pol will."

"How long will he last? Bingi's last apprentice didn't make it more than six months, right?"

"Pol is a special case. He has a lot to learn," Doara said.

Pol was amused by the fact that both of them spoke of him as if he wasn't even there. He agreed with Doara. He needed to learn a lot to discover who he was. He doubted that many apprentices didn't know who they were.

Pol expected the lime and chalk in two weeks. Doara promised Pol that he'd get the time to paint everything.

They had dawdled long enough to finally hear the cutlery merchant call for participants for the knife-throwing contest. Doara pushed him along. Part of the market had been roped off, and a board with painted circles was set up at one end as the contestants gathered.

Twenty people congregated around the merchant. Pol was surprised that there were all ages represented as well as a few young women. The merchant held up a hat. They all pulled out a slip of paper. Pol pulled one out but didn't know how to read Kirian script, so he gave it to Doara.

"You don't know how to read?" she said,

"I do, but not Kirian," Pol said. It was the first time he had ever called the language the villagers spoke anything.

"I barely know my letters, but a girl's got to know her numbers. It says seventeen."

Pol nodded and listened for the rules.

"There will be three rounds. We will cut the field to the top five, and then the top two go at it for the prize," the merchant said. He spread out knives on a folding table. "Pick your weapon. You get three practice tosses."

Pol looked the knives over and found one that had the best balance. He waited for a turn and threw the knife, hitting the center.

"Luck," Pol said a little louder than he needed to. He knew he had tossed knives before. He felt he could hit the center each and every time. Where did he acquire such a talent? He had to shake his head. When he tried to place himself somewhere, his mind refused to work.

He purposely missed the center of the target on his next throws. He didn't want to call attention to himself, but he did like the knife and wanted to win.

The first round showed Pol that many of the villagers hadn't practiced enough. Interestingly, two young women dressed in closer fitting mannish clothing remained in the second round of five. Pol barely made the next round, throwing just good enough to proceed, as did two men who looked to be in their mid-twenties. Bingi told Pol that he looked sixteen or seventeen, so they were older than he. He didn't know how old the women were, but they both looked youngish with looks of confidence on their faces.

The merchant walked over to the girls who stood close to Pol.

"Why don't you hold a contest at our village?" one of the girls said.

"I used to, but your brother always won. I tried to keep him out, but the village chief told me if I held the games, I'd have to let him compete," the merchant said.

Both of the women laughed. "So it's our turn?"

The merchant nodded. "If you beat the others, but only one of you can prevail. I can't give two knives to two sisters."

Sisters, Pol thought. He wondered what kind of warrior their brother might be to win all the contests. Like him? Maybe he could find out something about his knife throwing that might indicate his origins.

The next round forced Pol to use his new found skill. The two men quickly showed they couldn't keep up with Pol and the two women. One of the sisters hit a knot in the wood, and the knife wobbled and fell off the board. That gave the opening for Pol and the other sister to claim a position in the last round.

"You are good," the sister said. "Who let a Shinkyan in here?" she said rather loudly. "And you stink besides," she said even louder.

"I'm sorry. I'm an apprentice to the tanner."

"Someone who stinks worse than my brother," said one sister. The other laughed.

"What does your brother do?" Pol asked.

"He is a blacksmith trying to make arms."

"Loga's better at using them than making them," the other sister said, joining them.

Pol didn't know how to reply. They spoke so fast that Pol didn't quite get it all. He would have to persuade Doara to speak more quickly.

The merchant clapped his hands. "Time for the final round." He flipped the board over to reveal a set of smaller targets. "One pace farther," he said as he moved the stand back.

Pol's opponent groaned.

"Too far?" Pol asked.

She remained silent and stood squinting at the target, making motions to throw with nothing in her hand.

"You should do that with your knife in your hand, so you don't forget the balance," Pol said. It seemed logical to him. He smiled as he exercised some memories that hadn't vanished.

"I don't need your help, tanner," she said. Her mood had turned sour.

Pol shrugged. "Suit yourself."

"Ladies first?" the merchant said,

The sister shook her head and nodded towards Pol.

"I think she is giving you the first throw."

Pol thanked the sister and threw at the target the merchant had pointed out. His knife went into the center. The sister used a different target, and hers was a bit off. After three throws, Pol was clearly the winner.

"Thank you for the competition," Pol said.

The woman growled. Her sister smiled through it all. "Weya isn't used to losing, except to Loga, our brother. I suppose we should see who is better, you or our brother. You should come to our village some time and have a friendly match."

Pol looked at the silent sister. "I was hoping this could be a friendly match," Pol said.

The disgruntled sister turned on her heel and stalked off. "She'll get over it. I'm Toira, by the way." She extended her hand.

Pol looked at it. "I'm sorry. I lost my memories in a shipwreck and don't have any social skills. Do I shake your hand or grip it?"

"Shake it," Toira said, grinning. "You are a strange person." She looked at Weya walking away. "She won't stop until we get to our village. I'm serious about visiting us. Just wear, uh, different clothes."

Pol smiled back. "I will in a few weeks."

Toira waved as she left. The merchant walked up with Pol's new knife in a leather sheath.

"You have an excellent eye for knives and sharp edges. Those two sisters are something else."

"What about their brother?"

"Loga? He is too sharp for his good in a different way. He is too competent at all he does. He works hard to do that, and most villagers don't. It may be different in Kitanga, our capital, but we don't like people coming here to show everyone else up."

Pol looked at the merchant. "Is that what I just did?"

The merchant raised a corner of his mouth. "Maybe."

~ ~ ~ ~

~ A BIT ABOUT GUY

With a lifelong passion for speculative fiction, Guy Antibes found that he rather enjoyed writing fantasy as well as reading it. So a career was born and Guy anxiously engaged in adding his own flavor of writing to the world. Guy lives in the western part of the United States and is happily married with enough children to meet or exceed the human replacement rate.

You can contact Guy at his website: www.guyantibes.com.

†

BOOKS BY GUY ANTIBES

THE DISINHERITED PRINCE

Book One: The Disinherited Prince

Poldon Fairfield, a fourteen-year-old prince, has no desire to rule since his poor health has convinced him that he will not live long enough to sit on any throne. Matters take a turn for the worse when his father, the King of North Salvan, decides his oldest will rule the country where Pol's mother is first in the line of succession followed by Pol, her only child. Pol learns he has developed a talent for magic, and that may do him more harm than good, as he must struggle to survive among his siblings, now turned lethally hostile.

Book Two: The Monk's Habit

With his health failing, Pol Cissert takes refuge in a monastery dedicated to magic, healing, and swordsmanship. As a disinherited prince, he thinks his troubles are behind him, so he can concentrate on learning magic and getting his body repaired. He soon finds that his sanctuary isn't the protection he hoped for.

Book Three: A Sip of Magic

Expecting to resume his studies after a long absence, Pol Cissert is disappointed when he is drafted by the Emperor's Seeker to infiltrate into Tesna Monastery. His mission is to verify rumors of a new army being raised by the South Salvan King, a man he perceives as a personal enemy. Pol will face new challenges, not the least of which will be figuring out the mysterious roommate that arrives no long after he learns about the Tesnan's plans to take over the world.

Book Four: The Sleeping God

Carrying an amulet given to him by his late mother, Pol Cissert seizes on an opportunity to travel to a far off city in search of his roots. He has no idea that the journey is no easy jaunt. Chased by magicians, thugs, pirates, and priests, he seeks his legacy by seeking the Cathedral of the Sleeping God. Pol finds that the truth isn't always something everyone wants.

Demeron: A Horse's Tale - A Disinherited Prince Novella
Demeron, a Shinkyan stallion who can speak to human magicians, is cut off from his master and must find a way to return hundreds of miles to Deftnis Monastery, his master's home. To do so, Demeron must travel through the country of his birth, eluding humans who would eagerly take possession of him. Sixty pages long, Demeron, A Horse's Tale is best read between A Sip of Magic and The Emperor's Pet.

FANTASY - EPIC / SWORD & SORCERY / YOUNG ADULT

POWER OF POSES

Book One: Magician in Training

Trak Bluntwithe, an illiterate stableboy, is bequeathed an education by an estranged uncle. In the process of learning his letters, Trak finds out that he is a magician. So his adventures begin that will take him to foreign countries, fleeing from his home country, who seeks to execute him for the crime of being able to perform magic. The problem is that no country is safe for the boy while he undergoes training. Can he stay ahead of those who want to control him or keep his enemies from killing him?

Book Two: Magician in Exile

Trak Bluntwithe is a young man possessing so much magical power that he is a target for governments. Some want to control him and others want to eliminate the threat of his potential. He finds himself embroiled in the middle of a civil war. He must fight in order to save his imprisoned father, yet he finds that he has little taste for warfare. Trak carries this conflict onto the battlefield and finds he must use his abilities to stop the war in order to protect the ones he loves.

Book Three: Magician in Captivity

After a disastrous reunion with Valanna, Trak heads to the mysterious land of Bennin to rescue a Toryan princess sold into slavery. The Warish King sends Valanna back to Pestle to verify that the King of Pestle is no longer under Warish control. The Vashtan menace continues to infect the countries of the world and embroil both Trak and Valanna in civil conflict, while neither of them can shake off the attraction both of them feel towards each other.

Book Four: *Magician in Battle*

Trak saves Warish, but must leave to return the Toryan princess. He reunites with his father, but is separated again. Circumstances turn ugly in Torya, and Trak returns to Pestle to fight a new, unexpected army. Valanna's story continues as she struggles with her new circumstances, and is sent on a final mission to Pestle. The Power of Poses series ends with a massive battle pitting soldier against soldier and magic against magic.

FANTASY - EPIC / SWORD & SORCERY / YOUNG ADULT / NEW ADULT

THE WARSTONE QUARTET

An ancient emperor creates four magical gems to take over and rule the entire world. The ancient empire crumbles and over millennia. Three stones are lost and one remains as an inert symbol for a single kingdom among many. The force that created the Warstones, now awakened, seeks to unite them all, bringing in a new reign of world domination—a rule of terror.

Four Warstones, four stories. The Warstone Quartet tells of heroism, magic, romance and war as the world must rise to fight the dark force that would enslave them all.

FANTASY - SWORD & SORCERY/EPIC

Book One: *Moonstone | Magic That Binds*

A jewel, found in the muck of a small village pond, transforms Lotto, the village fool, into an eager young man who is now linked to a princess through the Moonstone. The princess fights against the link while Lotto seeks to learn more about what happened to him. He finds a legacy and she finds the home in her father's army that she has so desperately sought. As Lotto finds aptitude in magical and physical power, a dark force has risen from another land to sow the seeds of rebellion. It's up to Lotto to save the princess and the kingdom amidst stunning betrayal fomented by the foreign enemy.

Book Two: Sunstone | Dishonor's Bane

Shiro, a simple farmer, is discovered to possess stunning magical power and is involuntarily drafted into the Ropponi Sorcerer's Guild. He attracts more enemies than friends and escapes with his life only to end up on a remote prison island. He flees with an enchanted sword containing the lost Sunstone. Trying to create a simple refuge for an outlawed band of women sorcerers, he is betrayed by the very women he has worked to save and exiled to a foreign land. There, he must battle for his freedom as he and his band become embroiled in a continent-wide conflict.

Book Three: Bloodstone | Power of Youth

When usurpers invade Foxhome Castle, Unca, the aging Court Wizard of the Red Kingdom, flees with the murdered king's only daughter, taking the Bloodstone, an ancient amulet that is the symbol of Red Kingdom rule. Unca uses the Bloodstone to escape capture by an enemy and is transformed into a young man, but loses all of his wizardly powers. Unca must reinvent himself in order to return the princess to her throne. Along the way he falls in love with the young woman and must deal with the conflict between his duty and his heart, while keeping a terrible secret.

Book Four: Darkstone | An Evil Reborn

As the 22nd son of the Emperor of Dakkor, Vishan Daryaku grows from boy to man, learning that he must use his unique powers and prodigious knowledge to survive. He succeeds until his body is taken over by an evil power locked inside of the Darkstone. Now Emperor of Dakkor, Vishan is trapped inside, as the ancient force that rules his body devastates his homeland while attempting to recover all of the Warstones.

As the amulets are all exposed, the holders of the Moonstone, Sunstone, and Bloodstone combine to fight the Emperor's relentless drive to reunite the Warstones and gain power over the entire world. The armies of Dakkor and the forces of those allied with the three other stones collide on a dead continent in the stunning conclusion of the Warstone Quartet.

Quest of the Wizardess

Quest of the Wizardess chronicles the travels and travails of young Bellia. After her wizard family is assassinated when she is fourteen, Bellia seeks anonymity as a blacksmith's helper. When that doesn't work out as expected, she flees to the army.

Her extraordinary physical and magical skills bring unwanted attention and she must escape again. After finding a too-placid refuge, she takes the opportunity to seek out her family's killers. Revenge becomes her quest that takes her to a lost temple, unexpected alliances and a harrowing confrontation with her enemies.
FANTASY - EPIC/NEW ADULT-COLLEGE/COMING OF AGE

The Power Bearer

How Norra obtained the power and the extraordinary lengths she went through to rid herself of it.

What's a girl to do when all of the wizards in her world are after her? She runs. But this girl runs towards the source of her power, not away from it. Along the way she picks up, among others, a wizard, a ghost, a highwaywoman and a sentient cloud. Through thick and thin, they help Norra towards her goal of finding a solution in a far off land that no one in her world has even heard of.
YOUNG ADULT EPIC FANTASY

Panix: Magician Spy

Panix has life by the tail. A new wife, a new job in a new land that has few magicians and none of his caliber. His ideal life takes some unexpected downturns and Panix finds himself employed as a spy. He has no training, but must make things up as he goes if he is to survive the politics, betrayal, war and, at the end, his own behavior.
FANTASY - ADVENTURE

THE WORLD OF THE SWORD OF SPELLS

Warrior Mage

The gods gave Brull a Sword of Spells and proclaimed him as the world's only Warrior Mage. One big problem, there aren't any wars. What's a guy to do? Brull becomes a magician bounty hunter until the big day when he learns he not only has to fight a war with the magicians of his world, but fight the god that the magicians are all working to bring into being. He finds out if he has what it takes in Warrior Mage.
EPIC FANTASY

Sword of Spells

Read about Brull's beginnings and earlier adventures as a bounty hunter of magicians in the Sword of Spells anthology.
EPIC FANTASY

THE SARA FEATHERWOOD ADVENTURES

Set in Shattuk Downs, a reclusive land in the kingdom of Parthy. Sara Featherwood could be a Jane Austen heroine with a sword in her hand. There are no magicians, wizards, dragons, elves or dwarves in Shattuk Downs, but there is intrigue, nobility, hidden secrets, plenty of adventure and romance with a bit of magic.
FANTASY - YOUNG ADULT   FICTION - WOMEN'S ADVENTURE

Knife & Flame

When Sara Featherwood's mother dies, her sixteen-year-old life is thrown into turmoil at Brightlings Manor in a remote district of Shattuk Downs. Life becomes worse when her father, the Squire, sets his roving eye on her best friend. Dreading her new life, Sara escapes to the Obridge Women's School. Seeking solace in education doesn't work as her world becomes embroiled with spies, revolution, and to top it all off, her best friend becomes her worst enemy.

Sword & Flame

If you were a young woman who had just saved the family's estate from ruin, you'd think your father would be proud, wouldn't you? Sara Featherwood is thrown out of her childhood home and now faces life on her own terms at age seventeen. She returns to the Tarrey Abbey Women's School and is drafted to help with the establishment of the first Women's College in the kingdom of Parthy. Now in the King's capital of Parth, life confronts Sara as she learns about family secrets, which threaten to disrupt her life and about resurgent political turmoil back home that turns her scholarly pursuits upside down as she must take action and use her magic to save her family and her beloved Shattuk Downs.

Guns & Flame

At nineteen, Sara Featherwood has done all she can to help establish the first Women's College in the kingdom of Parthy. That includes a pact with the kingdom's Interior Minister, to go on a student exchange program as payment for eliminating opposition to the college. Little does Sara know that her trip to a rival country is not what it seems and as the secrets of the true purpose of her trip unravel, she utilizes her magic to escape through hostile territory with vital secrets, but as she does, she finds herself drawn back to Shattuk Downs and must confront awful truths about those close to her.

THE GUY ANTIBES ANTHOLOGIES

The Alien Hand

An ancient artifact changes a young woman's life forever. A glutton gladiator is marooned in a hostile desert. An investigator searches for magic on a ravaged world and finds something quite unexpected. A boy yearns for a special toy. A recent graduate has invented a unique tool for espionage. A member of a survey team must work with his ex-girlfriend in extremely dangerous circumstances. A doctor is exiled among the worst creatures he can imagine.
SCIENCE FICTION

The Purple Flames

A reject from a Magical Academy finds purpose. A detective works on a reservation in New Mexico, except the reservation is for ghouls, demons, ghosts, zombies, and the paranormal. A succubus hunts out the last known nest of vampires on earth. The grisly story about the origins of Tonsil Tommy. In a post-apocalyptic world, two mutants find out about themselves when their lives are in imminent peril.
STEAMPUNK & PARANORMAL FANTASY with a tinge of HORROR

Angel in Bronze

A statue comes to life and must come to terms with her sudden humanity. A wizard attempts to destroy a seven-hundred-year-old curse. A boy is appalled by the truth of his parents' midnight disappearances. A captain's coat is much more than it seems. A healer must decide if the maxim that he has held to his entire career is still valid. A fisherman must deal with the aftermath of the destruction of his village.
FANTASY

~ ~ ~

Guy Antibes books are available at book retailers in print and e-book formats.